# EYE STONE

By Sylvie Harrington

First Edition: Paperback

www.eyestone.co.uk

Published by Eye Stone Publishing in 2015

Cover Design by Andre Lucas  © Eye Stone Publishing

Edited by Eye Stone Publishing

Eye Stone © 2015 by Sylvie Harrington

ISBN  978-0-9934118-0-9

For Evan and Sioux, the brightest stars.

# Eye Stone

## Index

# Prologue

Suspended by his ankles, an old man dangled naked from a rope above a burning barrel of black tar. His eyes sealed shut in petrified prayer. He pleaded, "Show mercy, Lord," but his captors jeered. They sliced the rope and his carcass tumbled into the boiling black.

It was a spring evening in 1675 when the hot tar tore through The Brahan Seer's flesh. They called him The Brahan Seer because of his visions – his 'giftie' – the power of seeing into the future. Now, bubbling liquid fire fused through his skull, melting his visions, boiling his brain.

A sinister darkness spilled over the land. Thunderclouds pumped dirty rain, like murky oil weeping over the Chanonry Point. The folk of the township stayed indoors with bowed heads. They hid shamefully, for not one of them could save the Seer. None dared to confess belief in the Seer's visions. Too great was their fear of the law and the power of The House of Seaforth.

Earlier that day, Lady Seaforth had browbeaten the cowering Seer, as he knelt before her.

"I beg you Lady Seaforth, ask no more questions of me," he said. "The truth that I see will surely displease you, my Lady."

"I insist that you obey!" she shouted. "You will summon your powers immediately and tell me the whereabouts of my husband, the Earl of Seaforth. Friends avoid talk of his prolonged absence and I must know why."

With trembling hands, the Brahan Seer dutifully raised his magic stone to his left eye. He swallowed hard and then shared his vision.

"My Lady, I see the Earl in Paris. He crouches on bended knee, with lips pressed on the fair hand of a French maiden. They…"

Lady Seaforth bolted from her chair and stamped her foot three times with rage.

"You foretell evil, pure evil! I am infuriated by your effrontery!"

She dashed her silver wine goblet to the floor and screamed at the Brahan Seer. "I offer you my hospitality and in return you malign the good name of my husband." Flailing her arms, she grabbed a plate of roast goose from the table and launched it at the Seer's head. "You have slandered a noble chief in the house of his ancestors, witnessed by his loyal servants. For this you shall die."

The Seer turned and bolted. His heart pounded as he hurtled down the long staircase.

Back in the main reception hall, the incensed Lady Seaforth shrieked, "Capture the demon sorcerer. Burn him in tar for his witchcraft!"

For hours the Brahan Seer eluded his captors, but eventually found himself cornered by six burly pursuers. He stood trapped at the far end of a wood, his back to the shores of Loch Ussie. As he could not swim, escape proved impossible. Accepting his fate, he squeezed his prophesying stone one last time. "Curse the house of Seaforth!" he cried, and launched it into the murky waters of Loch Ussie.

As the Seer offered up his wrists to be tied, he shared his last prophecy. "Whosoever finds the stone will become my successor, the next Highland Seer. They will inherit God's 'giftie', the power of second sight. May the giftie serve them well."

They led the Seer to Chanonry Point, to the burning barrel of tar. His magic stone sank to the depths of Loch Ussie.

# Chapter 1

# Fish Out of Water

Having a grandpa can be handier than hip pockets on a haggis. I hope that's a compliment, because ever since I immigrated to Scotland I've felt so glad to have him near. Gramps became my best friend then, especially the day when we fished on Loch Ussie. Actually, back when I was the new kid in town, he was my one and only friend.

On the plus side, with Grandpa being my only buddy, no one ridiculed my boyish name, Brucie. I'd rather chew tin foil than chin wag with such mean buzzards.

You see, ever since my parents' divorce, I've felt scrutinized. Mom changed. Instead of being chilled and fun she became the chief inspector for symptoms of loss. Whenever I frowned, she'd spit fire at Dad for having cheated on us.

The day Mom and I boarded that Boeing 777 out of Texas, I felt her screen me closer than the baggage x-ray at passport control. I stared ahead and into space, imaging my welling tears sealed securely in two containers no greater than the regulatory 100ml and placed safely within a watertight, zip-lock bag.

Jet engines thrust us into a cool undiscovered blue, steadily climbing away from the baked Texas clay below. Wings tipped, banking right, pushing us north away from Dallas and aiming forward as the crow flies toward Hudson Bay. I avoided thinking about leaving Dad by concentrating on us flying like crows. A couple of hours later we banked right again, over Godthab, and I still didn't cry.

Below the plane, on the south coast of Greenland, shards of ice jutted, pointing up at me, like shattered fingers of glass. We'd flown 3065 miles away from Dad. I closed my eyes and tried to ignore the strobe light on the wing tip, but it prayed on my emotions like a paparazzi camera flash. *It's all Michaela's fault. If she hadn't lured my Dad away, with her cleavage and her pout...* and that thought stretched the entire width of the Atlantic Ocean, like a giant tightrope.

Finally, some 17 hours later, we arrived cold and weary at my grandfather's house in Ardcarron, Scotland.

The first night in my new Scottish home I dreamed the first of many tightrope dreams. I'd walk the tightrope from end to end, east to west and west to east, back and forth between Dad in Texas and Mom in Scotland. Over and over, I'd lose my foothold and gasp in fear of the giant grey swell below. I'd wake with a jump, searching with my hand to stroke Zoe my Labrador dog. Of course, I wasn't in my old bed and Zoe had stayed behind to live with Dad.

I tried to think positively; maybe with an ocean between them, Mom and Dad's squabbling would stop. However, thanks to Alexander Graham Bell, inventor of the telephone, Mom still managed to call long distance to scream at him "Jerk!" and "Adulterer!"

During these transatlantic battles, I usually bit my fingernails and looked to my Grandfather for support. Gramps would wink and smile one of his warm reliable smiles. He'd kiss my cheek, his breath smelling of musk, sweet like his pipe tobacco, and say something like, "I'm so chuffed you came to live with me, Brucie MacKenzie-Bice. You've made an old gadgie very happy."

It was a fine, spring, Friday morning in Ardcarron, the day I caught my first pike. The cool air smelled of pinecones. Before the fishing trip, I sat in my plaid pajamas drinking tea with my legs outstretched on Grandpa's cold back doorstep. All the new sights and sounds in Scotland amazed me. I stood up and stepped onto the grass with bare feet.

"Well, I'll be! Your grass is greener than a fifth grader," I told him. "Spongy too, like walking on dough. Texas dirt packs harder than a lawyer's heart. Ya'll must have real soft soles here compared to us corn-footed Southerners."

He laughed.

I watched little, wild rabbits chewing and skipping across the lawn, while I sipped on the cup of hot tea. Gramps tapped the ash from his smoking pipe on the outside wall and retired indoors to re-invent a recipe of infamously special porridge for our breakfast: oatmeal and milk with fresh heather honey, and bacon bits sprinkled on top like sunburned flies.

"That'll put meat on yer bones, Brucie," he teased, handing me a steaming bowl and a spoon. "Eat your brochan, and I'll take a trundle off doon to my hut. I'll get a couple of fishing rods and a puckle of hooks. Come on doon an' get me when you're done. We're going to catch a wee pike today."

I loved the up-and-down tones of his Highland accent. He almost made me want to like being in Scotland.

But then the phone rang.

I felt cold and trapped, like a wet blanket had been cast upon my shoulders. *Why can't Mom lower her voice?*

"No, Dustin, I didn't hang up on you. I dropped the phone. And, I didn't kidnap Brucie and take her out of the country illegally. Yes, I'm well aware she is only fifteen, and I did keep you informed throughout. It's not my fault you don't check your mail."

A pause followed.

"Yes, as her mother, I know Brucie is an American citizen, but I'm not American… and my family lives here in Scotland. Get over it, Dustin!"

Another pause followed.

"You started it by abandoning us!"

Pause. Mom drummed her fingernails on the hall table.

"After seventeen years of marriage, you leave me for a twenty-year-old dental nurse from Fort Worth…that pouting Michaela Whatserface? The very same day, you… you… announce that she's pregnant! How could I stay in Texas, miles from the support of my family? I had to leave, Dustin!"

A long silence followed, and I heard Mom sobbing.

Just before Mom banged down the receiver again, she yelled, "Fine! Get yourself a fancy lawyer, but Brucie will tell you she likes it here."

At times like this, I wish I had a brother or a sister. And I don't mean the fetus that's aiming to be my sibling. I mean an older kid, someone to talk to. Texas already seemed light years away, and so did Dad.

I showered, dressed, pulled on my hoodie and ambled down the un-tarred road. "Dry your hair, before you go," called Mom, but I didn't listen. We both have thick red curls, so she knew drying took an age. Besides, the blow dryer made my hair frizz out like a halo round the moon, so I settled for a casual 'hair don't'.

Grandpa's shed resembled an old Nissen hut, built during World War II. "Originally," he told me, "it housed Air Force mechanics who repaired sea planes in the nearby firth." The hut snuggled pig-in-the-middle between two more identical buildings. In a row, the three prefabs reminded me of homes where trolls might live. Each supported a wriggly tin roof of corrugated iron. The sheets of rusty-brown ridges and grooves looked like furrowed, hump-backed fields. I'd not seen anything like these sheds before.

To the rear, the huts huddled close to lofty grass-tipped sand banks. The front walls, facing a sea of frothy-topped waves, housed two windows on either side of a painted door. Grandpa's door looked creamy-colored, but flaking like shredded coconut. It hung ajar, so I pushed the handle inward.

Creak! Dry hinges grated together like feeble old bones. I knew by the bellow from his radio that Grandpa didn't hear me. A funny English accent on the radio informed him that the price of a barrel of oil had fallen again. He could also expect a shower of rain coming in from the west that afternoon.

*We'll need our waterproofs if we're fixing to fish on Loch Ussie,* I thought. I wondered if it had rained in Texas this month yet. Dad called rainstorms "gully washers," for when it rained in Texas it rained a mean old frog-strangler. Scottish rain mizzled, a mix between mist and drizzle.

As I stepped forward, my eyes adjusted to the dim light. Dusty, chrome-edged suitcases dotted the shed floor. I stifled a sneeze. *If I could only maneuver around these trunks,* I thought, *I could signal for Grandpa's attention.* The news program continued to blare.

Picking up an old tennis racket, I blew cobwebs off the strings. Dad used to play tennis with me. A small spider clambered down the handle and tickled on to my wrist. In Texas I'd flee from spiders, but yesterday Grandpa told me they're all friendly here. "Meet a lucky spider and it will weave a lucky future," he said. I lowered the little guy onto the curve of a wooden rocking chair, smooth dark wood that swirled into knolls at the end of arm rests. Tiny holes, where woodworm had burrowed, rippled under my fingertips. I slipped my hand underneath a canvas cover to stroke the soft, velvet pile of a burgundy foot stool. Beside the stool an open cardboard box begged further investigation but it merely contained a random pile of books, which all looked as dull as grey laundry, and an old cane basket full of… black crow feathers!

"Yuck!" I jerked my hand away with a shiver, as if I'd touched death.

I calmed. My curiosity returned and I continued to rummage through Grandpa's *midden*, a term Mom used to describe the strewn contents of his hut.

Golf clubs, steel cold to touch, lay askew on a green felt-covered card table. Dad loved playing golf. I shook a card pack, presumed it to be empty.

The King of Hearts tumbled to the floor. His beard curled blond like my dad's.

In the far corner of the hut, Grandpa wound heavy gut onto his fishing reel. He spotted me and flashed his gold front tooth as he grinned. It glinted like a fishing spinner, till it caught me.

"Ready to go, Brucie?" he asked.

I saluted. "Ready as a four-minute egg, Captain."

It felt weird sitting on the left-hand-side of Grandpa's car, as he drove on the right of the twisting roads heading for Loch Ussie. "This is freaky, Gramps," I said. "I keep thinking there should be a steering wheel on this side, like in Texas."

He laughed. "Och, it's being the right way up that's more important. We're okay, as long as the tyres stay on the underside."

I studied all the trees we past. They were endless, of every type; dense, elegant, gnarly, prickly, shaggy, short, skinny, swaying, thick, waving and welcoming. After a half hour drive, we parked the car in a small clearing, clambered over a large wooden gate and carried our kit through a small wood till we reached the water's edge.

A beautiful rainbow arched over the loch before us, and a family of swans swam our way. I thought about Mom, Dad, and me being together again, the two hugging me close like swans protecting their cygnet. The father swan moved away when Grandpa pushed our small boat into the water, taking his new family with him. Gramps held the bow with one hand and offered me his other hand for balance. I stepped aboard. The boat rocked, and he told me to stay to the middle as I made my way to the back seat.

"I need to give you a few pointers about catching a pike," he said. Gramps tied a float and attached this thick wire trace onto my line. "Pike have razor-sharp teeth," he warned. He threw the baited trace into the water and told me to watch the float. I panicked. "But how in the Jim Dickens do we pull the hooks from their mouths without them chomping off our fingers?"

My fishing line pulled taut and, quicker than a hiccup, I knew I would find out.

"That's it, my wee wifie. Haud the rod end way up high and reel him in as hard as you can," Grandpa said. "Go on now. Gie it laldy!"

"I can't, Grandpa. It'll yank me into the water," I shrieked.

"I've got a haud of you," he said, holding my coat.

I pulled with all my might, cranking the reel, straining against the fighting pike.

"What about its teeth?" I screamed. "Tell me what to do!"

Grandpa reached for his net as soon as the fish's head broke the surface of the water. Oh, my God, it looked nasty! The creamy, greenish, mottled, squeamish body looked the most obscene, dirty meanest thing . . . and, those teeth!

I hollered for my granddad to take over. One quick swing and the pike thrashed in the net like he had a conniption fit. Conniption fit is Texan for being real jerky.

"Get ready with those tools," Gramps said, pointing into the plastic box where various shiny instruments waited at the ready, each neatly labeled by name, sitting in a row in order of length.

I read the labels as quickly as I could. *Was he talking about the artery forceps, the hook-cutter, or the pair of long-nosed pincers?*

Gramps carefully slid his left hand inside the right gill of the fish, securing its jaw with his fingers on the inside and his thumb on the outside. With his grip secure, he laid the pike on its back and teased the fish's mouth open by curling his hand inside. He asked me to pass the artery forceps to his right hand.

"Hurry, Brucie, I need to nip the hook from its mouth, so I can hurl the cratur free again," he said.

"Set him free?! No way, Grandpa. This is the first time I've caught a fish," I protested. "Can't I keep the pike and send a photo to Dad with me holding it?"

For the first time in weeks, I'd mentioned my Dad's name aloud.

I looked at the pike's sharp teeth again and shivered. I thought about the dental nurse in Fort Worth, Michaela Marie McGraw. Dad called her Mike, for short. *Funny how Mike and the pike both have big teeth,* I thought. *And Mike even rhymes with pike!*

Grandpa whacked the fish on the head, jolting me back to the present.

"Best to gut it now, then," he said, flicking open his knife.

I looked away when he stabbed in with the blade. He sliced into the pike's long belly. From the side of my eye, I saw Gramps' hand go in and pull out all the guts. *P-U!* They spilled out like lumpy poo.

I sat back while Gramps fumbled with the fish, creating a moment of time for me to wonder if Dad would be at the birth of my little brother, and if Dad would look the other way. Or, would he stare at her lady garden, waiting to see a head appear? *Yuck! I can't believe that babies are really born that way.*

Plop! Something fell out of the fish: an oval-shaped stone suddenly squished from the pike's belly and onto my tennis shoe. At first I freaked, as I thought I saw an organ, like a giant fish heart that still beat. Next thing I whooped, "Yeehaw!" and rinsed the stone in the water over the side of the boat. "Wow! Look Gramps, it cleans up real pretty."

Grandpa's eyebrows shot so high they near shoved his hat off. "In the name of the wee man. . . sealbh math dhut!" He gasped at the stone and clapped me on the back.

"Speak English, Gramps, not Gaelic!"

"Good luck to you," he said with a grin. But then his expression darkened. Suddenly he scrunched his brows together. Raising his hand, he tweaked his top lip between his index finger and his thumb. His gaze drifted up and curled inward to a thought that he kept private.

"What's up?" I asked, caressing my find.

He seemed slow to reply, "Nothing." He smiled and nudged me affectionately with his elbow. "Nothing at all, Pet. Well done."

I wasn't so sure what he meant by that, but . . . "Oh Joy!" I beamed, and stared down at my hand in awe. Cupping the stone in my palm, I wiped it clean with my thumb, and then buffed the surface on my jeans to rid the last of the slimy film that layered over the surface. As I examined the stone, a hole became visible, slightly off-center: its eye socket.

Holding it up to the sky, I couldn't peel my eyes off it. "Look at all the subtle colors."

Gramps nodded.

"It's like coming home, Gramps. Finding this feels like finally coming home, weary after a long day. You know, Gramps, like when you need cheering up? I've really needed cheering up lately, haven't I Gramps?"

He nodded again and I polished my stone on my other leg.

"What's the odds of finding this inside an old pike, Gramps?"

He shrugged. "A quadrillion to one, I think."

"It's like finding treasure from a golden city lost to the age of time, fathoms deep beneath the water." I gazed and prattled on about imaginary tales of sunken treasure chests beneath the loch, guarded by shoals of pike with big teeth. The more I blathered, the more my imagination focused down into the mystical depths of the water, away from Dad and Michaela, away from their baby, and away from Mom, too. Lost within my mind's eye and rubbing my stone, I imagined myself sitting within a bubble on the bed of the loch. *Weird!* I could almost feel myself swaying in time with the gentle, underwater current. I closed my eyes. *Wow! It's so relaxing down there.*

"This stone is so cool, Grandpa! Maybe it's magical."

Gramps said nothing. He twiddled with some fishing gut. *It's not like Gramps to go all silent.* I panicked, and felt awkward like I'd done something wrong. Continuing to clutch my stone, I shifted uneasily on the seat of the boat, and my thoughts ran aground in Texas. *What's the big attraction with that Michaela Marie McGraw, anyway? Has Dad lost his brain?*

Grandpa tapped my arm. "There you go." He smiled and handed me a knotted chain that he'd woven from the gut. We threaded it through the eye of the stone and hung the stone like a pendant around my neck.

He said it looked good on me but I still felt uneasy. "Grandpa, is something wrong?" I finally asked. "Why are you suddenly so quiet?"

"Oh. . ." As he stalled, it felt like he tried to find a fib.

"I worry that soon I'm going to have to share you with others, Brucie, and not keep you all to myself each day," he said.

I answered him, regardless. "Hmm, is that really true, or are you trying to say that it's time I made friends my own age?" I said. I'd been hanging around Grandpa for weeks.

"When you're ready, lass," he said. "There's stuff you could share about your Dad, and that, with folk your own age that I suppose you couldn't blether about with an old gadgie, like me."

I clutched the stone in my hand and pressed it on my chest. It shocked me as much as Grandpa when I suddenly found these words. "You mean share things that worry me? Like my fears about learning to live in a new country; wishing Mom wouldn't let me hear so many of her negative arguments; being jealous of Dad's new girlfriend; feeling threatened by the arrival of a new baby brother; and . . . missing my Dad so much?" There! I finally said it all, aloud.

Grandpa's arms reached out when he spied my first tear.

"Och you wee soul. You're fair scunnered with it all, aren't you? Good girl. Let it all out," he whispered. So I did. I sobbed till my eyes stung raw.

He let me go after a few moments and pulled up oars, allowing our boat drift with the flow, and then Grandpa put his arms around me again. We bobbed and floated, turning gently east, as Mother Nature pulled us ashore. The evening sun warmed my back, together with Grandpa's hugs. Cupping the stone in my hand, I wiped my nose on my sleeve.

I wilted to exhaustion. Through blurry vision, I imagined I saw a silhouette on the horizon. I could only open my sleepy eyes halfway, which, through my long lashes, made the image look like a man on a horse, riding toward me, smiling. *Dad?* I blinked but nothing stirred, only a passing wish.

"Let's go home, Gramps. I'm whooped as an old lame mule." I yawned.

"Home, James, and don't spare the horses," he said, instructing an imaginary coachman.

That night, as I snuggled down between fresh, cotton sheets and studied my new stone... P-U, the whiffiest smell wafted through the room. Gorgonzola cheese? Roasting goose fat? Cat pee?

*Where's that strange smell coming from?*

## The MacKinnon Family

**That same day, a spectacled social worker stood by the open door of her car, a small white Fiat. She wore a bright red duffle coat to match the frames of her glasses. Slipping her feet into a pair of Wellington boots, she tossed her driving shoes to the back seat and locked the driver's door.**

**An over-sized bag held her laptop and she clutched a folder full of printed documents to her chest, like a shield.**

**She crossed the road, climbed over a wooden gate and squelched through a muddy field to the door of a static caravan. Despite repeated knocking and peering in windows, nobody answered the door.**

**Had she looked carefully, before crossing the road, the social worker might have spotted an old Land Rover, hidden in a thicket near**

the road.  Inside the Land Rover, the MacKinnons sat and watched her. They knew how to teach the authorities a lesson.  Nobody snooped into the MacKinnon's affairs for free.

"Don't worry," said Jake MacKinnon to his niece, Bethany, "That bitch won't take you back into care."  He slipped out of the Land Rover and returned a few minutes later, tossing a pocket knife on to Bethany's lap. "That's it sorted.  She won't come snooping round here again."

The signal from a mobile phone can bounce endlessly around the west side of Ardcarron, going absolutely nowhere.  It's impossible to make calls, without climbing the nearest hill.   It took the social worker an hour to summon someone from the local garage.  "All four tyres have been slashed," said the windswept social worker, standing at the top of Ben Struie.  "Please come quickly."

## Chapter 2

## *Dying to Meet You*

The next day, I felt as fresh as dew on the morning grass. Lemon sunshine peeled through the vanilla cream drapes. Straight away, I sent an email to Dad, attaching a photo of me with my catch. "This pike weighs 3lb 3oz," I wrote, proudly.

By afternoon, he emailed back with a short "Well done!" adding, "I have good news, too. As of 2 a.m., CST, you have a brand new baby brother."

The fresh dewy feeling turned soggy and damp. I wanted to barf. His reply should have celebrated me and my fish. *I'M his child! I don't want siblings. Babies stink of crap, especially this kid.* I kicked out under the desk in a temper. I sat in a mood for ages before caving to the temptation of reading more about the intruder, this newborn brother.

Dad said, "He weighed 6lb 6oz."

I eked out an ounce or two of inner sarcasm: *that is exactly double my pike's weight – Ha! A double pike… The boy will be a gymnast!* But, even sarcasm hurt. I stood up and knocked over the chair, pushing it with the palm of my hand. "I HATE this baby!" I shouted.

Lying face-down on my bed, I punched my pillow, sulking; fizzing about the little Double Pike till my brain ached and gave me rancid indigestion. *Hmph! He never even said anything about my dog, Zoe, and if he thinks I'm gonna cry he can forget it 'cause I won't.* But I did.

Seeking comfort, I touched my eye stone, to check it still hung securely around my neck.

Buzz.

That's the only word to describe it. The stone gave me a buzz. Not good buzz or bad; just buzz, like the anticipation when you ring a doorbell and wait for someone to come. I didn't know who or what I waited for, though. It felt frustrating, like trying to remember the name of something by its taste or smell. Confused, I slouched back into sorrow.

Mom called out, "Brucie, I'm making tea and cheesy toast. Want some?"

"No, thanks," I said, in the most cheerful voice I could muster, "I'm not hungry." That part held truth. If Mom knew about the arrival of little Double Pike, she'd cry like a gully washer in her room again, too. Some days she rarely changed out of her bathrobe. She's so sloppy these days.

My memories drifted back in time. Weeks earlier, waiting in the international departure lounge at Dallas Fort Worth airport for our flight to London, she'd said, "you won't regret this move, Brucie." We each selected a bottle of perfume from the duty free shop. I chose a scent called "Spark" by someone called Liz Claiborne. The lady at the counter volunteered the phrase, 'a blend of sensuality and warm awakening aromas of vanilla, musk, exotic woods, rose and caramel.' She added, "It's deliciously toasty and spell-bindingly erotic." I imagined myself being "spell-bindingly erotic" each time I wafted past a nose, but we also had a dog called Spark, once. He didn't smell erotic. In fact, one day Spark smelled of skunk – P-U! All the same, I said I'd have the large 20-oz bottle. Mom chose a scent called Blue. I'm wondering now if that was its name or a warning on the box!

I snapped back to the present when the top of Grandpa's tweed hat caught my eye, stalking past the window. Gramps whistled a song called "Tullochgorum." I know this because he taught me the words. "Come, gi'es a song, Montgomery cried, and lay your disputes all aside …" It's hard for me to sing some of his favorite Scottish songs with a Southern Texan accent like mine, but this one proved not too bad … even though it had to be sung fast.

I snuck outside, quietly past Mom in the kitchen, to hang out with my best buddy, Gramps.

"Here," he said, nudging me and moving closer to whisper, "there's a wifie doon the road that married a guy with a hair lip … aye … they bred like rabbits. Ha! Ha! Like rabbits! Get it?"

Sighing at his joke, I asked, "How d'y'all stay so cheerful here, Gramps?"

"I think happy thoughts," he said, unearthing some dirty, orange carrots from his organic vegetable patch.

"What happy thoughts are you thinking now?" I asked, inspecting my fingernails and searching for some know-how to lift my doldrums.

"I'm thinking about making carrot cake with roast rabbit-gravy icing," he said.

I smiled, weakly; *maybe I need to think happy thoughts, too.* And so began my practice of shutting out the bad and scary with all the funny and bright I could imagine ... *Squishing ice-cream into cookie sandwiches ... living in a brightly painted boat house ... ferret hammocks ... playing chess on the beach ... Toby, the teddy bear I'd had since I was a . . . baby. . . No no no! . . . Must get the word 'baby' out of my head. Try again . . . strawberry bubble bath . . . cute fluffy chickens . . . multi-colored beach towels . . .*

I wondered if Grandpa would let me explore inside his shed again. It's a real Aladdin's cave in there! Then I thought about my conversation with Grandpa, when we were fishing the day before: it really WAS time I found some friends my own age. 'You'll soon get to know more people around here,' he'd said. I think Grandpa let me know, gently, of course, that he needed me to let him off the hook. He should be swimming free with slow, old fish of his own age.

So, I said, "I think I'll explore for a while, Gramps."

"Good idea, Brucie," Gramps answered, as he exhumed and shook the ground from another dirty carrot.

I strutted off for a walk alone, up the old farm road by the house, to forget about Double Pike and to think over the whole deal of making friends. What a scary thought for an immigrant!

*Glitzy red and silver earrings ... monkey sounds in the Amazon rain forest ... hopping on one leg with eyes shut ... my bedroom back in Texas . . . Texas bluebonnets in the . . . No no no . . . don't think of Texas . . . hairy knees below tartan kilts . . . beautiful snowcapped hills above Ardcarron . . .*

On my walk, I estimated that the village of Ardcarron had no more than a hundred houses. Our home tucked into a sheltered dip near the top of Ardcarron Hill, overlooking the village. A lush, grassy field lay to the far off gable end of the house, the occasional home to a few sheep. When I first came to Ardcarron, Gramps told me that bad luck followed if you counted sheep aloud. He told me to end my additions by saying, "bless them." On account of me being a stranger to these parts, and folk felt superstitious about strangers, I did as Gramps told me. I never knew when Gramps talked serious or if he teased, but he advised to say 'bless them' if I felt the urge to count cows or people's children, too.

On the village side of the house, we had a few close neighbors, in a row of six similar bungalows with white pebble-harled walls and gray-brown roof tiles. No kids of my age lived there. Next door lived a woman that Gramps called Bunty Blackhead, "a bit of a nosy curtain-twitcher," he said. Only one home in the entire street housed kids and all three of them, bless them, stood less than three foot tall.

I decided that my first step to finding a friend involved a walk about the village, to smile at people. So, when I encountered an old woman carrying a cane basket, like the basket I found in Grandpa's shed with the crow feathers, I practiced on her and grinned with wide lips. At first, she gave me the strangest look and I felt a shiver of regret, but as we passed on the road she smiled back and winked. That appeared strange, too, but at least my smile provoked a positive response.

A large head poked over the wire fence to my left hand side, the face of a beautiful chestnut mare. As I grinned at her, she checked me out from the paddock, nodding quietly.

Suddenly, a smoky, old, Land Rover raced around the corner, backfired, and scared the be-jeepers out of the poor mare. I jumped onto the bank to avoid being hit. The horse whinnied.

"Easy girl!" I said in a calm voice. "I'm your friend, Brucie."

Yes. There were no rules to say that my first friend couldn't be a horse. Our hair color matched: *sufficient connection*, I thought. I stroked her mane and smiled in the hope that the horse could see all thirty two of my teeth, bless them. Under my fingertips, her wiry texture felt wild like my hair, minus the curls, of course. I hated my curls and still negotiated hard with Mom and Gramps to let me cut them off. The horse didn't have freckles, but we both had brown eyes. 'Sensitive and kind eyes,' says Gramps.

I love the veins that protrude on horse noses, their alert eyes and twitching nostrils. And, I adore the puckered skin on their mouths, like Gramps' old soft, suede slippers.

"Hello there, my new friend," I said. "What's your name, then?"

"Hi," said a short girl with long hair, carrying a large bucket with a small handle. I'd been so engrossed in showing my teeth to the horse that I hadn't seen the girl. She wore a dark green coat with riding boots over jodhpurs.

"You're Brucie, Ali Dubh's American granddaughter, aren't you?" she said. "I'm Rhiannon and this is my horse, Bracken." She smiled, lowering the bucket to the grass. Inside were cloths, a bottle of something, and stuff I couldn't clearly see.

"Hi," I said, feeling goofy.

"Want to help me hold Bracken still? I need to dress a cut on her leg," said Rhiannon. Bracken nuzzled around my neck, mouthing gently against my eye stone with her soft lips. I clutched the stone to prevent the horse from chewing it.

Buzz.

Actually, this time I sensed more of a wave than a buzz. A wave of misty rainbow colors that radiated around Bracken and moved with the mare. As Rhiannon spoke, the colors around her horse vibrated in tune with the tones in her voice. Above Bracken's head a light appeared; silver white... no purple, then turning mauve at her forehead and duck-egg blue down her neck. Her muscular chest shimmered steamy green into hazy yellow. Down her flanks and legs, the colors blended into shades of orange and then soft reds, except for her right leg. There, the color broke. Around the dressed wound, no color showed. Nothing; only grey.

"He-ll-o?" joked Rhiannon. "Can you understand me, Brucie? I'll speak slower. Do – you – want – to – help – me – hold – Bracken?" She laughed at my daydreaming.

"Eh? Yeah, sure." I grinned and squeezed through the fence into the paddock.

Rhiannon said she was sixteen, eight months older than me. Slim, she had long legs and she looked happy as a hog with the dirt on those big boots. Rhiannon sure knew how to handle horses. She had this funny way of blowing upward at her long, raven hair to blast the wispy bangs from her eyes without using her hands. When she laughed she let out a weird, horsy snort that I liked. Rhiannon said she played fiddle and loved singing. Her green eyes twinkled when I said I knew the words to Tullochgorum. "I can play that tune," she said.

In addition to Bracken, she owned four dogs, bless them, and favored Corrie, a Border Collie. She had seventeen hens, bless them, and a rooster called Henry, lots of farm cats, a couple of pigs and a white angora rabbit, bless them all. I told Rhiannon about Zoe, my dog, but I changed the subject when Rhiannon asked the whereabouts of Zoe. "It's a perfect day for dog walking," she said, and I answered, "Do you like playing the game Twister?"

Luckily, Rhiannon flowed into the change of topic and enthused, "Twister is such a hoot!" She loved strawberry milk, and I told her I that I did, too. With great embarrassment, she admitted that she still owned a collection of dolls, but she explained that they were costume dolls from all over the world. "So far, I've got dolls from most European countries, some from the Middle East and Asia, Peru, Jamaica, and two Canadian Mounties."

I replied, "bless them" and asked her if she had a Native American doll. She shook her head. "No. Not yet."

My most embarrassing admission had to be my parents' divorce, and I fixed to say that, but then I lost my nerve and lied about having a doll collection too. "I left it behind in Texas," I mumbled, as my voice trickled to a whisper.

Rhiannon smiled and asked me what Texas looked like.

"Well . . ." I had to think, as I'd never described it before. "I lived in a much bigger town than this, next to a lake . . . 'cept the lake done dried up, because in summer it gets up to ninety five to a hundred degrees, day after day. So, I guess you could say that we lived in a town next to a dried-up hollow of wasteland." My home town in Texas looked pretty, quaint with its old-fashioned main street, but my memory emptied to a blank.

Rhiannon laughed, "I love your accent," which gave me confidence to talk more.

"I had a big yard at my house but it only had one tree, a pecan tree. I always wished we had another. I'd get a hammock and lie in the shade. I never learned to climb trees, though. Zoe wouldn't let anyone near the tree. Silly dog thought she owned all the shade in the yard."

Rhiannon pointed over to the farmhouse where she lived with her elderly parents. The house stood two stories high, brightly painted with whitewashed walls and contrasting black painted window surrounds. A large green and red ivy plant grew up to the top of the gable end. Various outbuildings were newly painted, in black and white, too. She said I could visit her house any time. Her three brothers, bless them, were all much older. They had left home and were married with kids of their own.

"After my brothers grew up, my folks thought they were too old to have more kids, but then I came along," she said with a laugh. "I think I caught them off guard."

*I bet Dad felt caught off guard with Double Pike, too! ... The smell of basil ... circus clowns with painted faces ... beagle puppies with floppy ears ... stomping on bubble wrap with bare feet ...*

I wondered if I'd ever be able to speak as casually about my family, as Rhiannon spoke about hers.

Rhiannon returned her attention to Bracken. When she'd finished rubbing ointment on the horse's cut, she pulled strands of wool from her coat pocket – red, blue and green. As we chatted, she entwined the three strands into a pleat, knotting them together before tying the pleat around the stump of Bracken's tail.

"That's pretty," I said, and asked her the name of such a thing.

"It's a snaithe."

Curious, I wanted to know more about snaithes, but didn't want to sound like an ignorant American. Maybe Grandpa would tell me.

"Hey, how would you like to come and hang out with me and a few friends down at the local café, later?" said Rhiannon.

I watched her take a small gold ring from her finger. She put it, and a coin, into a bowl of water and then sprinkled some of the water from the bowl over the horse. How odd.

"I'll introduce you to the guys – Kyle and The Tubby Twins," she said. "Not many girls around here, I'm afraid. That's the trouble with wee country villages. There's a dire shortage of kids," she said, and then added, "Well, there is Bethany MacKinnon and her friends but ... I'll let you find out about Beth and her freaky friends for yourself," said Rhiannon. I mentally noted this girl's name; Bethany MacKinnon.

Rhiannon looked awkward as she clutched the small bowl with the remaining water. *What is she doing with it? Best not ask. Best just ask about this local café.*

"Do you mean the Gowan Café, down in the village?" I asked.

"Yes. Tell you what. I'll call for you at your house," she said. "Will you be there at 6:30?"

Would I ever? Hot Diggedy-Dog, I couldn't wait to tell Grandpa that he could swim free.

As I hurried home, I turned back to wave and I saw Rhiannon take the rest of the water and sprinkle it over the horse. Maybe I mistook the situation, but I thought she prayed. She said something like "in the name of the Father, Son, and..." Was she baptizing her horse?

When I arrived back home, at first I couldn't find anyone. Then I heard muttering and weeping coming from Mom's room. Grandpa sat in there with Mom.

"Imaging telling our Brucie in a cold-hearted email… about his floozy's baby! Has the man no respect for Brucie's tender age? She's still a sensitive child. Has he no decency? And what about me?" Mom wailed. "What am I to think? He could have phoned…"

*Dang it!* I hated having to share my laptop with Mom. I should've closed my email before I left the house.

"I know, Fiona," said Grandpa to Mom. "You're hurting badly, but we've got to think of Brucie now. Can't you get up out of bed and come ben the hoose? How about putting on a nice frock and doing your hair up all bonny? Brucie needs you to be strong for her. She'll be back soon, and we can't let her know that you were reading her private things. I think we should wait till she is ready to tell us about the baby. Here, dry your eyes and I'll get us a droppie of tea."

I snuck back out of the front door and came back in again, whistling "Tullochgorum" and calling a loud "Hey there" to Gramps as he came out of Mom's room.

"W… well… Hello. There's my favorite lassie," he stammered. "Come ben the kitchen and tell me all your craic. You look cheery. What have you been doing?"

"I found a friend, Gramps! I did. I really did." I felt genuinely excited, but fifty percent of my babbling camouflaged anger. Mom made me steam sometimes. *Why did she read my mail?*

I continued. "My friend is nice. Her name is Rhiannon and she'll be calling for me at 6:30," I said, escaping toward the bathroom. "Need to shower now and fix my hair, because we're meeting these guys at the café." I blurted quickly, trying to exit so that I could punch something.

"Hold it! Guys! Guys?" asked Grandpa, scowling.

"Yes, one is called Kyle and then there are twins called 'The Tubbies.'"

"Okay, hold your horses. Back up a bit, young Miss, and talk to your old Gramps." He caught my arm. "My goodness! You've made friends already? Why, only this morning…" He trailed off then changed tracks, "You mean Rhiannon up at Cnocnadarach Farm? Ah, yes, Ann and Charlie's wee one. Her brothers are much older."

I pulled my arm away. "Wee one!" I said, "Quit, Grandpa! Rhiannon is sixteen years old, I'll have you know!"

He ignored my correction and asked me to repeat the boys' names. *Will I EVER get to the shower?*

"I told you, Gramps, one is called Kyle and the other two are twins, called something like Tubby."

Gramps scratched his head, "Yes, I know Kyle, that's Marina MacKay's lad, but I've never heard of a surname called Tubby. Maybe it is Duncan and Donald you mean: Rev. MacLeod's boys from the church manse? They'll keep you right. Anything clever, weird or wonderful you need to know … go ask thon Macleod twins, they say."

"Who says?" I snapped, reaching for a clean towel from the closet. "Don't you know," and I imitated something Mom always said to me, "a gossip's mouth is the devil's mail sack."

Thankfully, Mom couldn't hear me mock her.

I felt unusually angry with Gramps and suddenly protective about my soon-to-be friends. My annoyance probably showed, because he didn't answer my question. Pangs of guilt churned in my gut, for acting so snippy to my faithful old buddy. I blamed Double Pike mostly, but also my mom, for reading about him in my email. In fact, I became so preoccupied, thinking about Mom crying every day and about Double Pike, I also blamed them for what happened next.


Unlike me and Mom, we have red hair, my Grandpa has black hair. Well, once upon a time his hair grew black. Obviously, his hair is now grey, but I only found *that* out by accident.

I'd already wet my hair in the shower when I realized my bottle of L'Oreal Elvive still sat on the top of the chest in the bedroom, so I used some of Grandpa's shampoo. It smelled okay, a bit like that herb-infused, olive oil that you dip crusty Italian bread in. If I'd been paying closer attention, though, I might have noticed its dark-colored lather. Instead, I tried to be happy … *Bart Simpson … the word "hiccup" … making picture collages from comic books … feeding nuts to squirrels in the park … reading road signs backwards …*

"Dry your hair, if you're going out, Brucie," called Mom as I unlocked the bathroom door. Well, at least she'd stopped crying. That seemed promising. Why does she always say, "Dry your hair?" She knows my routine:

towel dry, pull a wide-toothed Afro comb through the curls, and leave it to hang wet. I've done it so often I don't even need to check a mirror.

The doorbell rang, so I quickly pulled on my clothes as fast as I could: boot cut jeans, which I'd carefully laid out on the bed, my 'Frazzle Bo Dazzle' t-shirt, denim jacket, and my vintage-look cowgirl boots (ones that Grandma Centerville bought to remind me of Texas.) Pointing my toes, with thumbs hooked in the belt loops of my jeans, I practiced a few long leggy strides around the bedroom, doused "spell-binding erotica" behind my ears and on my wrists, and said to myself in a super cool voice, "Bling. Bling. Go strut your thang, Brucie MacKenzie-Bice." I swaggered up Grandpa's hallway to the front door, where Rhiannon waited outside.

Her jaw hung wide open.

I puffed out like a peacock, but when moments passed and she didn't speak, I asked, "What? Whassup?"

She stared at my head. "Eh, didn't you have red hair?"

"Yup." I had no clue what she talked about. Not even one.

Rhiannon pointed, "I wouldn't have mentioned anything, but you also have these dark streaks that run down your face."

I froze with my jaw open. "Do I?"

My new, very best friend rolled up her sleeves. "Yes, but the sooner you invite me to come inside, the sooner I'll be able to help you clean up."

"I'm sorry, yes, come in," I said, and scrambled to the mirror in the sitting room. Studying my reflection, I hollered my grandfather. "Gramps! Have you per chance concocted any experimental hair dye recipes?" I screamed.

He stuck his head around the corner and blushed. "Oops! I'll get you a towel and some fresh shampoo. Don't worry," he said. "It's not permanent."

"I'll wash it for you at the kitchen sink if you like," said Rhiannon.

"Yes, please. Could you?"

When the hair dye appeared almost gone, Rhiannon offered a choice of two suggestions. She held up a black marker pen, taken from her purse. "Either we both wear hats, or I can join up the remaining black dots by drawing a spider's web tattoo on your forehead."

"Only if you draw a web on your forehead, too," I said.

"Nah, let's wear hats," she said, and laughed.

As we left the house for the cafe, me wearing a sailor's hat that I found in Grandpa's closet and Rhiannon wearing our green knitted tea pot cozy, I told Rhiannon that Grandpa seemed to know everyone in the whole world here, and asked, "Are these Tubby guys called Duncan and Donald MacLeod?"

She smiled, "Yes. You'll get to know everyone soon, but all in good time."

I felt a bit jumpy as we rounded the corner at the bottom of the road, what with all these new friends to meet in one day and me still an immigrant, wearing a sailor hat. We passed the old war memorial: a stone statue of a kilted soldier pointing a rifle. Below the statue, a list of names of young soldiers from the village who had died during the war had been chiseled into the granite stone. A red poppy wreath lay against the base. My stride felt suddenly regimental, a march, keeping time with Rhiannon. As we neared the cafe, my stomach fluttered with butterflies, so I twiddled the stone pendant.

Buzz.

Weird! There it came again, that buzz; the doorbell feeling, the waiting for a reply. I felt heady, detached from my surroundings, so I stopped to ground myself by leaning my hand on wall outside the café. Reaching to catch my foot with the other hand, I pretended something had stuck to the sole of my shoe. Rhiannon said something like, "you should get yourself some comfier shoes," but I looked around, back toward the war monument, expecting to see or hear someone else emerge. Did we have company? It felt like we were not alone that night. *Who's there?* *Tell me who you are?* I thought. Nothing answered, so I stood tall again.

"Hey, look, guys. Here comes Hyacinth Bucket and Popeye," said blond-haired Kyle, when he saw me and Rhiannon in our hats. Rhiannon laughed, so I did, too. Kyle sat on top of a table inside the café, swinging his legs, which dented off a chair leg, until a woman's voice hollered from behind the serving counter, "Get yer backside off the table, Kyle."

Kyle continued to sit on the table. "Welcome to the Hard Roll Cafe," he said, ignoring the woman's complaint.

This boy had eyelashes to die for, like fawn-colored butterfly wings. He had grey-blue eyes with a small ski-jump nose. Kyle's head amassed with dark blond waves that swayed in the breeze of a nearby fan. He looked younger than the rest of us, but he's fifteen, like me. My birthday is September 28th and his birthday is September 30th, only two days difference. When he grinned, I spied his broken front tooth. "Lost half of it fighting with these guys in the lavvie down at the station, like," he said, jabbing a grubby finger at each of the two identical brothers.

The woman's voice beckoned again. "Kyle! Sit on a chair like everyone else, will you?"

"Sorry!" he called back, jumping down and clumsily dragging a wooden chair over the floor tiles with a loud scrape.

The twins spoke simultaneously. "Hi!" They were tall with square set jaws, high cheekbones and ruddy cheeks. Both wore identical round, wire-rimmed glasses and had the same short brown hair, but one wore jeans and a plain old khaki shirt and the other twin wore a long grey trench coat and a Dick Tracy hat.

"Great minds think alike!" The one in the hat chuckled, complimenting our headwear. "Glad that I dressed for the occasion, Madam," he said, smiling at me. Stepping forward, he bowed and shook my hand. "I'm Donald." *He's slightly taller than his brother, with nicer hands, too.*

"Hi Brucie, I'm Duncan," called his brother, more casually, from behind.

I missed the next few sentences as my eyes scanned the inside of the café. What a drab place, not the trendy hang-out that I'd expected. Horrid tartan wallpaper clung gingerly to walls, overloaded with a mish-mash of paintings with Scottish hills and glens; each painting dotted with scores of sheep and cows, bless them. Cream-colored net draped over wooden curtain rods, all in need of a wash. And, the tables, oh my God, people had scribbled names and messages all over them. In fact, the owners even seemed to supply pens for the purpose. Weird! But, after the initial shock, the café began to welcome me into its fold. I liked it. An old jukebox sat in the corner, which looked cool. I ached to check out the selection of music, and to pick up a pen and write my name.

Studying my face, Rhiannon whispered, "Ignore the grotty furnishings. The craic is good, the coffee's sound and it's cheap."

Kyle hopped from leg to leg in my peripheral vision, like he'd explode if he didn't get to interrupt my view and win my attention. "Hey!" he said to me, and pointed at the twins. "These guys are SO brainy, like, that they eat dictionaries for breakfast. For lunch today, they ate one of those boring books by thon Shakespeare gadgie, and for dinner they feasted on The Complete A – Z of Train Spotting for Nerds. You know what I mean, like?" Kyle paused to hoot at his own jokes and then said, "As for me, I had twelve pork sausages and a whole loaf of bread, like, and I'm much better looking than them." As he grinned I could see him checking out my boots.

"Kyle! Eating such large volumes of paper would eventually cause a blockage of the large intestine," said Duncan. "Given our distance from an adequate hospital, our intestines could rupture, prompting the need for an emergency colostomy by a proctologist. The risk of peritonitis would be high."

Donald, with the nice hands, added, "Peritonitis, following a messy intestinal surgery, is critical for the first twenty four hours, but I'd recommend seventy two hours of close observation in an intensive care ward, to be safe."

*Hmm ... he has a more muscular neck, too.*

"Hey guys, I once ate fifteen Cadbury's Cream Eggs," said Kyle, grinning into my face, and as he did two dimples appeared in his cheeks. He jumped, fidgeted, twiddled, stretched and lunged, like he seemed totally unable to stand still, adding, "Cool boots, by the way, Brucie."

"Thanks. Were you sick . . . when you ate all those eggs?" I asked, though doubting the truth in Kyle's story.

"Kyle doesn't know how to be sick," said the twins.

"You shouldn't listen to Kyle, you know," said Rhiannon. "We don't," she added.

Fidgeting, joking and bluntness aside, in the months to come, no other friends would prove to be as important to me as my new friends Rhiannon, Kyle, Duncan and Donald. In fact, without them, I'd be as good as a one legged cowboy at a butt kicking contest, especially with so much weird and freaky stuff waiting to transpire. And, especially, as I'd soon clash with the dreadful Bethany MacKinnon ... *Sweet puppy breath ...letting fine sand trickle through your fingers ... Swiss alpine peaks covered in snow ... slurping the bottom dregs of your milkshake through a straw and making the worst noise doing it ...*

After promising I'd be home no later than ten o'clock, I turned my key in the lock at 11.55pm. As I tiptoed in, I knew Grandpa would be waiting in the lounge. Through the crack in the door I spotted him doing the strangest thing. He stood by the fireside hearth, making a circle out of the smoldering remains of the fire and then, with his large claymore sword, the one that usually hangs mounted on the wall, he ceremoniously cut the circle into three sections of peat.

"Who's winning the fight, you or Peaty Pete?" Grandpa loved my puns.

"Come and I'll show you an old Celtic bedtime prayer," he said, forgetting to laugh, but also forgetting to reprimand me for being late.

As I knelt down with Grandpa, he pointed to each of the three peat sections in turn with his sword. "This piece is laid down to honor the God of Life, this one in the name of the God of Peace and the remaining third for the God of Grace."

I watched as he carefully laid ashes over each third section, creating a mound sufficient to smolder well into the night but not too much so as to extinguish the fire. He closed his eyes and held his hand gently over the hearth. In a voice so soft and with such warmth I'll never forget, he said this prayer. "Sacred are the Three, to save, to shield, and to surround. In this hearth, this house, on this night, this eve. Oh, this eve, this night, and each and every night. Amen."

Then, the strangest thing happened. As I stared at the amber glow of the smoldering peat, the eye stone around my neck grew warmer. I clasped it, to verify, and the minute my hand made contact I saw weird pictures within the fireside hearth. The orange embers anchored my gaze as a wavy mirage radiated from the warm core, upward and out toward me. I felt sleepy but my eyes were unable to close or look away. The illusion held me transfixed and curious as it tuned in and out, sometimes clearer, sometimes fuzzy, like I stared at a new television as it scanned for channels. Faster and faster, images jumped in front of my eyes. Faster... faster... faster...

"Grandpa! I think I'm going to vomit . . ."


## Bethany MacKinnon and the Rabbit's Feet

**Bethany MacKinnon rarely brought friends to the caravan. Her foul-mouthed uncle scared young girls. This made Bethany feel isolated, yet powerful, too.**

**But Jake's Land Rover could not be seen; so three girls dared each other to make an approach. They knocked on the caravan door.**

Bethany tweaked the curtain and shouted out of the window. "Hey! You're just in time to help." She grabbed her coat, stepped out and slammed the caravan door behind her, to prevent anyone snooping inside.

Hoisting a ferret from a cage, she also grabbed an axe, which she tucked under the same arm that held the ferret. Beth threw a pile of nets at her perplexed visitors. "Take them nets and follow me." The girls looked at each other and shrugged. Bethany quickly organized them covering rabbit exit holes with the netting.

Beth sent the ferret underground, pushing him down a hole. "Get 'em Zipper! Get them rabbits."

When the first rabbit launched out of a hole, netted, Bethany grabbed it. She grinned at her success.

Dangling the startled rabbit up by its rear leg, she snapped its head back until she felt the neck break. The little bundle of fur flopped limp and lifeless. Bethany laughed as the others squirmed. Then, raising the axe up to her shoulder, she chopped down four times on the dead rabbit's limbs. "Here. Have a lucky rabbit's foot." Bethany chucked a foot at each of the girls and chortled at their gaping mouths. "Who's staying for rabbit and mash dinner then?" she then asked. "Will I put the chitty over the fire?"

The friends were too dumbstruck to answer, and too aghast to hear the approaching Land Rover. Jake's vehicle skidded to a halt and by the time his boots hit the muddy grass the girls all turned in the direction of the town, each clutching a bloodied rabbit's foot. He watched them leave with a smirk. By the time he slammed the driver's door they were gone.

"Anything good today, Uncle?" Bethany studied the pile of boxes inside the Land Rover.

"Italian shoes," he said. "Help me stash them indoors."

## *Chapter 3*

## *Holy Smoke!*

<u>**Tuesday May 3<sup>rd</sup>**</u>

**1. Shopping Malls**

**2. Bueno Burritos with chilli sauce, cheese rice and beans**

**3. Our house and swimming pool**

Some mornings I lay on my bed and compiled lists of things I missed about Texas. My pen stalled at No. 3. I imagined wandering through our old house again. Entering each room, I reminded myself where ornaments sat, which light shades or chairs I liked, and I counted every mirror and picture on my fingers, bless them.

Yesterday Mom said that the estate agent had finally closed the sale on our house. A new family would move in. They'd paint me out of the picture with a thick coat of magnolia primer, like I never existed. Giant brushes -- Swish. Slap. Slop. Brucie's gone.

I recalled how Mom and I sat for the last time, dangling our feet in the swimming pool, and Mom said, "You'll love it in Scotland, Brucie, and once you get to know people there, everyone will love you, too."

She didn't tell me that while I'd be 'getting to know people' in Scotland she'd vegetate like a mushroom in a darkened bedroom, drinking tea and sighing.

*Damn that Michaela and her stinking baby for making my Mom so unhappy!*

I started to add a fourth memory to my list when Mom and Gramps got to arguing in the kitchen. Gramps said some strange word that sounded like 'Feess', "She has the 'Feess', Fiona," and Mom shouted back, "Poppycock! Stop those old wives' tales, right now." I then heard Gramps say 'we should tell her'.

*Tell who, what? What's going on?*

Pots and pans clattered in the sink and then I heard Grandpa shout. "…Dammit, Fiona, she'd be far better off going to school with the other village kids."

I snuck through the house and hid behind the kitchen door, to watch through the crack and listen.

"She's home schooled, Dad," cried Mom. "I'm still as capable of teaching Brucie here, like I taught her back in Texas. I simply need some time for *me* right now. That's all."

Gramps took a deep breath. He thought for a minute and then continued, "Look, I'm not criticizing, Fiona, love. Remember *why* you opted to home school? You spoke of gun threats and how you hated to see Brucie pass through a school metal detector each morning. You complained about the large class sizes, too. It's different in Scotland. These worries don't apply here… and Brucie is bored. She's bored senseless, Fiona!"

I stepped into the kitchen, so that they could see me.

"Mom, I think I would like to go to school."

I waited to see if she'd look at me, or answer, but she didn't.

"Rhiannon said that here in Scotland they graduate to higher classes in May, before the summer break starts. It sounds weird but she says that it makes the last few weeks before summer more productive."

Mom sighed, clasped both hands around her teacup and stared down into the steamy drink.

"Rhiannon told me all about her school," I said. "She is a year older, but I think I know as much stuff as she does, if not more. So, maybe, we could even get to be in some of the same classes."

Mom snapped. "'Rhiannon said this… Rhiannon said that.'" She mocked me.

I caught the look of warning in Gramps' eye and resisted the temptation to snap back at my mother.

"Mom, you were a fun teacher, and we had some great times. Not many kids my age can develop camera film, reconcile a bank account, write HTML programs, wire up light fixtures, change a car tire, and hybridize roses all on top of regular studies. But, I had other home-schooled kids to hang out with in Texas. I don't want home schooling here. I'm bored."

Grandpa's ears pricked up when anyone mentioned gardening. "You never said that you could hybridize roses?"

"You never asked, Grandpa."

"Hmm," he said, looking impressed. "Guess I didn't."

Gramps and I won the argument and we met with the local school headmaster, Mr. Arthur B. Campbell, the next day.

"Hello. Alistair MacKenzie, isn't it?" said the headmaster. (Only local folk called Grandpa "Ali Dubh", which means Dark Ali in Gaelic language.) He continued, "And this will be your granddaughter, Brucie MacKenzie?" Mr. A.B.C. shook both of our hands.

"Actually, I'm Brucie MacKenzie-Bice, the Bice is same as my dad, and Mackenzie is my Mom's name, but I like Brucie Mackenzie fine. So you can call me that and I'll call you Mr. Campbell, shall I?"

My knees buckled like a lassoed steer … *glittery Christmas cards … Grandpa speaking with a voice like Donald Duck … hedgehog feet and noses …*

I looked around his office, which I must say seemed very untidy for an educated man. In the corner of the room sat a mountain bike with muddy tires and a bright orange helmet sitting on top of the seat. Did he feel too old, too superior, or was he excluded from using the kid's bike shed? I meant to ask him, but he spoke first.

"So, let me see now… there are no up-to-date school transcripts, as you say you're home schooled. Well good … that's okay." He smiled, showing kind teeth like Bracken. "Let's talk and I'll ask some questions, Brucie, so I can get a good feel for what you've covered in your education."

We chatted and discussed my options. Mr. Campbell seemed like an animated child trapped inside a tight, grey adult sweater; Free Church grey, I think Grandpa would call it. His hands waved as he spoke, and then they quickly drew back to his side at the end of each sentence as if on elastic. In fact, midsentence, one arm looked like it hailed a taxicab while the other possibly beat eggs for an omelet. He spoke with a happy voice but his protuberant eyes stared from their sockets like a startled deer. He told me that, for a fifteen-year-old, I had a creative mind, my knowledge seemed advanced but I should join the end of the 3rd year classes and study toward the exams to be taken in 4th year. Thereafter, in 5th and 6th years, I'd study for Higher Grade qualifications. The 3rd year equated to 9th grade back in Texas, and so on, but Gramps and I already knew this.

My timetable soon filled up with English, Math, Physics, Biology, French, Social Studies, Computer Science, and looking at the sheet in front of me I felt overwhelmed. I had to choose between History and Geography, as I couldn't fit both, so I chose Geography. I'd never be able to remember all the dates of historical battles and names of all the Kings and Queens, even though I loved hearing about Scottish history. Physical Education scheduled into Monday last thing and on Friday mornings. I wondered how I'd get through the week and stay fit for a Friday work out! Before we left the school I couldn't help noting that the building smelled of antiseptic, custard and old tennis shoes.

Gramps shook the hand of Mr. A. B. C. and then we walked to the car without speaking. I think Gramps waited for me to speak first, but I didn't.

Back home in Ardcarron, I phoned Rhiannon right away, to share my news.

"Brilliant!" she whooped. "I'm coming down the hill to see you."

Rhiannon and I sat on my bed, singing Tullochgorum. We laughed when I mispronounced words. I discovered that we've both read some of the same old-fashioned books, like *The Swiss Family Robinson* and *Robinson Crusoe*. I asked Rhiannon what possessions she would grab if shipwrecked on a deserted island. "My lifejacket, dummy," she said, laughing. I told her, "I couldn't live without cheese burgers. I've eaten them since the time before they invented obesity." We agreed that we wear the same size in skinny jeans but my feet are a size bigger than Rhiannon's.

We decided to go sing outside in the front garden. Actually, Mom hollered, "Quieten down, you two!" I think we exuded too much cheerful energy for Mom's depression to handle.

Grandpa gave us two old tweed deerstalking hats to wear from the hook in the front lobby. I ditched mine, though, when Gramps told me why Harris Tweed cloth always smelled weird.

"After weaving the cloth they steep it in urine," he said.

Tossing the hat, I screamed, "P-U!"

Rhiannon suggested we lie on the grass in the sun, so I fetched a rug. She said she never knew any of her grandparents and I said that I only had one grandpa in Scotland and one grandma in Centerville, Texas. I also told

Rhiannon that Mr. A.B.C. had assigned a girl called Carrie Witherspoon to be my "buddy" for the first week or so, to help me learn my way around the school. Carrie would meet me at the headmaster's office first thing the next morning.

"NO WAY!" she exclaimed. "Carrie 'The Goth' is going to be your buddy?"

Somewhat hesitantly, I questioned her. "Carrie 'The Goth'?"

"Oh dear," she said. "The Goth is Bethany MacKinnon's friend. Look, don't worry. Everything will be alright."

Our school bus was scheduled to arrive in Ardcarron at 7:30 outside the corner shop. The shop belonged to the spinster sisters, The Misses MacGregor. It sat across the road from the war monument. My phone stated 7:45.

Despite the early hour, the plumper Miss MacGregor sister busied herself sloshing a soapy bucket of water across the doorway of the store. She then brushed the steamy bubbles across the sidewalk and into the curbside drain. Her skinny, jittery sister wore yellow Marigold gloves and teetered dangerously at the top of a stepladder, sponging the outside of the windows. As she stretched to reach, Kyle MacKay hopped and jiggled below, sniggering and pointing up her skirt.

Behind the shop, the small railway station sat quietly, empty platforms and no trains. I checked my phone again at 7:52. Rhiannon pulled up and padlocked her bicycle to a lamppost, just as the Tubby Twins also rounded the corner and crossed over to meet us. While everyone chatted, my stomach churned like Grandma Centerville's butter ... *The noise that dove wings make when they fly ... twirling dervishes who never get dizzy ... writing my name over and over as if I were famous, using multi colored gel pens ...*

*Ah ... Gothic!* I thought when Mr. Arthur B Campbell introduced me to Carrie The Goth. She looked like Morticia from the Adams family. Her long hair seemed even blacker than Rhiannon's. She wore a flowing black skirt, black boots, black eye-liner on pale, white eye lids but, as Gramps would say, "she had a soor face like a well-spanked arse," which is the same as a butt in Texas. She wore this weird rabbit's foot around her neck.

The Goth kept our small talk to a minimum, except to ask, "Is Brucie short for anything?" which I hate because everyone asks me that. I replied, "Nope, it's just Brucie, which is rare as hen's teeth." She didn't smile. I guessed that she didn't really like her job of being my buddy. Her 'well-spanked arse face' had tight prissy lips, much like a butt hole.

The Goth didn't walk: she floated along, with her head so erect like she balanced a book on top. When she wanted to look to the side, she turned her whole body. I wondered if she acted weird, posh, or if she had a sore neck. Maybe Mr. Arthur B. Campbell and I needed to have a few more words about a better choice of buddy, but in the mathematics class Rhiannon said, "N – O!"

By lunch The Goth seemed to like me more; in fact, she asked me to sit with her and two of her friends in the canteen, at lunch. They were called Gemma and Dawn, also dressed in black. I suddenly noticed that they all wore the same rabbit's foot necklaces. Weird! So, there I sat, wedged in the middle in my glitzy pink t-shirt, 'like a pig in a poke,' which is another of Grandpa's expressions.

"Nice French fries," I said, tasting one, but The Goth stared at me, oddly. I corrected myself, "Sorry, you call them chips here, don't you? Nice chips."

After a few minutes, Gemma burst out giggling. I wondered if I'd said something dumb, again, but she seemed generally flighty, tapping her feet to an imaginary rhythm, waving her arms as she spoke, eyes darting around the room. She fluttered like a moth, not unlike Kyle MacKay. I later found out that the two were cousins.

Gemma, Dawn and Carrie began discussing music lyrics by groups I'd never heard of, like The Dead Dairymen, Funeral for Jane, and Infected Vomit.

"Anyone like country music?" I asked.

They stared but no one replied.

I caught sight of Rhiannon, sitting at a table to the back of the canteen. *Look at me Rhiannon. I'm over here. THIS way! Hear my thoughts. PLEASE come and rescue me ... Dag nab it! ... Swimming with dolphins ... pillow fights on giant four-poster beds ... finding the last seat in a crowded cinema ...whistling through front teeth ...*

Chomping on a mouthful of pizza, Dawn, to my left, suddenly coughed. A pink chunk of pepperoni launched from her throat and stuck to the side of my Pepsi can.

"Oh, that's okay. You didn't mean to do it," I said, before realizing that she hadn't even apologized.

I scarfed down the rest of my sandwich and stood up.

"Okay, thanks for inviting me to sit with you. I'm really getting to know my way around quite well now. So, I'll go now and maybe see you all later."

As I turned to leave, another girl joined us and pushed me back to a sitting position. Boy, this girl could talk ten words a second, with gusts up to fifty! She stood tall, with an athletic build, chiseled cheekbones, hard, ice-grey eyes, and short, blonde, spiky hair.

"Hi there, I'm Beth. Bethany MacKinnon. What's your name?"

"Brucie short for nothing," I said. *Hmm,* I thought. *So you're Bethany MacKinnon.*

I warmed to Bethany. She asked me tons of questions about myself and she had great shoes. They looked expensive, very Italian. She even invited me to hang out with her and the other three girls any time I wanted. So, for every lunch hour that week, I somehow did. Maybe, though, I did so because every corner I turned, I would bump into Bethany, who would lock arms with me and sweep me away like a hawk with a rabbit.

"Be careful," said Rhiannon, but I didn't get it. Beth and I were getting on fine. I gave Rhiannon my "spell-binding erotica" bottle. "You can keep it for a week," I said. I wanted her to know she remained my best friend. She gave me a packet of spearmint tic tacs and a picture she'd cut from a magazine showing Taylor Swift wearing boots like mine.

In the school corridors, without Rhiannon or Beth with me, I tried not to appear like the lone immigrant. I did try. But, so often these irritating kids flocked around me.

"What's Brucie short for?" they'd ask. Or, "Say something Texan," they'd say, and gawk at my mouth as if expecting to *see* the words come out.

"Something Texan," I'd say and walk on.

"No, say something American... like 'Howdy Pardner'," one kid would start.

Then another kid would complete the mockery. "That sho-iz a purty dress, Emmy Lou. Lemme go cut sum far wud so's y'all can cook dat possum." And they'd all fall about in hysterics.

"Y'all quitcherbitchin'! Fiezyu I'd git outa here," I'd holler, sounding like old Grandma Bice back in Centerville.

Oh, why couldn't I learn to zip my mouth? I was still an immigrant!

Sometimes, after that, I'd get Rhiannon to speak for me. Or, if we were in the same class and I didn't understand something, I'd tap her leg under the desk, rather than ask the teacher out loud.

"Brucie, people love your name and your accent. They do. Pay no attention to those kids," she'd say, but I felt self-conscious. Coolness doesn't stick overnight. I'd work on it, though.

Bethany told me that she understood how I felt, too. "Here, take a puff of my cigarette," she said. "It'll make you feel better. Give you confidence."

"No, thanks." I said. "It sure smells weird for a cigarette."

She laughed. We stood behind the gymnasium, in between a large padlocked building and the store for all the soccer nets and track equipment. The stiff-necked Goth, the fluttering Moth, and Dawn with the pepperoni cough all took a puff of this musky cigarette. I felt muddled as a goat on Astro-Turf when Beth put it in my hand. Other kids gawked, staring at me, grinning, sniggering, and nudging each other.

In my head, I heard Mom's voice lecturing me on smoking. She'd made me vocalize the routine. 'Keep an eye out for potential trouble, understand when you need to make the right decision and have the courage to act upon it.' But when you see all those peering eyes fixed upon you, for real…

I held it between my index finger and thumb, like Beth did, and pretended to suck in a tiny amount of smoke.

"Have another puff. Breathe in deeply this time, and hold it in your lungs" said Beth.

My stomach heaved. It smelled awful. I put my hand to my chest to stop myself gagging and I clutched my stone.

Buzz.

A door eased open inside my mind. I felt something step out from inside my head… like a shadow bursting out from my imagination. This shadowy figure stood inches from my face, watching me. I stared at two big eyes; eyes that looked back at me. They were my eyes and they beckoned for me to look upward. I couldn't resist. As I glanced up, I felt a physical pull, elevating me to a position about 8-10 feet off the ground. My body suddenly felt heavy and I split in two. The heavier part of me fell to the ground, while my lighter body now hovered above. I stared down at my other self, lying on the ground.

*There are two of me! My body has split in two.*

A purple haze of light shimmered over my lower self and over other people standing below. Someone bent over my body below, asking, "Are you okay, Brucie?" Everyone spoke and moved so slowly.

*What's happening? I'm lying there motionless with my eyes shut. Am I breathing? Am I ...dead?*

I expected to see Beth, The Goth, Moth and Cough down there but in their place I saw four old hags, like withered and witchy versions of the girls. The four hags grinned through rabbit-like teeth. The first, resembling Goth, clutched an ugly ulcer that bled inside her belly. An aging Cough gagged with swollen lungs that bubbled mucus, thick and dark as molasses. Old Moth's bones looked so thin that they crumbled and snapped like powdery twigs. These three crones looked evil. I tried to lower myself closer, to see the fourth crooked figure. Suddenly, Beth's head turned and snarled up at me. She snapped with pointed teeth like a rabid hound, mouthing threats up at me. I struggled to hear. *What did she say?*

OH MY G... WHAT THE H...

SLAM!

The crash back into my lower body happened so sudden that my lungs emptied of air. I lay stunned, on the ground. Just one of me, looking up...

"Come on, Brucie. Get up!" barked Beth, shaking me and slapping me hard. "Someone, get the school nurse, call a doctor, or..."

"Why d'ya make the kid smoke it, Beth? You idiot! Where did you get the joint from anyway?" asked a voice from the wavy sea of faces above me. "I think she has asthma, or something, because she's wheezing now."

"At least she's breathing," said another.

A third joined in. "Hey, that's the American kid. It'll serve you right if she sues you, Beth. Americans always sue people."

"Shut up all of you, with your smart comments and questions," said Beth. "Brucie chose to smoke. No one forced the stupid dork to do anything that she didn't want to do."

*Stupid dork, huh?*

Donald pushed through the crowd and helped me to my feet, closely followed by Duncan and Kyle.

I remember being led indoors. After an 'all clear' by the school nurse, Mr A.B.C. told me to sit in the rest room and wait for someone to take me home. He said something about 'rumors of cannabis', 'further enquiries', 'disappointing conduct,' and then rambled on about being 'willing to make allowances' but I felt too overwhelmed to listen.

*How could there be two of me?*

Soon, the door to the rest room opened and Mom stomped in, raging. "Cannabis!" she said.

Driving home, I begged. "Mom, please don't take me out of school because of this."

She kept replying, "Cannabis, Brucie! Cannabis! My daughter! In school! Smoking cannabis!"

"But Mom, I didn't even smoke anything. I just pretended to do it."

*How can I get her to believe me?*

That night I researched the effects of cannabis on the Internet but I found nothing about 'out of body experiences'. I did read that cannabis, when taken in large doses, can contain some chemicals that may induce auditory and visual hallucinations.

*But I didn't smoke anything. I only held the thing and pretended to smoke it!*

Mom lodged a bullying complaint with the school but, 'without any witnesses', Mr. A.B.C said he was 'powerless to act'. He said, "The matter seems to concern rumor, without evidence. Unfortunately, this is Brucie's word against that of Bethany MacKinnon, who adamantly denies involvement or possession of cannabis or tobacco. I have spoken to both girls, spelling out the seriousness of the situation. They both assure me that there will be no future problems so I have to consider the matter closed."

A week passed. Mom raged for a while and then slipped back into her darkened room, drinking tea and slouching about in her bath robe all day.

Grandpa gave her a hug. "Maybe you need to see a doctor, pet, and get some antidepressants." He stroked her hair. "I can't remember the last time you bonnied yourself up and wore make up."

"I told you, I've already seen the doctor, Dad, some weeks ago. I have an appointment at the hospital tomorrow to see a psychotherapist. I hate hospitals, though, ever since..."

Grandpa finished her sentence. "I know, ever since your mother passed away."

"I'll go with you, Mom," I said, trying to make up for the upset. I also had a plan in mind.

Gramps smiled. "Go on, Fiona, pet. Let her help. The company will do you good."

I left school early, the day of Mom's appointment. Mom explained in a note that I had to go to the hospital. We just omitted to say that the appointment was not for me. At the psychiatric hospital we sat in the waiting room until the receptionist called Mom's name. With limited time available until Mom's appointment ended, I then began to scan every available magazine and leaflet in the waiting room, looking for information on out of body experiences or hallucinations. All I found were some handouts on Overcoming Anxiety and Depression. I took one for Mom. Finding nothing else, I approached the reception desk.

"Excuse me. Do you have any self-help leaflets?"

"What sort of self-help do you need?" she asked.

"Oh, it's not for me. It's for a friend." I lied. "She's hallucinating."

The receptionist frowned. "All we have is what you see on the tables. I'd tell your friend to contact a doctor."

I nodded.

It felt clinically weird, sitting there. Freaky paintings adorned the walls, designed by some of the mental health patients (according to a typed notice). To keep my eyes off the artwork, I chatted to a man with a checked shirt. He said he had severe arachnophobia and so I told him about Texan Brown Recluse spiders and Black Widows. I thought he'd be happier to know that Scottish spiders are friendlier, like Gramps said. However, he began to smell of hot sawdust, so I guess I'd made him real nervous. Sweat dripped off his brow; he fumbled with a ruler in his back pocket and he quickly left without seeing his doctor."

"Brucie!" Mom exclaimed, when I told her.

As Mom's happiness steadily increased, my sanity took a nosedive. Following Mom's complaint about the bullying and cannabis, Beth began to hunt me down on a daily basis. She spat on me and pressed chewed gum into my hair, and that was only the start ...*supermarket baskets full of butterscotch sundaes ... thousands of waving candles in a dark auditorium ... multi-colored magic carpets ... and Grandpa's face when he invents a new cooking recipe...*

"Carrot Frizz Ball" she'd call, and trip me with her foot. "You'd better not stand on the street corner with hair like that," she'd say, "folk will think you're a traffic light."

One day she pushed me into the boy's toilet and held the door shut ... *berry flavor lip gloss ... my friend Rhiannon ... playing the game 'Twister' ...*

On June 27th, I sighed, SO relieved to hear the ring of that noon bell. *I've done it! I made it through my first few weeks of school.* A rousing cheer filled every classroom and kids ran down the corridors singing *School's Out for Summer.* Boarding the bus, heading to the back row of seats, I grouped in a huddle with Rhiannon, Kyle, Duncan and Donald.

As bus engine revved up, the last passenger boarded. I'd recognize that blonde spiky hair anywhere. Beth strode up the bus aisle. She stared straight at me, and then dragged her pointing finger horizontally across her throat, and mouthed, "You're dead."

I suddenly remembered. Those were the words that she, I mean the old hag, had mouthed, the day I hovered over her; "You're dead!" I clutched my stone and felt fear, intense fear, like grave trouble lay ahead.


## The Fate of Bethany's Foster Family

Bethany scowled at her friend Carrie. "Brucie reminds me of this kid I used to know, a spoiled red haired kid just like her. That kid was the blood daughter of my first foster family. I ran away from them."

Beth rarely spoke about her past. Bugged by bitterness and Brucie, she spat out her tale.

"They always treat you different from their own kids, these do-gooder fostering folk. Uncle Jake says they only become foster families for one of two reasons; to get extra benefit money or to impress God. It's never because they want us kids."

Carrie listened but stared ahead, expressionless.

"That kid and her fat mother crossed me once too often. I stuck it to them good and proper, though, before I left."

Carrie turned. "What did you do?"

"I put a curse on them."

"What happened then?" asked Carrie.

"Car hit a tree, rolled down an embankment, burst into flames. All dead."

# Chapter 4

## Chills at the Icehouse

On the black and starless night of July 1st, I wrestled with insomnia. I felt weary, like the last aching runner hobbling toward the finishing line of a marathon. Fixing my gaze in the direction of the bedroom window, I waited for the dawn. *Please be a sunny morning as warm as Texas and then... let me sleep.*

Finally, a glint of light split through the glass and bounced down to reflect off the Eye Stone around my neck. My weighty eyelids sprung open as pink, green and yellow sparkling prisms danced over the stone. My body felt weightless and warm like feathery down. Closing my eyes, I surrendered to the opened door inside my head. I entered into a room where voices called to me.

They said, *Of course, parents tell lies. Little girls were never made of sugar and spice! Your insides are much more complex, Brucie. You've always feared your insides, haven't you?*

"Who is there?" I asked. "Am I dreaming? Who is this talking in my head?"

*It's you! You are thinking these thoughts, Brucie. You are thinking back to Texas now.*

"Am I?"

*Remember the hot Texas nights? Your Mom and Dad slept, and you lay awake listening to the hypnotic whirr of cicadas, droning in the Magnolia tree outside your house. Then, you tumbled into unexplained fear, terrified behind your eyelids, fighting the fearful sounds of your own pumping heart. Your heartbeat scared you, didn't it?*

"I don't remember. Who is this, please?"

*What if your heart stopped, Brucie? So many rigid nights you spent locked in your worries, ear pressed to the pillow, listening, listening, and listening. Do you remember now?*

"Why am I thinking this?" I said. "Am I awake or asleep?"

*It's time to let go of fear now, Brucie.*

"I don't understand."

*You can't run from your bed and cry to your Mom now, Brucie. Let go of your fear.*

"Yes, I remember running to Mom when I got scared in the night."

*Her words helped you only until the next night, when you'd hear your heartbeats race again.*

"Stop it. You're frightening me now!" I said, but the voices continued.

*Your dad said that boys were made of rats and snails and puppy-dog's tales. He stroked your head and gazed all gooey and lovingly at you when he said that. You asked how wide he loved you and he said as wide as the ocean. You asked how high he loved you and he said as tall as the sky. But, you barely cleared five foot tall and he left you, didn't he?*

"Stop it!"

*It's you that is thinking this, Brucie. You.*

"Am I?"

I felt myself tumbling inward again, listening to my heartbeat. I remembered the fear. Horses and dogs began to chase me. I stumbled into stone mazes of inner shadowy rooms looking for somewhere to hide.

"Why am I so frightened? Am I bad inside? Is it my fault that Mom and Dad separated? Is Bethany MacKinnon going to hate me forever?"

*It's time to let go of fear, Brucie. Nothing will harm you. It's time to let go of fear. You don't need to hide, Brucie. Search for an exit.*

"Okay. I'm searching."

Out on the horizon a tightrope appears.

"Oh no, not the tightrope dream."

*…Try to cross it, Brucie. Don't be scared. A giant sea will swell below your feet but don't look down. The rope is swaying now, Brucie. Concentrate on breathing. Listen to your heart. Ba-boom! Ba-boom! It's getting louder! Ba-boom! Ba-BOOM! Ba-BOOM! BA-BOOM!!* .

I jolted awake with a scream. "AAHHHHHHH!"

Grandpa burst into the room. "You look like you've met a ghost, Brucie," he said.

"Maybe I have," I said, shaking sleep from my eyes.

He fetched a cup of hot tea and sat on my bed. The tea comforted me. It soothed and oozed me out from a dark inside world, like a butterfly unfolding from its chrysalis. My inner world healed as Gramps held my hand. I suddenly felt larger, stronger and safer; more like myself.

By the time I showered and dressed, Gramps appeared outside the window. He walked into the distance, following the dyke down the southwest field to the rear of the house. These were the fields where I mustn't count sheep without saying, "bless them."  I wondered if he'd lost something, for he paced about searching at his feet.  In the verdant meadow, he shuffled about amidst the clover and daisies.  As Gramps turned, something shiny glinted in his hands. *What's he holding?*

As I continued to watch Gramps, Mom swung the door open and entered my room, clutching a large pair of binoculars.

"He-ll-o?" I said to her, "Didn't we agree that grownups would knock now instead of bursting into my room?"

"Oh, Brucie, you're so pernickety.  Don't get your knickers in a knot. It's only me," she said.

"I could have been standing here naked, Mom!"

She laughed.  Her hands fumbled to focus the lenses on Gramps. Sometimes Mom annoyed me so.

"I think I preferred you with depression," I muttered.

Using a pen, I extracted ten pounds from the belly of my piggy bank and quickly chose between the black beret and the baseball cap, so I could leave.  Baseball won.  Mom asked what I'd muttered, but I didn't answer.

She peered again through the binoculars.  "What's he doing out there, the old fool?  Go out and ask him what he's doing, will you, Brucie?"

"He's not an old fool, and I'm not your servant," I said, glad to slam the door and exit.

I joined Grandpa pacing up the 'bless them' field.  He held two, thick copper-colored rods, bent into L-shapes.  Gramps gripped the shorter lengths as handles while the longer bits protruded about a foot in front of him.  Like guns they were, one in each hand.

I asked, "Aren't you a bit old to play at The Lone Ranger with those pretend guns?"

"No, these are divining rods and I'm trying to find the location of an old well."

My fingers twirled and fiddled with my Eye Stone and I really don't know why I said the next five words.

"The well is over there." I pointed.  To my astonishment, I continued speaking about the well.  "It is right there, where that thorny tree grows, by the two dark rocks covered with yellow lichen.  It's dried up, though.  An old tramp washed his dirty clothes in the water, and it dried up.  Wells do that if you don't respect them."

Gramps raised his eyebrows and stared at me, lifting his cap to scratch his head. His puzzled expression made me panic.

"Who told you all that about the well?" he asked.

"Eh . . . Rhiannon," I lied.

*The well IS over there. I just KNOW it. But how do I know it?*

Gramps hesitated and then grinned. "Fancy you young lassies knowing that. Oh well, no need for these then," he said, tucking the rods into his back pocket.

*Wait a minute,* I thought, *is that a tramp over there?*

I tried to ask Gramps if he saw the tramp, too, but he raised his arms, palms up, and spoke over me. "Lived here all my years and I'll be darned if I've heard that tale about the tramp and the well before," he said. His arms fell to his sides and he sighed. "How can a well move such a distance?"

*Weird! I could have sworn I saw a tramp.*

"Look," I said, "I'm going to Rhiannon's now so I'll see you later, Gramps, okay?"

Gramps' mind wandered elsewhere. A bumblebee landed on his hand. "Hello there, Delius," he said, "and how can I help you today?"

"Are you speaking to that bee?" I asked.

"It's a foggie-toddler," he said. "a seillean mòr, and she's asking the way to the dahlias and snapdragons. . . "

"I'm starting to think that I inherited my strangeness from you, Gramps."

While Gramps pointed the bee in the direction of the neighbor's garden, I snuck away.

All the way up the road to Rhiannon's house, at Cnocnadarach Farm (Hill of the Oaks), I thought about what I'd told Grandpa about the well. And, then I thought about last night's dream. My skin rose with goose bumps and I shivered, even in the bright sunlight.

The craggy-faced boulders and gnarled oaks that I passed en-route suddenly seemed to have faces. They stared out at me from the fields, watching, so I fixed my gaze on the mountains in the distant west and tried to ignore everything else.

*What's that? Did I hear a footstep on the road behind me?*

I checked behind me.

*No. My imagination is playing tricks.*

I walked on the soft grassy verge, next to the ditch where tadpoles swam, to eliminate the noise of my own feet on the gravel.

*No. I don't hear anything now. I'm safe.*

I persuaded Rhiannon to walk back to the town with me, but via a different route. The thought of trees with faces scared me. My best friend and I cut through the fields and down the hill again. While squinting to see if any rocks had craggy faces, I thrust my hands deep into my pockets. It stopped my fingers trembling.

"Are you okay, Brucie?" Rhiannon asked. "You're very nervous today."

I nodded. "Yes. I'm good thanks." But, I wasn't.

We stopped on Ardcarron Brae at Gargoyle House where the twins live. I call it Gargoyle House because it has these carved stone faces with gaping mouths on the eaves and on the archway above the front door. (Donald swears the faces are cherubs, but I say gargoyles.)

Gargoyle House was built in 1853 by a landowner called Sir Edwin Shearer Ross. The church bought the big house, in a state of disrepair. They modestly renovated the building to house Rev. MacLeod and his twelve children. How the twins survive amidst ten other siblings I'll never know. Kirsty-Morag, Ailsa, and Alistair Hugh are at university in Edinburgh, but the rest all live in Gargoyle House together. Mhairi-Ann and Fiona are in the two senior classes in our school. They are followed by the twins Duncan and Donald, Catriona, Caitlyn, Kirsten, John-Alexander and baby Callum. I think I got that right. Bless them!

When we knocked on the front door of Gargoyle House, Duncan and Donald stood waiting for us, both wearing identical black hoodies. I couldn't compare the twins' necks, so I checked their hands to identify Donald. We four ambled down the rest of the Brae, onto the main street and turned left, crossing the road toward the circular metal bench in the village center. My head still buzzed with dreams, wells and tramps.

Kyle joined us all near the bus stop, outside The Misses MacGregor's store. He had something purple, like blackcurrant juice, spilt down the front of his grey t-shirt. Bouncing toward the twins, he beat his chest like an ape, boasting that he had secured a summer job with the spinster sisters in their shop. "Hey guys, I'll be working there for a couple of hours in the morning, you know, like. . . collecting morning papers from the train, mopping floors and stocking shelves with stuff. . ."

" . . . And nosing up old wifies' skirts, no doubt." Rhiannon sneered.

As far as local shops go, The Misses MacGregor's store loomed dark and baron as an old mare's womb. Since the construction of the Firth Bridge and bypass road, business dwindled in the town of Ardcarron. The sisters' shop sold a mish mash of newspapers, party balloons and birthday cake candles, Vick's chest rub in preparation of foreseeable cold snaps, sun screen in case of unlikely heat, day-old sandwiches in a sparsely-stocked fridge, some postcards, local maps, fishing permits, and boat hire could be purchased, too. Practical teenage food, like Pot Noodles, would never secure a place on their shelves.

"I don't know how those two old biddies stay in business," said Duncan. "They're so naïve, never traveled south of Inverness in their lives. I mean, for God's sake, they still rave on about the wonderful invention of traffic lights, 'Aye, in Inverness, the red lights stops the cars so that you can cross the busy street. How wonderful!'" he mocked. "Don't expect the shop to sell anything more modern than staple goods like porridge oats and tatties."

Kyle stirred up fervor, though. Still bragging about his job, he said, "And, hey guys, with my wage I'm going to buy a 75cc moped from my cousin. He'll give it to me for a steal, like."

Suddenly, Kyle paused, pointing out frown lines on my forehead. "What's wrong, Brucie? You're looking a bit flustered there, like. Oops..." he said, covering his mouth with his hand and leaping backward and then forward again. "Did I say the wrong thing? Is it your period... you know, Pre Menstrual Stuff?" Without waiting for an answer, he raced into the next three sentences and then ended with, "Hey, let's go into the Gowan Café? We could loosen the tops on all the salt shakers again?"

"I've got a headache, that's all. Maybe some fresh air will help. Let's just keep walking."

We strolled up the single-track road that circled around outer reaches of Ardcarron. Over and over I told myself to relax.

*There are no faces in those boulders and these are my friends. I should trust them,* I thought. *I'm safe. Everything is good.*

Many times, I'd wanted to tell Rhiannon about some of the weird stuff I'd been experiencing, but I didn't want her confusing me for crazy. My number one fear: friends thinking I turned crazy. My second worst fear: actually BEING crazy.

Sometimes I felt like an impersonation of an American girl who had come to live in Scotland. People expect me to fit the mold of a 'typical American girl'; if ever such a thing actually existed. At school, they place me in a pigeonhole and forget my individuality. The reality of my life, when I thought about it, seemed too surreal, like my life happened to someone else and not me. I wanted to be me, the real me, but lately I couldn't decide if I'd forgotten who I was or if I hadn't found myself yet.

Meandering along past a hedgerow of wild raspberry bush, I wondered to what extent people had prejudged me in Scotland. Ironically, we approached a funny red-roofed house with a hand-written sign propped against the gate, and my own naïve prejudgment kicked in.

**Palm readings.**

**Cross my palm with silver.**

**Minimum donation Five Pounds.**

I'd read a book once about a girl, Betsy, from a travelling family in the south of Scotland and my excitement grew. I recalled how Betsy read someone's palm in exchange for some flour, butter and sugar, which she proudly took home to her mother. Family meant everything to that travelling family and I loved the tales about Betsy's humility and her kindness to animals.

But, suddenly, a sharp pain seared through my forehead. At the same time, I saw one of the curtains move. An old woman peered out from behind the glass, staring right at me.

"How can you cross her palm with silver when the minimum charge is five pounds? That would take at least ten silver fifty pence coins. Nobody carries about that much change," said Duncan.

"Fisher Skeelie can't even count up to ten." Kyle laughed, slapping Duncan on the back. "That's a weird name. Who's Fisher Skeelie?" I asked, noting pain in my forehead again.

"It's that ugly woman at the window," said Kyle. He added, "My mother said they used to call her Scaly Fish, but then over the years folk called her the Fisher Skeelie Woman."

"Yes, but you really don't want to know her," said Rhiannon, popping some gum into her mouth and offering round the remainder of the pack.

I looked back at the croft house, with its wiggly lean-to and rusty, red tin roof.

"Why don't I want to know?"

"Because she's a phony… a con merchant… and a liar." They all agreed.

"Is she a gypsy, I mean does she have Romany blood, I mean…?" I paused. "Oh, never mind, I'm probably using the wrong terminology here."

"Yeah, she's something like that," said Kyle. He then changed his mind, unsure. "No, maybe not. I don't know what she is exactly. All I know is that she's bad news, like."

"I think the term for her is maybe 'scaldie'," said Duncan. "Which means that she may have originally descended from Travellers but she, or her family before her, chose to break away from that life and live in a town."

As we sauntered on, backs now turned to the red house, prickles tripped up and down my spine. My Eye Stone burned uncomfortably hot like fire against my chest. Something felt wrong. The old woman looked scary. I got the feeling of her hiding secrets, bad ones.

I decided that Fisher Skeelie couldn't be from a travelling family like Betsy's. When I read about Betsy and her kinfolk, I felt passionate and connected to their working struggles, living close to the edges of life, taking nothing for granted. I felt warmth, much laughter through hardship, all fiercely connected through strong family bonds. Fisher Skeelie, on the other hand, felt… dangerous, like a lone wolf.

I concentrated on the sweet whistle of blackbirds until the fieriness vanished from my chest. Grandpa had taught me to recognize birdcalls. "Pink! Pink!" The blackbirds then called, warning us to keep our distance from them.

Liquid trills of a fleeting skylark passed overhead, left to right. The sharp, "Tooreep!" of a wagtail pinched my eardrum until the high, screechy, "Mee-oo" of a spying buzzard turned my head the opposite way. "Clack. Clack." Jackdaws startled, flapping in the branches of a beech tree. "Caw!" they scolded.

Around the next bend a familiar landmark emerged into sight, one I had always meant to ask about. "What is that grassy-topped building, set into the side of that hill?"

"An icehouse," said Duncan.

The icehouse was partially buried.  Grass grew over its roof and the back of the building stretched underground into a hillock.  The front gable peaked up in a triangle, to roughly the same height of a two-story house.  It had a wooden door at the front, but no windows.

"Okay, this may be a stupid question but what is the icehouse for?" I asked.

"It was built in 1785," said Donald, "by some entrepreneur called George Dempster.  Fishermen stored ice inside and packed it around fresh salmon.  Prior to 1785, they could only preserve salmon by salting, smoking, or drying them.  The icehouse is abandoned now.  It's really creepy inside, though, isn't it Duncan?  Anyway, Mr. Dempster was well known.  In fact, the poet Robbie Burns even wrote about him."

Duncan quoted Burns, "*A litle Dempster merits it, A Garter gie tae Willie Pitt,*" which I loved, but Rhiannon complained, "You're such a bore, Duncan," so I pretended to yawn, too.

Staring at the icehouse, everyone's voices around me gelled into a droning hum.  I didn't even touch the stone.  It tingled all by itself on my chest and my eyes cocked up toward a cluster of cumulus clouds collecting above the icehouse.  The puffy white globules shifted and swirled.  Gently, they fluffed into one big cotton-candy mass, rotating slowly and pulling downward until a pointing tail formed below the mass.  A small, white vortex had formed, turning in slow motion.  Stretching thinner, the bottom tip formed into an arrowhead, which aimed below toward the icehouse.  All rotation stopped.  The arrow pointed.  Down.  It pointed at the icehouse.  I looked at the door on the gable, knowing it itched to be opened.

"Can we go inside?" I asked.

"It's too dark in there," said Rhiannon.  "We'd need a light."

"I can get a torch, like," said Kyle.  He jumped up and down, pointing to a row of houses.  "My uncle lives there.  He's got lights."  And, before anyone could stop him, Kyle darted off into one of the houses.  He returned with two torches, an oil lamp and a box of matches.  In Texas we call torches flashlights, but I knew what he meant.

The twins laughed.  "Kyle!  We're not spending the night in there.  Brucie just wants to look inside."  When they smiled at me, I felt accepted, worthy and included.  I felt that they really liked me.

"Thanks, guys!" I said.  "You know…" I stalled, wondering how to phrase my words. "Earlier today, something very strange happened. My Grandpa searched for a well today and I helped him find it."

I aimed to tell my friends all about the other strange things, too, but the twins interrupted. "We already knew about your Grandpa looking for the well."

"How come?" I didn't understand.

Kyle nudged Duncan again. "Go on, tell her what happened. I don't think she knows."

"Thanks for dropping me in it, Kyle" said Duncan. He turned to me. "Och, your Grandpa had an argument with our dad, Brucie. They had a major battle over the Garlic Festival and the well."

"What argument? And what's a Garlic Festival?" I asked. I felt tensely protective at the mention of my Granddad.

"I thought you knew," he said. "Your Granddad wants to hold this Pagan festival," said Donald.

"And, I get it. Because your dad is a minister, he objects about Pagan stuff, right?" I guessed.

*Why has nobody told me about a festival or this feud before now?* I felt feisty like Betsy, the girl in the book, when someone threatened one of her family members.

Rhiannon avoided eye contact, staring down to pick at her fingernails.

"Well, yes. But, there's more to it. The village stopped holding festivals and carnivals." He paused. "You see the travelling carnival folk came each year, because they owned the fairground rides like the dodgem cars. They'd park their vans in the field by your house and they'd cause trouble."

*He must mean the 'bless them' field.*

Betsy's story returned to my mind. "Travellers are not trouble-makers. That's unfair to judge them like that," I said.

Kyle said I sounded just like Gramps.

I listened to Duncan talk about 'carnival folk' and began to think about what he'd said earlier about Fisher Skeelie being a 'scaldie' and then I thought about the girl Betsy, trying to make a rational connection or comparison between them all.

"Most of the tinkers were quiet folk, no trouble," said Duncan. "But the local scaldies are troublemakers and their relations started coming here."

I remembered Betsy's reply in the book when someone called her a tinker. She said, most indignantly, 'I've never tinkered in my life before!' I took that to mean that she didn't fix up old broken kettles and sell them, but Betsy could've been joking, too.

My anger grew. "I'm confused. You seem to lump everyone together when you refer to tinkers, scaldies, carnival folk, and Travellers." I looked at my friends. "I mean surely these folk are all different and yet you seem to lump them into the same meaning… and negatively."

"Good point, Brucie," said Donald. "I suppose they are indeed different."

"I mean…" I continued. "Just because I was a girl born in Texas doesn't make mean I'd grow up to be a cheerleader for the Dallas Cowboys. It doesn't make me George Bush's cousin and I sure don't sing like Carrie Underwood."

"Who?" said Kyle.

I didn't answer his question. Instead, I concentrated on keeping calm.

Duncan continued. "Your Gramps wants to revive the gala. People in Ardcarron don't want tinkers…okay, sorry, I mean outsiders who might cause trouble, gathering in the field again but your Grandpa insists on holding this festival. He's even contacted the carnival folk and invited them here."

"Gramps sees the good in things," I said, miffed. "He doesn't put people into pigeon holes." I stood my ground. "We're all different and I think that's a good thing."

"You definitely sound like old Ali now. Why hasn't he told you about his Pagan festival?" asked Donald

"Er… I don't know." I grew so fiercely protective of my Grandpa that my cheeks flushed hot.

*Wait till I get home and speak to Gramps. Why would he keep this from me? I bet Mom knows, too.*

Duncan apologized. "Sorry, Brucie. You see, our dad, being the Free Church minister, went to visit your grandfather about the whole Pagan deal, this Garlic Sunday festival. Your Grandpa wants to find the well so that he can turn it into a Clootie Well, and he's going to re-invent all sorts of old Celtic ideas into a celebration similar to Lughnasa. Dad said that they came to blows and your grandfather hit him."

"NO! You must be wrong. My Gramps wouldn't do such a thing," I said. *Would he?*

"Oh, don't worry Brucie. It happened some time ago. I think the argument has been going on since before you came here, Brucie. Don't worry about it," said the twins.

"So when is Grandpa's Garlic Sunday festival to take place?" I asked, feeling stupid that I didn't even know about it.

"It's the day after the twins' birthday, on July 31st," said Kyle, surprisingly subdued, and now studying his fingernails, too. He raised his head, shuffling to life again, "Hey, are we going to the icehouse now?"

Rhiannon interrupted. "Yes, Kyle. And, can we talk about something else? I think Brucie looks embarrassed. It's not her fault so let's not upset her anymore."

Everyone agreed. Duncan called for group hugs to show support for me, which helped somewhat to calm me down. I'd talk to Gramps when I got home.

The icehouse wasn't locked but the twins had to shoulder the door several times to get it to open. Kyle handed one torch to Rhiannon and one to me. The boys fumbled with the box of matches, eventually lighting the oil lamp. Duncan carried it and led the way inside.

Before following, I meant to check the sky for the white vortex arrow but I felt myself being pulled to go inside.

My torch flickered off and on, like it had a faulty bulb. Simultaneously, I had this flash of a memory, where once, as a child, I chewed dirt. I recalled lying on my belly and sucking the tail of a gritty, old worm to stop him from burrowing down his wormhole. Entering this large underground room, I could taste that same metallic earth and recall the bitter saliva from crunching down on the worm. I clamped a hand to my mouth, easing the nausea from damp, flavorful air.

As we walked inside I felt it immediately. I knew. I'd entered THAT door; the one that had been waiting for me... the same door feeling that buzzed me when I touched my Eye Stone.

Something yanked at me, pulled me though the entrance... some invisible, magnetic force, and I stumbled.

"Watch out, Brucie!" called Rhiannon.

I tripped, fell against the inside wall and landed on the ground.

Rhiannon shone her torch on my face, as I lay on the ground. The twins stepped forward with their oil lamp.

"I'm fine, guys," I said. "Help me up." But, something caught my eye; a white board sat against the wall. It measured about 2 x 3 feet, with bold black alphabet letters written in a circle around the edge.

"Look!" I pointed. "Shine your lights on that over there. What is it?"

"Holy Moly, it's an Ouija board," said Donald.

"And, look here," said Duncan. "It's a glass. Someone has been in here trying to contact spirits."

"That's it! I'm out of here," said Kyle, making for the doorway.

*Don't be afraid!* I kept hearing those words in my head. *Don't be afraid!* So, I said it out loud. "Don't be afraid!"

The twins spoke. "You know these boards can be dangerous. People have developed deep seeded phobias and psychoses from using Ouija boards."

*Don't be afraid!* I heard it again. My heart began to boom. *Ba-boom! Ba-boom!*

Kyle's eyes were huge.

"What's wrong?" I asked him, trying to ignore my beating heart.

"Nothing," he stuttered and twitched. "Are we, like, going to contact dead people?"

Rhiannon pulled me up from the ground and whispered in my ear. "Brucie! Kyle's father died last year?"

Behind us, Kyle's silhouette gingerly edged against the doorframe.

"Aw, no! Don't worry, Kyle. We can go if you feel frightened."

*Don't be afraid!*

Kyle puffed out his chest. "Me? Frightened? Never. What the heck... let's have a go of it, like. We are game for a laugh, aren't we?" Kyle laughed, trying to be brave. "Nothing will happen anyway, will it?"

The twins looked at each other. "Dad would kill us for messing with Ouija boards."

Rhiannon backed them up. "Yes, it's silly. You don't have to impress Brucie with bravado, Kyle. Let's leave."

But, we didn't leave.


*Don't be afraid!*

We'd barely placed the glass on the board, when the icehouse suddenly filled with the strongest stench... a familiar stench . . . gorgonzola cheese?

Roasting goose fat? Cat pee?

*You're late!* he said. I spun around, searching, but saw nothing. His deep throaty bellow resounded with gruffness, like boots on gravel.

"Did you hear that voice?" I said.

"Shut it, Brucie," said Rhiannon. "Quit trying to scare us."

I listened again. Nothing. Not a sound. I asked again. "Seriously! Didn't any of you hear him?"

*I said, "You're late!"* he growled again.

"Do you hear that?" I asked.

"Hear what? We don't hear anything," said my friends.

*They can't hear me!* He laughed.

*Maybe I have schizophrenia. Or, my God, it's a ghost... spinning round on an office chair...cuddly Koala bears sitting in eucalyptus trees...munching toasted marshmallows... Bunty Blackhead in a polka-dot bikini...*

*What is a polka-dot bikini?* he asked.

*In my head... Oh no, I have incoming trouble. I have voices in my head again.*

"Come on Brucie. Don't stand there with your mouth open. Let's do this, so that we can get out of here," said Donald.

I tried to act as normally as possible. "Yes, normally, let's all act normally and do this thing very normally," I blurted.

"Are you okay?" Rhiannon looked concerned.

"Sure. I'm pert as a cricket. But, you can't get lard unless you boil the hog, so let's get this show on the road and go boil a hog."

She shook her head. "Brucie, sometimes you act like you're a sandwich short of a picnic."

Donald placed the glass upside down in the middle of the board.

"Is there anybody there?" he asked. His voice shook like the tail of a rattler.

*Yes, I've been here since eleven o'clock,* the voice sneered.

I tried to keep my cool and ignore the voice. "Is there anyone there?" Donald asked again. "Move the glass if you want to speak."

*I don't need to move the glass. You can hear my voice quite clearly.*

*Who is this?* I spoke into my thoughts.

*At last! So you've decided to speak to me, have you?*

*Who is this?* I asked.

*You'd better do your table-rapping thing again or your friends will think you're not paying attention,* he said.

*Who are you?* I asked again.

*I don't know. You tell me what my name is.*

*What? But, I don't know who you are.* I grew frightened.

*Easy! Put your finger back on the glass and spell out my name.*

*But, I told you, I don't know your name. Do I?*

He fell silent.

"Put your finger back on the glass, Brucie. Try one more time. It's getting cold in here," said Rhiannon, checking behind her shoulders. "I'm playing my fiddle at a ceilidh tomorrow and I need to practice."

Before I could say anything more the glass began moving towards the letter C.

"Ha! Very funny, Brucie," they all said. "Stop pushing the glass."

"I'm not. My finger is barely touching it," I said, as the glass then moved to the O, then, I, and then N. It stopped there for a minute.

*"COIN?"*

*Yes? Nearly there. Keep going.*

"But I'm not doing anything," I told everyone, including the voice.

*Oh yes you are,* he said. *Well done. Okay, there is more to come. Ready?*

The glass spun around and landed back on the N, then it slid to the left, E, further left to the A, and finally right to the C and the H.

"NEACH? What does NEACH mean? COIN NEACH?" I asked.

"Coinneach!" screamed Rhiannon. "It spelled out Coinneach. You're a hoot Brucie. How did you manage to spell that?"

"I didn't spell it. And, what does Coinneach mean?" I asked.

"I saw you push the glass, Brucie. It's pronounced Conn-Yach. The 'ch' sounds the same as in loch. Coinneach is Gaelic for the name Kenneth," she said.

"Neat trick, Brucie. Has your Gramps been teaching you Gaelic?" asked Kyle.

I backed away. "Okay, that's it. Show is over."

Rhiannon and Kyle were psyched-out, but then they laughed. "Brucie, you are hilarious. What made you think of Coinneach?" They fell about laughing. "Okay, Brucie, tell us who Coinneach is?"

"I have absolutely no idea," I told them. "And if that ain't the truth, then I'm a possum. But, let's not do this any more."

"Good idea. It's too cold in here. Let's go up to the café and you can tell us who Coinneach is," said Kyle, happily fidgeting again.

Duncan grew quiet. He flung the board to the far darkened corner of the icehouse. He looked scared. I felt scared, too. The sooner I could get away from the voice, the happier I'd be.

Donald appeared quiet, too. "We shouldn't have done that," he said. "My dad would go mental if he caught us."

"I'm out of here," I said, and ran for the door.

"Slow down, Brucie," my friends called.

They caught up with me at the Gowan Café. "Sorry," I said. "I'm cold and I need a coffee." I opened the door. That day the tablecloths were bright red.

Stirring multiple sugars into my coffee, my heart beat loudly. Memories triggered back to my dream, listening to my heartbeat and then to the voice in the icehouse.

*I swear . . . I'll never go inside that icehouse again!*

I shivered, SO relieved to leave that voice behind.

*Ah!* Coinneach sighed. *It's been a long time since I frequented this tavern. How kind of you to take me out of the icehouse and invite me to join you all here.*

## Bethany's New Curse

**Bethany MacKinnon sat with her grandmother. They shared a pot of tea by the fireside.**

**"Last night I cast another curse, Gran. I cast a real juicy, bad one."**

**The old woman chuckled. "Aha, ha. Yer just like yer Ma, so you are. But, you be careful with those curses now, mind. Remember what happened to yer Ma; what goes around comes around?"**

**Beth ignored the warning. "It's another 'Curse of the Red Head.'"**

**The grandmother laughed, "I know exactly who that's for."**

**"It'll happen soon, you'll see. The shadows will creep up on her. She'll wish she was dead, instead of crazy."**

"Did ya use the blood of a mare and seal the curse over the fire?" the old woman asked. "Ya have to bleed the mare at night, if ya want to give her nightmares."

"Even better, I took blood from her friend's horse. I cut its leg again."

"Ahaha!" cackled her grandmother. "I hope ya remembered to pay the darkness for yer curse. Ya have to give the darkness a gift, something special. Yer Ma forgot a gift, didn't she? I bet ya forgot, too."

Beth flinched uncomfortably.

# Chapter 5

## The Well 'To Do' List

*If you don't quit talking, I'm gonna open up a whole can of whip-ass here! And P-U, is that smell coming from you? Don't you ever wash?*

Coinneach explained that his bathtub doubled up as a pig trough, but I cut him off.

*Won'tcha quitcher gabbin', old man! You've followed me about for days now, chattering incessantly inside my head. It's 7:30 am. I'VE HAD NO SLEEP!*

My phone said the date was Saturday 30th July. "Oh no! It's the twins' birthday today. I need to get up."

Dressing slowly, I hoped to eat breakfast alone. To my frustration, when I entered the kitchen, Mom sat at the table, reading the Northern Star. I said "Hi," politely.

Mom asked if I was feeling okay and I nodded. She pressed further. "I heard you talking to yourself again, Brucie." I shrugged.

Mom put down her paper, poured a fresh cup of tea and swiped fruit flies from the bowl of apples. She rummaged into a box, which sat on the floor beside her, and removed an old, white bed sheet.

"What'cha doing?" I asked, diverting the attention on to Mom. I didn't want to talk about me.

"Making clooties, for Grandpa's festival. We're going to sell them tomorrow for a donation of one pound."

*Shaness! I meant to ask Gramps about the carnival folk and his fight with Rev. MacLeod.* I tried real hard to act normal.

"A POUND, for one of those rags?" I said. "That's robbery!"

"Ah, but you can tie your clootie to the Clootie Tree and make a special wish with them," she said. "And, the profits go to charity."

"Why didn't Gramps tell me about the festival?" I asked.

She shrugged. "I thought he did. You've been muttering to yourself so much, Brucie, that I swear you don't hear when people talk to you."

I changed the subject again and tried to look helpful. "Need a hand?"

*Hmmm, maybe I could make a clootie and wish for Coinneach to leave.*

*I heard that, young lady*, he said.

"Okay," Mom replied. She handed me some cloth and scissors.

Bonding with Mom sometimes felt like trying to bail out a leaky boat with a spoon, but I kept trying until it felt like we'd stay afloat. Busying our hands, we then bunched wildflower posies for the festival. Wrapping flower stems in wet tissue and polythene may have kept the blooms from wilting, but it did nothing to stop my shoulders from hunching forward as I worked.

"Pass me a couple of those Oxeye Daisies, and some Tansy, Brucie, please?" said Mom.

*I used to poke Oxeye Daisies in the holes on my Kilmarnock bonnet, and sometimes Tansy Ragwort, too*, said Coinneach.

Ignoring him had no effect; so I answered with indifference into my head, *Yawn! How interesting. That'll be alongside the feathers, chicken bones and dirty rags, will it?*

*No! The bones hung from the chin chain, but that attached to my Wide-awake hat, not the blue Kilmarnock bonnet. I only donned the blue bonnet on days when I hung the cutlass on my belt.* He snipped at me when I got the details wrong.

*Oh yes, I remember now, and on the days you wore the Wide-awake hat, you also wore the brace of cast-away pistols with your Mexican powder horn, instead of the cutlass, right?*

*And the medals!* His stern prompt me made me jump in the chair.

Mom frowned. "Brucie, you're muttering again."

"Sorry" I said.

*So, if you didn't have a house, what did you do with the cutlass and the Kilmarnock bonnet on days when you only wore the Wide-awake hat, pistols and powder horn?* I asked.

*I left them at the hut in the tree trunk, the Barracks, with my collection of shoes. The frogs and the crows watched them*, he said confidently.

*You really don't sound very Gaelic to me.*

*Why should I speak Gaelic?*

*Well your name is Coinneach, isn't it?*

*Yes, but you wouldn't understand me if I spoke Gaelic.*

"Brucie!" Mom said, sighing sharply. "Stop mumbling and pass me those flowers!"

I sighed. "Sorry, again."

Grandpa entered from the garden. He stirred a pot on the cooker containing stovies -- mashed potato, onion and ground beef goop. I suddenly caught him staring at me. He whispered something to Mom, "Taibhsearach! I'm telling you."

"Dad! Enough!" Mom threw a stem of yarrow at Gramps.

"What's that word you just said?" I asked, Grandpa.

"Ignore him," said Mom with tight lips. "He said you look tired."

"No I didn't," said Gramps.

I didn't want to explain my tiredness, so I opted out of the argument. Coinneach then fell silent, too.

Some days, my fuel gauge drained so low, like I'd been siphoned of the last drop of energy I needed to prevent my emotions from breaking down. With Mom I felt inadequate. Once upon a time, she'd fill me full of praise, like, "What a clever girl!" She'd call me her 'pretty little picture' and make up sweet songs to sing about me. I remembered looking into Mom's happy smile and feeling complete, like I had the sun on my skin and the coolness of a light breeze brush on my cheek, both at the same time. She made everything better.

Sitting here with her now, despite all the colorful wildflowers, the atmosphere around the kitchen table hung as grey as an old sock. It felt like a dank sea mist had rolled in from the Firth. So, when I finished my last posy, I stood up.

"I'm leaving now," I said in the direction of Mom's empty stare. "I have to give the twins their birthday gift; I've burned a compilation CD for them."

No response.

I left the house, yawning, and trudged down Ardcarron Hill.

Adding to the day's anxiety, the outdoor mizzle frizzed my hair. On the approach to Gargoyle House, I tried to flatten the fuzz with spit on my palms. As the sun broke through the misty grey, I cringed at my shadow stretched out in front of me. My head looked like a large toffee apple on top of a thin stick.

*Maybe I should've stayed back in Texas with Dad*, I thought.

Suddenly, a scrawny crow squawked and peered down from up in an overhead telephone wire. Something about the crow on the wire reminded me of the tightrope dream. I realized that no matter where I lived, the Atlantic Ocean would always separate my parents. As long as I had a Mom and a Dad, I'd always have to walk that wire between Texas and Scotland. Gramps: always my comforter, never my judge. He anchored me here. But, the bird squawked again, as if trying to warn me about something else.

Up the driveway to Gargoyle House, another shadow caught my eye. I saw a strange shadow on the wall. A builder's truck, MacKay's Contractors Limited, sat parked by the front door and the shadow appeared to move from behind this truck. Something blinked in my head, flashing like a migraine, pricking hair follicles on my scalp. I felt oozy, like time slowed, and I could not make sense of what I was looking at. Then, without further warning the shadow leapt toward me.

"WHAT THE FRICK!"

A female apparition, swaddled in a shocking-red shawl, squeezed out from the stone in the wall beside the large bay window. THROUGH the brick, THROUGH it! Her face contorted, body constricted, until she looked like a giant blister. She burst free with a silent pop and lunged at me.

I froze.

*Help me, someone! Coinneach? PLEASE! What is going on? Who is she?*

Silence. I stood motionless, not moving a muscle.

Donald, or was it Duncan... *No time to check for a muscular neck, or hands* ... opened the front door. "You look like you've seen a ghost." He laughed.

My finger wouldn't point to the woman, even though I urged it to. Words scrambled to clamber over a tongue, which braced to ram down my throat and choke me. I gulped air.

"Are you okay, Brucie?" Donald, or was it Duncan, stood right next to the woman, but he obviously couldn't see her.

No matter how hard I fought to control my breathing or to stiffen the muscles around my eyes, I couldn't stop tears from erupting. They flowed down my cheeks, first one, then two, and then the floodgates opened.

"Why me?" I cried.

"Why you what?" asked the twin, "I don't understand," he said. "Here, come inside. You look terrified."

"No, I can't come in because you said your Dad dislikes my Gramps," I bubbled. "You said he was angry with my family because of my Grandpa's festival," I told him.

*Why can't I tell him the truth? ... A woman emerged from the wall of his house!*

"Is that what's wrong? You're frightened of my dad?" The twin smiled, gently cocking his head to the side, and from the thickness of his neck

I saw it was Donald.

I nodded and handed him the gift, "Here, Happy Birthday!" Spinning around, I dashed for the gate at the end of the drive, legged it up Ardcarron Brae. I kept running and running, across the 'bless them field' toward Rhiannon's house.

*She came OUT of the wall! She did, she came OUT of it.*

I ran till my lungs hurt. At the top end of the field, seven modern caravans now clustered and flames rose from a communally centered campfire. Several adults shouted at a huddle of children, who whacked at a tin bucket with sticks. The children looked happy. They stopped their game to wave at me. I sprinted straight through the middle of their camp without speaking.

For the entire distance up to the farm, I didn't stop running, not even when an old Land Rover pulled up at my heels and backfired beside me, like a gun with its sights set on a trespasser.

Rapping on my friend's front door, I called out, "Rhiannon, I've GOT to talk to you." I gasped, breathlessly.

Once inside her bedroom, with door shut, I breathed slower and blurted my troubles.

"Rhiannon, I saw an aura around your horse and I saw Bethany as an old hag and then I have this man in my head called Coinneach and he talks and talks all day and night and I knew there was a well in the field and I don't know how I knew it but I told Gramps about a tramp spoiling the well water and I don't know how I knew that either and then this woman squeezed out of the wall at Gargoyle House... OUT of the wall, I tell you, and...do you think I'm schizophrenic, Rhiannon?"

"WHAT? Woah! Slow down, will you?" she begged. "Brucie, what is wrong with you? You're gabbling like a crazy person."

"Maybe I am a crazy person, Rhiannon. Maybe I'm schizophrenic."

We both stood staring at each other.

Rhiannon's so honest you could shoot craps with her over the phone, but on this occasion she was simply stunned into silence. She cupped my face with her hands and I buried my head into her shoulder. Never had I felt so distraught. She stroked my hair, like the big sister I longed for.

"I don't know how to help you, Brucie. What's this about hearing the voice of Coinneach in your head? That's the name from the Ouija board in the icehouse, isn't it?"

I nodded my head into her shoulder.

"You mean there IS such a person?"

"Yes," I said. "I hear him talking in my head."

"Can you hear Coinneach's voice now?" she asked.

"No. He turns up whenever HE feels like it, which is usually in the middle of the night, or when I'm watching a movie, when I'm peeing or trying to read."

"WHAT? He's there when you're peeing?" she squealed. Rhiannon backed away.

"Well, not every time, but once he was there when I peed. I told him, "Git!" and he left. What am I going to do, Rhi? Coinneach won't hurt me, will he?"

"Brucie, I have absolutely no idea, but this creeps me out." She took another step away from me.

"I need you, Rhiannon. Help me? I don't like this anymore."

She looked stunned.

"You've got to believe me!" I begged her.

"Will I phone for a doctor?"

"NO!" I said. "Please don't."

"Okay." She thought for a minute. "Look, Brucie, I know who might help you find out more about schizophrenia, or about demons," she said.

"Please don't say the brainy twins because I fled from Donald just now. I'm too embarrassed to tell anyone but you. They'll think I'm crazy. Please don't let anyone take me away and sedate me on drugs." I looked up right into her eyes and asked, "You don't think I'm crazy? Do you?" I stared, serious as a preacher on the television.

"Yes, I mean no. Aw, I don't know but I can see that you're scared," she said, and handed me a tissue, on which to blow my nose.

"Do you want me to talk to the twins for you?" she asked. "Honestly, they'll be really supportive."

After some convincing, I finally nodded. "But promise you won't tell them about the ghost at their house? I don't want them scared, too."

Rhiannon shrugged instead of answering.

She spent nearly fifteen minutes outside on her mobile, the only spot where she was able to get a signal. She relayed my tale to the twins. I stayed in her bedroom, with the window open, listening. I felt nervous about repercussions from Coinneach.

I talked gingerly into my brain. *Now look here Coinneach, I had to tell someone about you. You won't . . . you won't . . . make anything bad happen to me, will you, Coinneach?*

He didn't answer me. I interpreted that as a positive thing. Nonetheless, I sat on the bed and bit my nails to pieces.

Unable to handle the suspense, I swung the window open wider and stuck my head out. "Don't be long," I called out.

Rhiannon's voice now muttered inaudibly against the sound of cows mooing in the byre. I watched her pace back and forth by the cowshed, talking into her phone, gesturing with her free hand. I waited, sucking on the drawstring cord of my hoodie. A few phrases carried in the wind, "How about typing "banishing spirits" into Google, Duncan?" and "Okay, don't bother if Donald has it in hand." She paused. "Great. Come as quickly as you can then. I can't handle this alone," she said.

I joined Rhiannon outside, when the twins arrived. It felt so awkward, talking to the twins, in fact I felt a bit ashamed when we all sat down and talked about my troubles.

"I'm sorry. Maybe I should have listened to you when you said that Ouija boards were bad news!" I said to . . . *nice hands, yup* . . . Donald.

"It's okay," he said.

Rhiannon looked at me warily, which made me cry for disappointing everyone.

My sniffing interrupted when I hear the sound of . . . *putt . . . putt . . . brmm . . . putt . . . putt.* A small engine strained to climb the hill, and Kyle rounded the corner on his new moped bike. His crash helmet had a very old-fashioned peak on the front, which made the twins laugh.

"Not Kyle! Please!" I panicked. "If you tell him, he's bound to tease me."

But he didn't.

"Here, Brucie," he said, carefully handing me a steaming cup, like the kind you get in the Gowan Café. "It's tricky work steering a bike without spilling your coffee. Thought you might need one. Four sugars enough, like?"

I nodded.

We hung about the farm and I made them all swear not to tell anyone about the voices.

"We won't. Don't worry," they all said, but I felt . . . yes felt . . . something move behind a large copper beech tree. I kept my eye trained on the trunk. Its girth looked more than wide enough to hide someone, but nothing moved again.

"It's probably a deer," said Rhiannon.

I felt unconvinced.

"There! I saw another movement," I said in a loud whisper. "Someone's listening."

Nobody looked around.

"Brucie, what's that odd stone around your neck?" Duncan quizzed me with an odd expression. "Where did you get it?"

With one eye on the tree, I struggled to tell coffee from split peas. How could I tell a boy that I wore a charm around my neck that fell from the stinky guts of a dead fish? Plumb tuckered out, I'd already said too much.

"I found it! Right?" My mood snapped.

"Okay, well, here's what we're going to do then," said Donald. "I read about this in a book once. It's called a Soisgeal and…"

*That's the bossy twin, isn't it? Ha! Ha! He's funny. He's going to try the old wife's soisgeal on you, the cure for a weak mind. This should be amusing,* whispered Coinneach.

"Oh, shut up, will you!" I screamed.

Donald stepped back, astonished, "Sorry, I…"

"Not you Donald," I said. "It's HIM, Coinneach. He's laughing at you."

*Tell tale! Tittle-tattler! Clype!*

"Then, I'll continue and he can laugh all he wants," said Donald. He whispered into his brother's ear, whereupon Duncan lifted my arm and held it out.

*Darn. I can't hear him. What is the bossy one saying now?*

"Open your mouth, Brucie," Donald ordered, and he placed one end of a length of green twine across my tongue. "Okay, now you can close your teeth but keep biting on the string."

"Don't hurt me then," I mumbled.

*Ha! Ha! He's going to try and restore Grace to your poor soul with that string. Tasty is it?*

63

*I swear you are so low Coinneach that you'd have to look up before you'd see hell.*

Donald handed the other end of twine to Duncan, who, still holding my arm, wrapped the twine around my shoulder.

"Poor Brucie," said Kyle, bouncing up and down on the seat of his bike. "She really looks so dumb standing there with green twine in her mouth, like."

Rhiannon kicked him and he sulked defensively, "I was only saying! Anyway her coffee is getting cold." He drank the last of it.

"What's next?" I tried to ask Rhiannon, without dislodging the string.

She looked at me, shrugged and then turned away like she'd had enough of it all.

"Now we have to read a scripture, hymn, or some spiritual words written by a priest, so I came prepared," said Donald, pulling some paperwork from his backpack.

"What's that, like?" asked Kyle, nosing into the backpack.

"It's a copy of Dad's Sunday sermon."

"The whole thing?" asked Rhiannon, squinting at her watch.

I stood very still, string in my mouth, shoulder bound, while Donald puffed out his chest and began to read. He praised the virtues of abstinence, lest we all burn in hellfire and damnation. After a sentence or two, he checked our faces to see that we were all still attentive and then, seeing his captive audience, he abandoned the notes and continued ad lib: he praised and preached like Billy Graham. His anomalies and alliterations were so brilliant, I wanted to applaud, but Duncan held my arm.

When Donald finished, a full ten minutes later, Coinneach cheered. *Excellent delivery! This boy should join the Kirk like his father.*

"Well?" asked Donald. He cocked his head in that sweet way again. "Do you feel stronger, Brucie? Are we helping to combat anything?"

What could I say? He grinned so . . . hopefully . . . so enthusiastically. *His neck is so...so...muscular...and...* I found myself admiring his shoulders. "Sorry guys," I said, removing the twine and rolling it up. "This is not working."

Coinneach sniggered.

"I don't feel any different. Look, you've all been great, though. I'm sorry for getting so upset and I should never have used that Ouija board. This would never have happened if I hadn't done that. I'll be okay. The voice is not frightening me now. In a weird sort of way, Coinneach is actually quite stupid."

*STUPID? What do you mean, stupid?* Coinneach raged.

I winced, waited for repercussion, expecting Coinneach to swivel my skull around on my neck until it faced backward.

*Sorry.* I said to Coinneach inside my head. *You're not the type of spirit that could project green demonic froth out from my mouth, are you?*

Coinneach laughed. He really didn't seem to pose any threat . . . other than his constant talking.

"Donald, I don't really think Coinneach will harm me, so I can live with the voices for now." I hoped that my assumption was correct.

"Well, I guess," said Donald, sad that he'd failed. "There are other things, alternatives that we can try. Duncan has printed out a list of plants that might help, natural remedies, sians?"

Rhiannon turned to the twins. "What about asking your Dad to help?"

"NO way! He'd kill us for meddling with Ouija boards!" they replied.

I felt calmer in the company of my friends. In fact, I tingled all over, as I noticed something new about Donald. *His voice soothes like velvet.* He really believed in everything that he read from his father's sermon. Enthusiasm can be so addictive. I studied them both with their same round glasses and identical blue-grey eyes. Donald definitely looked the more confident of the two twins

"You said something about a sian?" I asked, searching deep into Donald's eyes.

"Yes. Charms that protect you from danger," said Rhiannon, "like hanging horse shoes above your door and stuff."

I remembered the day I met Rhiannon and her horse. "Is that snaithe you put on your horse the same sort of thing the thing, like a sian?"

"I suppose," she said, quietly.

"So you believe in Pagan stuff," I said to Rhiannon.

"I didn't say I *believed* in this stuff," she said. Her face flushed pink. "I'm not a Pagan! I read about the snaithe in the Horse Monthly, an article about this horse whisperer who practiced alternative equestrian healing. It was just to help Bracken's leg." She looked angry.

"Sorry," I said.

Duncan shared the compilation on his list, with Kyle jumping on his back and breathing over his shoulder. "Rowan, elder, pearlwort and ivy all have protection qualities, as do marigolds. Phew! Kyle, did you eat dog poo for breakfast?" He continued, holding his nose, "St. John's wort, milkwort and dandelion, if woven together."

"Hey, guys, it says here that some of these flowers can be used as love potions, like," said Kyle, grinning and ignoring the insult.

*Oh? I think I smell love in the air,* said Coinneach.

"We have some of these wild flowers at our house," I said to Duncan. "I left Mom sitting at the kitchen table making all those posies for the festival."

The twins looked awkward. "Yeah, sorry we won't be coming along to support your Grandpa's festival. You understand, right?"

"Sure, I do."

Duncan checked his watch. "We need to be going, too. Our sisters will be throwing a "surprise" birthday party for us. It's a bit of craic for the younger ones really. They're all fond of celebrating birthdays in our house, and just as well, since there are so many of us."

As the twins left, I realized that Rhiannon couldn't have told them about the apparition at their house. Did they need to know? I suddenly wished that I could go to their family party, too, but I couldn't quite think why, as I wasn't very patient with young children.

Kyle broke into my daydream, with gushy enthusiasm. "Hey, I'm not working today, like. Can I come and help you and your Grandpa, Brucie, like, you know?"

Rhiannon backed away. "Don't look at me to help you, Brucie. I have stuff to do, too." I felt a distance in Rhiannon's voice, like she wanted me to leave.

"Okay," I said to Kyle.

"Then, I'll take you home on the back of my moped," said Kyle. "You can squeeze my muscular torso all the way home, if you want to, like."

*I smell love in the air?*

*Shut up Coinneach. Kyle's only a friend.*

I lifted my leg to straddle Kyle's moped, when suddenly, in my peripheral vision I saw a head pop out from behind the copper beech tree -- a head with dyed peroxide-blonde, spiky hair.

"Aw, Kyle, I told you that I saw something . . . Someone heard us . . . Oh no! Look! It's Bethany MacKinnon!"

Bethany chuckled loudly. "Ya beauty!" she squealed. "What wonderful gossip. I've been standing here pissing myself laughing at you lot. Wait till I tell everyone about this! Brucie has voices in her head. She IS a witch!"

## Bethany and the Cat

Bethany MacKinnon cussed up a storm. "Brucie Bice is an effing witch."

It was 10:30 pm. She walked home from Ardcarron to her caravan near Ben Struie, after visiting some of the travelling folk in the 'bless them' field. A stray cat followed. The cat slinked along behind her, warily. Its yellow eyes flickered mysteriously, glowing like luminous beacons in the night.

Travelling folk say cats were born of the moon; the sun makes the lion and the moon makes the cat. They always respected cats.

Bethany turned around, intending to stroke the cat. But then, she remembered what her grandmother said, 'I hope ya remembered to pay the dark moon for its curse. Yer Ma forgot, didn't she? I bet ya forgot, too.'

The cat arched its back at her approach. It hissed like a lump of black coal smoldering on a fire.

Bethany kicked at the cat and then stamped her foot at it. "Aw, piss off then, ya manky beast!"

The cat shrieked. The moon vanished. The sky turned jet black.

# *Chapter 6*

## *Garlic Sunday*

My face glowed red, taking a boy into my house. Gramps seemed okay about it.

"Hello there, Kyle, my man," he said. "That's a cracker of a wee motor bike."

"Aye, I got it from my cousin, cheap, like." Kyle answered, while keenly eyeing a plate of sandwiches on the kitchen table. Instinctively, he licked his lips. "I came to see if you want a hand with anything for the festival, you know?"

Gramps picked up the plate and offered a sandwich to Kyle who, with both hands, lifted them all. "We could do with some help to erect a couple of bell tents in the field," said Grandpa. "There will be lots of folk selling crafts. Gazebos are arriving later for the musicians, together with some temporary flooring for a stage. The public address system is all in hand but we're running behind time."

Kyle, who munched and spoke with his mouth full, squinted out through our kitchen blinds, over in the direction of the 'bless them' field. "I see the travelling folk are here, Ali? Isn't that risky, like?"

"Aye, there's many more Travellers than I expected, Kyle, but they'll be no bother, you'll see. Let me tell you a story."

Gramps lit his pipe and slowly began his tale. "When I was a lad of about 7 years old my mother became very sick, so sick that she nearly died. My father worked on a farm and couldn't stop work to look after her or me and my brother. A family of Travellers took me, and my brother George, to live with them. We slept six in a bed head-to-toe with their boys. We were fed well and treated as part of their family. They looked after my mother, too, until she recovered. I'll never forget their warmth and kindness, Kyle."

"That's cool Ali. Good story, like," he said, interrupting. I don't think fidgeting Kyle really listened. "What are those rag strips for?" he asked, rummaging in a box by the table.

"They're clooties," I said. I felt that the power of Grandpa's message was lost on Kyle and I didn't really know how to react to such a poignant story. Gramps, looking teary eyed, blew his nose on his handkerchief.

Feeling somewhat inadequate, I tried to speak for Gramps.

"Grandpa wants people to tie them on the thorn tree by the well, to make it a Clootie Well Tree."

I tried to continue talking to Kyle about the festival but Coinneach began his chatter in my head. He rambled on about canons and explosions.

*You can't hold a festival without gunpowder. When will we be setting off the gunpowder?*

*What gunpowder? Go away!*

*Well, I won't be attending if there is no gunpowder,* said Coinneach.

True to his word, he didn't appear on the day of the festival. I enjoyed almost a whole day without any interruptions in my brain. What bliss!

Mom seemed more agreeable on the morning of the festival, too. She didn't brush my comments aside, or draw attention to the zit on my chin. She even complimented the French braid in my hair. "It makes your eyes look nice and big," she said. I felt my heart and soul fill up with energy, like she loved me again. I even felt confident enough to ask Grandpa about his tiff with Reverend MacLeod.

"What's the problem with Reverend MacLeod, Gramps?" I asked, while helping him carry the clooties and flowers over to the 'bless them' field.

"Well, what's your take on the situation, Brucie? Why do you think we argued?"

"Does he think you're mocking him, by encouraging people to celebrate a Celtic God? We're not really doing that, though, are we? Or, has it got something to do with the Travellers being here? I think you're trying to befriend everyone and pump creativity into a stale village gala." These were my assumptions.

Grandpa shrugged at all my comments.

I continued. "Garlic Sunday is really about celebrating the start of the crop harvest, isn't it? You did ask Reverend MacLeod to lead the procession up to the Clootie Well, didn't you? And you encouraged him to hold an outdoor church sermon, didn't you?"

"Yes, but. . ."

I answered for him. "But when he declined, you decided that you'd dress up as a priest and take his place. Wouldn't that insult his role here as minister here?"

"I suppose so. But. . ."

"But, I know, you'd already made up your mind about the festival... didn't you? You wanted it to be a success, not for you but for the good of the village. That's it, isn't it, Gramps? Don't you worry now, Grandpa, because it WILL be a great day! You'll see."

Grandpa didn't look convinced. "But..." he said again.

"It's okay," I said. "I understand about the travelling folk. That was such a kind thing for them to do, to take you and your brother to live with them. No wonder you feel protective toward them. I can't wait to meet them all."

"Yes, but..." he said.

"It's okay, Gramps. I understand," I said. I wondered how I could explain to Gramps that I appreciated sensitivities involving minority groups, as I supposed Travellers were a minority. When you are culturally different you stand out more and people, who don't know better, can say some pretty mean stuff to, or about, you. I should know! At first, when I was a minority, kids followed me about goading me to 'say something Texan'. I wanted to say just that but instead I asked Gramps a question.

"I heard some people say that this is more of an Irish festival. Do you think that some people are upset because you're hosting an Irish festival idea here in the Scottish Highlands?"

"I think I want people to enjoy themselves and have fun," he said. "Don't you?"

I had to think about my answer. "Sure, it's good that we can adopt cultures and traditions from others. I remember when I thought that more people would wear Scottish kilts here in the Highlands, Gramps. You see, lots of people wear kilts at Scottish festivals in Texas. Mom took me every year to hear the squealing bagpipes and to visit all the clan tents. When I said in school that more people should wear kilts here, they told me that I had an Americanized view of Scotland, and everyone laughed. So, maybe Reverend MacLeod thinks your festival is a bit too touristy, a bit like us Americans wearing your kilts. You already have other Clootie Wells in the Highlands and Garlic Sunday is not one hundred percent traditional in Scotland, so maybe

70

that's why some people don't take you seriously," I said.

"Are you trying to say that people think I'm eccentric?" he asked, flushing pink-faced.

"Maybe. But, that's good, right... to be different?" I said.

He still looked distraught. I wasn't helping him to resolve his disagreement with the minister, so that's when I had the idea. "Hey Gramps, maybe after the festival you and I could visit the Reverend MacLeod and we could give some of the proceeds to his church. Why don't you dole out the profits? Maybe then the Reverend would see the good in what you are doing and he won't be so offended?"

"I'd have to apologize first," said Grandpa.

"Why?" I asked.

"Ochone. Ochone. You see he didn't know what a tansy ragwort was. When I called him a fish brain, he stepped on the new seedlings I'd planted. He wouldn't apologize, so I cuffed him on the chin and emptied a bucket of fresh garden manure over his head."

"GRANDPA! No wonder Reverend MacLeod stopped speaking to you! I thought you argued about Travellers, traditions and religion...!"

"Not really. Whatever gave you that idea?" He laughed. "Come on," he said, pulling on his priestly costume. "Or, I'll be late for my own procession."

Our assembly (the Nasad) gathered in the square outside the Gowan Café at ten o'clock. Young boys carried sheaves of corn, to celebrate the coming harvest, while girls wore corn garlands. Some people clutched clootie rags in their hands. Others carried flowers (which Rhiannon and I sold for one pound each), as offerings to the sun God and the fairies. A true Garlic Sunday (or Lughnasa festival) procession would traditionally climb to the top of a large hill, but our town procession only climbed Ardcarron Brae and we walked as far as the 'bless them' field. Gramps wanted the walk to be accessible to people of all ages and disabilities.

As we passed Gargoyle House, I glimpsed a flash of red and shivered. I looked away, as the piper, who walked to the front with Grandpa, played a haunting lament on his bagpipes.

I thought about Donald, as a distraction. Strange, I forgot about everything, even the woman that bubbled out of the wall, until Rhiannon asked, "What's that silly grin for?"

I didn't answer.

The chatter and hum of a waiting crowd of Travellers grew louder ahead, as our procession approached the field. I smiled at them and waved, grateful for their kindness to my Grandpa.

Craft stall sales commenced. Sweet and savory smells filled the air. The travelling folk called out from sideshow stalls, "Roll up. Roll up. It's two pound for five shots. Lovely prizes!"

Beside the well, about twenty feet to the left, Grandpa and Kyle had dug a neat hole, now sectioned off with bright orange warning tape. I saw Kyle fastening the tape and ushering the crowd to move back, with a look of importance.

Grandpa positioned himself between the hole and the well, where the tree grew. If I hadn't still been thinking about Donald, I might remember exactly what Grandpa had said in his opening speech. I recall he looked earthy and spiritual. He probably invited the crowd to toss their flowers to the depths of the earth, asking them to wish for good health and bountiful harvest, but I only remember wondering if Donald MacLeod had ever kissed a girl before, and if so, who?

"Brucie, you're grinning again," said Rhiannon. She nudged me. "Come on, we're all waiting for you to throw the first flowers into the hole."

As I let my flowers fall to the earth, I scooped soil over them and wished . . . *Please, God . . . Please can Mom and Dad get back together again? I don't mean any harm to Little Pike but he can see Dad now and then, at holidays. He'll be okay with Michaela to bring him up. I'll make sure that Dad pays his child support. I mean Pike probably doesn't even know that Dad is his Pa yet. He might smile at my dad but Pike won't know him yet . . . not like I know my dad.*

My eyelids shut so tight in concentration they near squeezed my eyeballs backward into the nape of my neck.

*And can you make me prettier, so that . . .* I sighed . . . *oh, it doesn't matter . . . Donald will be a preacher one day and I don't know how I feel about that yet.*

I opened my eyes and then quickly closed them again.

*One more thing . . . can you keep Bethany quiet, PLEASE? Don't let her tell everyone that I have voices in my head.*

I waited my turn to tie a clootie to the tree. As I repeated the same three wishes, I felt my neck and cheeks flush warm like I had fever. My hair felt full of static and my head oozy with dizziness. A strange magnetism radiated out from the tree pulling me toward the well. Sweat glistened on my palms and my heart raced, but I also felt sleepy. The earth appeared to spin faster. My thoughts took on the rhythm of the folk tunes being played in the distance. I spun around as songs sprouted forth from my head, words all twisted like limericks.

Fiddlers fiddled, dancers danced, round and round in tempting trances. Games and races, happy faces smudged with pink cotton candy laces and sandy feet all tripped and tapped in rhythmic time, clippity clap, clippity clap. Potatoes and meats, tasty to-eats, painted whiskers on sunburned cheeks and noses red as clowns and sounds around all blended to hues and hints of happy treats. Old friends greeting, children squealing as toffee apples stuck to teeth and mothers scolding "no more money," but funny how a child can scheme and beam a smile so sweet and triumphant. Hand-painted pictures, puppets and leather belts and sweaters of wool sitting in the cool of light airy tents, striped white and blue and…

The spinning stopped and I fell over, giddy, clutching my Eye Stone.

*Wow! What happened? How did I get over here?*

I now lay on the ground at the other end of the 'bless them' field, outside a tent with a hand painted sign. It read: *Palm Readings. Cross my palm with silver -- Minimum donation five pounds.*

I quickly rose to my feet. Lifting the door flap, I snooped inside.

*Hmmm. I bet I know who that sign belongs to!*

More curious than scared, I dug deep into my shorts, retrieving a five-pound note, and entered the tent. Suddenly, the pain in my forehead returned, the same searing pain as when I walked past Fisher Skeelie's house.

*God she's ugly!* I thought, when we met face-to-face inside the tent.

Fisher Skeelie and I sat at opposite ends of a small table, both silent. I held out the money, which she swiped with her left hand. Her other one, withered and deformed, curled inward to her black sweater like a crow with a damaged claw. Twitching her head with a tic, she repeatedly tossed a tousle of badly dyed hair until she could see me through the matt of frizzy black. As she studied my face, her gaze lowered to my necklace and her eyes widened when she saw my eye stone.

I offered both palms, "Which one do you want?"

Three women hovered to the rear of The Skeelie's back; one smoked a clay pipe, another tall woman restrained an inquisitive mongrel on a rope. The third, a short, stocky woman with a harshly wrinkled face, stepped forward and muttered something into Skeelie's ear. She pointed at me. I didn't understand, their language sounded too coarse and they spoke too fast.

I heard Fisher Skeelie say back to her, "Be gone. Dinnae stir. I winnae troosh her."

The three women promptly left the tent, as told, shaking their heads in disagreement.

Fisher Skeelie waited till we were alone. She stared deep into my eyes, paused and then spat on the ground. "Get out!"

"What?" I said, confused. My palms were still outstretched, waiting like an idiot.

"Leave!" she ordered. "Or I'll scud ya."

"What's wrong? I don't understand," I told her. "I've given you my money."

*Oh! Oh!* Bethany MacKinnon entered from the back of the tent, and stood behind Skeelie.

"This girl is a witch, Grandma," said Bethany to The Skeelie. Bethany grabbed my left hand. I pulled away from her but she held my palm open, "Yup, as I thought, Grandma. Look at the lines here. She's got crazy voices in her head. She's a witch!"

"A ha ha ha ha!" Skeelie laughed. "Aha ha ha ha ha!" laughed Bethany.

"Get out of here, WITCH," said Fisher Skeelie, "and take your evil voices with you."


## Around the Campfire


**A quarter moon struggled to light the sky, as a clique of male Travellers gathered around the campfire, talking and drinking yellow tea.**

**Jake said, "Beth don't want to visit her mother in the jail, not after what her Ma done."**

**A fat man, called Joseph, said, "Beth's become a selfish scaldie, Jake; just like you. You've lost the ways of the good traveling folk."**

Jake moved to punch Joseph but a gruff voice called out. "Hey! No fighting. We gave our word there'd be no trouble in this camp."

The same gruff voice pulled rank again. "Bethany needs to respect the old ways. We respect our kin, no matter their crimes. She'll see her mother in the jail. Family comes first and that's the end of it."

"I'm no scaldie!" shouted Jake. "I'm only staying put so Bethany isn't taken again."

"That's not true, Jake, and you know it."

Jake insisted. "I'll tell you, Bethany won't go to the jail," he said. "She'll do a runner again."

"Enough," said the gruff voice. "We've had a whip round. Forty quid for her Ma. The girl can take it to her. That's the maximum she can get in."

"Post it," said Jake. He turned to leave and spat in the fire.

A large hand grabbed Jake by the shoulder. "Her Ma's booked a visit in Bethany's name. The girl needs to be at the jail in Stirling 30 minutes before visiting on Wednesday. So that's 1:45pm. Got it? And, her Ma's sent a pro forma for some new clothes. We've gathered some nice things for her. So, Bethany needs to bring them."

Bethany appeared from behind a truck. "I ain't going!"

An older woman stepped toward Bethany, attempting to reason with her.

WHACK! Beth hit her with a stick.

# Chapter 7

## Detention Tension

Summer over, we sat on the sandstone window ledge of the Misses Macgregor's shop, waiting for the morning bus to take us to Glenaldie High School.

I turned to Rhiannon. "I said that someone hid behind that beech tree, watching, listening. Didn't I say that? I told you."

"Sorry," said Rhiannon. "I should have known. Beth ruined the festival for you, didn't she? In fact, because of her fighting, she's ruined things for everyone. It's been over a month now. I wish she'd back off and leave you alone. Even Kyle has asked her to stop goading you."

My shoulders lifted, to reply with a shrug. I sighed when the tall double-decker sway around the corner. The lower deck looked full, so I knew we had to join the bullies upstairs.

"Rhiannon, what if Beth and her friends threaten to throw me out of the top window again?"

"No, they won't. We'll tell the driver and have them kicked off the bus this time," said Rhiannon. She pushed me up the stair way and we slipped into the first available seat.

"I used to think that Goth, Cough and Moth were okay, but they are as bad as Bethany now," I told her. "I can just 'bout deal with Beth when she's on her own, but when the four come a-callin'. . . I'm dead as a strip of ol' beef jerky."

I thought about some of my Texan sayings. *Maybe I should try harder not to sound so Texan. My accent thickens when I get stressed, though.*

"Have you told your mother and your grandfather about this bullying, Brucie? Maybe today you could see your school counselor?" asked Rhiannon.

"No. It's cool. I can handle it myself," I said, but the taunting jeers whooped up as soon as the bus pulled away from the stop.

Cough pretended to be Coinneach's voice and mocked, "My name is Coinneach. I'm the schizophrenic voice that lives in Brucie's head." She laughed.

Beth answered in a high pitch, "And I'm Mrs Coinneach. I live in Brucie's head, too."

They howled with laughter when Moth squeaked, "And I'm Baby Coinneach. I live in her head and dawg gone it, some hawg's gone and eaten up my bowl of breakfast grits."

Coinneach objected from inside my head.

*Lies! Lies! There is no Mrs Coinneach or baby. I never took a wife. Never married the wench. Turned my back for a minute and she stole my best sword from The Barracks.*

*What Barracks?* I asked.

*The Barracks in the tree. I told you about the tree with the shoes, guarded by the crows and frogs. And, of course, that day my wide-awake hat hung there too, and the brace of cast-away pistols and my Mexican powder horn because on that day, the day she stole my sword, I wore my blue Kilmarnock bonnet and the short cutlass. I'm so thankful that she only took the sword and not my wide-awake hat and...*

*Okay, I get the picture...* I had both eyes on Bethany, determined not to quit staring before she did.

*The wench traded my good sword for John Barleycorn, because when I caught up with her she staggered drunker than a sailor's strumpet. Sprawled face up in the ditch spouting raunchy seafaring songs.... Are you listening to me? I'm trying to distract you here.*

*How very kind, but I'll distract myself, thank you.*

When Beth finally looked away, I turned to peer outside the bus. Condensation steamed up the windows, so I gripped the cuff of my shirt and wiped the glass with my forearm. Trees whizzed past my eyes, one by one by one by one by one, rhythmically hypnotizing me.

Mom and I had been arguing again that morning, too, before I'd left the house. I wanted a new iPhone, REALLY wanted one. My friends all had iPhones, but she didn't seem to understand.

"You don't need an expensive phone, Brucie. You are only fifteen!"

"Sixteen next week! And, I'm going to be the only sixteen-year-old on this planet without a decent phone, for fizz sake!"

"Well, who will you call?" she said, and then answered her own question with, "It certainly won't be me, because you hardly speak to me these days. You are with your friends all day, so who is there to call?"

"That's not the point, Mom. What if I got into trouble and needed help and this old phone stopped working?"

"In my day we didn't need mobiles, Brucie."

So, I mocked her, "In my day this and in my day that. I'm fed up of hearing about how things used to be in Scotland. It's obviously different now, Mom."

"These arguments exhaust my patience, Brucie." She walked away.

I felt so frustrated that I tossed my old phone to the floor and left the house, shouting out, "Here! Have the phone if you think it's that good. I really hate you, Mom."

I jolted back from the memory of our argument, forced back to the present when a roar of laughter echoed from the front of the bus. Beth had found other uses for the window condensation; she wrote with her finger, "Brucie is a Schitzo Witch."

Coinneach continued chattering on about his wench, as if trying to distract me again. *Sober, she washed my shirts . . . and I brought her a dead cow to butcher once.*

I humored him. *Okay, so where did you find the dead cow?*

*I shot it with my brace of pistols but missed, so I used the gunpowder.*

He paused long enough for me to think he'd shut up and then he said . . . *Yes, there was one lady I loved once, and she loved me, too . . .*

He twittered on in my head all day and in every class. I got real angry with him, as he kept saying that History lessons would be much more beneficial than geography. Forgetting my surroundings, I argued, "That's shit!" out loud and then returned to private thoughts.

*Look! I can't take history because it won't fit my timetable!*

*But, there are people you need to know about from history.*

*Who?*

*Well, if you read history books you'd find out.*

"What garbage you speak!" I said aloud again.

Greasy O'Hare the teacher suddenly hollered at me. "Right! Miss Bice. Report to the school secretary's office, and make arrangements to stay behind after school. Maybe some after-school study will stop these outbursts of swearing at me in class."

When I tried to explain that I wasn't swearing at him, he pointed to the door. "Enough! Out!"

I heard someone whisper, "She's talking to those voices in her head again."

Gathering up my books, I then sauntered to the offices by the front entrance, knocked on the second blue door and entered when the voice said, "Come in!"

When I spoke to the secretary she seemed surprisingly kind and, with one finger dialing my home number, she asked, "Will your mother be angry when I tell her about your detention?"

I shrugged. "No. Anyway, I'd rather take a later bus home and not the school bus."

She asked, "What do you mean?"

"It doesn't matter," I said, leaving her office.

"Brucie, do you want to speak to a counsellor about something?" she asked.

"No thanks," I said.


I endured my after-school hour of detention, sitting in the library. After completing most of my homework, the librarian nodded for me to leave and I scuttled out of the school gate toward the town. The regular service bus, going to Ardcarron, would leave at six o'clock from outside the Post Office. That gave me twenty minutes to browse inside the few remaining shops still open. Kyle's birthday neared. I wanted to buy him a gift.

I love the way that towns in Scotland are built around a hub of activity. Everything grows outward from a core, in this case the High Street. Old ladies meet on shop corners to chat about the weather, workmen leave their engines running while they dash into the baker's for a hot meat pie, the fishmonger parks his van to sell a few fresh pieces of haddock, landed that morning, and secretaries scuttle with bundles of pre-franked mail to the post office. Neighbors pass on opposite sides of the street. One of them calls out. "Hello, Annie. I've got gossip for you. Pop next door for a cuppa tea when you get home."

I stood momentarily to drink in the atmosphere, realizing how much I'd miss this if I left and went back to Texas.

Kyle's gift, a sticker for his bike, only cost 75 pence in the newsagents,

so maybe I'd burn a CD for him, too, like the one I made for Duncan and…
Time halted.

How long had I been standing there thinking about Donald? I caught sight of my reflection in the glass of the newsagent's window, wide-eyed and grinning again. My hair looked messy. I wondered if he preferred long hair or short hair. *Maybe if I got Rhiannon to weave another French pleat, he might notice my eyes looking bigger? Grrr, I'm so hopeless at doing my own hair.*

My watch confirmed enough time to find a washroom before the six o'clock bus arrived, so I hurried toward the sign that read 'Ladies.' A cheerful attendant with a tortoiseshell cat sat in a small office, fronted by a glass wall with a hole in it. She called out through the hole, "Money please," so, I handed over a pound coin. I hopped from leg to leg, as she slowly counted out eighty pence change into my waiting hand. I gasped, "What? Twenty pence to empty my bladder!" She smiled, and joined the chorus of a Charlie Rich song "Behind Closed Doors" playing on a portable CD player behind her.

I dashed into a cubicle and, from behind my closed door, I heard someone else enter the public restrooms. Plastic bags rustled, shoes shuffled and I heard the voice of a person moaning, as if in pain. When I flushed the loo and opened my cubicle door, I saw a woman slouched in the corner beside the trashcan. At her side lay an empty cane basket. I'd seen this woman before somewhere. Was she tired or unwell? She lay sprawled on the floor, her legs outstretched, bare feet poking through worn stocking soles. I suddenly recognized her face and remembered having seen her in Ardcarron one day. Was she the lady who winked at me, the day I first searched for a friend?

"Are you okay?" I asked.

"Oww! Oww!" she groaned.

"What's wrong? Are you in pain?"

"Oww!" she said again, holding out her hand.

I checked her palm but found no bruise or cut, so I asked her what she wanted.

"Oww!" she said again.

"Look, Ma'am, I think you should maybe get yourself home, if you are not well. Do you need a doctor? Can I help you to your feet?"

"No! I'll get the bus," she said.

"You're going on the bus? Yes, well, you'd better hurry because the buses will be leaving soon."

"Oww!" she said again, holding out her palm.

I didn't understand but she looked scruffy, so I asked her if she had money for the bus. She shook her head. *Poor woman.* My back pocket held eighty pence and I added another one pound and thirty pence from my schoolbag. After all, my school bus pass would get me home.

"Here," I said, handing her the coins. "Take this. But if you're going to Ardcarron we'll have to hurry."

"Go on ahead," she mumbled.

I ran ahead, to ask the driver to wait for her, but when I boarded the bus I couldn't find my pass. Maybe I dropped it, so I retraced my steps back to the cubicle.

No bus pass, no old lady, and by the time I returned to the bus stop the bus had vanished, too. *Oh great!* I'd have to call Grandpa for a lift. But, I remembered throwing my old phone at Mom in my morning rage. When I saw the 'out of order' sign on the one available public phone, my only option was to walk home, all thirteen miles!

*This is your fault for twittering on about history classes,* I told Coinneach, as we left the town and joined the A9 road.

*Ladies can be so accusative. Once upon a time a local farmer's wife broke her large wooden porridge spurtle on my brow because her pig died.*

*Did you kill her pig?*

*Of course not! The pig died from the fall.*

*What fall?*

*When I dropped him.*

*Dropped him where?*

*Over the cliff's edge, of course.*

"I swear you're meaner than a skillet full of rattlesnakes, Coinneach!" I shouted aloud.

With each passing car, I held my thumb high. I hoped for a lift, but due to my animated conversation with Coinneach, I guess I looked like I'd lost my vertical hold and everyone drove on by. *Tarnations!* I comforted myself with the thought that Mom would throw a hissy fit if she knew I was there hitching a lift. Despite this, I stopped hitching and walked... and I walked, till my feet hurt and my belly and my back bumped together with hunger.

Then, I heard someone else speak to me, a... a... stag. Yes, I know how crazy that sounds. A stag spoke to me. Well, not so much spoke, not in words. It lured me and I felt pulled to its energy. Drawn, like when the door opened in my head and like when I knew someone listened behind the beech tree. This time I trusted my senses. The stag stood on the other side of a roadside hedge. Tucked behind some dog rose bushes, he waited for me and all I had to do was find a gap in the thorns so that I could push through. I knew I had to go to him, find him. I clutched the stone around my neck; *he's beckoning me.*

The scratches on my arms and face didn't hurt, as I pushed through the thorny hedge, not at first. For there he stood, right in front of me, in front of a group of tall Cypress trees, next to an abandoned plough. Immobilized by his majesty, I locked into his presence. The stag towered, all consuming. I smelled his sensual musk, saw his piercing eyes, and, even though I stood apart from him, I swear I felt his hot breath on my skin.

*Fire is coming! Stay alert! Forewarned is forearmed! Be careful of the fire! Fire is coming!*

His warning swirled in my head again.

*Fire is coming! Stay alert! Forewarned is forearmed! Be careful of the fire! Fire is coming!*

I sensed a gradual release from his pull. Slowly, my thorn-scratched skin started to nip and sting. The stag leaned left, turned, and faded into the Cypress trees.

Though I searched, I couldn't find the spot where I'd squeezed through the bushes. The hedge bulged so thick with rose hips, some as big and shiny as crab apples, and I couldn't see any gap for all the thorny branches. *How did I get through?* Water trickled nearby, and my feet squelched, sodden. Had I crossed a stream, a ditch, or had I found a well? Suddenly a break appeared in the hedge. *But I had looked there. I could have sworn it.*

Clambering back through the bushes, I reached the verge of the road again, just as Grandpa's white car whizzed on by. He headed in the direction of town. I jumped up and down, waving my arms in the air. Momentarily, his red brake lights flashed on. *Good, he's seen me in his mirror and he's going to turn and come back.* But, he speeded up again and drove out of sight. *Perhaps he braked to avoid the stag? Darn it! He must be going into town to look for me.*

The sun sank into an orange glowing sunset behind the hills to the west.  And then, I shivered cold.  If only I hadn't given that old woman my change.  I could have used that money to get myself home.  I doubt she even caught the bus.  Amidst the wondering about where she went, Coinneach interrupted my thoughts.

*You might not want to walk in the middle of the road, young woman.*

*There are no cars coming,* I replied.

*Cars? Whoever said anything about cars?*

*You did.  You said I might not want to…*

*Move! Quickly!* He screamed inside my head.  Coinneach had never shouted before.

I looked around but the road looked clear ahead, right up to the church on the corner some half-mile away.  Behind me, the road also seemed clear for a good two hundred yards.

*Move! You must move!* He insisted.  *Come to the fence and ground yourself by holding on.  Imagine white light around you.*

*What are you talking about?*

*Don't ever walk in the middle of a road, especially not near a church.*

I continued walking down the white line in the center of the road, to purposefully annoy him.  After all, my detention was HIS fault.

*No! Not the middle of the road!*

*What's wrong with the middle of the…*

At first the clips of the horse's hooves were faint but they grew louder, escalating to a clatter in my brain like the repetitious clapping of hollowed-out coconut shells.  But where?  The noise . . . which direction?  I searched, listened.  In front?  Behind?  Then, finally I spied the steamy, black stallions, wearing black head plumes and pulling a wooden cart.  On the cart a coffin, dressed over with thick black cloth.  A funeral procession!  *But, why is it traveling so fast?*  Suddenly surrounded by wailing mourners, dark mesh veils draped over their elongated faces, I fought to breathe, choking, claustrophobic.  Their grief began to swallow me like a vacuum, expanding my head, augering my eyeball sockets, like trying to thrust a large rubber ball down a thin plastic pipe.  I felt myself being sucked into the procession.

*I MUST pull away.  Must leave the middle of the road, NOW!*

Coinneach screamed at me inside my head.  *DO AS I SAY…Think of a white light.  See the light shine all around you and imagine you are a huge tree.  Ground yourself!  Imagine you have huge roots securing you to the ground.  DO IT NOW.  See those roots holding you firmly to the spot. Now HOLD ON TIGHT with those roots.*

"Okay! Okay! I'm closing my eyes. I see white light. I'm a tree. I have roots going way down underground. They are holding me. The roots are holding me."

My ears popped and a searing pain pierced my brow. It felt like some invisible force snapped, and the forceful release catapulted me across the grassy kerbside. Lying on my back, the clatter of hooves faded to silence. Sunlight slithered into nightfall. The last wisp of pink cloud dyed to charcoal black, and the phantom funeral procession vanished into the dusk. Gone.

Grandpa's tires screeched to a halt when he spied me lying in the grass at the side of the road. He sprinted from the car like a sprightly youth. Crouching down, he hugged me tight.

"Lassie, you'll be the death of an old codger like me. Whatever are you doing out here on the road alone? It's nearly ten o'clock and I've searched all but a puckle o' places for you! We were worried sick, your mother and me. I called Rhiannon and she said you were being bullied and . . . Are you hurt? Can you walk? Did you fall? Speak to me, lassie."

Poor Grandpa cried.

"I'm SO sorry, Gramps. I've had such a horrid day."

"Come. Get into the car and tell me about it." He sniffed and blew his noise on a large white handkerchief.

I told him about the detention, about giving all my change to lady with the cane basket, about missing the bus, about the phones, "…and I did thumb a lift, even though I didn't want to take rides from strangers, but nobody stopped, so I walked all this way, and my feet hurt and I'm hungry and I'm tired and I want to go home and I'm so glad to see you Grandpa and…"

"Poor lassie," he said. "Poor lassie."

Poor Grandpa, too. How could I put him through all this worry? He gushed with emotion, so completely overwhelmed with tears that he could hardly see to drive. We held hands all the way home, except for when he had to change gears.

As Grandpa pulled into the driveway of the house, the front door opened and Mom stomped out from the threshold, a huge scowl on her face. She held my old mobile.

I tightened my grip on Grandpa's hand.

He whispered, "There's a marag and jeelie piece in the kitchen with a glass of milk. Get it and go to bed, lassie. Coorie down and I'll see to your mother."

As soon as I cracked open the car door she started, "Where do you think you have…"

"FIONA!" shouted Grandpa.

Mom gulped.

"Later, Fiona. There will be plenty time for questions later," said Grandpa, assertively.

Mom breathed in and held her breath, tightened her lips and glared at Grandpa. She looked livid at being reprimanded. But she let me pass so that I could grab my food. I scuttled quickly to my room.

While Mom and Gramps squabbled in the kitchen, I stood at my bedroom window gazing out. The moon illuminated the solitary tree at the Clootie Well at the back of the field and all the white rags fluttered in the breeze.

What a beautiful old tree. Then, I remembered the lesson in grounding myself. *Thanks for saving me, Coinneach. From now on I'll be surrounding myself with imaginary white light each and every day!*

I closed my eyes, imagined pure white light all around me and then called out to the tree, "Hello tree. My mind's full of worries, too many to mention. Help me out here! I'm one bubble off plumb. What am I to do? Speak to me."

Neither Coinneach nor the tree answered, so I flopped onto my bed and buried my head into the soft, down pillow.

*No way Mom will buy me an iPhone for my birthday now!*

Exhausted, I curled into a tight fetal position. Outside, the pale moon shone. Orange glows sparkled from the Travellers' campfire in the 'bless them' field and I could just see the white clooties fanning and dancing in the distance. My eyelids drooped, eyes half shut. In the reels of flickering light, the dark branches of the Clootie Tree became the velvety antlers of the majestic stag.

*Fire is coming! Stay alert! Forewarned is forearmed! Be careful of fire! Fire is coming!* The stag whispered, warning me again, and again, and I shivered beneath the duck down duvet, first acknowledging him but then trying not to listen.

As I squeezed my eyes tightly shut, I concentrated hard on imagining white light but I couldn't. I tried to think of my happy words, but found none.

Pleading for distraction, all I could think of were raindrops, so I begged the rain to drum off the window outside. I also asked the tree, nicely, "please can everyone leave me in peace now."

But suddenly, the stag's pounding heart began to thunder in my ears -- *Ba-Boom! Ba-Boom! Ba-Boom!* It escalated to a loud, roaring bellow, like the stag competed with the thumping in my own chest. My heart pummeled and pounded against my breastbone, beating in tandem. *Ba-Boom! Ba-Boom! Ba-Boom! Ba-Boom! Ba-Boom! Ba-Boom!*

"No! Not hearts! Be-jeepers, anything but hearts! Okay, I'm listening now . . . I heard you . . . Fire is coming . . . Yes . . . Fire is coming."

## Visiting Time

"I hate that bitch more than ever," said Bethany to Jake. "She's pathetic!"

"The American girl?" he asked.

"No, I mean Ma. I hate Ma."

Jake chuckled. "You hate everyone, Beth."

"No I don't." Her eyes narrowed to slits as she spoke.

"I go to see Ma in the jail and all she wants me for is to get her pills, diazepam. Where am I supposed to get her that? 'I need them, Bethany' she says. 'It's stressful in here and the guards won't search a nice kid like you,' she says in her lovey-dovey voice. No feckin apology. Nuh, not her... not for times she left me starve half to death, while she lay wasted beside her dirty needles. When she knifed that guy for his wallet and left him for dead, she might as well have knifed me. 'It's stressful out here, too,' I told her."

Jake clipped his niece on the ear with his hand.

"Ouch! What was that for?'"

"Get over it and stop yer complaining. I'm here for ya now, ain't I?" Jake's mood suddenly changed, softened. He touched her gently on the cheek with his index finger.

Reaching into an old tin that he'd extracted from a cupboard, Jake produced a hand rolled joint. He lit the joint of marijuana, inhaled its smoke deeply into his lungs, closed his eyes and grinned.

"Here. Drag on this till you chill," he said, and handed the joint to his niece.

Beth puffed on the joint, till they both fell about laughing.

"Like I said, Bethany, I'm here for you now. You don't need your druggie mother. I'll be your stoner buddy form now on, Babe, okay?"

"Okay, Babe," she answered, and they laughed again.

## Chapter 8

## *Ladies in the Walls*

"Woop! Woop! I've got another message on my brand new iPhone!"

I squealed and told Mom it was the best birthday gift, ever. "Am I popular, or what?" I said.

But, I choked on my spit when I read the message.

"WITCH!"

*Who sent this? I don't recognize the number. Why don't these people leave me alone?*

Oblivious to my anguish, Gramps chuckled with excitement, holding out a bottle of maple syrup.

"I spied a wee puckle o' these jars at half price in the supermarket," he said, frying up a batch of pancakes for my breakfast. But the sweet smell tasted sickly. My chest ached as I tried to swallow the emotional lump in my throat.

"I'll just have the pancakes and the syrup, Gramps, no beetroot for me." I sighed.

"You're such a joker." He laughed.

No joke; I'd grown so used to his cookery experiments that I genuinely mistook a pot of raspberry jam for beetroot. This was a genuine error, but I was tired of seeing things that others didn't... *Oh no, tonight is Halloween!*

"Gramps, I don't feel like going to school this morning," I said. "I could say that my stomach hurt and I felt sick, but that would be a big old lie. Truth is that it's Friday, last school day of the week. They're doing a lot of goofy stuff for Halloween today, and I want to stay at home. I'd rather not say why. Is that okay, for once?"

He leaned back against the sink folding his arms. His eyebrows wrinkled together and he drew breath to speak in a serious tone... but then he smiled and simply said, "Aye, good idea. Yes, why not have a day off. I'll call the school to say I'm keeping you at home because you seem a little beetroot."

"Thanks, Grandad," I said. "I think I'll go out for a walk in the fresh air."

"Here then," he said, handing me some coins. "Fetch me The Raggie from the paper shop on your road home, so I can read the latest hatches, matches and dispatches." He referred to page two, where all the births, marriages and obituaries notices were posted in the newspaper.

Grabbing a pair of binoculars on the way out of the front door, I also swiped Grandpa's fishing hat from the hall coat rack and buried my exhausted brain deep within its musky smell of pipe tobacco and Brylcreem. I loved the colorful fishing flies that he'd hooked into the khaki green cloth. Grandpa had told me all their names: McGinty the fly clung like a bumble bee, striped yellow and black; Butcher Kingfisher had brown wings, and an orange belly with a turquoise tail; and Brora Ranger reminded me of red and black wasps that would build their nests on our front porch in Texas.

I hadn't thought about Texas in days and suddenly my mood dipped again, overwhelmed with guilt about Dad. I'd been ignoring his emails again. He wanted to know if I got the birthday present that he'd sent. If I thought for one minute that he'd bought my gift himself, I'd rush back a note of thanks. But Dad would never have chosen a flowery t-shirt for me, not in red. He knows that red clashes with my hair.

I sat on a wooden bench at the top of Ardcarron Brae and peered through the binoculars, which I'd focused on the bottom of the hill. Rhiannon, Kyle and Duncan stood outside the Misses MacGregor's shop, waiting for the school bus.

"Sorry, Rhiannon," I whispered, when I saw her clutching the giant pack of Andrex toilet paper. We had planned to wrap ourselves up as mummies for the Halloween Fun Day at school.

*I don't think she can hear you from here,* said Coinneach.

Weird! That time I could've sworn his voice came from behind me, not in my head. I swung around with the binoculars still fixed to my eyes.

At first, the view through the lenses appeared like a kaleidoscope, vague pink and green patterns floating and changing, adding brighter hues of amber and yellow, stronger mauves, shuffling together then splitting apart into diamonds and triangles, and finally blending into curves and circles. Coinneach emerged through the center of smoky blue clouds, sitting on a bench much like the one I sat on. His legs were crossed. The boot on his left foot had a large flap in it, where the sole had come loose. Long, dirty fingernails curled around a wooden cane that he leaned upon. He smiled. Gaps appeared where front teeth once lived. A matted grey beard framed a crooked mouth, his moustache growing way down below a ruddy, bulbous nose. His clothes were plain freaky! Rusty chains encircled his coat-clad torso, all jingling and dangling. And, the weirdest of things hung from these chains – wishbones, feathers, claws, bits of fur – a whole menagerie of possessions. He looked scruffy and tattered, like a right tatterdemalion, as Gramps would say.

"Coinneach?"

*Yes. I'm a handsome fellow, wouldn't you agree?*

"Holy Macaroni! You're a tramp!"

The words flew out before I had time to think.

*TRAMP? TRAMP!* Coinneach spat, furiously.

I chuckled and he vanished from inside my binoculars.

Once the Glenaldie High School bus departed, I returned the binoculars back to their case and ambled downhill to the Misses MacGregor's store to collect Grandpa's paper. I zipped quickly past Gargoyle House where… *did I perceive a flash of red? No! Don't even look.*

An old fashioned bell tinkled as I opened the village shop door. "Hello dearie," said Miss MacGregor, the thinner sister. She squeaked with a high-pitched voice, always with shocking pink Marigold gloves and a matching pink apron. One of her eyes drifted toward the till, while the other squinted west to the tinned peas and I didn't know which one to look at when she spoke. I moved my head back and forth but neither eye seemed to follow me. Bifocals perched on the end of her long, thin nose. The glasses anchored to her head with a gold cord that dangled from the frame and disappeared into the folds of a silvery grey chiffon neck scarf. Miss MacGregor stood alone behind the shop counter. However, she spoke as if she were talking to her sister, the other Miss MacGregor, who was nowhere to be seen. She addressed me in the third person, like this. "Oh she's got such lovely red hair, so she has, hasn't she?"

The doorbell tinkled a second time and an old farmer-type with dung-splattered boots entered behind me. She greeted him the same way. "Hello, Alec. How's himself today? Oh yes, he'll be wanting his pipe tobacco now, will he? And, he'll be getting his Farming Monthly, too, once I've seen to herself here."

*Why does she speak like that?*

I fixed my gaze at a mid-point between each of her eyes and tried to reciprocate with her Highland banter. "I . . . I mean she, that's herself here, will be wanting her Grandpa's paper, so she will." It worked, because Miss MacGregor handed me the Northern Times. I then asked, "How much would she, herself behind the counter, be wanting to charge me for her papers?"

Suddenly, Miss Macgregor's thin lips drew tight and she scowled, no longer addressing me in the third person. "Now, don't you be so cheeky young lady, or I'll tell Ali Dubh about your insolence."

"What?" I exclaimed, but she didn't answer.

"Sometimes I don't get this stupid Highland culture." I dumped the correct money into her bony, upturned palm, and turned to leave.

On my exit, I skirted past Alec and his stinky boots. Weirdly, I had this sudden urge to warn the man about something in connection with a tractor, but since I didn't feel like hanging around to speak to anyone else, I said nothing.

Standing outside the door of the shop, I stared ahead at the war memorial and sighed at the unfairness.

*I don't get it. Why do people pick on me?*

Coinneach spoke. He said, *Since you insulted me, calling me a tramp, I'm going to ask you a question. Instead of asking yourself why people pick on you, why don't you ask yourself why I am here, living in your head?* he said.

He'd never done that before; ask me stuff. Until now, his ramblings, always self-centered, barely acknowledged my existence. I didn't answer him, because I didn't know why he'd begun asking me uncomfortable questions.

*Brucie, why do you think I am here, living in your head?*

His tone felt freaky, stunning me to silence. I felt suddenly vulnerable. Someone lived in my head and I hadn't invited them there. I would call the police if someone entered my house without asking so what was I thinking of, letting Coinneach into my brain? Suddenly scared, I acted tough, like I didn't care.

*Pink and tangerine clouds from a summer sunset... March hares racing, bounding across a green meadow... eating corn dogs drenched in mustard at the Texas State Fair... the sweet smell of skunk, oh how I love the sweet smell of skunk...*

*Don't act tough with me,* he said.

I started to cross the road.

"BANG!"

An old Land Rover backfired from its exhaust. As if that wasn't enough to scare me, the driver honked his horn. A filthy man, with eyes dark as ravens, rolled down the window. "Watch where you're going, Sweetheart!"

I'd walked straight out in front of him without looking.

Red faced, I lowered my head again, checking out the truck from the corner of my eye.

*Oh my God, there's Bethany MacKinnon, sitting in the passenger seat beside him. Any minute now, I thought, she'll roll down her window, and cuss me, too.*

Bethany saw me okay, but she looked away without acknowledgement. Nothing! In fact she looked sadly troubled sitting there. The truck sped off into the distance.

*That's odd!*

Passing the memorial, I quickly glanced back over my shoulder. It felt like a battalion of eyes followed, waiting for me to answer Coinneach's question.

*Well?* said Coinneach.

I ignored him as best I could.

The air bulged pregnant with silence and a large thought bubble burst when I clattered into . . . *muscular neck*. . . Donald. Hands clad in a large pair of goalkeeping gloves, he dove out of the entrance to Gargoyle house, chasing a soccer ball. Our skulls collided.

"Ouch!"

We each rubbed palms to our foreheads. *Mmm . . . he looks different without his glasses!*

Desperate for a quick distraction, I blurted, "Not in school today either, huh?"

A green MacKay's Contractor van parked in the driveway.

Donald massaged his forehead and laughed. "I like your hat." He paused. "Actually, I missed the school bus. My parents are getting estimates for a house extension, so they are too busy to give me a lift. I'll get the eleven eighteen bus, though. Thought I'd kick a ball with John Alexander till then. It's the second time I've missed chemistry this week, though."

"I don't think you should worry about your chemistry," I said. Donald had more chemistry than I could handle. "I think it's mostly Halloween nonsense today."

A small boy with a freckled nose and large blue eyes stretched out his arms and clung onto Donald's leg, grinning coyly as he sucked on a chubby, wet finger.

Donald knelt down and coaxed the wee guy, "Say hello to Brucie, John Alexander. And, why don't you ask her if she'd like to come to our party tonight."

"Hi Boosy," said a shy John Alexander. "Want to come to party?"

"Yes, I'd love to come, John Alexander."

Donald asked me, "So what's your excuse for skiving?"

"Ah, which excuse would you like? I could lie and tell you that I broke my leg…"

"Nah, your legs don't look broken to me."

*Eek, why did I draw his attention to my legs?*

"What's wrong?" he asked. His concern made my heart race and my cheeks burned hotter than a habanera chili. *Why do I struggle so to keep eye contact with Donald? It's like I'm frightened that he'll see what I'm trying to hide from him.*

When I didn't answer, he asked again, "You okay?"

*Get a grip, Brucie,* I told myself. *Just because you think that he's hot doesn't mean that he's going to think that you're hot, too. Keep your cool. Don't spill your guts!*

"Oh, I needed a day off to help Gramps," I lied.

"You're coming to our house later tonight, though, right?" He continued to rub his forehead.

"Oh well," I exclaimed. "I guess I won't need a disguise for Halloween now, not with this giant lump disfiguring my head." I lifted the hat. "Does it look scary?"

"Naw, you're still pretty."

*DID HE REALLY SAY THAT? DID HE?*

John Alexander tugged on Donald's leg. "Play with me."

Donald ignored his little brother. Instead, Donald raised his finger to the lump on my forehead and… touched my skin! He cocked his head to the side like a curious spaniel. "Sorry, I'm clumsy and blind without my glasses. Should've seen you there. Does it hurt?"

*Oh no!* I panicked, turning on my heels to leave. "I have to go!" The wall of Gargoyle House had begun to flash red again. And, like a photographic image floating in developing fluid, her image slowly materialized in front of me. I froze in a moment in time, caught between flight, fright and fascination. My throat felt choked and I wheezed the words again, "I have to go." But my eyes fixed on her. She floated forward, circling around Donald, huddled into the red shawl that she wrapped around her feeble frame. When she opened her mouth, her pale lips and boney jaw moved as if at half speed. Words fought to squeak from the hollow of her mouth, distorted high-pitched tones and squeals, like the blings, pops and crackles of an old-fashioned dial up modem. She struggled to connect to me.

"BAY BAY. GAY YO TOT IT OW IT."

Frozen to the spot, I made no sense of her strange sounds.

"What's Boosie doing, Donnie?" I suddenly heard John Alexander speaking and felt acutely aware of everyone staring at me: Donald, John Alexander, Coinneach and the woman in the red shawl. All seemed to be asking me various questions that I couldn't answer.

"Go inside, John Alexander," said Donald to his brother. "I want to speak to Brucie alone."

"Och!" John Alexander muttered. He hung his head and dug his chubby hands into the depths of his large coat pockets before ambling off in doors, kicking at a stone en route.

"What's up, Brucie? Your face turned pale. What are you hearing? Is it Coinneach again?"

"Turn around, Donald." I pointed to the area behind his left shoulder. "Tell me what you see over there by the window."

The woman in the shawl screwed up her eyes and batted a hand at me before huddling deeper into her shawl and fading out of sight. I wanted to call to her, "Don't leave! Tell me again what you said. Speak slower this time . . . deeper, faster . . . speak English, or whatever."

Donald looked puzzled. "I see plant pots, a bike, a garden hose, the football..."

"It's okay, Donald." I said. "She's gone."

"Who?" he asked.

"Nobody." I lied.

"But, then why..." He changed his mind and stopped asking questions. "I thought I saw someone standing behind you, but, never mind. I have to go. I'll see you later. Six o'clock? And no Halloween costumes, right?"

He didn't need to reply. I knew his father forbade any reference to Halloween. It would be just a friendly gathering.

"Yeah, that's right," he said, as I spun around and ran.

Back at my house, Gramps stood by the cooker in the kitchen, icing bag in hand, ready to frost some rusty colored tomato and basil fairy cakes. A text arrived from Rhiannon, "Y u not in skool? R U going to the party?"

I text back, "Soz I woznt @ skool. Yes. Im going. Will I CU after skool?"

Rhiannon confirmed that she'd see me later.

"Here is your newspaper," I said to Gramps. "Will I leave it on the table?"

"Aye, sit it there. Who served you in the shop today?" he asked, licking some yellow icing off his finger.

"The thin, short-sighted one," I answered, watching, opting not to ask the flavor of the icing.

"Ah, but she's got the eyes of a good Catholic woman, she has . . . always crossing themselves." He laughed at his own joke before politely spitting the icing into a waiting napkin.

At 4.40 pm Rhiannon rang the doorbell and walked straight in, calling through to the kitchen to Grandpa as she headed for my bedroom, "Hi, Mr. MacKenzie. How are you today?"

"Fine Rhiannon, but I keep telling you... call me Ali."

Rhiannon blushed. "It doesn't feel right to call you that."

"Then call me Gramps, like Brucie does," he said.

"Okay, Gramps." Rhiannon smiled.

If there is one thing that I can usually guarantee it's that Coinneach will stop talking as soon as I have company. It's like he doesn't want anyone to hear him, which is stupid because no one CAN hear him, except me. As Rhiannon walked into my bedroom, though, Coinneach began his incessant chattering.

*You still haven't asked me why I am here.*

"Oh, for God's sake, what are you doing here, then?" I shouted at him.

"Besom! I'm here because you asked me to come see you, Brucie Bice!" Rhiannon wore a new, blue cashmere sweater, which complimented her long dark hair beautifully. I suddenly felt scruffy in comparison.

"No. I didn't mean you, Rhiannon. I meant Coinneach."

"Is he here?" she asked.

*Yes. I'm here.*

"She can't hear you," I told Coinneach, and then I relayed to Rhiannon, "He says yes, he's here... and this is plain silly now, delivering messages back and forth between the two of you."

Giddy. I felt giddy, so I sat on the bed. Leaning slightly back against the pillow, I felt weird in my throat. My voice deepened, as I spoke.

"Hello Rhiannon. Charmed to make your acquaintance," he said, in a big, gruff tone that made me gasp in need of a glass of water.

Rhiannon leered at me, open mouthed. She let rip a high-pitched scream. She screamed and screamed and screamed, until Gramps and Mom entered the room.

"What happened? What is it?" demanded Mom, searching around the room for clues to Rhiannon's sudden terror.

Rhiannon had a beige face, like puked-up porridge.

Quick as a wink, I lied. "Nothing is wrong. She thought she saw a rat under the bed but it is only my hairy slipper."

Gramps laughed, shaking his head. "Come on, Fiona. Let's leave those two daft lassies to their rat jokes."

The minute Gramps and Mom left the room, Rhiannon grabbed my arm. "HE spoke to me!" She grabbed both of my arms and shook me hard. "I mean YOU spoke to me. Like, HE spoke to me with YOUR mouth, or something. Brucie, what the... Are you possessed?" She began to cry. "Don't you EVER do that again! NEVER AGAIN! RIGHT? EVER!"

"Sorry Rhiannon!"

She gulped and choked on her own spit, furious with fright and rage. Her words tumbled and jumbled into a ball. She fumed. The horror that I saw in my friend's eyes made me angry, too.

I shouted at Coinneach inside my head. *NEVER! Don't EVER do that to my friend again! In fact, NEVER do it to ANYONE again. GOT IT?*

But, he'd scarpered, taken himself off like a guilty thief, to hide in the shadows of my brain.

"It's okay Rhiannon," I said, "he's gone."

But, Rhiannon turned on her heels, too. "This is way too spooky for me, Brucie! I can't handle this. I'm sorry but I'm out of here. You are freaking nuts." She tossed her long hair with her hand, zipped toward the hallway and slammed my bedroom door behind her.

I scolded Coinneach. *Now look what you've done!*
He still didn't answer.

By six o'clock the night folded an eerie darkness around Ardcarron. Faulty street lights left me fumbling back down the hill to Gargoyle House, under a pitch-black sky. My mood darkened deeper, too. I trembled with apprehension and clutched my Eye Stone. *Will Rhiannon still go to the party? What if she ignores me? We were supposed to be going there together.*

Suddenly, an orange glowing streetlamp hummed and buzzed to life above my head, "Hmm bzzzruzzie bzzzruzzie hmm."

Orange flashed on. Off. On. Off.

Red bubbled out of the wall.

*Not again! Won't y'all just quit cher colors flashin' 'bout 'n' leave me alone.*

"BAY EE BAY EE!"

"Go away," I said to the woman with the red shawl, "I can't understand you." She flew up the driveway toward me, screeching like a rusty hinge. I darted for the twins' door, but she blocked my path. "Leave me alone," I screamed. "I don't know what you are saying." Lunging forward, she zoomed in two feet from my face. I stepped back till the heels of my boots wedged against the garden wall.

*I'm trapped!*

Protuberant eyes, white with red thread-veins, fixed on me with a glaucous stare, bulging out from their puffy grey sockets. Her cheeks were taught and gaunt, pale, and waxy, gouged into hollows beneath sharply carved cheekbones. With mouth open and head elongated, her whole face stretched into an ugly scream.

"BAY EE BAY EE!"

The porch door flung open and John Alexander called out, "Boocie! Why-oo standing atta wall?"

Flash! The red shawl extinguished into the smoky dark night. She switched off, like a television… but I could still feel the electricity of her presence. Her energy crackled, raising all the small hairs on my neck like static. She followed me inside Gargoyle House, as John Alexander beckoned, "Come in Boocie. Come and play wif me ata party."

"Hmm, bzzzruzzie," I heard her static hum around me, "Hmm, bzzzruzzie."

In the living room, Rhiannon leaned against the large, oak mantle piece, chatting to Kyle, picking at a bit of cold wax that had dripped down a brass candlestick. I know she saw me enter the room, but Rhiannon looked back toward Kyle, completely snubbing me.

*Please don't do this to me, Rhiannon. I need you. I'm under so much stress.*

Twenty-three people filled the room, including most of the twins' siblings, Reverend Macleod and his wife. An elderly woman in a tweed coat buttoned to the neck sat by the fire on a wooden kitchen chair, cradling a cup of hot tea in her hand. She smiled at me, revealing a toothless set of bright, pink gums.

The drab room looked more like a morgue than a party venue. No wonder the house had a ghost! If not for the welcoming fire, a large mirror and some glitzy, gilt pictures frames which twinkled reflecting light, I might have excused myself and gone back home. Solemn oil paintings hung on oatmeal textured wallpaper, scenes of brown and purple heather clad hills, old croft houses, or cattle meandering along country roads. Four armchairs, of which only two were the same grey-green velvet, grouped around a large bay window with cream net curtains. A half-moon table supported a crystal vase full of yellowing-white carnations. A giant rug in autumn colors covered most of the wooden floor in the room, except for the outer three feet in all directions. Conversation droned rather than bubbled.

*Where are the party balloons?*

The twins looked around, as if longing for someone to crack a joke. Kyle fidgeted and sighed. Old Beatles songs played on an ancient mono turn table and trays of food were scattered around the room with sandwiches and cakes, but nobody ate.

*Oh, well, might as well dig in*, I thought.

As I grabbed some chocolate cake, though, the music died and everyone bowed their heads to give thanks. I said, "Amen" with my mouth dripping chocolate.

"Tut tut," said the lady with the gums, "irreverent eating is not the way of the Lord."

*Lord, if you are there, can't you transport me to a good ol' Texan trick or treat party?*

Texans love to celebrate everything. Back in Texas, stores bulged with ghoulish masks, tubes of fake blood, candy galore and every kind of battery operated toys that screeched. Wal-mart would be strewn with Halloween costumes as kids squealed and trampled on them. Looking around at the somber faces in front of me I yearned for a dose of good ol' Southern fun, like going to Fright Fest at 'Six Flags Over Texas' with Dad.

*Sometimes Scots people bore me. I need to be entertained!*

I stood awkwardly alone and counted everyone again. Twenty four this time! The extra guest hovered and then perched at my side on the arm of the large floral sofa, adjusting her red shawl. She watched me, constantly. No one else noticed her... except, John Alexander stood by the heavy oak door with his finger in his mouth, glancing from me to the sofa, me to the sofa, me to the sofa. *He can see her, can't he?* The boy edged toward her, still sucking on his wet finger. John Alexander kicked at the sofa arm and giggled.

His father scolded him from across the room. "Don't do that to the furniture."

"I'm not," he argued. "I'm playing wif the lady."

*He saw her! I knew it! John Alexander saw her!*

"Brucie is no lady, like, if you know what I mean?" said Kyle, laughing. "Hey Brucie, do we smell or something? Come over here and join us."

Rhiannon scowled and looked down at her fingernails. I wanted to say something to her, like 'sorry Coinneach scared you,' but it really wasn't my fault so I didn't speak.

*I hate you, Coinneach.*

He didn't even have the decency to hate me back. Nothing. No response.

We moved from the sofa over to the mantelpiece: me and the woman in the red shawl. She hung by my side. Rigid with trepidation, I swore I could even smell her breath on my face; moldy and stale like a musty old second-hand bookstore, or the inside of a museum. Her lips parted and she burbled like scraping gravel into my ear "Bay Bay." Then again, louder, "BAY BAY." This time her face filled with anguish, until the frequency and tone of her voice lowered and the tones were more distinguishable. She spoke slower. At last I understood.

"Baby," she said, followed by, "Go, get it. Get the baby."

I looked around quickly to see if anyone else had heard, but everyone chatted and droned liked bees, oblivious. All except for little John Alexander, who could not keep his eyes off me.

"Baby," he said and giggled. "I've got a baby brother," he told her, and grinned.

*He can HEAR her, too!*

"What did the lady say, John Alexander?" I asked, seeking confirmation.

His little leg kicked out in the direction of the woman in the red shawl but his foot went right through her and he kicked me instead. He laughed.

"Okay, time out, John Alexander. Say sorry to Brucie and then go to your bedroom, young man. I saw you kick her," said a stern and watchful Rev. MacLeod, who then turned to me. "I'm so sorry, Brucie. I hope he didn't bruise you."

I shook my head. "No, it's fine."

John Alexander left the room, grinning.

"I swear that wee guy only misbehaves when you are around, Brucie," said . . . *yes, nice hands* . . . Donald.

"Did you know that your brother is psychic?" I asked.

Rhiannon freaked. "Oh Brucie, give the weird stuff a rest, will you? Leave John Alexander out of your psychic-babble. He's only a kid."

"There's actually no such word as psychic-babble. It's psychobabble," said Duncan, trying to help.

"No, psychic-babble is what I mean and I'm tired of her psychic-babbling," said Rhiannon. "You're so . . . you're so . . . American sometimes, Brucie. If you want to fit in here you'll have to stop this freak show and act normal like the rest of us . . . or . . . or, I don't want to have anything more to do with you."

"Rhiannon? What are you like?" said Kyle. "Girl fight! Girl fight!" he chanted, clapping his hands.

My pressure gauge blew. I snapped and launched myself at her, yelling, "It's not a freak show!" But, I stumbled and lost my balance, knocking Kyle's arm and spilling his cola all down Rhiannon's new, blue sweater.

"Brucie! My Mum will go crazy. You've ruined my jumper. I'm going home. Why don't you do the same? In fact, why don't you go home to America?"

"Ladies, ladies, ladies!" the Reverent MacLeod called out, but Rhiannon had already left the room and I followed her, trembling.

"Rhiannon, don't go. I'm sorry about the psychic-babble," I called. "You've no right to be mean, though. I'm trying to fit in here but it's not easy being an immigrant."

I tried to chase after her but she ran up Ardcarron Brae faster than a hungry whippet. My breath panted out in clouds before me, even after I gave up running.

A couple of fake Halloween ghosts, kids dressed in white sheets, called, "Woooo!" as they passed by. I sat on the sidewalk and smirked at the irony of their façade. The two phony ghouls hung around, Wooing stupidly, and I wished they'd leave me alone. Then, I heard one of them say, "She doesn't need a costume. She's already a witch!"

Donald called to me from outside Gargoyle House, "Brucie!" but I didn't want to speak to anyone now. I'd had enough; the spirit voices in my vocal chords, the red-cloaked ghost shouting about some baby, my best friend hating me, being an out-of-place immigrant, and ... I missed my dad.

I don't know why but I snuck into a gap in the curbside hedge to hide myself away and cry. Maybe the hedge space felt snug and secure, womblike. I sat on my heels surrounded by privet, bubbling over with emotion. I didn't want to be found, either, so I kept my flashlight in my pocket. My soul found some relief within the crawl space, where I could hole up and escape.

"What am I going to do?" I cried over and over, crouched down in the cold. "I miss you, Dad. If only you could see the mess my life is in."

Suddenly... a hand touched my arm.

"AAAAAAAAAH!

"Got any chocolate for an old guiser?" She shuffled in beside me, into the hedge. I knew immediately who it was and pulled my arm away quickly. The moon slipped out from behind a cloud and outlined the shape of her cane basket.

"I nearly wet myself, lady!" I said, wiping my wet eyes on my sleeve. Then, I remembered the bone that I had to pick with her. "Oh yeah, last time we met, I missed the bus because of you! I gave you all my change and lost my bus pass, so I had to walk home."

"Is this whatcha call a bus pass thingummy?" she said, holding up my pass.

I fumbled to twist the top of my flashlight, shining a beam down on her hand. "Where'd you get that from? It's mine, my bus pass."

"You dropped it in them water closets in town, Miss," she said, and handed it to me.

"Water closet? Don't you mean toilet or wash room?"

She nodded, and then asked, "You been fighting, Miss? I saw yer friend scarper up um hill, like uh beat up dog. None too pleased she wuz, if y'ask me."

I put the nosy, old crone in her place, "Well I didn't ask you. Did I?"

She sighed on me, with more bad breath, and I felt so gross huddled next to her, in the privet hedge. I shone the light on her hands again. They looked bony and her hair and skin dark, like a gypsy's. She reached her scrawny hand out to touch my Eye Stone.

"Git cher hands away from my stone!"

"I'll buy it orf ya, that stone there round your neck. A'll give y' a florin, if it's bringin' ye bother, Miss. But, if I were you I'd be wantin to keep it safe 'cause that stone's special, 'n it?"

She reached out to touch it again.

"Git cher paws off!"

I wrapped my hand around the stone, protectively. As we touched hands, a massive surge of energy bubbled around me. My head spun with dizziness and I saw these strange rays of white light. This sensation changed to the middle of my forehead. More spinning radiated purple up through the privet branches. Then my throat vibrated, like a force within, rotating clockwise. Hues of eggshell blue beamed and brightened from my neck and throat, widening out into the road. Ba Boom! Ba Boom! Ba Boom! My heart pulsed out green. All around, the night began to resemble an aurora borealis with stunning lime-green lights. I cupped my hand on my stomach and the light changed to yellow.

"Oooooh, luverly yellow solar plexus," she said.

"Solar what? What's happening?" I asked.

"It's yer chakras, Miss," she said.

"What are you talking about?" I called out.

And, then a bright orange ball arced upward from my abdomen to connect with the streetlight above. Tzzzzzz! Tzzzzzz! Sparks flew around like darting bugs, before blending into a steady red glow. A shriek emitted from down the hill. I looked around expecting to see the woman in the shawl. But, the two silly folk draped in the white sheets returned.

They gasped, speaking in silly disguised voices. "Whoa! Cool light show. Where d'ya get the fancy colored torch from, Brucie?"

But, light didn't shine from my torch. It was me that glowed.

I bolted uphill toward home with the two childish ghosts following in pursuit.

*Oh, please go and annoy someone else. This is not the time. I take back what I said about missing the tackiness of Halloween. This is SO freaky now. Please go away!*

It felt that if I ran faster I could detach from the colors. Instead, I dragged this tail of light behind me, like a giant firefly in the night.

"Woooo! Woooo!" they chanted. "The witch is burning. The witch is burning."

Within reach now, home would feel safe, with Gramps and Mom to protect me. I fumbled desperately in my pocket to find my key. My whole body glowed like a rainbow, charged with electricity. When I touched the key to the door lock... ZAP! Sparks flew and the lights cut dead, like I'd hit a trip switch.

"Wooooo! Check what happened there!" the two called from outside, followed by much senseless giggling. "She blew a fuse!"

I quickly locked the door behind me.

"Mom! Gramps! I'm home. I need help. Where are you?"

The fear in my voice echoed down the hallway. Frantically, I searched every room. The kitchen clock said nine fifty. Nothing. Nobody. My heart raced, palpitating.

I flicked on the light switch in my room. "Darn this stone!" Ripping it from my neck, I chucked it inside my jewelry box on the window ledge, slamming the lid and locking the box with a small silver key from the top right hand drawer of my desk. I drew my curtains, to shut out the two silly tricksters, who peered inside, watching me through the glass.

I massaged my bare neck till it perked like a soothed foot, free from the blistering constraints of walking in tight shoes.

*Why had I not thought to rid myself of that stone sooner? I'm done with it!*

The house rippled with a jarring quiet. No notes of explanation stuck to the refrigerator door, to say where anyone had gone. The smell of Blue perfume suggested that Mom had gone out somewhere. A small compact mirror and an open Rebel Rouge lipstick lay abandoned on her dressing table, confirming the theory. Grandpa's favorite hat and his down-filled Parka were missing from the coat stand and his large coffee flask had vanished from the kitchen countertop.

Another text message buzzed into my iPhone.

I froze, alone and frightened. The message read, "**B** a B y ! S av e thE B aby . "

## Shhh!

"Halloween was awesome last night," said Goth to the Moth. "We need to tell Beth what we saw. Have you seen Beth today?"

"Not since this morning," said the Moth, "But I heard stuff."

Goth asked, "Heard stuff like what?"

"When Bethany speaks to her uncle on the phone she calls him Babe." The Moth fluttered, nervously. "I heard her say to him, 'Hey Babe, where ya going at nights? I'm really missing ya Babe.'"

Goth's eyes opened wide, trying to warn the Moth to shut her mouth.

But, the Moth continued. "Isn't it weird to call your uncle 'Babe'? I hate him. You don't think she has… "a thing"… for her own uncle, do you? What's going on there?"

From behind, a hand grabbed around her throat and squeezed till the Moth began to choke. Her eyes protruded from their sockets and her face turned blue.

"So, you had an awesome Halloween?" said Beth, as she tightened her grip. "Anything else?"

The Moth struggled to speak.

"Not got much to say now. Cat got your tongue?" said Bethany MacKinnon to the Moth.

# Chapter 9

## The Crack Between Two Worlds

In all my sixteen years, one month and five days, I'd never been alone in a house after eleven o'clock at night. Normally, I'd be glad of the freedom and space, but...

*Please Mom, please Gramps; please come home.*

By eleven fifteen I'd bitten all the fingernails of my left hand. At eleven fifty five, I sat down at Mom's dressing table mirror to talk myself out of hysteria.

"Come on, Brucie. Anyone would think your life was over. Stop this fear-fest NOW!"

I studied my face.

"Look at you. What happened to happy Brucie?"

I sighed. I thought. And then, I discussed these thoughts with my reflection.

"I think your reaction to these problems is growing bigger than the actual problems themselves, isn't it? So, cool it, Brucie. Everything will be good. The Eye Stone is locked away now. Chill. Okay?"

Midnight ticked by with me studying my own face. I calmed, returned to my room and shut the door.

BANG!

The back door slammed.

"Mom! Is that you? Grandpa! Are you there?"

*Oh, Help? What if it's not them? What do I do now?*

I grabbed a heavy paperweight for protection and leapt into my closet. With arm raised, clutching my weapon, I breathed in. And then, Mom's bedroom door banged shut.

Silence.

Braving the hallway, I knocked gently on the outside of her door. No answer.

*Why did she creep in like that?*

"Are you okay in there, Mom?" I asked.

"Fine Brucie. Go away and I'll speak to you in the morning."

"I'm okay, Mom, in case you were worried about me?" I said, sarcastically.

"That's good," she said, and then I heard her snoring.

The hallway stunk of cigarette smoke and I could smell alcohol.

*Is she avoiding me because she's drunk? Maybe I should check Grandpa's room in case he snuck in too. Nope! There's no sign of him.*

I sat on my bed and began to chew the nails on my right hand, when a faint light flickered through the curtain. Whipping back the drapes, I watched the light grow larger, weaving a path down from the hill above. Someone, carrying a flashlight, headed toward the house. At one twenty-three, Grandpa reached for the latch on the gate, stepped through and clicked the bolt behind him. His feet crunched up the driveway gravel to the front door. I waited by the door, agitated.

"Oh-oh, caught!" he said, guiltily.

"Where were you?" I demanded, like a scolding mother.

He laughed. "What are you doing up so late?"

"I could ask you the same. No one was home tonight. I came back to an empty house," I said.

His eyes widened when he saw my tears. "What happened, lassie? Where's your mother?"

"In bed. But, she didn't come in until late. And, she's drunk."

"What? She was here when I left at eight o'clock. Said she was going to have an early night."

I shrugged.

Gramps stared at my neck and the red mark where I'd ripped off my necklace. "Your stone?"

I shrugged again. "Gone. I hate it now. It's caused me nothing but trouble."

Without warning, Gramps cussed like trailer trash born on the wrong side of the blanket.

"Gramps?" I'd not seen him like this before.

"It's okay. Go to bed and sleep," he snipped. "We'll speak about your stone in the morning." Gramps looked away. "Yes," he said. "I should have done this long ago. We need to speak about your stone."

"Speak about my stone? Why? Don't you mean we should talk about Mom being drunk?" I didn't want to talk about my stone. Not even to Gramps. But, suddenly I realized that perhaps Gramps knew more about the power of that stone than I'd thought to ask.

"It's late, lass. Go to bed. We'll talk in the morning. I should never have let your mother stop me, but…yes, we need to speak about your stone." He left me standing in the hallway and closed the door to his room.

He'd never dismissed me like that before.

*What does he mean, 'speak about my stone' and he should never have let my mother stop him?*

I knocked on his door to ask a question. "You mean that you and Mom…?"

"Not now. Tomorrow!" he called, and he left me standing in the hallway with my mouth open.


Despite puzzling about Gramps' strange comments, for the first night in an age, I slept motionless. No dreams. No voices. *YES! I should've ditched that stone sooner.*

Immediately, when I awoke, I remembered that I needed answers from Gramps. Ready for a confrontation, I burst into the kitchen but a note on the table said, "Back soon, Love Grandpa."

I made some tea and waited. Grandpa returned around 9 a.m. with the morning paper tucked under his arm. He fumbled nervously, jingling some change in his pockets. As I scanned slowly over Grandpa's frame, I noted he stooped like a man with worries.

My mood softened. "Let's go for a walk, Grandpa."

He smiled, but not his usual smile. "Yes, that's probably best." He paused. "As I said, there is something I want to say. A wee stravaig up the hill might help."

Nervously, I laced my blue hiking boots and togged up for the wind's bite with a green waterproof jacket over my fleece.

"What hats shall we wear?" I asked Gramps. I wasn't as cool as I pretended to be.

He scratched the top of his head, checking out the choices on the hooks by the door, and picked out the same cap that he wore every day. "I'll have this one for a change."

"If you want to bring about change, Gramps, you should try wearing a different hat," I said.

"In that case, I'll borrow your lime green toorie with the dangly pom poms," he said, donning my hat. He did! Why did I open my mouth? He refused to take it off; so then I had to walk outside with him looking like an idiot. In case he changed his mind, I kept his favorite hat in my pocket. Until then, as a car approached, I steered his elbow, diverting him through the large wooden gate and into the 'bless them' field, out of sight before anyone saw us.

"Let's cut through the field here," I said, trying not to look at his luminous head.

After a few yards, we approached the Clootie Well. Gramps stood still. I waited for him to talk about the stone but he raised his hand, signaling me to stop and listen.

"Water!" he said. "Running water."

"What do you mean?" I asked.

"The old well," he said, picking up a stone. He heaved aside a large bolder, secured over the well head, and dropped the stone down the hole beneath. It plopped at the bottom. "Fancy that! The old well is active again," he said, removing the green hat and scratching his head. Grabbing the opportunity, I nabbed luminous green from his hand and replaced it with safe khaki and fishing flies.

I parked myself down on the grass. It felt cold and a bit damp. The butt of my jeans soaked up the wet, so I changed to a crouch. I felt my back pocket. *Darn. I forgot to bring my iPhone.*

"Gramps, do you ever get lonely?" I asked, filling in time.

He leaned forward and peered down the well. As he answered his voice echoed in the crevice below.

"It's really quite impossible for humans to be lonely, Brucie."

"No it's not. I'm often lonely. In fact I was lonely last night when I came home to an empty house." I didn't understand what he meant.

"Brucie, my pet, we humans are made up of multiple personalities." He kept his head down the hole as he spoke.

"I don't understand," I said, feeling panicky again. *Did someone tell Gramps about Coinneach's voice in my head? Is that what he means by multiple personalities?* I backed off from questioning.

"Well, I am not simply your grandfather. Inside my head I am also a father to your mother, I'm a spiritual person, sometimes I'm a rogue, I'm a true Scot, a friend to my buddies, a pensioner, a fisherman, and, in my memories, I am many other people, too, like a child growing up during the war, the boy who once lived with Travellers, and a husband who lost his dear wife. With all of these people inside of me, each with a slightly different perspective on life, and with all of them queuing to be heard, how can I ever be lonely? Especially, when sometimes all these inner personalities clash together."

I heard him but then my thoughts drifted off on a course of their own. *When is he going to speak about my stone? Hmm. Since I ditched the stone, I haven't heard Coinneach.* I thought for a minute. *I wonder if he's inside the stone, like a genie in a bottle. No. Of course he's not, because I heard him inside my head.* More thoughts came. *Hmmm, I saw him through the binoculars, too, so he must be separate to me. Or, was he following me because I carried the stone? Rhiannon heard him speak, too, though, through my voice....so how does that happen? Whew! He sure smelled; goose fat, Gorgonzola cheese, and cat pee. I'm sure glad to smell the back of Coinneach.*

"So, have I got multiple inner personalities, too?" I asked Gramps.

"You tell me," he said.

"Well, I guess I am a daughter and a granddaughter and a friend and a student and . . . I don't get what you mean, Gramps. Yes, I agree that I am all of these people but I still get lonely and panicky. The more parts of me there are the more difficult life gets, trying to please everyone. How can all these different parts of me keep me from being lonely and from feeling fear?"

He still had his head stuck down the hole so I let the conversation go.

A gathering herd of cows mooed in the adjacent field, some stopping to munch on grass as they plodded forward. The cows seemed to console each other. I felt that they were comforting some sad ones in their midst. *Hmmm, how do I know that?* Rhiannon's dad herded them with a stick and, Corrie, the sheepdog, crouched and then circled behind the beasts, edging them on toward the large byre over at their farm in the distance.

"Why is he leading the cows inside, Gramps? They're not dairy cows, are they?" I asked. My legs grew stiff, so I moved to sit on the bolder.

Gramps pulled his head back out of the hole and looked at me. "Today is Samhainn, Brucie; end of the grazing season. It's time to winter the beasts, but first they'll have to be sorted either for breeding or slaughter. It's the start of the Celtic New Year and new beginnings in the old Celtic calendar; a time to renew earthly prosperity to ensure the success of the community." He returned his head to the hole in the ground where his voice echoed.

I flashed with anger, sickened by the thought of slaughtering poor cows. No wonder I sensed sadness. These animals knew their fate!

"How can murdering these cows ensure the success of Ardcarron?" I stood up and peered over at a big-eyed cow. Images of its destiny unfolded before me: the shot, the knife, the blood, the saw, the guts, the hose, the drain, the hook, and the pinky-red carcasses hanging and then swinging across a rail that suspended from the roof of a very cold building. *Ouch! That vision was way too vivid for having no Eye Stone!* Before Grandpa answered, I vowed to be vegetarian.

"It's the old way, Brucie," he said, now standing, too. "Here, help me roll that boulder back now."

I helped him to cover the wellhead again and we walked, mostly in silence, for a good mile, heading Norwest until we reached the River Dubh.

*When is Gramps going to speak about my stone?*

"Let me tell you about Samhainn and the salmon here," he said.

*Is he consoling me? What's he leading up to?* I sensed his nervousness. He fidgeted, cleaning his nails a lot, drawing breath to speak but then saying nothing.

So, I cut to the core. "What did you want to say about my stone? And why would Mom not want you to talk to me about it?"

"In a minute. The salmon first," he said.

Standing by the riverbank, the deep, blackcurrant-colored water moved quietly, not rushing by like the shallower flow downstream. The air nipped cold but a peaceful quiet blanketed all around.

"Here," he said, pointing. "Salmon have returned to this point in the river. They've swum uphill from downstream. They've come here to die. It's the way, Brucie. First, the skins of the old ones turn splotchy yellow and they begin their homeward journey, swimming upstream in October. Their souls wait until the Feast of Samhainn, before they can cross over into the 'Other World'. I watched the salmon yesterday."

"Then where are they today? I can't see any fish. " I asked, checking around but not seeing anything in the water.

"Gone to another world, Brucie. Last night, the night you call Halloween, is also 'the night outside time'. It's a weird night neither in the old or the new Celtic year. It's a crack between two worlds. Anyway, last night I came here to sit with the fish."

"What do you mean, 'sit with the fish'?"

"Just that. I sat here talking to the fish, to calm them before they departed into the Other World," he said.

"Cross your heart?" I gulped. "Is this where you'd come from when I opened the door for you last night?"

With hands buried deep in his big green coat, he nodded.

"So, what is the significance of the salmon going to another world? Why did you bring me here to tell me this?" I asked.

*Why is Gramps beating about the bush? Get to the point about my Eye Stone, Gramps.*

He paused.

"Brucie, do you ever see things?" Gramps looked me square in the eye.

I stepped back away from him. "See what 'things'?" I asked.

"I think you know what I mean," he said. "Do you have visions from the Other World?"

Caught off guard, I lied. "No, I don't get visions from the Other World and I don't know why you took me all the way up here to the top end of the River Dubh to ask me a stupid thing like that when you could have simply asked me in the house."

*Why am I getting so angry and fidgety?*

"Ca canny, lass," he said. "Don't be so defensive."

"I'm not!"

*Don't lie Brucie,* I told myself. *Defensiveness is growing out of your ears.*

"Brucie, did anything happen when you held your stone? Did you see things?" He continued, regardless of my answer. "Why did you say that you hate the stone now and it had caused you nothing but trouble?"

"I SAID already, I DON'T have any visions."

*Why am I being so defiant?*

He took my arm. "You can tell me, Brucie. You see, I have been watching you, Sweetheart, and I have seen changes in you since you found the stone. There is something I need to tell you about the stone, and about you." He smiled, hopefully.

I didn't want to shout at Gramps but it suddenly rang clear that I wasn't the only person keeping secrets.

"WHAT DO YOU MEAN?"

I started to physically shake now. I filled with suspicion and distrust; two emotions that were new to me in such concentrated forms. ... *jumping on to bales of hay . . . multicolored hot air balloons floating in the Texas sky . . . freshly mown grass . . . bowling a perfect ten strike . . .*

Grandpa spilled the beans. "Brucie, I believe your stone is very special and I need to tell you about it. I think you have 'the giftie'."

I snipped at him. "Oh yeah? And exactly what is 'the giftie' and when did you come to this conclusion?"

"To be honest… the minute the stone fell from the pike's belly, I knew what it was. I just didn't want to frighten you."

He tried to put his arm around me but I pushed his hand away. My voice bit steely cold, "I don't know what you are talking about."

He began, "Long ago, around the middle of the seventeenth century, there lived a man called Coinneach Odhar."

*OMG! Is he talking about Coinneach in my head?*

"Coinneach has since been named The Brahan Seer. The Seer earned fame for making many predictions here in the Highlands of Scotland, many of which have come to pass and some which have yet to be fulfilled."

*. . . jumping in puddles . . . finding a coin on the road . . . pinging elastic bands through the air . . .*

Grandpa reached into his coat pocket and pulled out a small book, *Prophecies of the Brahan Seer.*

I grudgingly took the book out of his hand.

*…knitting pink socks . . . Why can't I look Gramps in the eye when he's trying to help me?. . rolling painted Easter eggs down a hill . . . remember what I said to myself in the mirror last night. . . my reaction to the problem is growing bigger than the actual problem. . .but I'm so full of anger I can't stop myself…*

"Brucie, I'm trying to help," he said, "but I don't want to push you to listen, if you don't want me to speak."

My thermostat neared blowout. "So why are you telling me about this Brahan Seer guy?"

"Take the book home and read about him for yourself, but the reason I am telling you comes at the end of the book. I wondered if you wanted me to save you some time and tell you how this tale ends."

I shrugged.

*What's wrong with me? Why am I being so difficult?*

Gramps cleared his throat, "To cut a story short, the seer worked on a local Estate for a wealthy family called Seaforth." I listened. "Lord Seaforth traveled to France and kept postponing his return. Lady Seaforth called upon the Seer to tell her why her husband delayed. She summonsed the Seer's wisdom concerning this matter."

"The Seer told Lady Seaforth not to concern herself. He tried to persuade her not to ask again, but she insisted on knowing the reason for her husband's absence. Bullied, the Seer divulged that the Lord lay in the arms of another woman. Lady Seaforth steamed. Outraged, she accused him of witchcraft and ordered his hasty death sentence. She ordered him to be burned in a barrel of tar."

"I don't understand the point of this story, Grandpa. Why are you telling me this? Are you suggesting that I will be burned in a barrel of tar because people think that I am a witch?"

*Why is he mentioning witchcraft? I'm not a witch. I'm not.* I started to fume again, kicking my boot at the base of a dead tree by the riverside.

"Dinna be raising a stour. No, I am not saying that you are a witch, pet. Nor will anything bad happen to you."

I muttered under my breath. "How do you know that bad things haven't already happened to me?"

When he asked what I meant, I refused to repeat it.

"Don't be upset, Brucie. All I want to tell you is that the Seer cast his prophesying stone into Loch Ussie and said that one day his successor would find the stone within the belly of a pike. The person who found this stone would inherit his second sight and become the next Highland Seer."

"So, you knew that all along and you only thought to tell me now? ... Seven months later? Thanks a lot Gramps." I kicked the dead tree stump again.

"Brucie, remember the day you sat at the table making posies with your mother? You heard me say the word "Taibhsearach" about you to your mother, remember? It's Gaelic. It means The Giftie: the power of vision. Your mother didn't want me to tell you. She wanted you to have a normal teenage life without my 'meddling old wives tales', as she puts it."

"NORMAL? You think my life has been normal? Ever since I found that darn stone I lost my vertical hold!"

I squeezed the book in my hand, considering how hard to throw it at Grandpa. Instead, I bolted and ran away. I called back, "I'm in one sod-pawing mood now! There's liars, damn liars and then there's you and Mom, Grandpa!" I added, "I'm gone! Out of here! I'm going to Rhiannon's house. She totes level! You can hang your hat on my girlfriend. She don't squat 'n watch me diggin' dirt. If she saw my horse kept headin' home with an empty saddle and she knew why, she'd spit it out right away, not leave me stewin' for over six months. She don't lie. Not like you! I wish my butt never came to this place. And if that ain't a fact then I'm a possum. I'm not a Seer. I'm NOT! I hate you. Liar!"

"Come back, Brucie," he called, but I didn't.

I cut through the woods and ran until I tripped on the jutting root of a gnarled old tree, landing face down with a sore shoulder and a scraped, bruised chin. Sprawled out in a damp, brown, leafy bed of broken branches, rocks and rotting fungus, I cried. I cried for my Dad. I cried for my Mom. I cried for Grandpa. I cried for me, and I cried for all the multiple people I'd become. Most of all I cried for me because I felt so very sorry for the childhood that had left me. I felt alone in a strange land and strange things had been happening to me, so I reckoned I deserved to cry.

When I stopped crying I looked up and ... right in front of me ... Dog bite my buttons, I saw Coinneach's house, The Barracks. Tucked inside a tree, guarded outside by crows... *I FOUND IT! Holy Macaroni! It's just like he said, complete with bones, shoes, frogs, bits of tin, a musket and an old hat. Dang! Look, it's his wide-awake hat!*

At first I rummaged through his possessions and laughed in disbelief, but then I grew angry and bored. Minutes, then hours, shuddered past in jerky flashes of frigid thoughts, as I shivered and squatted, shifted and squirmed inside the Barracks. Gingerly shuffling my back up against the termites inside of the large, old tree trunk, I hid out, suspicious and daring each and every notion in my head to impart the truth. My hands both stung and ached, before they turned blue. The wind wound up from intermittent bursts and blurts to a whistling strident whine outside. I yelled out into the din. "Why didn't you tell me the truth sooner, Grandpa? Why give it to me now. Why didn't you tell me the truth ages ago? Why didn't anyone help me?"

Of course, I knew Gramps wasn't there and he wouldn't be able to hear me.

Flopping forward, exhausted, I placed the book at my side. Red-brown leaves from the forest floor suddenly spirited upright. Leaves swirled and gusted, driven by the force of the November northeasterly.

My eyelids felt heavy. They drooped. Through the half-light of spidery lashes, I looked out into the distance. The wind stalled to a swift hush. Leaves hung in the air, settling, floating gently one upon another, weaving, weaving, weaving, until... the form of a tall man in a floor-length trench coat stood in the middle of the leaves, with his left hand leaning on a cane.

The leafy man stood statuesque amidst a stagnant backdrop of oak, pine and sycamore. In the unexpected hush, black crows suspended in the air with outstretched wings, beaks open mid-caw. The muted tranquility lingered, except for a whispering rustle resonating from the leaf man. His leafy coat drew open, like a set of stage curtains, and Coinneach stepped out. He dusted himself down and sneezed.

*Achoo!* he said. *Leaf mold gets to me every time. Achoo! Ah! I see you've found the Barracks. Achoo! I hope you haven't moved anything about in there. I'd know if you've moved anything.*

I spoke aloud. "What are you doing here? I thought I got rid of you when I ditched my stone. And, why didn't you tell me that you were a Seer?"

*No, you don't get rid of me that easily,* he said. *And, I'm not a Seer. That's my father you are talking about.*

I glowered upward as Coinneach stared down at the book Grandpa had given me.

*The Brahan Seer? So that's what they call the old man now. Fancy that!*

I rose to challenge Coinneach but I hit my head off the inside of the tree. The pain made me even more furious.

*I didn't know him personally. But, my mother knew him well enough. Blind in one eye, she said of him, and, temperamental. They didn't marry.*

"You mean temperamental, like you?" I snipped, rubbing the same spot on my head for a second consecutive day. "So why didn't you tell me this sooner, about your father being a Seer? You're just as mean as my Gramps."

*And risk being burned in tar, too? I only ever disclosed the connection when asked by people I trust. I invited you to ask but you refused.*

"You smell like a barrel of smoky tar," I said.

He ignored my insult, so I threw more at him.

"You and my Grandpa are sharper than a pocket full of toothpicks. Oh how funny. Ha Ha. I'm happy as a hog in mud to know that you've both been keeping secrets from me. You knew my stone belonged to this Seer, so I bet you said to yourselves, 'bless her little cotton socks, let's all keep this information about the Seer and the stone from Brucie and wait until she gets herself overdrawn at the memory bank, and see how many times people call her a witch before we'll eventually tell her there is an explanation for it.' Is that it? Is that your idea of a joke?"

Under attack now, he stepped back inside the leaf man's coat. He quickly buttoned it shut. From inside, I heard a muffled sneeze.

"Oh no, you don't! You're not escaping that easily. You can stay right here and explain yourself, Coinneach or Odhar, or whoever you are!" I shouted. "And why are you still here when I haven't got the stone with me?"

He didn't reply.

"You come right back here, mate, coz we've got a whole barrel of possums to pluck."

I ducked, taking care not to bump my head again, and dove out of the tree. My fingernails spread for attack and I spat like a wildcat. But, as soon as my brow cleared the opening of in trunk, the northeasterly roused again and blasted me from the side. It knocked me to the ground. A flying twig scratched my face. With one huge gust, the leaf man blew away. He scattered into a scramble of random leaves, all fleeing into the distance. In the moment that Coinneach vanished, a torrent of rain poured from the sky.

Holding my hood with both hands, I turned my back on the woods and leaned into the wind, pushing on a course downhill. I followed the sheep path on an old drove road that I hoped would lead me to Rhiannon's house. The gale's ghastly gusts ripped tears from my eyes. Tears then mixed with rain, lashing on my cheeks. I needed shelter from the storm, so I edged onward, fighting a nor'easter that fought me back each step of the way.

*Am I going the right way to the farmhouse? Will Rhiannon let me in after last night?*

## Bethany and the Badgers

The torrential downpour ceased.

Outside the MacKinnon's caravan, Bethany sat cross-legged on top of a hessian sack, adding driftwood to a campfire. The ground was damp and, despite the heat from the fire, she shivered and wrapped her arms around herself. She stared into the flames.

Midnight passed and still she sat alone, in the dark.

Jake must've taken his tobacco tin with him and she needed a joint to calm her anxiety. She bit on her nails, wondered about her uncle Jake, why he hadn't come home again.

A curious young badger entered the field, immediately followed by its mother; the eyes of the two black and white figures illuminated by her campfire.

Bethany picked up a crossbow that sat by her feet. She'd intended hunting rats to pass the time, but quickly loaded an arrow and aimed at the baby badger. They locked eyes. Bethany swiveled left and pulled the trigger, killing the mother badger instead.

"Take that, bitch!"

The baby sniffed at its mother, lying dead on the ground. It looked back toward Bethany, uncertain what to do.

"Don't look at me," she said. "I'm no role model."

# Chapter 10

## *A Dawn Raider*

I battered on Rhiannon's door.

"Can someone let me in, please, before I catch my death out here?"

The door gust open and Rhiannon stood with a glower as fierce as the storm.

I dared to ask. "Please can I come in?" My cold hands thrust deep into my pockets and I looked down at the puddles on the ground. "Please?"

Grabbing my arm, she pulled me into her house and bolted the door.

"Brucie, you make me SO mad," she shouted.

"I know," I said. "But, I need a friend right now."

"You talk crazy, though, and I don't know if I want to be your friend." She paused. I allowed the silence to hover, waiting.

"These voices and paranormal things that you see…it gets so hard to defend you. At school, people are mean to me, Brucie, because I hang out with you. I constantly have to choose sides."

"I'm sorry, Rhiannon. I am, truly sorry," I said.

My hair plastered wet to my face and I knew I looked miserable. I certainly felt it.

*She hates me. This is pointless.*

I reached for the door handle, ready to brave the weather once more, but she caught my arm.

"Brucie," she said, and hugged my sodden neck. "Sometimes you are the most infuriating besom I've ever met. Let me get you some dry clothes."

*YES!* "Oh, Rhiannon, I thought you hated me. Thank you. Dry clothes would be great."

"What happened to your face?" she asked. "It's cut."

"Oh, that happened in the Barracks… I mean, nothing. Never mind. It's okay."

"Here, take off that soaking coat. I'll get you a towel first," she said.

My mood flipped a full 180 degrees, once inside the cozy farmhouse with the smell of hot soup and baking bread.

"Hi, Mrs. Sutherland," I called to Rhiannon's mother. Hands dusted with flour, she rolled out pastry on a white Formica table by the window. She smiled, but she didn't answer. As I unzipped my coat, I saw her from the corner of my eye shaking her head.

I hung my sopping coat over the back of a kitchen chair by the big wood-burning range, near Mrs. Sutherland. It dripped onto her floor and I started to ask for a mop, but the phone rang out.

"Oh, no! For goodness sake! Fancy that. How awful," I heard her saying to someone called Maggie. Silence cut the air, and a gasp, then, "Alec's tractor overturned! He's broken BOTH legs and he's crushed his pelvis, TOO? Och, he must be in a bad way, then. Poor soul."

The smell of dung-ridden boots filled my head, "The man in the shop... Oh shit!"

Mrs. Sutherland cupped her hand over the mouthpiece, and stared at me, "Brucie! We don't use that sort of language in this house, thank you."

"Sorry, Mrs. Sutherland," I said, and slipped away to find Rhiannon.

I sat at the dressing table in Rhiannon's room, fingering my tousled ringlets of wet curls when she threw a fluffy towel in the door. "I'll make us hot chocolate, if you want to dry off. You can take my black jeans and a t-shirt but you're not getting any of my underwear. That's too gross to share."

"I wouldn't wear your stinky underwear, anyway." I laughed. "But, I'll turn up the heater, if that's okay. We'll never sleep in here, it's so cold?"

Rhiannon crooked her head back in the door. "Did you say 'WE'll never sleep in here'?"

"Uh yep, sorry, I didn't have time to tell you yet... I had a fight with Gramps and I ran away and my Mom is losing it because she snuck home drunk last night and I don't know where she got to and I had a horrid time last night with all these colors following me and I'm all confused, but I've turned over a new leaf... and since you are my best friend... and I'm sorry for frightening you, and I need to stay here, Rhiannon. Please, can I?"

"Okay. Okay. Slow down!" she said. "Gees, Brucie!"

"Sorry," I said, "again."

"You really do need to get a grip, Brucie. And, I tell you that because people care about you. I care."

"I'm trying, Rhiannon. I took off the stone. Dumped it. No more. Look," I said showing her my bare neck.

"What has the stone got to do with anything?" she asked. Her expression looked puzzled.

So, I told Rhiannon all about catching the pike, how I found the stone in its belly, and then I shared what Grandpa had told me earlier that morning about the Brahan Seer. "He tossed the stone into the waters of Loch Ussie and said whoever caught the pike with the stone in its belly would become the next Highland seer. Grandpa said I could read all about it in the book ..." I paused to think. "Ah, the book. I must've left it in Coinneach's Barracks."

"Brucie! Coinneach's Barracks?" She grew angry again.

"Yes, I know. I'll try to stop talking about freaky stuff and I'll be normal," I promised her. "But, the Barracks do exist! I'll show you."

She glared a 'No Way Jose' warning at me.

"Okay then, what about this ... I KNEW that Alec's tractor would overturn!"

"Brucie, sometimes your mouth needs a filter. Please just quit before we fall out again." She shot me another stark glower. "Does your Grandpa know you are here, Brucie?"

I shook my head, "But he'll have a good idea by now."

"Why don't you call him on your mobile?" she asked.

"I forgot to bring it. Well, actually, when you and I had our argument I ditched it to my desk drawer, as you are the only person who calls me ... except for the person who texts 'WITCH' all the time."

"Who's that?" she asked.

I didn't answer, so she shook her head and said, "I'll get my mum to call your Gramps. He's probably worried, what with this storm ..."

I sighed but she insisted, "I don't want the blame for hiding you out up here, especially if no one knows where you are."

She left to get our hot chocolate, and I overheard heard her talking to Mrs. Sutherland.

"I've already spoken to Ali," said her mother. "It's as well that lassie is in a wee place like Ardcarron now, because I'm sure if she went running off in Texas, then ..." Her sentence trailed off.

*If I ran away like this in Texas... who knows where I'd end up?* My imagination ran rampant. I envisioned nightmare scenarios; wandering lost at night down city streets, traffic horns and sirens blaring, panhandlers begging for cash. *Eek! What if some creepo abducted me . . . stuffed me in a dumpster. . . dead?* Rhiannon spoke sense; people cared about me here.

I remained deep in thought when Rhiannon brought in the steaming mugs of hot chocolate.

Rhiannon's jeans felt a little slack on me. She confirmed my thoughts. "Brucie, you've lost weight. When's the last time you ate?"

"Um, yesterday lunch time."

She fetched us a plate of fresh, hot sausage rolls, which we ate as we listened to CDs and read magazines.

"I would have brought cake, too," she said, "but Mum is making us lasagna for dinner and she's a great cook."

She sure was! Half way through my second helping of beef lasagna, though, I remembered the sad cows and I left the last few forkfuls.

After dinner, Rhiannon and I rolled on her bedroom floor holding our stomachs like two fat cats. We giggled.

"Cut the noise in there!" shouted Mr. Sutherland.

"Sorry, Dad, I forgot you were in bed." Rhiannon called back. "He'll be off early to the cattle auction tomorrow. I hope prices are fair or he'll be in a bad mood all winter," she told me.

I remembered the sad cow faces again. *I hope he sleeps in late and misses the sale.*

We played 'Consequences' on sheets of paper, where we each wrote down a girl's name on the top of the paper. We folded over the paper to hide the name and then swapped sheets to write a boy's name. We folded it over again and swapped and then wrote where they met, then what he said, and then wrote what she said. Before the final fold we wrote down the consequence of the meeting. I unrolled Rhiannon's paper and read the contents out loud.

Rhiannon (met)

Mr. A B Campbell

In the cow byre

She said, "I think I have chicken pox."

He said, "Your eyes are as pink as flamingoes."

They robbed a bank and stowed away on an ocean liner to the Caribbean.

She unrolled hers.

Brucie (met)
Donald
By the River Dubh
She said, "Why do you have a cactus on a leash?"
He said, "Your shoes are on backward."
The sky rained orange juice, so they kissed beneath an umbrella.

I guess my blush gave my thoughts away.
"Brucie Bice, I do believe that you're in love with Donald MacLeod!" she squealed.
"Keep the noise down in there," called Mr. Sutherland again.
*That's it. Don't sleep. Maybe the cows will be safe.*

Rhiannon made up the sofa bed for me in the corner of her room, but then we lifted it quiet as we could over next to her bed. It weighed a ton but we wanted to talk.
"Has Donald ever had a girlfriend?" I asked, gingerly.
"I doubt he'd know what to do with a girlfriend." She laughed. "… Unless, of course, she gave him some mathematical equations to solve."
"That's not fair. He can be really cute," I said.
"Woo hoo, Brucie, what have you and Donald been up to?"
"Nothing," I said, honestly. *Why did I have to go and blush?* "Is your dad really going to take all those pretty cows to auction tomorrow?"
"Stop trying to change the subject, Brucie." Rhiannon teased.
"I saw their faces today, Rhi."
"Whose faces?" she asked. "Duncan and Donald's?"
"No the cow's faces. I'm vegetarian now. I respect animals too much." I said.
"But you just ate beef lasagna and loved it." She laughed.
"I know but starting tomorrow, I'm vegetarian."
"Have you kissed yet?" she asked.
"Kissed who? The cows?" I laughed.
"No, Donald!" she said.
"Goodnight, Rhiannon!" I shut my eyes and pretended to sleep.
Silence.
"Are you going home tomorrow, Brucie?" she asked.

I gave half an answer; "It depends."

I wished she'd fall asleep and not ask me any more questions. My wish came true but then I couldn't sleep, tossing from one side to the other.

"Rhiannon? I'll talk to you now if you want me to."

Her slow and heavy breathing told me to forget it.

*Brr!* The room grew suddenly chilly. I clutched the covers up to my nose and peaked out around the room. The curtains were thin and the moonlight strong, a calm night after the storm. Shadows played off the walls, changing as I blinked. Amazingly, the night glowed bright enough to distinguish colors still, though barely. I could tell the walls were pale green, or were they pale blue? I saw the black outline of Rhiannon's fiddle case. Dolls? Rhiannon had such a fabulous collection of dolls. I studied them.

*Hey! ... That Dutch doll moved! The one wearing the clogs and the funny hat, it moved! She lifted her little doll hand and scratched her little doll nose. And, I didn't imagine it. In the name of... she's waving!*

I waved back at her.

*Sliding on polished floors in your socks ... diving into a swimming pool on a hot day... eating toffee popcorn... Again! Her hand moved again.*

Dutch doll twirled around, and then pointed to get my attention.

"Who, me?" I whispered.

Her nod freaked me out. She pointed to the Peruvian doll who sneaked a sly kick at the little Mexican in the wide sombrero.

"What on earth...?" I said, and then hushed when I saw the movement of a Spanish matador ducking down behind the flamenco dancer. She lifted her right arm and clicked her tiny castanets at him, which appeared to summons the Russian Cossack dancer. He folded his arms and kicked out alternating legs clad in long black boots.

"I don't believe this!"

The old doll lady, making Belgium lace, twisted her yarn around the tail of the Canadian Mounties' horse, and giggled. The doll horse whinnied and bolted across the shelf, knocking into the Venetian gondola and tipping out its oarsman. He cursed in Italian, probably vowing vengeance, when an Asian doll in a turban came to his aid. Excited by the commotion, a smiling figure clad in lederhosen began slapping his thighs and skipping till the Morris dancer joined in, with bells a-jingling at his ankles.

"Rhiannon! Wake up, Rhiannon," I whispered. "Look at the dolls!"

Rhiannon snored on.

Suddenly, a tiny arrow like a sharp pin shot from a taught bow and hit me in the forehead, followed by a small Viking axe that sliced my hand like a paper cut.

"Hey!" I called out, but too late . . . a world war ensued as dolls from one country attacked dolls from another country. Limbs severed, heads rolled. . .

"Stop it! Stop it!" I cried.

"Huh? Whassup? What's wrong?" Rhiannon bolted upright in bed. With clumsy fingers, she rubbed her eyes and squinted. She fumbled for the bedside lamp. "Is something wrong Brucie?" she asked, yawning, "What's happening?"

"Ah! Well ..." When I looked at the dolls on the shelf they were all composed again, back in orderly rows, motionless and unblemished.

"Brucie?" Rhiannon asked, "Why were you shouting? It's the middle of the night."

"Sorry. I had a nightmare." I lied. *What a wimp! I wish I could tell her what I saw.*

"Oh! Then try to get back to sleep, Brucie," she said. Rhiannon lay down and began to snore again.

I thought about Grandpa. Why had I shouted at him so? Poor Grandpa! And, the book he gave me, *Prophecies of the Brahan Seer*, I left it in the Barracks. Afraid that the rain might have ruined the book, I decided to rise as soon as it was light and retrieve it.

*Maybe I should read the book. How else can I find out about my Eye Stone? It's not like the stone came with a manual. What I REALLY need is an A-Z on how to become a Highland Seer without losing my mind. I'll check Amazon.co.uk in the morning.*

I wrestled with the remainder of the night, waiting for the chorus of bird's song to begin. Tiptoeing to the window, I pulled back the curtain searching for the first hints of dawn. Wow, it felt so cold. Even the inside of the windowpane sparkled with frost, so I rubbed it. Pale winter light struggled to climb over the dark foreboding hills. A lone seagull flapped across the sky, calling out. Silent crows fleeted past, followed by three white geese. No sound. A flurry of starlings darted from the telephone wire, landing on the byre roof about 100 yards away. More seagulls appeared, calling out in the direction of the sea. Beyond the byre, daylight grew a bit stronger. I saw the clachan of Ardcarron, nesting at the foot of the hill below, and Cambuscurrie

Bay beyond that. The orange glow of Ardcarron street lights switched off, so I presumed it must be around six o'clock. Still, the sun had not risen.

Silence surrounded me, except for the ringing in my own ears and the ticking of the clock beside Rhiannon as she slept.

I closed the curtains again, dressed quietly, and picked up a marker pen and a sheet of paper. Writing in the dark proved tricky.

"Rhi, Gone to get clean clothes. Will speak to Gramps too. Text you later or meet you in café around noon. Love B x"

Snug in my coat, warm and dry from being next to the range, I snuck out. Not even the hens were out pecking. No goats, rabbits, or dogs in sight. All remaining cattle slumbered in the byre; bless them. *I wish Mr. Sutherland didn't have to sell their buddies,* I thought.

I hauled opened the large gate, secured it again behind me, and followed the old drove road back up toward the Barracks. Every tree seemed familiar and I could have sworn I stood in the exact location of the Barracks. But, it wasn't there. Combing the edge of the wood over and over, eventually I gave up.

*It's not here. I've searched everywhere.*

Fatigued, with a rumbling stomach, I headed downhill again, toward Ardcarron. Veering off the old path, I decided to cross the pastures heading toward the 'bless them' field, a quicker route. With no cows in the fields, I could cross without the fear of being nudged by giant, wet noses. The grass, both green yet crispy white with frost, soaked inside my shoes and up the leg of Rhiannon's jeans, as they trailed off the ground. Wet denim flapped the chill of the morning against my ankles. I doubted the sky would turn very blue today, as dank clusters of dewy clouds hung over the hilltops. Visibility appeared reasonable though, so it would stay dry for a while.

I could see our house, down beyond the Clootie Well. Every time I looked at the Clootie Tree, with its white rags draped from all branches, I saw something new. Today the tree looked like a group of contemporary dancers who waved their arms in the air... pretending to be a tree. Weird!

But, something else caught my eye. *What is that person doing at the window of my house?* I stopped walking to focus. My bedroom window gaped wide open, much like my mouth now, and I watched in disbelief as a dark-clothed figure clambered out of my window.

"HEY! YOU," I yelled. "WHAT ARE YOU DOING?"

I ran as fast as I could toward my house.

The figure turned around, hesitated momentarily, and then bolted away down Ardcarron Brae. I knew pursuit would prove hopeless. The gap between us widened as I tripped over the wet bottoms of the long jeans.

"Come back! What do you think you're doing in my room?"

I called over and over, but the person slipped out of sight.

*Who was that? Male? Female?* I only saw bulky, dark clothing with a dark beanie hat pulled down, which made it impossible to tell facial features.

Chase over, I burst into the house via the back door. Mom sat in the kitchen, hugging a steaming cup. "Someone's broken in to my room!" I panted to Mom, "I think we've been robbed!"

She calmly reached out for a cigarette. "Well, it certainly wasn't you in your room last night," she said, in a very sarcastic tone. She sipped from a mug and didn't even look up at me.

"Mom! I am serious. I just saw someone climb out of my bedroom window."

Now, I had her attention.

We opened my bedroom door together. Sure enough, my curtains flapped outside the open window. Muddy footprints crossed the entire length of the beige carpet from the window to the closet. Rifled drawers lay askew with contents strewn on the bed.

"We've been burgled!" my mother exclaimed, indignantly. "And, I didn't hear a thing."

We checked every room but only my bedroom had been touched.

"Brucie, check what's missing. I'll find your Grandpa. He went out to get lentils and melon for a new soup recipe," she said.

"You're not going to leave me here alone now, are you?" I said.

"Don't be silly, Brucie," said Mom. "This is Ardcarron, not Spooksville in a horror movie." She handed me one of Grandpa's walking canes. "Here, if anyone jumps out at you, whack them hard with this."

"Mom?" *What's gotten into her lately?*

"If you are tough enough to stay out all night and not come home, then surely you can stay here by yourself for five minutes until I get your Grandpa." She stormed out of the house.

*Point taken.*

I held firmly onto the cane as I checked through my possessions.

Nothing seemed amiss.

*Why would anyone want to break into my room anyway? I have nothing of interest to anyone. It's not as if I have any valuable jewels, or ...*

*My jewelry box! They took it. Why would anyone want to steal a box of cheap glitzy bangles and earrings? Or, steal my Eye Stone...? Oh No! My Eye Stone, it's gone, too...*

The gravel outside of the window crunched.

"Who is it?" I called out. "Who's there?"


## Bethany's Sacrificial Altar

Bethany avoided her granny, Fisher Skeelie, for days. For every time she saw the old crone, Skeelie would ask her, "Have ya paid the darkness for that curse yet?"

Finally, though, Beth could put an end to that question.

"Come outside Granny. I have something to show you."

Skeelie laughed when she saw the home-made sacrificial altar that Beth had built in her back garden -- two concrete blocks with a hessian sack laid over the top. Lying on top of the sack... a dead badger, positioned as if it were sitting up.

"Har Har Har," Skeelie laughed. "Is that yer offering to the moon tonight?"

"Yes, Gran, but look closer at the badger. Look what it's got in its paws."

"Oh my!" exclaimed Skeelie. Her eyes lit up. "It's like a prize. Me likes prizes!"

## *Chapter 11*

## *Backfire*

Grandpa poked his head in through the open window to my bedroom. I startled.

"It's only me, Pet. I'm so glad you're back home," he said.

Spying the mess, he continued, "What a burach! Having a clean out, are you?"

"No! I've been burgled!" I told him. "Mom has gone to look for you."

"Burgled?" He ran his fingers over the window frame. "Ach! Look at that," he said, checking the damage. "The window's been forced open." He polished a mark on the glass with his sleeve.

"Shouldn't you leave the window alone, so the police can dust it for prints?" I asked. Mom pulled up in her car but sat talking to someone on her phone. She played with her hair in the rear view mirror and pouted in between comments.

*Eh, Mother!* I thought. *In case you've forgotten, I've been burgled here.*

"Finger prints?" said Gramps. "Oh, I don't know if the local bobby would know how to work a finger print kit. We don't experience many break-ins in Ardcarron." He stroked at the stubble on his chin. "Anything taken?"

"Yes," I said. "My Eye Stone is gone!"

"Hmm." Gramps mused a bit. "Well…" He studied my expression. "I wonder if that might be for the best, considering yesterday's conversation." He smirked. "I suppose there won't be any predictions on whether we'll catch the burglar now, then?"

"Gramps! That wasn't funny!" I said. Then, I added, "Sorry about yesterday."

"Apology accepted." Gramps scuttled away, and then turned. He popped his head back in the window. "I'm sorry, too." He winked and made a funny face.

Laughter felt good, much like offloading a sack full of rocks from my back.

*Ah, who cares about my stone? I hope it brings the thief as much trouble as it has brought me. Yes, they've done me a favor. Maybe Coinneach will stay in the woods. I can be normal again.* But, I remembered the dolls fighting in Rhiannon's bedroom. *I wish I hadn't lost the book. I'm still seeing stuff, even without the stone.*

As Gramps expected, the policeman didn't dust the window for prints. PC Anderson, or 'Frank' as Grandpa called him, sat at the kitchen table. His black, police notepad lay untouched and he drank at least two cups of tea. Actually, due to a large bottom lip, he slurped the hot tea with a mouth like a bucket. When I sniggered, Mom kicked me under the table.

During Frank's entire visit, my mother dominated the conversation. She discussed *'their'* teenage years from back in the 1980s. *Did my Mom date this man?* Frank fidgeted, crossed his right leg up onto to his opposite knee, and then picked at his teeth. I noted his mismatched socks, one blue, and one black. When he saw me stare at his socks, Frank twitched and dropped both feet to the floor. In a bid to hide the offending blue sock, he used his left foot to cover his right ankle.

Mom, unusually bubbly, invited Frank to stay for Sunday lunch, and without waiting for his reply she said to Grandpa, "Do you remember the rollicking you gave Frank, Dad, when he brought me home late from the school dance?"

*Wow, Mom's a bit flirtatious here.*

Frank blushed and, finally, after three failed attempts to interrupt, he said, "Och, Fiona, don't be bringing that up. I'm a happy hen-pecked husband now… and the wife will have a meal waiting for me."

*Ah!* I thought. *Hen-pecked…that explains the swollen lip, then.*

The sparkle cleared from Mom's eyes. She whisked his cup from the table, and rinsed it under the tap, tossing Frank's tealeaves to the fate of the drain.

Sensing Mom's annoyance, Frank announced, "Okay, I'll get back to the station." He paused and pulled on the protruding lip. "Before I go …" He scratched his head. "You said the burglar stole your daughter's stone? Was this a gemstone? Was it valuable?"

Grandpa looked at me and then answered for Mom.

"It's a semi-precious gemstone and quite rare. It's called an Eye Stone."

Frank's mouth hung open, unsure of what to say. His tongue rested on the lip, as if waiting for the sun to shine, or a passing fly to land. "What's it worth, this stone? A hundred, two hundred pounds?"

Gramps replied, "No. It doesn't have a monetary value, Frank."

Frank nodded his head, "Right then," and buttoned the blank notebook into his breast pocket again. "I'll speak with your neighbors down the road. Maybe they saw something."

Before he left the house, Frank said to Gramps, "I'd get that window latch fixed if I were you, Ali." He donned his black and white police hat and ducked out of the door without looking at Mom.

"What a dork!" I said. "It's a blessing that Ardcarron has low crime if that's the intelligence of the police here."

My mother scowled at me.

While Mom and Gramps chatted in the kitchen, I escaped to tidy my room, but shortly before noon, I sent a text to Rhiannon and tiptoed out of the house.

At 12:05 pm, Rhiannon and I chose a window seat at the Gowan Café and ordered two coffees. Rhiannon immediately asked, "What did your mother and Gramps say about you staying over at my house?"

When I shrugged, and said, "Nothing," she gasped in disbelief.

"They never said *anything* to you?"

In my defense, I said, "Well, I caught a thief robbing my bedroom today, so the burglary distracted us all."

"Hell's bells, Brucie! A Burglar? Whatever next?" Rhiannon lowered her voice and moved in close to my face. She whispered. "Who was the burglar? What did they steal?"

I pulled back a bit. "I didn't recognize the burglar. They took my jewelry box. My Eye Stone was inside it."

Wide-eyed, she drew in a sharp breath and covered her mouth with her hand. "You mean there's a stranger in the village, stealing things? No way!"

I told her the story, working my way back from Frank's visit to when I saw the crook climb out of my window.

"Wow!" she exclaimed. "Brucie, your life is such a whirlwind of drama."

"I know," I said. My fingers picked nervously at the brown tablecloth. Instinctively, I reached for the Eye Stone. The empty space felt weird.

To cheer me up, Rhiannon joked about Frank's odd socks.

I laughed. "How could my mother ever have dated such a dork?"

She chuckled.

"Rhiannon, why would someone steal my jewelry box?" I asked. "Apart from the stone, it only contained a few earrings and some cheap necklaces. Oh, and my watch."

"You must be upset, Brucie," she said.

"Actually, I don't think I care any more." I looked away, hiding any disappointment. "Anyway, we agreed, no more weird stuff, didn't we? So, just as well the stone has gone."

Rhiannon agreed. "Hmm. That would be nice, but…"

I didn't hear the rest of her sentence because I spotted the woman with the cane basket, outside of the window, leaning against the café wall.

*I wonder what she's doing?*

I moved closer to the window but the old woman disappeared. She vanished.

*Strange! Where did she go?*

Rhiannon said, "Maybe we should forget about burglars and talk about something more normal."

"Yeah, like when I can ride your horse? You always make excuses whenever I ask," I said.

But, before she could answer my mobile rang.

"Brucie? Where are you? Grandpa called you for lunch and you were gone." Mom's voice echoed in my ear.

"Sorry Mom. I'm coming home now."

"And, I wanted to tell you about a surprise," she said, "But, it seems you're not interested in surprises when you keep running off." Silence. She hung up.

"Sounds like you are in trouble again, Brucie," laughed Rhiannon.

I nodded and downed the last dregs of my coffee. "Sorry, Rhiannon, time to split."

"Will I come with you?" she asked.

"Good idea," I said. "Mom won't yell at me in front of you."

I pushed Rhiannon in the door first, as a shield.

"Okay, what's the surprise?" I asked Mom.

She played a defensive role now. "You'll see tomorrow."

"Aw Mom! I thought you said today? Can I have a clue? I mean, is it a good surprise, or is it bad?"

"Tomorrow!" She snapped.

"But, I'll be in school tomorrow!" I protested. "Can't you give me a clue?"

"It's a late birthday present from your dad," she said.

"But, he already . . ."

She interrupted, "I know, but we both know who chose that awful t-shirt for you. This is something special from your dad."

"Then, why can't I have it today?" I asked.

"Wait until tomorrow!"

Somewhere between the mention of today and tomorrow, Rhiannon waved and tiptoed out of the back door.

I heated up a small plate of left over roast beef dinner in the microwave. Half way down the hall toward my bedroom, I remembered my vegetarianism and realized I'd have to make do with soggy potatoes and limp broccoli. I returned to the kitchen.

"Why are you scraping good food into the trash?" Mom yelled at me.

"Later, Mom. Please? Let's have this argument later," I said, standing in the doorway, holding the plate of vegetables. Mom backed down so I headed to my room.

*Am I really the next Highland Seer? It seems ridiculous,* I thought. *The last few months have been crazy. But, what happens now that my stone has vanished? Maybe I shouldn't have been so frightened of things that happened.*

Something Rhiannon said came back to me. I asked her how she could eat meat and live on a farm with all those pretty cows. She said, "Sometimes you have to ignore the distress and concentrate on what is good for you." She said she taught herself not to see sad cow faces when she ate lasagna.

*Maybe I should've learned to ignore my distress with the stone and tried to find out what good it could bring me.* I sighed. *Easy to say that now it's gone!*

When I took my dirty plate back to the kitchen, Mom smelled of Blue perfume. I asked if she wanted to talk to me about my stay at Rhiannon's and about me running away.

"No, just don't run off like that again," she said, gazing into the depths of her compact mirror. Out came the Rebel Rouge, black mascara and green eye shadow.

"Going out again?" I asked.

"For a while," she said, but refused to elaborate.

*Maybe it has something to do with my surprise gift. Is she going out to get it? Or, is she meeting Frank?*

It felt such a relief to have my own thoughts in my head instead of Coinneach twittering away.

*If Coinneach's father was the Seer then why is it Coinneach who bugs me? Why not the Seer himself? Hmmm. Coinneach wanted me to ask him why he followed me around, but I never did. I was too scared. Too late now! He's gone to live in the Barracks ... the elusive Barracks. Maybe I'll never find him again.*

I felt a heavy sigh well up in my chest, like ... I'd changed my mind and I actually missed Coinneach. *How weird is that?*

Grandpa broke into my trail of thought. "I think I'm coming down with a cold, so I am going to bed," he said. "A hot toddy drink and a good book is what I need."

"Okay, Goodnight." I worried about Gramps. What would I do without him? He's my soul buddy. "Gramps?" I called after him. "Do you think someone stole my jewelry box deliberately? I mean do you think they knew my stone was inside?"

"No idea. But if it is meant for you, Brucie, you'll find it again." He walked away from the door but returned to add, "Oh, and your mother is out again, in case you are wondering."

"Okay, Gramps," I answered.

Through the wall, murmurs from his radio preceded loud nasal snores. Mom's bedroom door sat ajar. I snooped around in her wardrobe for a while. No hidden surprise from Dad, so I ran back to bed. Brr, the nights are cold, much colder than Texas.

*Texas ... I could google a few pictures of Texas on the Internet! That would warm me up.*

As I moved toward the computer, the book caught my eye. It sat on the chair by my desk, *Prophesies of the Brahan Seer*, the book I left inside the Barracks.

*But I couldn't find the Barracks. The Barracks vanished. So how did the book arrive here in my bedroom? Did Gramps bring it back? I guess he did.*

I leafed through the pages.

*Wow! This is cool. It's about the stone. I need to memorize this story to tell Rhiannon.*

I closed the book and tried to recall a short piece that I'd read.

*Okay, in the first half of the seventeenth century, the Brahan Seer's mother tended cattle near a burial ground. At midnight she witness ghosts leaving their graves. An hour later, all the spirits returned, but one tomb remained empty. She placed something across the grave and waited for the last ghost to return. On arrival, the ghost spoke to her, "Please uncover my grave so that I can enter." Then . . .*

"But wait!" I spoke aloud. "How can I tell this story to Rhiannon? We made a pact not to talk about any more spooky stuff." I memorized the rest of the story, regardless.

*Then, the Seer's mother asked the ghost, "Why are you later to return to your grave than the other ghosts?" She answered, 'I'm the daughter of the King of Norway. I drowned at sea. My journey is, therefore, longer than that of other ghosts because I have to go all the way to Norway. If you let me return to my grave, for your courage, I will tell you where to find a stone. When you find this stone, give it to your son. It's a magic stone.'*

I lay in bed, engrossed in the story about my stone, when . . .

BANG!

*Gun fire? OH my God, someone fired a gun.*

"Grandpa! Someone's shooting at us!" I yelled.

*What do I do? Quick, think, Brucie.*

I dove to the floor, covered my head with my arms and waited.

BANG!

"GRANDPA! WAKE UP!" *Oh, darn his whisky toddies!*

Trembling, I crawled right under my bed and curled into a tight fetal position. *Please, No. Don't shoot!* I held my breath, waited, and prayed for insight.

Tires spun onto the gravel outside of the window. BANG!

*Oh thank God, it wasn't a gun . . . it was a vehicle backfiring.*

*Mom? I can hear Mom's voice outside.*

"MOM!" I called.

She giggled like a schoolgirl, drunk as a sailor. The door of an old Land Rover opened with a creak and her laugh grew louder.

"Oh, you naughty, naughty man, Jake. Now look at the state I'm in. Are you not ashamed of yourself?" She roared and laughed. "Shhhh!" she said. "Shhh! You'll waken my daughter."

I sprang to the window, and peered outside.
*I don't believe what I'm seeing!*

## The Prize

As the moon rose in the sky, the dead badger lay where Bethany MacKinnon had placed it; in her Grandmother's back garden, on the homemade altar. The crows removed the badger's eyes. Fisher Skeelie removed the prize from its paws. The badger's soul departed, too. Only the body remained.

Inside the house, Skeelie stroked the prize, which she'd removed from the badger's paws -- the prize which Bethany had intended as a gift to pay the darkness.

"Oooh, yer loverly so yer are," she said to her prize. She stroked it again.

The old woman thought for a minute and returned to the garden. She picked up the dead mother badger by the leg, walked back to the house and threw it into the freezer.

"Waste not, want not," she said, and laughed.

Bethany wondered if the darkness would notice the missing prize and the missing badger. She called out to the moon. "It's not my fault that Grandma took it."

Later, when she returned home, Bethany hunted for the joint tin again. Unsuccessful, she took another large swig out of her uncle's vodka bottle. The smell of Jake's cheap aftershave filled the caravan. She cursed him for her leaving her empty-handed again.

## Chapter 12

## *Dogs in the Manger*

My Mom swayed in the driveway, as she swapped spit with . . . that dirty guy . . . the one who drove the backfiring truck. *GROSS!* Her butt stuck out of the door of his truck, and as they leaned over the passenger seat, the two of them locked jaws. *PU!*

One look would tell you that he sucked, but obviously not sufficiently, though, because Mom fell out of the truck and landed on her butt on the gravel.

*Right! That's it!*

Pulling on my sweater, jeans and a pair of boots, I stomped out to the driveway and stood over my Mom.

"Get up!" I ordered.

"Hello, Sweetheart, my little angel pie, light of my life," she said, slurring and spitting.

I offered a hand. "Here, hold on to me and I'll help you to stand."

Mom ignored my outstretched arm and giggled uncontrollably. She rolled over and over on the gravel and guffawed from her chest and gut, gurgling like an overflowing drain.

"Mom!" I shrieked. "He can see your underwear. Get up!"

A deep voice bellowed from the truck. "Your mother had fun tonight, pet. Don't dampen her spirit."

"And who are you to offer me advice?" I asked, hands on my hips.

Still stretched over the passenger seat, he spat on his hand and offered it to me. "I'm Jake."

*Totally gross!* I didn't answer, nor did I shake. *No way!* He looked evil.

"You're the lass 'at wants to get herself knocked down, aren't yer?" he asked.

"No. You're the varmint in the truck that needs more toes on his brake pedal and more eyes on the road. And, I'd get your engine fixed, if I were you. That back-firing is 'bout as neighborly as a flea to a dog," I said.

"Ah, ha, I see you have your mother's fiery spirit." He smirked. "And her good looks, bonny lass."

I made a face at him. "CREEP!" I said. Then, I told them both in a loud voice, "Y'all 'r stewed as prunes."

*Is Mom crazy, going out with THAT?*

"Mom, GET UP!"

This time, when I shouted, she stopped giggling and reached toward me, but her pupils struggled to focus. As I pulled her to her feet, she staggered wildly back and forth before hitting the gravel again with her butt. We tried a second time.

"Can I get another kiss then?" asked Jake.

"Inside, Mom. NOW!" I ordered. Physically, I maneuvered her feet up the two front steps and in through the threshold. She wobbled so much, like she couldn't find a hole in a ladder.

Jake's truck fired up again. BANG! He rammed the gears into reverse. SCREACH! His engine skirled until the thick black smoke cleared, and then backed out of the drive. "I'll call your landline tomorrow, darling!" he shouted, and sped off down the hill. The air stunk of burning rubber.

"You GAVE HIM our phone number?" I protested.

"Oh, Brucie, he doesn't have a mobile and our number is in the phone book for all to see," she said.

We ended the night in silence, but later I heard her barfing down the toilet pan in the bathroom.

In English class next day, I stared out of the window then I yawned my way through Math, and shifted in the seat from buttock to buttock until Geography ended. Any excitement about a late birthday surprise had vanished. On my way to the lunch hall, I broke sweat with a pounding heart when blonde spikes appeared in front of me. Suddenly, I recalled the morning that I saw Bethany MacKinnon in Jake's truck. *Hang back, Brucie*, I told myself. *Sneak down the corridor with your head lowered.* I slithered and rounded the corner.

In the canteen line, I bit my nails to the quick, in fear of a 'Beth encounter.' *Please don't let Bethany know anything about my Mom and that awful Jake.* Fortunately, I spied Rhiannon and we ate at a table together.

"Right I'm done. Let's go," I said.

"What's the rush?" she asked, munching salad.

"I have a headache and need to get painkillers from my locker," I said.

I rummaged in my locker, with my back to Rhiannon. It felt easier to ask the question when she couldn't see my face.

"Rhiannon, what is the connection between Beth and that Jake, you know, the guy who drives a rusty old truck? I've seen Beth with him before. Who is he?"

She spun around. "Why do you want to know about Jake?"

She made me tell her about Jake and Mom.

Rhiannon shrieked. "Oh my... Brucie, Jake is Beth's uncle." Frown lines wrinkled her forehead. "Your Mum needs to stay away from him. He's totally bad news."

"I know. I found that out last night."

"Poor Brucie," she said.

"Oh no, look out," I warned. "Here comes Beth now, with the Three Stooges – G C & M."

Cough started first, "There's carrot cake ..."

But Beth stopped her. "She's not worth it, girls. Let's go pick on some first years instead."

Rhiannon and I stared at each other, wide-eyed.

"What happened there?" I said. "Dadgum it! Someone finally took the yellow jacket out of the outhouse. I can go pee again."

"Brucie! You're talking all Texan. That mouth needs a filter again."

"Sorry, Rhiannon, but sometimes Texan is the only way I can say stuff."

"I know." She smiled. "It's cute."

That afternoon, I successfully filtered my mouth but I couldn't filter my thoughts. From two o'clock until the end-of-day bell at Glenaldie High School, my mind jumped from Mom and Jake, to Dad and Michaela, to Bethany MacKinnon and then back around to Mom and Jake. A few times, I fumbled and fiddled, searching for my necklace stone, but ... *I keep forgetting. It's gone.*

Riding home on the bus, I didn't chat much with friends. I watched the scenery pass by.

*I wonder who took my stone. And, why is Beth so quiet? But she's been quiet since before the theft. Something is up with her. She's letting me off light and I don't know why. Is it something to do with Mom and Jake?*

As I left the bus and climbed up Ardcarron Brae with Rhiannon, I wondered if Mom would apologize for her drunkenness. After all, I have to apologize for stuff!

*Even her depression was better than dating Jake. I liked her more when she festered in her darkened bedroom all day. She better not see that creep again!*

At my garden gate, I breathed easier, relieved when Rhiannon said, "I won't come in."

"Thanks for understanding," I replied. "It's best I go in alone."

Immediately, the minute I opened the front door, I picked up the weirdest energy from Mom and Gramps. And, I could *smell* something strange.

"What's that whiff?" I said, sniffing the air. "It's like sea weed, moldy blankets, or mildew."

Mom and Grandpa stood in the kitchen grinning from ear to ear.

"What? Why are you both so smug?" I asked.

"Maybe you should check in your room," said Mom. "Remember? A surprise . . . coming today . . . from your dad?"

Despite dark circles beneath her bloodshot eyes, Mom looked okay. I expected worse. She ushered me through the house. "Go and see," she said, but I resisted and took my time. I feared that the gift would be a disappointment and . . . I still boiled inside, angered by Mom.

*After last night, how can she stand there so brazen, so jovial?*

I rehearsed in my head how to fake gratitude, how to simulate excitement. Then, I opened the bedroom door.

"Zoe!" I cried, "My dog! My dog! Zoe, you're here!"

"Woof!" said Zoe.

"YES! I'm totally pumped Mom!" I cried and laughed simultaneously. "Is she for real?"

Zoe wagged her tail and pranced around in circles.

"Zoe, Oh Mom, Oh Grandpa, Oh Dad… He's sent Zoe to live with us? When did Zoe arrive? How come? Oh I love you, Zoe!"

"She landed in Glasgow airport four days ago. We collected her from the quarantine kennels today," said Mom.

"You drove to Glasgow today? With a hangover?"

She never answered.

"But, I thought that animal quarantine lasted six months?" I asked. "Wasn't that the main reason why we left her with Dad?"

"Changed rules now, Brucie. Zoe flew over on a pet passport scheme."

"What's that?" I asked.

"Well, if you can prove that your dog is free from rabies, they can fly with a pet passport. She had something called a Titer blood test, to check for rabies. It was clear so Zoe had booster rabies shots. They chipped her for I.D. and waited 180 days before retesting her. When she checked out, still free from rabies, Dad applied for an International Health certificate and they declared Zoe free to fly. She didn't have to endure six months of quarantine. The kennels here issued an early release, once a Scottish vet cleared her paperwork."

"Hear that, Zoe?" I said. "You might smell stronger than a garlic milkshake but at least you ain't got rabies. No you ain't, lovely girl."

I hugged my precious dog.

"Thanks, Mom," I said. "I love this dog more than anything in the world."

"Don't thank me. Go and call your Dad. He's waiting to hear from you."

As she said that, the phone rang. "Maybe that's Dad now," I said, and I galloped down the hallway to the phone. Zoe bounded after me.

"Hello?" I sparkled with happy tones.

"Hi, darling. Is your mother there? I've been trying to call her all day but she doesn't answer."

I clapped my hand over the mouthpiece, "Mom! It's the creepy guy. It's the man that took you home last night."

"Oh, please, tell him I'm not here," she urged, in a loud whisper.

"No, you tell him," I said, holding out the phone.

"Brucie, PLEASE? I'll explain later. Please tell him I'm not here."

So, I did and then I hung up before he could ask any questions. Jake freaked me out. I knew that wouldn't be the last we'd hear from him.

I concentrated on regaining my composure and I dialed Dad's number --001-469-955-4441.

"Dad? I love you SO much," I screamed when he answered. "Thank you. Thank you."

I started to write daily emails to dad from Zoe. Like this.

"Dear Paw, I ain't had so much fun since the legs fell off old Yeller P. McGraw's cat. Other bitches here are so gone yonder lazy. They got to lean up against a fence to bark, but there's a whippet I saw. He's faster than lickety-split, so as long as I got a dog biscuit, he's got half. Woof, Zoe."

I wished I could joke like that with Mom. She said she regretted swapping spit with dirty Jake. "He was a huge mistake, Brucie."

*Whew. What a relief!*

But each time he called, Mom left me to fend him off. She'd slip out of sight.

"Does she do that with you, too, Gramps?" I asked. "You know, disappear from a room, even sometimes when you're in the middle of talking to her?"

"Sometimes," he said, "but your mother has always been deep and creative."

"Creative?" I didn't understand.

"Yes, creative people are often aloof, especially when they muse about something,"

"So, what is she musing about?" I asked.

"We'll have to wait and see, won't we?" he said. I wondered where he got his patience from and if I could inherit some, too.

I told Grandpa, "Jake called again. He left a message to say he'll meet Mom at the Christmas dance down in the village hall. What should I do?"

"Simply pass on the messages, Brucie," and he smiled.

"But, *I'm* going to that dance!! What if I meet him there and he asks about Mom? He's sweet as a slop jar, Grandpa. I hate him."

"Then I'll speak with him next time he calls," said Grandpa. "Say nothing and hand the phone to me."

But, Jake didn't call again.

On the night of the dance, my hands shook as I paid my entrance money at the door. I stuck behind Rhiannon, who didn't have to pay because she'd been asked to play her fiddle with the band for a couple of tunes.

"Is anything wrong?" asked Rhiannon. "You're nervous as a deer caught in headlights."

I nodded. "I've never been to a dance, Rhiannon, much less a Christmas dance. And, that dirty Jake might appear. I've also never worn panty hose; sorry, I mean 'tights', before. They feel horrible, like my legs are two link sausages encased in skins."

"But, you look lovely in that dress, Brucie." She gave me a hug.

"It's brown as strong tea, and my make-up smells oily. How am I supposed to feel glamorous, dressed like a full Scottish breakfast?"

Before she could answer, Kyle butted in.

"Wow! Look at you," he said, and drooled.

*Typical, I remind him of food,* I thought. Kyle couldn't take his eyes off me.

"What?" I asked him.

"Nothing. Only … Wow!"

Kyle wore a blue shirt that matched his eyes. He sprouted a large, green plant from his breast pocket.

"Why have you got a plant growing out of your shirt?" I asked.

Rhiannon pulled my arm. "Ssh! It's mistletoe," she whispered.

"And, so?"

"Kissing beneath a sprig of mistletoe is considered lucky," she warned.

"Yeah, I know, but isn't a sprig a tiny bit? Kyle's carrying near two pounds of plant there," I said.

Kyle closed his eyes and puckered his lips.

"Shh! Run," whispered Rhiannon.

The village hall smelled hot and musty, like mothballs. Drab beige curtains hung like limp rags and a few tacky decorations glittered from the ceiling.

"What do we do with our coats?" I asked Rhiannon.

"Here!" She handed me her coat. "Take them both to the cloakroom next to the toilets. I have to go and play my fiddle now."

Some older girls that I didn't know sat in the cloakroom. They swigged from the necks of concealed bottles.

"Want some?" one asked, pushing the bottle in front of my face.

"No, thanks, it's nasty," I said. The group laughed.

This time, I didn't care who laughed at me.

Alternating voices echoed through microphones from the stage in the main hall, "Testing, One, Two," said a gruff tone. Another musician added, "Two. One, Two. One, Two." Then a deafening screech of feedback hurt our eardrums, and the whole counting process started over. "One. Two. Testing. One. Two."

I edged away from the drinkers and caught up with Kyle. He grinned when he saw me and patted the parasitic plant that peeped from his pocket.

"You quit cher grinnin', boy!" I quipped.

He sighed. "Okay, like."

"Will Duncan and Donald be coming tonight?" I asked, trying not to sound too keen.

"Nah! Reverend Iron Fist won't let them go to a heathen dance like this. Actually, they're granny-sitting again. Their old dear from Benbecula is still here."

"Oh yes, the old lady at the party with the pink gums," I said.

"That's her, like."

Once the band burst to life with a rowdy jig, talking became impossible. So, I watched Rhiannon get into her groove with the rest of the musicians.

*Gee! She's fabulous!*

Everyone else thought she was brilliant, too. Feet tapped. Hands clapped. Kyle whistled through a curled finger and thumb pressed to his teeth, piercing through the music with his shrillness. Dancers locked elbows and swung each other around in circles. The wooden floor bounced with the thudding rhythms and reels. Feet kicked. Armpits sweated. Tongues parched. My ears rang with drums and chords, riffs and strums, and then …

*Ah! There's nothing like a good teuchter's ceilidh,* he said.

*Oh, no! Coinneach. I thought you'd gone back to live in The Barracks?*

*Gone? I only come here when you want me,* he said.

*Want you? But my stone has been stolen. You shouldn't be here. I didn't ask you to come back.*

*Are you sure? You wanted to dance, didn't you?*

*Oh, no!* I protested. *DEFINITELY NOT! Don't think for one moment that I'm going to dance with you!*

*I'm very light on my feet. I don't step on ladies' toes. Come on, dance …*

My feet moved.

*Go away!* I concentrated really hard, and repeated *Go away!* But, hard as I tried to resist, my arms swung back and forth.

*Oh yes, I do love an Eightsome Reel. We have to join in.*

*Go away Coinneach! I don't want to dance with you. Quit making me look stupid.*

I couldn't understand why he turned up out of the blue like that.

*Why don't you ask me why I am here, then?*

*Grrr! Not now, Coinneach. This train's leavin' the station, Buddy. Church is out. I need some air.*

"Where you going?" asked Kyle. "Neat moves you were making there, Brucie. I thought you said that you didn't know these dances?"

"Later, Kyle," I said. "I'm going outside. The heat 'n' the sweat's done addled my brain."

*Brrr! I wish I'd grabbed my coat before coming out.*

I coughed in the frosty air. Holding my breath, I edged passed a group of smokers, hunched together in the cold. I didn't want my dress to smell of barbecued nicotine, so I pushed my way through quickly.

"Excuse me, please?" I said politely.

In the hurry, though, my foot knocked against...

*What's that?*

...a cane basket. Its owner sat on the steps outside the building.

"You looks pretty, Ma'am," she said. "But, yer not wearing that luverly stone of yours, are you?" she said.

It was cold and I wasn't in the mood to explain.

"No I'm not," I said. "Sorry, I can't chat. I have to go back inside to see my friend," I lied. "Pardon me," I said, as I turned back around and bumped my way back past the smokers.

*Why does everyone congregate by the door? No one can get in or out.*

My hand reached out to touch this girl's arm. "Can I squeeze past you, please?" But ... Oh my God! ...I nearly grabbed Bethany MacKinnon's arm.

*What am I going to do?*

I froze, turned my head and self-consciously cupped my palm up to the side of my face, as if my hand might magically shield me from sight. I waited. Wedged back-to-back with Bethany and stuck in the middle of the crowd, I heard Beth talking to Goth and Cough. The little fluttery one appeared to be missing. Beth slogged back gulps from a bottle and swore like ... like ... well, like Bethany MacKinnon.

" ... And see if I catch hold of his woman tonight ..." she said, "I'll flush her head in the ladies bog and close the lid on her face."

*Damn! Is she talking about Mom?*

I slithered and squeezed forward, but ended up jammed tight next to a large man in leather jacket. The night had turned ugly.

Beth slurred her words. "I bet she's a floozy. I bet she'll be here with her fancy dress and her high heels. She won't look so nice when I'm through with her."

*Mom? Thank Heavens Mom didn't come.*

I waited for someone to spot me, for my hair to pull, my dress to rip, my arms to bruise, my leg to swell in pain. Nothing!

*They haven't seen me. Oh, thank heavens. They haven't seen me.*

Another slurred voice joined the conversation. "Och, you don't know that he's dating anyone. You're drunk Bethany. Forget about it. Tell us about the craic with your Grandma."

I knew the voice: Goth.

Cough joined in. "Aye, tell us about the stone."

*THE STONE? Did I hear her say 'the stone'?*

My ears near turned inside out, as I strained to hear more. My brain filled with humming sounds. I wanted to say Shh! *How can white noise ring so loud?* The suspense drove me crazy, waiting. I bit my knuckle, and killed dark ages within that time lag. *What about my stone? Tell me about my stone.*

"Ha! Oh yes, the stone. Granny's pleased with her new stone. She calls it her prize. Folk are flocking to have their fortunes told by her. She's charging twenty quid a reading now."

"Wooooo!" one of them said. It was Cough. "Wooooo!" said the other.

*The Halloween tricksters! I recognize that 'Wooooooo'... Of course, they followed me home. The night when I ripped my stone off my neck, they were looking through the window. They were there when I put it in the jewelry box... but ... how did they?*

So many questions filled my head.

Spitting wild, I spun around.

"You're a dirty thief, Bethany MacKinnon. You're just like your dirty uncle. You'd better both keep away from my house because I've got a big dog now. Tell your filthy uncle that my Mom can't stand him any more. She completely regrets going out with him, now."

Goth and Cough shuddered.

"What?" Bethany said. "What did you say about my uncle and your mother?"

"You heard me." I said. "She regrets dating him the other night."

Two of the three stood staring at me, hands over their mouths. For some reason, though, Bethany backed away into the crowd, away from the hall doorway. I swear she looked like she was going to cry.

Inside I seethed with anger and fear, yet on the outside I managed to smile and stay calm. Rhiannon would be so proud of me.

*I did it! I must go and tell Rhiannon how I stood up to Bethany MacKinnon. YES!*

"Excuse me, please." I said to the man in the leather jacket. "Can I squeeze past?"

My stomach lurched when our eyes met.

"Hello my darling." He grabbed my arm. "You can squeeze me any time you want to."

*Oh no! Not Jake.*

## Bang! Bang! You're Dead.

Beth couldn't see very well, not after consuming so much vodka, but she managed to find the keys to Jake's Land Rover. Jake never took keys with him. He always threw keys to the floor of the vehicle before slamming the door.

Sitting in the driver seat, her legs were much shorter than Jake's. She fumbled to insert the key in the ignition.

As Bethany MacKinnon revved the engine, loud bangs emitted from the engine. She crunched the gearstick into first, locked the wheel to the right and slipped the clutch.

BANG! BANG!

Beth drove off like a bat leaving hell, driving in the direction of Brucie's house.

"I'm coming to get you, Mama MacKenzie-Bice. You're dead!"

# Chapter 13

## Carry Out the Drunken Lout!

Jake stunk of raw meat, soapy cologne and stale cigarette smoke. I shook off his grip and stepped back, but he towered over me and blocked my escape. His smirk revealed a large gap between his two front teeth, plugged with a spent match, which he twiddled and teased with his tongue. Charcoal-black eyes ignited and flashed. He hissed with the cunning of a preying feral cat. Stroking the dark growth on his unshaven jaw, Jake cocked his head left to leer down the bodice of my dress.

I squirmed and folded my arms, to obstruct his view.

"So where's that pretty mother of yours?" he asked, and leaned to his right to stare at my butt.

"Why don't cha go fix your bug eyes on something else, huh?" I snapped at him.

"You're such a feisty one," he said, and grabbed my wrist, again. This time, he pulled me inside the hall and toward the center of the floor. "Come and dance."

I fought against him, shouting, "Get char dirty hands off me!"

Immediately, a group of guys inside the hall turned their heads.

The tallest one warned, "Lay off, Jake. Leave the young lassie alone."

"Yeah, leave her alone, you're drunk and you're scaring her," quipped a shorter man.

Jake dismissed me quicker than spit, launched himself toward the second voice and swung a clenched fist. "Drunk? What d'you mean 'drunk'?"

BAM! Jake's fist struck nose cartilage with a crunch and blood spurted everywhere.

"Fight! Fight!" The crowd chanted, "Fight! Fight!"

Within seconds, a ring of onlookers dove into the centre of the scuffle. Rousers, jeerers and the all-curious shoved forward, straining for a better view. Unwittingly, they slammed me against a row of wooden seats. *Ouch! My shin!* Tossed left, thrust right, I tottered on my high heels like a deaf, dumb and blind kid, pinging like a pinball from person to person.

"Help!" I cried. "Let me out of here."

*So much for the cool Brucie now!* I thought.

The music cut. A voice shouted, "Calm down everyone!"

I rammed an elbow between a tall, red-haired woman and a kilted man, forced them apart with my shoulder and furrowed forward. I channeled ahead until I reached Kyle. He grabbed my hand.

Suddenly, a posse of six burly bouncers wrestled Jake to the ground and the crowd heaved left again, like a Mexican wave. Carried like a cork on choppy water, I squeezed Kyle's arm.

"Fight! Fight!" they called again, but Jake lay prone, face down and pinned by the posse, who then carried him out of the door and out of sight.

"Are you okay, lass?" asked the tall guy from the corner group. Simultaneously, he dug into his pocket for a handkerchief, which he then handed to his friend with the bloody face.

"Yes, I think so." I said. My hands trembled.

Kyle wrapped his arm around me. "She's with me now. She'll be fine," he said, puffing out his chest like a strutting cockerel. Rhiannon jumped down from the stage.

"What happened?" she asked.

She stomped with rage when I told her about Jake. "Brucie, stay with Kyle, will you?" and I didn't argue.

*Darn it! I forgot to tell her how cool I was with Bethany MacKinnon.*

A burly, red-faced man called Rhiannon back to the stage and music resumed.

I turned to Kyle. "Is this behavior typical of village dances? Do people always cheer at fights like this?" I asked, aghast.

"Dunno," said Kyle. "I'm only sixteen, too, like."

The plant in Kyle's shirt pocket hung limp, berryless, shrunk to a mere twig. He spied me checking out the remnants.

"People keep stealing bits," he said, and frowned.

When I backed away from the plant, he offered the last piece to a couple standing to our right. Kyle then held out his empty palms to show me. "Look! All gone now!" he said.

Sometimes Kyle can be sweeter than a Laffy Taffy.

"Thanks," I said.

He grinned. "Can I walk you home? I've seen enough action for one night."

"Yeah, me too," I said. "I'll grab my coat and I'll meet you outside."

Outside the hall, I fixed my stare toward the moon, rather than look for Bethany MacKinnon. Jake's rumpus seemed harder to ignore. He yelled and banged on the inside of Frank's police van.

Ardcarron Hill sparkled with glittery ice. I struggled to steer my new high-heeled shoes up the road ahead, so I took the shoes off.

"Your feet will freeze, like," said Kyle.

"Better than a broken neck," I laughed.

Bless Kyle. He removed his shoes and insisted that I wore them.

We walked in silence and I thought about my stone.

*I can't believe they broke into my house and took it? I should have realized that the Moth was one of those stupid Wooing ghosts. She saw where I put my stone. I wish I'd shut the drapes first. Will I phone Frank and tell him about the conversation I overheard? Nah, he's got his hands full with Jake.*

"What are you thinking about?" asked Kyle.

"Promise you won't tell anyone." I said.

His eyes grew wide. "Honest," he said, with his hand on his heart.

So, I told Kyle about the Eye Stone.

He grinned, "Cool!" Then he switched to a serious face. "I mean not cool that it's gone, like, because you could be famous like that whats-is-name, Yogi Geldoff, bending spoons and that, like."

"Don't you mean Uri Gellar?"

"That's the guy, like. Whatever… we need to get your stone back," he said.

"I'm not so sure, Kyle. I seemed to get into trouble with it. And, Rhiannon would be mad at me."

"Naw, she's not mad at you. It might be tricky but we should get it back. You'd be happier then, wouldn't you, like?"

I smiled. "Yes."

As we rounded the bend at the top of the road, Kyle suddenly jumped in front of me. "Don't look, Brucie," he said.

"What is it?" I asked, trying to see around him.

"Stay there," he said and he ran forward to where the back wheels of a Land Rover stuck out of a ditch. A recovery vehicle pulled the truck backward till it landed again on all four wheels.

"That's Jake's Land Rover, isn't it?" I called to Kyle.

"Yep, it is, like," he said.

"But, they've just taken Jake away in the police van." I said. "Is anyone there? Is anyone hurt?"

Kyle asked the bystanders and came back to tell me the answer. "No one there, like. One of your neighbors heard the crash but when they came outside to investigate the Land Rover was empty."

I shivered.

"Don't worry, Brucie," he said. "I'll look after you."

Thereafter, Kyle assigned himself as my personal bodyguard. He convinced me in great detail and frequency that I needed him around for protection. During the time leading up to Christmas, he became my shadow. As bodyguard, he even commenced a workout regime. He said he built muscle, lifting concrete bricks above his head... one in each hand, before going to bed and after getting up. So, on December 23rd, I gave him the gift of a body-building magazine, called, *Ab Zone*.

"I was going to get you some proper hand weights but they were a little expensive," I told him.

"Oh, that's okay," he said. Kyle then stammered, saying that he had a present for me, too, but, he told me he would deliver it on Christmas Day. Oddly, he left, muttering awkwardly, with the magazine stuffed under his jacket.

He pestered me with weird phone calls. He'd begin a sentence then change his mind and hang up.

*Why is he so flustered?* I thought. *I worry about Kyle, sometimes.*

Coinneach became my other concern.

*Why did he turn up at the dance like that? I haven't seen him since. It is like I have to need him for something specific. But how do I know in advance what I need him for? Grrr! I don't understand.*

By Christmas Eve, I felt smothered by Kyle's peculiarity, so I ignored my mobile whenever he called. I needed to deliver my gifts to the twins, and I didn't want to accept any of his odd phone calls while I visited Gargoyle House.

All around, the sky clung dark and damp, as I entered the MacLeod's driveway. Suddenly a pair of headlights switched on in front of me. The beam shone in my face, separating me from thoughts about Kyle and Coinneach.

MacKay's Contractor's van revved to life in the driveway. A ladder hung out of the back door, with a white rag attached to the end. Cement mixers and various tools lay covered by a large tarpaulin in the corner of the yard.

*Hmm, looks like work will begin soon on their new house extension.*

The guy inside the van, rolled down his window as he passed me. He looked so familiar.

"Tell your mother and Grandpa Merry Christmas, will you? Say that Johnny MacKay said hello." When I studied Johnny MacKay's face, I realized that I had met him before somewhere.

*Yes, I've come across you before. But, where? It's the shirt that I recognize. Brrr! Don't these Highlanders feel the cold?*

The van pulled away before I could figure him out. I'd encountered so many new people and so many new places that sometimes everything blurred together.

Looking around the empty front yard, I saw no sign of the figure in the red shawl, so I rang the doorbell with confidence and waited. Singing and laughter emanated from inside. Someone played "Oh come all ye faithful" on a piano, accompanied by a screechy violin and a very loud trumpet. I felt suddenly envious and backed away from the step.

*What's wrong with me?*

I fumbled. The din reminded me of our old family Christmases and my heart ached. Tears pooled in my eyes.

*I wish Dad was here. Christmas is not the same without him.*

Clearing my throat, I told myself aloud, "Come on Brucie. Snap out of it."

Thankfully, I found a distraction within my plastic sack containing gifts for the twins. With my head down, hands rummaging inside the sack, I didn't notice the door open. Maybe it opened very slowly or maybe very quickly, but it opened in total silence. One minute I faced a pane of glass and the next minute she stood there and peered into the sack with me. The sudden chill announced her presence. That, and the tiny hairs all over my skin that began to stand on end.

*Oh no! I thought when I lost the stone that SHE would have gone too.* I double-checked my neck, in case I had imagined the stone's absence.

"You must save the baby. You must!" she insisted. Her eyes and her tone filled with such bitterness that I backed away, feeling quite afraid of her.

*Remember what Rhiannon said about the cows*, Brucie, I told myself. *Sometimes you have to ignore the distress and concentrate on what is good.*

But, the ghost scared me.

The twins' father, Reverent Macleod, approached the threshold, "Brucie, if you are going to open the door then come in, child. Don't loiter, creating a draught." He stood in the same spot as her. I could see them both, the minister standing *inside* of her. The yellowish, grayish haziness that surrounded her now surrounded him, too.

I've always feared that the Reverent thought me crazy. Now, yet again, I couldn't do anything to defend myself. I stood there gawking at him like a lunatic.

"What's wrong, Brucie?" he asked. "What are you staring at?"

She looked straight through his face and moved her lips at the same time that he did, but then an even weirder thing happened. The minister said, "You must find the baby. He'll be wrapped in swaddling clothes, lying in..."

Astounded, I demanded, "What baby am I supposed to find, wrapped in swaddling clothes?"

Reverend MacLeod sidestepped to lean against the door frame, stumbling to the left and separating himself from her body. He held on to the wooden door frame, apologizing and muttering that he couldn't think why he had even mentioned a baby. "I've been preparing the Christmas service. Yes, that must be it." Now, HE looked crazy. "I am talking about the candlelight service," he said, but without conviction. "Come in, Brucie. Come inside. Yes, that's it, you must come in, I think." Flustered, he patted moisture from his bright red brow with the sleeve of his ministerial, plain grey sweater.

"Actually, I'll not stay. Can you give these gifts to the twins?" I asked, and I dumped the sack in the doorway. Rev. MacLeod gaped at me, with an open mouth, and then he gazed up into the darkness.

*Maybe he's looking for the North Star*, I thought.

"Wait, Brucie," I heard Donald calling. He pushed past his father, who searched the sky in awe. The Reverend Macleod returned indoors, shaking his head and muttering. Donald held out a small home-made box, with elephants drawn on it.

"They are supposed to be drawings of your dog, Zoe. It's a small gift for you. Merry Christmas," he said handing me the box.

*Our fingers touched!*

"Thanks, I'll put it under my Christmas tree," I said.

Before he had time to question my gooey expression, I blurted, "Donald, I can see ghosts."

One of Donald's most endearing qualities must be his calm matter-of-factness. "Don't worry, Brucie. I'm sure it will be okay." He thought for a second and quickly offered a suggestion, "Why don't you distract your mind?"

*Why are boys practical, rather than romantic?*

He continued, "Did you know that there are multiple ways that you can get the digits 1-9 to amount to the number 100 by adding and subtracting? The numbers have to run in ascending sequence, though." He whipped out a pen and a small notepad from the back pocket of his jeans. "Look," he said, and wrote down "123-45-67+89=100" He stood back with a smug grin and said, "Clever, eh?"

It took every ounce of concentration for me to soak in even an ounce of that information. I smiled.

*He's so smart! And hot!*

"There are ten more ways to do this. Next time you feel panic strike and need something to think about, try finding another solution," he said.

"No way!" I laughed. "I'm never smart enough to figure that in my head." I thought, *What a nice nose he has. I've never noticed his cute nose before.*

"Oh, I think you're way smart enough, Brucie. Didn't you get top marks on the Maths test?" he said, with his head cocked to the side like a spaniel puppy again.

*And, I like his teeth. And… Okay, Brucie that's enough. Go home before he sees you drooling,* I told myself.

Later that night, sitting by the fireside at home, coal cracking and hissing below the dancing flames, I looked around the sitting room. Christmas Eve felt cozy. No television. Mom, Grandpa and me grouped together with Zoe at our feet. For ages, we sat quietly in the dim firelight. No one spoke about anything, not even about the fact that no one spoke. I sipped on a warm fruit drink that Grandpa had concocted for me.

"It's a special drink I invented called "an Ikit"," he whispered. "The Christmas version is called a "Yule Ikit.""

I did.

Laughing, I asked, "How do you make a Yule Ikit?"

"Ah well, you gather pumpkin eggs while they are still fresh and…"

I cut him off mid-sentence. "Hey, speaking of pumpkins …you know what? November passed by and we completely forgot to celebrate Thanksgiving! How on earth did that happen?"

"But Thanksgiving is not a holiday here, Brucie," said Mom.

"I know, but …" I felt a pang of sadness, and even shame for forgetting such an important American holiday. How could that happen? Had I become too Scottish, too quickly? Grandpa said my Texan accent sounded less pronounced. Texas slipped away a little more each day. Sometimes an identity crisis infected my brain, scary as a split personality, like my Texan past and my Scottish future squared up for a fight and, in the confusion, I'd forget who I was.

"We can celebrate Thanksgiving right now," said Gramps, immediately healing the cultural rift within my head. "I think I still have a turkey sandwich in my bedside table, since the end of November. We can share it."

"Sure, and I'll go heat up some left over snow," I said. "What about you, Mom?"

She replied, "Oh, I'll pass on your kind hospitality and simply give thanks that Jake has stopped calling me." She looked at Gramps and me and added, "I'm so sorry."

"Oh, I just remembered something," I said. "Johnny MacKay told me to wish you both a Merry Christmas. I met him down at Gargoyle House."

Gramps smiled. "That's nice," he said, while Mom sat up straight and fluffed with her hair, as if someone important arrived at the door.

*Why is she blushing?*

The big Grandmother clock struck eleven and Gramps poured himself a small measure of ruby port. Flickering golden flames reflected beautifully off his delicate crystal glass, casting shades of amber on the wall. He raised the glittering vessel and offered up a toast to the air above him, "Slainte Mhath, sweet Edna," he whispered.

After a pause, he said, "I always think of your Grandma when that big clock strikes, Brucie. I wish you had known her, Lassie. She loved children." Gramps reached into his trouser pocket, pulled out a handkerchief. He dabbed his eyes and then smiled. "Och, I'm sure she's up there smiling down upon us."

Grandma died when Mom was young. I closed my eyes and imagined a pretty young woman with red hair like mine and Mom's. Her eyes were brown, though. She smiled at me, winked, and vanished from my inner vision.

As the image faded, I relaxed and the arm chair molded to my frame. My limbs flopped, irresistibly heavy, supported gently by something unseen. Something unknown. . . Something more than solely the chair. . . My body felt delicately cradled. It swayed, encased in a womb-like bubble. Concentrating on the bubble feeling, I closed my eyes and floated out of my body to the ceiling, where I peered down upon myself. Yes, I looked relaxed down there, and. . .

*Shit! What am I doing up here?*

The bubble burst and I jolted uncomfortably in the chair. Zoe sniffed at me. Grandpa, who had been sharing memories of my Scottish Grandmother, Edna, stopped talking.

"What's wrong, Brucie?" he asked.

I'd not talked about this in front of Mom before. "Gramps," I said. "Do you still think that I could have 'the Giftie'?"

Mom looked at Gramps for his reaction to my question.

He winked. "Most certainly," he said, reaching over toward the Christmas trees. "Which giftie would you like to open first?"

"Not that kind of giftie. . . I mean second sight."

Mom laughed. " Och, let's open ALL of our gifties now."

Gramps moved to the floor with his legs outstretched in front of him, like a little boy.

"Okay, I'll be Santa," he said.

It suddenly dawned on me that Mom only had three presents. One came from me, one from Gramps and the other said, 'Love from Zoë.' I noted that Mom's eyebrows knitted together and she sighed a lot, gazing wistfully into the fire.

Six gifts bore Grandpa's name and I hoarded seventeen.

*Poor Mom!*

I nudged Grandpa's arm, "Maybe we should wait until the morning," but he had already torn the Christmas paper off a box of Cadbury's assorted chocolates and removed the cellophane wrapper to offer them around.

"God bless Bunty Blackhead," he said, stuffing a strawberry cream into his mouth. "She knows I have a sweet tooth."

Mom handed me the little box with the Zoe elephants and grinned. "Open this one."

"No, I'll em, er… I'll open that one later." My cheeks flushed red hot, exposing my thoughts.

"Who is it from?" she asked.

"Oh … nobody." *Why can't I say his name? Now I'm drawing attention to myself.*

Grandpa removed the box from my hand and exchanged it for another. "Try this one instead," he said. "It's part of my gift to you, an extra that you might like."

Inside the package, I found a large diary. It had a lock and key. "Great! I can write down all my secrets and keep them safe. Thanks, Grandpa!"

Mom yawned and said she needed to sleep. She switched off the tree lights, bundled up the torn wrapping paper and heaved another sigh. Gramps handed me the Zoe elephants' box. "Why don't you open that one in your room?" he winked.

So, I did.

"What the…?" A nine volt battery sat inside a metal casing. Some connecting wires ran to small cogs. These cogs shifted small plates back and forth. I turned the contraption over and realized I held a crudely-shaped green metal animal, obviously homemade. A note said, "Attach wires to battery, to make Zoe walk." Since three of the toy's legs were longer than the other one, it limped forward for a few inches and fell over. "Ha! How sweet!" I smiled. Thinking for a moment, I fastened a paper clip to lengthen the shorter leg and the green dog walked all the way across my window ledge.

*I absolutely love it! And, he made it with his own hands.*

I drifted toward sleep, like a fluffy cloud floating across the sky. Clutching Donald's toy dog, I felt this deep and soothing peacefulness. But, not for long...

At 3:49 am, I crashed back to consciousness. I screamed. I choked. I gasped for air. Petrified, I gripped the toy tight in a clenched fist, calling out into the dark, "No! Don't drown, Donald."

The same visions spun on and on, even though I lay awake. I couldn't move. The visions filled me with horror. My mouth rasped, like I'd swallowed a bucket of salt. Flashback after flashback haunted and taunted me.

I saw a large boat floating upside down. Metal scraped on metal. Legs scrambled in front of my eyes. Mouths gaped and choked underwater till only bubbles emerged. Screams screeched so loud that a glass porthole shattered, seawater gushed inward, a torrent raged, and eyes, white with fear, popped from their sockets. Open hands thrust upward, desperately clutching for help. They seized and clenched at swirling whirlpools and then disappeared, sucked below a rolling ocean of putrid, oily water. Donald floated into view, with blue and bloated skin. He somersaulted, first slowly, and then faster, dragged into a clockwise vortex by an underwater current. His lungs gurgled, muffling and swallowing his words. I felt myself choke, too. Suddenly, the sea spat him high into the air. He bobbed and floated on his back, arms tangled and broken. His eyes stared at me helplessly, until their sparkle faded to opaque and his head vanished down . . . down . . . down . . . into the deep. But, in the final seconds, Donald held my stare.

"Why didn't you save me, Brucie? Why didn't you use your stone? You could have foreseen this."

## Shooting the Moon

Bethany lay on her bed blaming the darkness. 'This is revenge,' she thought. 'I couldn't pay the darkness, not since Gran claimed the 'prize'.' The walls spun and she felt sick. She rubbed her head where the bruise had appeared and winced at the cut on her left arm.

'Gran might as well keep her prize now. I only put it on the Altar to please Gran anyway, to get her off my back. But, next time I make curses, I'll pay the moon and the darkness, too. I won't forget next time.'

Her memory jolted back to driving the Land Rover; skidding, rolling… the thump to her head and the long walk home.

'Oh well, I've had my bad luck. There won't be any more,' she hoped.

Outside the window a wild cat screeched. An owl screeched, too. She found Jake's gun, loaded it. Aiming up at the moon, she fired the gun out of the caravan door.

"Quit the noise out there!" she called. "Before someone else gets it."

# Chapter 14

## *Overboard!*

Mom hit the light switch. "What are you doing on the floor, Brucie?"

"Bad dreams, Mom." I said, "I'll be okay in a minute."

"Oh my God, you're bleeding," she exclaimed.

My hand throbbed. I held it up and blood trickled down my wrist.

Mom rushed from the room. "I'll get the first aid box from the bathroom cabinet." She returned with a wad of cotton, soaked in something that smelled of hospitals. Gently, Mom took my palm and wiped at the blood with soft strokes. "Looks like you cut it on that toy dog."

I'd clenched it so tightly, the metal dug deep into my skin.

Gramps looked in the door. "Have you been fighting with the ghost of Christmas past?"

"No." I said, as Mom finished tending to my hand.

Gramps cooking smelled of savory herbs.

"When will Christmas lunch be ready?" I asked, in a bid to divert the fuss.

"We'll eat at one o'clock and everything is under control, pet," he said. "The cock-a-leekie soup is clucking in the pot and the turkey is gobbling in the oven. I've made roast potatoes, Brussels sprouts, turnip, and carrots. There's bread sauce and pigs-in-a-blanket, too. For desert you can have either plum pudding and brandy butter or Scottish trifle."

"Lovely, Gramps, I'm hungry." I said, fibbing.

I stood up too quickly and immediately sat down on the bed. *Wow! The room is swirling.* As I lay back against the pillow it felt like I sank to the bottom of the ocean.

"You're very pale, Brucie," said Mom.

"I'm okay," I lied, again. "I'll get dressed in a minute. I want to play with my new digital camera."

"Oh good. I'm glad you like it." Mom added, "I'll leave you to get dressed."

*Yes, Mom. I need to be alone. I need to call Donald. Check that he's okay. But, how can I call him on Christmas Day. His dad will freak.*

Mom popped her head back in the door. "I charged the camera battery, ready to use," she said, and then she left me alone with my thoughts.

DING! DONG!

After lunch the doorbell rang.

"I'm too stuffed full of turkey to drag myself off this chair, Brucie. Can you get the door?"

"Sure." I said to Mom.  After all, I'd only eaten a very little.

As I turned the handle, I secretly hoped to see Donald standing there. *Don't be silly, Brucie. Donald wouldn't call here, especially not on Christmas Day. Oh, what if he's in danger, though?*

"Can I come in, or are you going to stand there dreaming, like?" said Kyle.

"Eek! You're wet," I squealed. He stood on the doorstep, dripping like a leaky backyard faucet.  Outside, the wind whipped all ways. Sleet darted at my face as I zipped behind the door.  When Kyle entered I pushed my shoulder against the door until it clunked shut.

"Mercy me, where did that storm suddenly blow from?" said Grandpa. "Come ben the hoose and take your coat off, Kyle. You're like a drookit rat."

"Thanks, Ali," said Kyle. He sniffed the air. "Ah! Smells like you've had a lovely lunch, like."

"Aye, are you hungry, Kyle?" asked Grandpa. Without waiting for an answer he said, "Let me fix you a plate."

"Oh, I've had a huge meal, Ali," said Kyle, but Grandpa ignored him. He piled up a feast of turkey and all the trimmings and set the microwave for two minutes.  Gramps turned to Kyle. "So how is your mother keeping these days?"

"She's not too bad, like. Her cough was bad last night, so she stayed in bed today," he said.  Kyle's eyes didn't leave the microwave oven. The minute the bell timer dinged, he grabbed the plate and tucked in like he hadn't eaten in a week.  Meanwhile, I snapped some photos of him with my new camera.

"For someone who's eaten a huge meal, you sure seem hungry," I said.

Gramps poked my side and scolded me by knitting his eyebrows together.

*Why is Gramps staring at me like that?*

*Ah!* A light flicked on in my brain and I started to read the scene more clearly. Actually, I only fully twigged when Kyle rose to leave, two plates of turkey later. Before going, he pulled a present from his pocket and handed it to me.

"Merry Christmas, Brucie," he said, and stepped out of the door into the volley again.

I felt sorry for Kyle but the wind snatched away all thoughts of pity and exchanged it with the sound of scraping metal, the screams, the gurgling, the fear. . . I slammed the door quickly and took my gift to the sitting room, where I hugged up next to Zoe in front of the warm fireplace.

Ripping open the wrapping, I found another tag stuck to the box of chocolates inside. It read, "To Kyle, Love from Mum. Sorry it's not much. xxx."

Grandpa stood watching closely, waiting for my reaction.

"I don't understand," I said. "He's obviously given me the wrong gift."

"No, love," said Grandpa, "think again," and he left me to work it out for myself.

"Oh, no! Poor Kyle," I said. "How sad is that, Gramps? He's given me the gift that he got from his mother."

I picked up my lovely new digital camera and realized how much I took expensive gifts for granted. Flicking the 'on' switch, I checked the photos I had taken of Kyle eating his meal.

"He was starving, wasn't he, Gramps?"

But, I didn't hear Grandpa's reply because something caught my eye in the photos.

"What are these globes floating around Kyle's head?" I asked.

Mom tilted the camera, so that she could see the screen.

"I know what they are," she said. "They're orbs!"

I shot her a stunned look. Mom forever reprimanded Grandpa for dabbling in mysticism and now. . . her description of an orb sounded suspiciously mystical to me.

"Orbs are translucent balls of light that hover above the ground or above people," she said. "They are usually seen in historic or haunted sites, but it is interesting that these orbs are floating around Kyle."

"Why is that interesting?" I asked. I had to keep my voice low while Grandpa listened to the Queen's Christmas speech on the kitchen radio.

"Orbs are believed to be the soul or spirit of a human who has passed on," she said.

"You mean that a dead person is hovering over Kyle?" I asked.

*Weird! How can I see people like Coinneach, ghosts that bulge out of walls, I can detect auras around horses, and yet I didn't notice anything odd about Kyle?*

Coinneach suddenly appeared from behind my mother, stepping out to stand by her right shoulder. He waved and then disappeared again.

*Don't go! I need to speak to you.*

But, he didn't show again.

Mom replied to the question I'd forgotten asking. "Maybe someone close to Kyle is watching over him." She added, "I've also heard that orbs found outside at nighttime are the spirits of trees. They come out in the dark when the tree is at rest and return at dawn when they are needed again."

*I bet there are orbs around the Barracks!*

I had no idea about my Mom's spiritual interests and our conversation left me wondering why I hadn't confided in her before now.

*Should I tell her about my nightmare? Ask her advice about the stone?* I hesitated. *No. I can't. Oh, why do I keep my Mom at such a distance these days?*

The reason presented plain as white bread, inevitable as fleas on a farm dog, when the phone rang and I heard her speaking to Dad.

"You're such a liar, Dustin." Mom hollered into the mouthpiece. "You didn't even send her a Christmas present!"

Silence.

"If you sent a gift, then where is it?"

Silence again.

"You should have posted it sooner, then," she snipped.

As my parents argued, I quietly zipped up my waterproof jacket, pulled on my boots and left the house.

Outside, the wind calmed. Inside, the barometric pressure had escalated. Angry emotional outbursts gust upward from a gale force of six or seven. I walked out before the roof lifted off. Yes, that's the reason why I kept my distance from Mom. That... and I withdrew because of her having dated Jake MacKinnon.

Dad's parcel arrived on the 27th of December but I could tell that Michaela chose it, again … a yucky, pink handbag, patterned with sparkling horseshoes and … I don't do pink leather skirts.

"It's itsy … more like a belt," I moaned to Mom. "And nothing in Texas tarnations would make me wear such a trashy top. I'm not a hoe!"

"Brucie! Watch your language," Mom warned. But, I caught her expression in the mirror, as she turned away to smile.

Resentful and disappointed, I didn't call Dad at all that Christmas week.

On New Year's Eve, Rhiannon told me, "Sometimes, you are not the most tactful person, Brucie."

Rhiannon and I headed down Ardcarron Brae to join the midnight street party. We wore our 'See You Jimmy Hats' (that's a tartan bonnet with fake ginger hair attached) and layers of warm clothes.

"What do you mean, 'I'm not tactful'?" I asked.

"Because I heard you ask Kyle why a dead person might follow him around," she said.

I asked, "So what's wrong with that?"

"Think, Brucie. His dad died, remember?" Rhiannon shook her head and handed me half of her packet of sparklers for the midnight celebrations. "Maybe you didn't mean to be cruel, but…" Her voice trailed off.

"Sorry," I said. "I'm always goofing up, ain't I?"

"Well, you could've shown him the photo and waited until he asked about the orbs. But, no… you tell him that dead folk are following him, without explaining about the photo. He's totally spooked. Anyway, I thought you agreed not to talk about any more creepy stuff."

I sighed, feeling lily-livered. "Sure. No problem." Texas blood still ran through my veins; a hog was still a hog. Sometimes, when it came down to tact, I missed the mark and I couldn't hit the floor if I fell out of bed.

*Oh wait; I did hit the floor…*

*Hmm…I wish I could tell Rhiannon about my dream on Christmas morning. It's a warning. I know it.*

I cleared my throat. "Eh, I need to tell you about something I dreamed about."

But, Rhiannon didn't hear me. She'd spied MacBean's Hot Dog Van, "I'm st-aaa-r-ving," she stressed, and disappeared.

Rain drizzled endlessly, so I made for the shelter of the café doorway. Gazing down at a pool of water by my feet, I continued to obsess about Donald.

*Don't think of him drowning, Brucie*, I told myself. *Think of . . . 12+3-4+5+. . . It's no use. I'm all whoomperjawed!* I tried my other happiness trick . . . *finding a coin on the street . . . pinging elastic bands through the air . . . singing down the drain hole in the bath and listening to the great acoustics . . .* but nothing took the misery away.

A covered flatbed trailer stood next to me, outside the Gowan Café. The trailer, set like a stage, hosted amplifiers and microphones rigged up for a band. Electrical cables ran along the ground into the café via the side door. I discovered one of the cables when my shoe snagged it and I tripped, tumbling toward the ground. A hand stretched out to catch me and I instinctively grabbed it, breaking my fall.

Without looking up, I said, "Thank you," but...

"And you had the nerve to chew out your mother for being drunk! You need more water in your whisky, lass," he said. The foul stink of raw meat and cigarette smoke immediately disclosed his identity. I jerked my hand away, as if I'd touched a cottonmouth.

"Get lost. I tripped, right? These cables should be kept out of harm's way. I'm not a drunkard. Not like you," I snapped, staring him out.

*Ick! He gives me creeps. Demons must've possessed my Mom. How could she kiss him?*

He laughed and grabbed for the ginger hair on my hat. "What do you need this for when you already have a carrot top of your own?"

"You have all the personality of linoleum flooring and the sex appeal of a wet paper sack. Don't know what possessed my Mom to go out with you. Who let you out of jail anyway?"

He didn't answer so I turned away from him.

The old woman with the cane basket watched us, stern faced. As Jake staggered away, I saw her lean toward him and mutter something in his ear. He kept walking, so she swiped at the back of his head with her gloves. Jake put his hand up to his neck, as if bitten by a mosquito, but he didn't respond or turn around.

"What did you do that for?" I asked her.

She shivered. Apart from an old-fashioned headscarf and gloves, her only protection from the blustery night was a thin blanket wrapped around her shoulders. Her fawn, tweed skirt hung tattered and her stockings threadbare above her old, black, hobnail boots. As usual, she carried the same basket. Tonight it held a bottle, something wrapped in a little white cloth, and a lump of coal. Presumably she would be 'first footing' later. (Grandpa explained to me that 'first footing' meant a tradition whereby after midnight you would visit a neighbor to bring a drink of whisky, a piece of clootie dumpling to eat, and a piece of coal to place on their fireside hearth.)

"Jake needs a slap, an' that's why a cuffed him," she said. Her voice growled and her eyes closed as she spat on the ground.

"You know Jake?" I asked, curiously.

"I'd say I do," she said.

"What's your name?" I asked, wondering about her connection to Jake.

"Sissy, call me Sissy."

I didn't know what else to say to Sissy. New Year seemed a good enough time to call a truce with her, though. So, I told her my name, "I'm Brucie," and said, "Have a Happy New Year, then, Sissy."

"Who are you wishing a happy New Year to?" asked Rhiannon, with a mouth full of sausage. She carried two hot dogs and handed me the one with everything on it, ketchup, mustard and onions.

"Sissy," I said.

"Who is Sissy?" she asked, and took another large bite.

I turned around to point, but Sissy had wandered off. "Oh, she stood here a minute ago. I'll show you when she comes back." *That's odd! Where'd she go?*

"How come you know this Sissy?" Rhiannon asked.

"She must live around here somewhere. I see her quite a lot."

Rhiannon shrugged, "I don't know anyone called Sissy and I know everyone around here." Rhiannon winced, fanning her hotdog-filled mouth with a flapping hand. "Outh, this thauthage ith hot."

From behind me, two hands clamped over my eyes. "Guess who this is?" said a phony, gruff voice.

But, I'd recognize his hands anywhere.

"Freshly-mown grass! Multicolored hot-air balloons! Bouncing on trampolines! You're alive!" I shouted, spinning around, flinging my arms around his neck and burying my head on his shoulder.

"Of course, I'm alive, Brucie. What do you mean?" said Donald, red-cheeked with eyes as round as white dinner plates. He backed away with a look of discomfort on his face.

"Oh!" I said. I quickly let go and stepped back two awkward paces. Staring at my feet, I couldn't think what to say or how to explain myself.

*What in the Jim Dickens did I do that for? I lost it! I completely lost it!*

"Brucie! You're a bit enthusiastic tonight!" said Rhiannon, giggling.

Everyone laughed at me, except for Kyle. "No one ever hugs me like that," he mumbled.

"I'm so sorry, Donald, but I thought you were Sissy," I lied.

Donald's face color now flushed a lesser shade of pink, as opposed to its previous screaming scarlet.

And, then I said. "…I thought you were Sissy and I'd been worried that she had died."

Rhiannon stared at me. "What the hell are you talking about?"

"Sometimes he is a big sissy," said Duncan.

Donald asked, "Who is Sissy?"

"Sissy is Sissy. You *must* know her; the woman who wanders around the village, carrying the cane basket," I said, hoping that if I kept talking they'd forget what I'd done.

Rhiannon screwed her index finger into her temple and nodded at me. "Ignore her, folks. She's got a screw loose."

"Cane basket?" Kyle asked, checking everyone's expressions and shrugging.

Rhiannon began to stir trouble. "Brucie, you said you saw this Sissy woman only a few minutes ago, so why would she be dead?"

"Maybe I heard her name wrong? Maybe …" I said. I desperately searched my brain, completely stumped as to how I could answer Rhiannon's question …

"Brucie, if you keep biting your nails like that, a finger will grow in your stomach," said Duncan.

Suddenly, much to my relief, someone called out, "Look at the sky!"

Above us we could see green shafts of light, slowly moving and changing from arches to swirling waves.

"Cool, an aurora borealis!" said Rhiannon. "I wonder how that happens?"

"It's a solar storm," said Donald, and he continued, "a collision of charged particles from in the magnetosphere with atoms in the Earth's upper atmosphere. How cool!"

"Hey! There goes a shooting star," said a voice from the crowd. "Make a wish, everyone."

I wished very hard but God wasn't listening, because immediately after I opened my eyes Donald said, "We have to leave soon."

*Stay, Donald. Please stay until I know you're going to be safe.*

My wishing fingers crossed behind my back, and I quickly scanned the sky for more shooting stars.

None.

He continued, "Dad has put Duncan in charge of ringing the church bell at midnight. The other problem is that our granny from Lewis, who is staying with us, has suddenly gone dotty in the head. She wanders the garden in her nightclothes, looking for the out-house. We told her that the bathroom is indoors but as soon as we repeat this she forgets again. Our mother caught Granny peeing in the corner of the potting shed yesterday."

Another sheet of green light rippled across the sky like tumbling dominos. My body felt as if it swayed with the changing shades and patterns of light. I thought of the sea, deep murky green water, sinking, my body felt heavy, and I heard Donald's voice in my head again.

*Why didn't you save me, Brucie? Why didn't you use your stone? You could have foreseen this?*

The sky softly crackled and hissed, as green hues swept overhead. Simultaneously, with a shiver, I felt the imminence of the next sentence. My heart stopped.

"When Granny returns to Stornoway, after the holidays, my parents want me and Duncan to travel back on the ferry with her. They're concerned that she might fall overboard or something. Our mother is trying to get Gran to stay a bit longer, but she's adamant she wants to go back home. I am on the midnight watch tonight at the potting shed, so we'd better leave now."

I panicked, "Yes, you must get her to stay with you. Don't let her go back on the ferry."

"Well, eventually she will have to go home, Brucie, and we'll travel back with her, but we'll keep her as long as she will stay. In Lewis, my aunt keeps a good watch over her, but she can't come and get Granny on account of her twelve cats," he said.

*Yes, she can! Make your aunt come and get her. Don't go on that ferry Donald! 123+4 is... oh, I can't think, -5, eh, +67, and what is next, oh yes -89 = 100.*

"I did it!" I blurted.

"What did you do?" said Donald, frowning. "I don't understand"

"Mental arithmetic," I said, proudly.

His confusion turned to a smile. "You mean solutions for ascending sequences adding up to one hundred?"

*Run, Brucie. Run away.* I thought. *You're making a fool of yourself.*

"Yes," I replied.

He checked to his left and to his right and then leaned toward me, whispering close to my face, "Did you see a ghost? Is that why you are adding in your head?" His breath warmed my cheek. *What a fabulous smell! He's been eating tangerines.*

"Not really. It's something else that I saw," I said.

*Dadgum it! Don't tell him about the dream, Brucie! Not until you are sure of your facts.*

"Maybe it's the Northern Lights," he said. "They scare some folk you know. Some people say they are really ghostly riders romping across the sky and. . . ."

I missed the rest of his sentence. My mind flipped back to the vision of him drowning, his gaping mouth screaming at me to help.

"Really?" I gulped. Pealing my eyes away from his face, I focused back on the sky.

The bright green faded. Around us, the charcoal night settled in and stars shone visible once again. There are so many more stars to be seen in Scotland, compared to Texas. The Plough sat up high to my right. I could see the Seven Sisters, too.

*One day I'll buy myself a night vision red flashlight, a telescope and a star map. I'll invite Donald to come stargazing with me. We'll lie out on a blanket and ... but what if I never get the chance? What if he drowns first?*

I hadn't noticed the band playing on the trailer, until a short man with a big moustache commandeered the microphone to make an announcement.

"We have only fifteen minutes to go now until the midnight bells sound throughout the village, so don't wander away. I have a request for a song called..." and the chatter fed back into the night. Duncan rushed to leave, so I walked with Donald.

"When are you planning to take the trip to Lewis on the ferry?" I asked.

*Maybe if I knew the date of the trip I could work out what to do, sit and think about it.*

"Not sure exactly, Brucie.... Around the end of the month, I think. I'll let you know," he said. "Why?"

*Think of something, quickly... something connected to the Isle of Lewis.*

Coinneach appeared in my head. *Ask him will he be going to visit the Callanish Stone Circles?*

"Because I wondered if you'd be visiting the Callanish Stone Circle," I said.

Donald seemed impressed. "How do you know so much about Lewis and the stone circles?"

I don't remember answering his question and I don't remember leaving him behind at his gate.

*That gives me only a few weeks... I really need your help, Coinneach.*

I waited but Coinneach didn't show again.

*Okay, why do you keep appearing and disappearing, since my stone was stolen, Coinneach? Why did you come to me in the first place? I'm ready to know now, so please tell me. I'll listen. I promise. The stone was important, wasn't it?*

No answer.

*I need to get it back, don't I?*

No reply.

*But, I don't understand... if the stone gives me prophesying powers... and if I don't have the stone... then why am I having these vivid dreams. Maybe I dreamed a regular dream. Everyone has bad dreams now and then, right? PLEASE speak to me Coinneach.*

Zilch!

I'd reached home, but I wasn't ready to go inside.

I peeked in the window. Gramps entertained a couple of his old friends. Together, Mom called them *The Three Monkeys*. Gramps speaks no evil. Finlay MacAngus is half blind and Donnie the Post is as deaf as a ... *Ah!* A thought dawned. *Up until now, I simply assumed that Donnie used to be a Postman!*

Leaning against the wall of the house, I noticed the stars spangling in the sky. I thought of the American flag and tears welled in my eyes.

*I wonder what Dad's doing now? Is little Pike sitting on his knee? I wonder if he's kissing that Michaela right now.*

With a face all wet with tears, I couldn't go inside yet. From the corner of my eye I saw white flags waving to me in the breeze. *Yes.* The Clootie Well tree seemed a good place to hang out.

Standing next to the tree, I looked down over the lights of the village and listened, waiting for Duncan to ring the church bells.

DONG. DONG. DONG. DONG. DONG. DONG. DONG. DONG. DONG. DONG. DONG.

In the gap between the Old Year and the New Year, while waiting for the twelfth chime, a noise distracted me. I turned my head to the right.

The stag stepped out from behind a large, baron oak tree and raised his nose to sniff the air. Raising his chin, he called out into the night, first a high-pitched rasp and then sliding down to a controlled bass-note bellow, which echoed around the hillside and down over the village. Lowering his head, he stood statuesque. His coal black eyes glinted at mine. We stared at each other in silence. I counted twelve points on his regal antlers. The bell rang out twelve times. Twelve words flowed through my mind, bless them: *reflection, connection, power, focus, grace, awareness, balance, truth, endurance, sacrifice, calmness, and gratitude.*

"Why am I hearing these words?" I asked myself

Then I heard the warning again. *Fire is coming! Stay alert!*

He bowed his head, stood majestically tall for a minute, and then disappeared back into clump the oak trees.

Instinctively, I reached for my Eye Stone, but...

The sky lit up with fireworks from the village, gleefully swirling, fanning, bursting ... spraying out waves of sparkling blues, pinks, greens, yellows, glittering gold and silvers.

Bang! Bang! Bang! Bang! Bang!

"Happy New Year," I whispered to the stag. But, he'd gone.

My mobile phone rang out.

"Hello?"

"Where are you, Brucie?" Rhiannon scolded. "I can't find you anywhere in the crowd."

"I'm up here at the Clootie Well," I said, recalling the word 'truth.'

"Where?" She squealed down the mouthpiece. "Brucie! Friends don't do this to each other. You vanished and didn't even say where you were going? One minute we were talking to Kyle and the twins, the next you were gone. If you want to be my friend, you'll have to quit acting so weird."

"I know," I said. "I'm sorry. Mom wanted me home by midnight. I've been distracted lately."

"You can say that again," she said. "But, I have craic for you, Brucie. Bethany MacKinnon is covered in bruises and her face and arms are cut. Frank the Bobby and Dr. MacDougal are here talking to her, but she won't say what happened. Frank has gone looking for her uncle Jake, because Beth says she won't say anything unless he is there. Jake's Land Rover was all bashed up, lying outside the garage. But, someone said that he got the engine going and he was seen driving it up Ardcarron Brae just now. Be careful, Brucie. Go home and lock your door. That man seems to have a strange attraction to you and your mother."

A dreadful thought suddenly registered. *Those loud bangs . . . did they really come from fireworks . . . or . . . were they closer to hand . . . like, coming from. . ?*

Jake's truck blocked the gate entrance to the field. Bits of the front radiator grill hung off and one of the front headlights bashed out.

He staggered toward me, swiped my mobile phone, threw it to the ground and crunched it under his boot. "Don't plead innocence. It wis you, Carrot Curls, wisn't it? You hate Bethany. It wis you that hurt her, weren't it? You an your big Texan mouth, telling her stuff."

### Freshly Roasted.

**Fisher Skeelie greeted the New Year alone.**

**She tucked a white napkin under her pointed chin and licked her lips. Picking up her knife and fork in one hand, she toasted the Moon with a tumbler of rum in the other.**

**"Thanks for my prize," she said, and laughed. "I knew that one day it would be mine."**

**And, then she tucked into a hot plate of roast badger.**

**"Mmmmm," she said, and laughed.**

**As the clock struck midnight, Skeelie reminisced to olden days. Seventy-five years passed by since the last time she saw the prize;**

seventy-five years since Skeelie did the very bad thing; seventy-five years passed by and nobody ever found out.

"Mmmmmm," she said, again, as she chomped down on the roast badger leg.

# Chapter 15

## Destination Nowhere

"January 01 – 11.30 a.m. - Dear Diary, Granddad gave you to me for Xmas. I've never kept a diary before, but I need to talk to someone. Gramps said you'd be good for that.

I wish my first entry here could be about ordinary teenage things, like school, music, clothes, and boys. No such luck, though. Life is too complicated. You see, I'm terrified that Donald Macleod is going to drown, and last night that dirty Jake MacKinnon attacked me! It gets worse. I think I'm losing my best friend, Rhiannon. She hates me speaking psychic babble, but spooky stuff keeps on happening. I'm a Wednesday's child, and man do I have woes!

I'm so confused. Take last night and the twelve bell rings, and the twelve words I heard when I counted the twelve antlers, bless them; reflection, connection, power, focus, grace, awareness, balance, truth, endurance, sacrifice, calmness, and gratitude. What's that all about?

And what's going on with Bethany MacKinnon and her family? First she bullies me; she calls me a witch, steals my stone and gives it to her granny. Then her uncle Jake lunges at me, drunk as a stewed prune, hollering it was me that hurt Bethany… (Are you following all of this?) I hate them all! ~~Yes, even Rhiannon.~~ (Cancel that last comment.)

Jake grabbed me and slobbered his filthy puckered-up lips all over my face. Yuck! He smelled putrid and felt soggy as a chamois leather cloth. I pushed him back hard as I could, and then aimed my shoe at his crotch.

I sure can scream, too, because the whole street came running. More wired than electric fences, Grandpa and his two friends jolted to my rescue. Grandpa launched a rock at Jake and cracked him on the head. When I screamed Jake reared, back rigid as a cobra, ready to strike me . . . but when the rock hit him, Jake's legs folded like a card table and he shut off like a light. I thought Gramps killed him.

Bunty Blackhead ran from next door in her blue bathrobe, wielded a long, brass fire poker. She cracked Jake on the legs and then whipped the belt from her robe to lasso his hands behind his back. Gramps covered his eyes when Bunty's bathrobe opened. Meanwhile, Jake lay prone, tied like a steer.

PC Frank Anderson's tires smoked rubber as he sped up Ardcarron Brae. Steam spewed into the air as his hot engine clashed with the frosty night around."

*Darn it, I'm running out of space on the page.*

I put my pen aside and lay back on the bed to relive my relief when I saw Jake safely handcuffed, inside the Frank's car. Then I laughed, recalling when Gramps took everyone back to our house and made them hot chocolate.

"I didn't hear Brucie scream. Did you?" said Deaf Donnie the Post, blowing on his mug.

"Aye, I heard it but I couldn't find my glasses in time," said Finlay MacAngus.

Grandpa said nothing. He gave me a hug.

"Does anyone know what happened to Beth?" I asked.

Everyone shrugged.

Deaf Donnie said, "She must've been bitten by a snake because Frank told me "he had to take snake venom from her"."

"No, Donnie," Finlay interrupted, "Not snake venom. He said he'd 'take a *state*ment from her'."

"Ah!" said Deaf Donnie, realizing that his ears had let him down again.

I picked up the pen again.

*I'll have to write smaller to finish what I have to say.*

"People are saying that Jake caused Bethany's cuts and bruises but I think it was her who crashed the Land Rover. That's one weird family! Gramps said Jake's in jail for the time being. He said that Bethany is with her Grandma, Fisher Skeelie, until Jake gets out of jail. Methinks that someone in authority should ask more questions about that family, like 'why does a sixteen year-old girl live with her perverted uncle?' I need to ask more questions about that family, too… like, how I'm going to get my stone back from them.

I'll write more tomorrow.

Love Brucie x"

With the little key, I locked my diary and hid it under my pillow.

Zoe pawed at my knee with her leash in her mouth.

"Okay, big girl," I said. "Come on, then. Let's go for a walk."

Zoe and I left via the front door and walked uphill, toward Fisher Skeelie's house. I chose that route to prove that I wasn't frightened of Bethany any more. As I scanned the red roof and grubby whitewashed walls, to my horror, the old crone leaned out of an open window. I waited for the pain in my head but it never came.

Fisher Skeelie's window was large, with a pull-up sash. It quartered into four, square panes of glass and the window sat to the left-hand-side of the brown, front door. With her bare elbows on the stone sills, she cupped her bony hands to support her chin and chuckled when I passed by.

"Coming in for a cuppa tea and a reading with my fancy new stone, young un? Since it's the Sabbath I'll do you a special deal - half price, ten quid. You can take the dog in wiff you. I likes doggies. They're very tasty. Pwahahaha."

Zoe bared her teeth and growled. Skeelie threw her head back, opened her mouth and guffawed.

I searched my memory bank for an insult with which to decline her offer but a car raced around the corner, narrowly missing me, and I had to jump out of the way. A wash of sludgy puddle water sprayed out from the nearside tires. I grabbed Zoe and hugged close to the walls of Skeelie's house, much too near to the old fraud for comfort.

Skeelie's left pupil glazed, smoky grey and drifted upward. The right one homed in on me, black as a crow's beady eye.

*She's like an evil relation of the thin Miss MacGregor*, I thought.

Locking my gaze onto this right eye I felt sick. The color grey swirled around me, accompanied by a horrid smell and scenes of scorched hair and flesh.

*What was that?*

I shivered, backed away. She scraped her scraggy grey hair down to cover her dull eye in a curious way like a nervous thief might stash a stolen egg under a wad of straw.

"Let's go," I said, to Zoe. Further on, I let Zoe off her lead. Zoe's nose plowed through a puddle and then she bounded ahead toward a winter turnip field. For a second, I thought how youthful Zoe looked, perfectly puppyish.

All the way home, I screwed my face up like sucking lemons. I mocked

Skeelie out loud, "Coming in for a cuppa tea and a reading with my fancy new stone, young un?"

*Young un, indeed! I might be young but I ain't green as guacamole. It's not her stone. IT'S MINE! Mind your own biscuit, y'ol' witch!*

Insult after insult raged inside me. How I wished I had thought of saying these things earlier.

*No, of course I don't wan'cher reading,* I thought, *because you smell like you want to be left alone. I'll come in for a reading when there are whales in West Texas. There's too many nooses in your family tree, Lady. You're more crooked than a cowbird... so crooked that you'd meet yourself coming home. You're so crooked that you'd swaller a nail an' sick up a corkscrew, wouldn'tcha, Fisher Skeelie? You'd lie like a tombstone to get your twenty quid out of me, wouldn'tcha?*

On and on, the slurs reeled in my head.

*It's MY Eye Stone, you old barrel of fish hooks! And, I aim to get it back. That'll blow your skirt up. I don't care if it harelips the minister, I ain't fadoodling when I say that you ain't heard the last from me, Fisher Skeelie! I'd sooner pick cockleburs out of a skunk's butt than leave this bed unmade. I don't cotton to thieving, Fisher Skeelie. It's time to circle the wagons 'cause I'm gonna drain your swamp till I find my stone.*

*Oh I do like a woman with passion,* said Coinneach. He sat on the open gate by the Clootie Well field, next to my house, swinging his legs and drumming his fingers on the wood.

"Forget it, Coinneach. You'll never move the gate, no matter how hard you swing your legs," I said, sarcastically. I spied two vigilant ramblers with wooly hats and backpacks, and reverted to the private ranting of my thoughts, rather than speaking aloud.

*What's up, Coinneach? Stuck at College 101 in Paranormal Phenomena? Maybe they don't teach movement of gates until your Poltergeist lecture in the next semester...* I said to him in my head.

*I have no idea what you are talking about,* he said, *but I am smart enough to recognize when you are insulting me,* he snipped. *Your time would be much better spent asking me questions. After all, I have waited for months to give you some answers. I'm very impatient today, due to a large carbuncle on my left foot and because I lent my best hat to a sailor who absconded overnight with my prize Glengarry bonnet on a voyage to France. Now,* he said, *my head is chilled.*

He sighed and stilled his legs. *Well, you said you wanted to ask me questions, so here are your first three answers. Yes, No and Yes.*

Quicker than God could get the news, Coinneach vanished. I rage in a temper.

*I'm sick of you and your cryptic, mystic, twisted, shifty, willow-the-wispy ways. Don't disappear on me! You can't say 'Yes, No and Yes' and then not explain. You can't do that! Coinneach, I am talking to you. Can you do that? Are you going to answer me? Do I have to stand here like a clown trying to figure out what you mean?*

Despite the startled ramblers I called out aloud. "I ASKED, CAN YOU DO THAT? ARE YOU GOING TO ANSWER ME? DO I HAVE TO STAND HERE LIKE A CLOWN TRYING TO FIGURE OUT WHAT YOU MEAN?"

*I already told you the answers to those questions,* he said.

"Excuse me," said one of the ramblers. "Are you okay?"

"Yes, No and Yes," I replied.

I left them shrugging and scratching their heads at the gate, as I walked up toward the Clootie Well. Sitting down on the large bolder by the tree, I leveled with Coinneach.

"Okay, I get it. You are smarter than me. I don't know how come you've figured what I'm going to say next. Who are you?"

*I already told you that my name is Coinneach and I was the son of The Brahan Seer, before they fried his brain in tar.*

"I know but WHAT are you?" I waited for an answer. He hovered there, but this time he chose not to show himself, or speak.

"I know you are there. Coward! Why don't you show yourself?" I asked.

*And how do you know that I am here?* asked Coinneach.

"I simply do." I said. "I know. My eyes are waiting to focus on you," I replied.

*And how do your eyes know what they are about to see?*

"I don't understand. I don't know what I am going to see. I simply know that I should focus on you, and when I do focus… then you appear."

*So why can't you see me now?* he asked.

I tried to focus on him but he remained invisible.

"I don't understand. Are you trying to say it's my fault that I can't see you?"

*Let me put it this way,* he said. *If I were Zoe and you wanted me to appear then what would you do to see me?* he asked.

I'd completely forgotten about Zoe. I held an empty leash in my hand, one without a dog on the end. "ZOE!" I called.

*Zoe is safe. She went home. Look! See her at the window of your bedroom? Now I'll ask again, if I was Zoe and you wanted me to appear then what would you do to see me?*

Indeed, I could see Zoe at the window.

"But it is different with anything else. Zoe REALLY is at the window. Everyone can see her there. I can't make her materialize out of thin air. It's different with you. When I see you here I know that you are invisible to everyone else." I said to Coinneach.

*Then how can you see me? Why do you see me and others don't see me?*

"Hey! I thought that I asked the questions?" He fell quiet again. "I swear, Coinneach, that you are one of the most frustrating people on this earth."

*Au contraire, it is you that frustrates yourself.*

"I DON'T UNDERSTAND!" I screamed. "Why are you teasing me?"

*I'm trying to tell you that it is you who has the control over me and not the other way around.*

"That's crap! I have no control over you. You turn up whenever you want to turn up."

*That is only because you haven't learned control yet.*

"Control of WHAT?" I screamed with frustration. "And why can I still hear you when I no longer have the stone?" My tongue got so caught in my eyeteeth that I couldn't see what I was saying.

*You answered your own question there.*

Clarity suddenly dawned. "You mean I've already been given the gift of second sight. That is why I can hear you, but I needed the stone in order to learn control of that gift?"

*At last! It took some time for you to figure that one out, didn't it?*

"Okay, but why you...? Why are you here?" I asked.

*You're young and your gift could turn you into a psychological mess without guidance. So, my father entrusted me with the job of being your spirit guide, Brucie.*

"Spirit guide! That's rich. My spirit guide is a tramp?"

He fell silent again. Insulted, no doubt.

I thought for a minute and asked, "Wait. Why didn't your father act as my spirit guide, instead of you? After all, it's his Eye Stone, isn't it?"

Coinneach muttered something about his father having brain damage, due to boiling tar.

"Hello?  Earth to Coinneach, come in Coinneach?  Am I getting a signal or is there no network again today?"

I waited but he vanished, so I continued to speak, regardless.

"So, if you are my guide, why are you not guiding?  You're leaving me to ask all the questions here.  Hello?  Coinneach, I swear your phone is clean off the hook."

*I DO need to get my stone back, don't I?  If not...*  I mulled over the consequences.  *If not, I might be stuck forever in limbo; unable to control this weird gift I've been given.*

I left the 'bless them' field and walked toward home.

*Guides are supposed to lead the way, aren't they?*

I didn't expect him to answer.

Surprisingly, he did.

*First, before I can be your guide, you must be able to tell me your destination.*

And, with those last words of the day, Coinneach fell silent.  I punched the air around me with my fist.  "Come back here and tell me what you mean?"

Gramps watched my air-sparring from the open front door.

"Come in about the house, lass.  You look frozen," said Gramps.


Gramps and I sat by the fireside, and he offered me a plate of some sort of dark cake.  "Want some of my clootie dumpling?"

"What's a clootie dumpling?"  I asked, suspiciously eyeing the black-spotted lump of brown dough.  "Is it something that you fished out of the Clootie Well?"

"Ha!"  He laughed.  "I never thought about that.  No.  There is no connection to Clootie Wells.  A clootie dumpling is a traditional New Year food.  It's a spiced fruit pudding that is boiled in a cloth – a cloot."

"Sounds ugly," I said.  "Isn't the cloth a bit chewy?"

"Brucie, don't be such a facetious brat!"  Mom glowered over the top of her reading glasses, and then turned her pen to the next clue on her crossword puzzle.

"Why am I a brat?  What did I say?  I only asked..." I shouted at Mom, tears breaking into my eyes.  "Anyway, I didn't speak to you, Mom, I spoke to Grandpa, so there's no need for you to be so nasty."

My head choked with conflicting emotions. My memory bank flashed full; chockfull of Jake MacKinnon, Bethany MacKinnon, stags, Rhiannon, Donald, my stone, Fisher Skeelie, orbs, and Coinneach. All of that, and I still tried to find my own identity, too! The complexity of clootie dumpling seemed the last straw and I found myself sobbing into Grandpa's shirt collar. He, in turn, stroked my hair.

Mom stormed out of the room, "Oh, stop babying her, Dad," and she left muttering something about wishing she'd left me with Dad and Michaela Marie McGraw.

"Poor Lassie," Grandpa said to me. "Your mother is upset since the last phone call from your father. She doesn't mean to hurt you." Then he said, "Why didn't you stay and speak to your dad when he called?"

"Because, Mom and Dad argued again, Gramps. When they do that I lose my way. Everything falls to pieces inside me. I don't know what to do. Where am I going to, Gramps?" I asked. "How can someone find out what their destination is?"

He looked at me with a wrinkled brow. "I'm not sure I understand your question."

I tried to explain. "Imagine that you are a guide and you want to take me somewhere, okay?"

He nodded and I continued.

"Well, a guide can only lead you, if they know where you want to go. How can people guide me when I don't know where I am going? I'm totally lost."

Gramps thought for a minute.

"First, you need to tell me what is important to you, Brucie. What do you believe in? What gives you passion, makes you want to fight, and puts the sparkle in those pretty eyes of yours?"

"I don't know, Gramps." I said. "What has that got to do with deciding a destination?"

"Never you mind, lass," he said, "You're tired. Don't worry about these things for now."

With a yawn, I excused myself from the room, whispering to Grandpa, "It's Mom. She tires me out sometimes. I think I'll go lie on my bed and read a book."

"Good idea," he said, with a smile, "and I'll have a quick nap here by the fire."

I picked up the book about The Brahan Seer. Sitting on my bed, I read on from the last bookmarked page but I grew sleepy. I nearly shut the book, when this caught my eye.

The Isle of Lewis will sink without trace. That's all. No more information about the prediction, only that the Isle of Lewis will sink without trace.

"OH MY GOD!"

### Let me out!

Jake battered on the inside of the thick jail door.

"Get me out of here now before someone else gets a fat lip!"

"Calm down Jake," said Frank. "I told you, you'll probably get bail after you've appeared in court on Monday. There's nothing anyone can do until then."

Jake spat at him. "Then next time you see me in here, it'll be for murder."

Frank wiped the spit off his cheek, with a cloth handkerchief.

"You're not doing yourself any favors, Jake. Quiet down in there."

"Let me out! Let me out! Let me out!" he called.

# Chapter 16

## Storm in a Tea Cup

The house phone rang.

"Hello?" I grunted.

"Hi. Brucie? It's Donald here. Can I ask you a big favor? I need to speak to you in person."

"Yes, of course. And, I really need to speak to you, too." I trembled.

We agreed to meet at his house so I left immediately, running all the way down Ardcarron Brae, and right to his door. I rang the bell, half expecting to see the woman in the shawl. No sign of her, though. Donald came to greet me.

"Happy New Year," he said, and quicker than a knee jerk he moved forward to kiss me. His puckered lips took me completely by surprise, though. I moved awkwardly toward him, over-compensated with my feet, and my mouth landed on his left earlobe.

"Oh well, Happy New Ear," I said, like a dork with flushed cheeks.

He laughed, thankfully.

"What's the favor, Donald? How can I help?" I said.

*Will I tell him about the dream now?*

"Thanks for coming here so quickly. I wanted to show you something."

Guiding my arm, he led me upstairs into John Alexander's bedroom. I had no idea why I stood there. John Alexander, wearing a pair of Spiderman pajamas, sat on a single bed by the window, on top of a . . . red . . . shawl. He sat beside the ghost looking miserable. I looked at John Alexander, the ghost, and then at Donald.

"What is going on, Donald?" I asked.

"What do you see, Brucie?" asked Donald.

I wanted to lie, crack a joke to ease the shock.

*. . . focus, grace, awareness, balance, truth . . .*

"Quickly, Brucie. What can you see?" he said again.

"I see John Alexander sitting next to a woman and she is telling him to get a grown up to find her baby for her."

"Hells Bells, Brucie!" exclaimed Donald. "I can't see her. I thought that John Alexander invented these stories.

"Boocie, if you find the lady's baby, will she go away?" He started to cry. "I don't like the lady because she shouts."

I crouched down to talk to the boy. "It's okay, John Alexander." His little eyes welled with water. "If you go out of the room with Donald, I'll talk to the lady about her baby and then everything will be fixed. She won't bother you again."

He nodded and took Donald's hand. When the two left the room, I squared up to the fight.

"Look here Lady. Listen to me. Quit talking to that kid. Ya hear me?" But, she kept flashing in and out of sight.

*Darn, I wish I had my stone and I knew how to use it.*

I continued, regardless. "The boy is scared as rain barrels. Speak to me if you want something, but I warn you, Lady . . ." I trembled, "I'm stubborn as a splinter and no one will look for your baby unless you leave John Alexander alone. Now move outta the kid's bed and GIT!"

I waited a few minutes, both to calm my nerves and to check if she'd gone, before fetching John Alexander. All I could do though was hope for the best.

"Come on in, John Alexander."

He edged his way gingerly back into the room, looking all about to see if the woman had gone. I crouched down to his level and spoke softly.

"I spoke to the lady and told her to leave you alone," I told him. His big eyes, opened like giant search lights, screening all four corners of the room.

"But will you find her baby, Boocie?" he asked, sweetly. His little finger twisted and glistened inside his wet mouth, eyes still as large as twin moons.

"Yes," I said, "but not tonight."

"Wow!" said Donald. He stood behind John Alexander, holding on to the boy's shoulders, protectively. "I'm sorry to involve you, Brucie, but John Alexander looked so upset and I couldn't tell Dad about this. I thought we could deal with the problem ourselves, quietly. Do you understand?"

"Of course," I said, passionately. The only stronger passion I felt at that moment was a pressing need to tell Donald my fears about the ferry. I nearly told him. I came SO close. The time seemed so right, but then something caught my eye. Outside in the dark, toward the rear of the minister's garden, something triggered the sensor on the outside security light. A deer stepped out of the woods and peered up at me through a gap in the hedge. I saw the glint of its eyes.

*Reflection. Focus. Awareness. Calmness,* I thought. *Donald doesn't need to know yet. But, why not? Why am I changing my mind?*

"I have to go now, Donald."

"Yes. Of course. It's late. And, thanks," he said, and then paused. "Aw, Brucie. I'm sorry. I completely forgot to ask if you were okay after your encounter with Jake. Did he hurt you?"

"Na. He's a jerk. I'm not scared of him." I lied.

Donald smiled. "Brucie Bice," he said, "you're so different."

*I'm different! Yeah!*

"Oh yes, and what did you want to tell me?" he asked.

"Nothing much. It will keep for another day," I said, while definitely feeling different.

My spirits rose like a corncob in a cistern. All the way up Ardcarron Brae I grinned.

When I reached home, Gramps commented on my lighter mood.

"Tea?" he offered.

"Go on then, a small cup," I said, watching him scald the teapot and drop in two measured spoons of loose tea.

I sat down at the table. Mom's blue coat hung on the back of my chair. Waiting for the brew, I tucked my hands into her coat pockets and felt around with my eyes shut, trying to guess the contents, *a fifty pence piece, a pen, an elastic hair band, a dog biscuit, a dog's nose...*

"Okay, Zoe, you can have the biscuit," I said.

Zoe crunched the treat and then licked her lips, as I continued to rummage in Mom's pockets.

*...and this must be a small business card methinks.*

I removed the card to study it.

*Well cut off my legs and call me Shorty!* I thought, reading the print. *What is she doing with this?*

"Gypsy Palm Readings - Cross my palm with silver - Minimum Donation Twenty Pounds. Telephone - Ardcarron 276341."

Written on the reverse, in Mom's handwriting -- *January 6th – 2:30pm.*

"What's that you have there?" asked Gramps, handing me a mug of steaming tea.

"Some of Mom's pocket junk," I said, acting out a blasé tone. I slipped the card into my own back pocket and sipped my tea until I reached the dregs at the bottom of the cup. My eyes gazed down into the leafy patterns left by the tea.

"The proper name for it is tasseography," said Granddad.

"It's the proper name for what?" I felt confused.

"Tea leaf reading; it's called tasseography. So, tell me…what do you see in the cup?" he asked, leaning toward me.

"Hmm! I see a shape like a horse." The horse came alive in the bottom of the mug. I felt a warm glow. "And, I see an arch next to it." The arch seemed significant to the horse. The two seemed connected. I turned the mug around to see it from the other side. "A coffin shape, too." The coffin scared me. I paused, put the mug on the table again.

"What does it mean?" I asked. Gramps appeared to have knowledge he wanted to share.

"The horse is usually a soul mate and the arch signifies travel overseas," he said. "Do you know someone close to your heart, someone who will soon travel overseas?"

I gave nothing away.

With every ounce of my being I yearned to ask Gramps about the coffin shape, but I lost my nerve.

*Travel overseas and a coffin… Does this mean that …?*

## She's Back!

On the first working day after the New Year, a spectacled social worker stood by the open door of her car, a small white Fiat. She wore a bright red duffle coat to match the frames of her glasses. Slipping her feet into a pair of Wellington boots, she tossed her driving shoes to the back seat and locked the driver's door.

An over-sized bag held her laptop and she clutched a folder full of printed documents to her chest, like a shield.

She crossed the road to the whitewashed cottage with the red corrugated roof and knocked on the door.

The curtain twitched at the top window, the window to the left of the brown front door. The social worker waited but no one answered the door. She tried turning the handle but the door was locked.

She wrote a note, inserted the note into an envelope, and posted the envelope into the letterbox.

Inside, Bethany MacKinnon caught the envelope before it hit the ground. She opened it quickly and read the note.

Bethany laughed and took the note to the sitting room hearth, to burn it in the fire.

"She can forget it. No way am I meeting with her."

# Chapter 17

## Phantom Power at Zero Miles Per Hour

January 3rd felt unseasonably warm. Perhaps nervousness made me sweat. With Mom safely out of earshot, I called the number on the business card. I waited as the phone rang out, biting my nails to the quick.

"Come on," I muttered. "Why don't you answer?"

Back straight, tummy tucked in, I stood taller in a bid to sound more grown up and to disguise the crooked lie that I prepared to tell.

Eventually, a croaky voice answered, "Hello?"

"Hello. My name is Fiona Bice... We spoke earlier about an appointment on January 6th? At 2:30 p.m., I believe?"

My heart pounded when she said, "Yes."

"You see, I've realized that I have another appointment that day, so I want to cancel..." I paused and waited for Skeelie to say something. She kept silent, though.

*Is she buying this?*

"Hello?" I said. "Did you hear me?"

"Yes, I heard you, Mrs. Bice," she said, "as, I told you before, though, there will be a ten pound fee for short notice cancellations."

*Short notice? Cancellation fee?*

I didn't have ten pounds so I stalled for time, while I thought.

*How can I stop Mom from seeing this evil woman? Is Mom looking for advice about Dad, or even Jake? I don't want that old jailbird knowing any of our family business.*

My plan was simple; cancel the appointment. Later, I'd tell Mom that it was *Skeelie* who phoned to cancel. That would give me enough time to persuade Mom not to reschedule.

*What am I going to do now? Quick, Brucie, THINK FAST!*

I found myself saying, "No problem. I'll send someone else in my place, so you won't need a cancellation fee."

"And who would that be?" Skeelie asked.

*Shoot my hound dog! Who am I going to send in Mom's place? I can't say my name, and Rhiannon wouldn't go. The twins are out, as their dad would throw a hissy fit...*

"His name is Kyle MacKay." The words blurted out before I could stop myself. "There are orbs floating around his head."

"January 3rd - Dear Diary, What on earth am I going to do? How do I tell Kyle?

12-3-4+5-6+7+89 = 100.

I've only made matters worse. Now I will have to find twenty pounds for Kyle, to pay for the reading. And, how can I convince Kyle to go and see Skeelie? He freaked when I said that a dead person followed him. I didn't even get to explain about the picture with the orbs above his head. Why can't I mind my own business, Diary?"

I lay awake for most of that night, listening to Gaelic language on the radio, hoping the foreign garble would induce sleep. It didn't.

At sunrise, which dawned at exactly 08:06, I snatched Zoe from her doggie dreams and led her quietly down the hall to the kitchen.

"Want to walk, Zoe?" I whispered.

She wagged her tail and pawed the back door, while I grabbed my new camera from the table.

I also stopped to write a note. "Mom. A lady called to cancel your appointment for Friday 6th at 2:30 pm. She said she is sorry but she can't give you a replacement appointment. Brucie. x"

At the far side of the village, Zoe and I cut behind the Free Church. A path wound uphill, heading northeast.

Zoe stopped at the top of the hill, cocked her head to one side and barked at me. As there were no signs of sheep in the surrounding fields, I unclipped her leash.

"Go on then, Zoe. Go play with the rabbits."

She bounded off to the right and disappeared behind a clump of jagged whin bushes.

Looking back down toward the village, I stood directly uphill from Kyle's house. His curtains were open, unlike those of his sleeping neighbors.

*Should I go down and knock at his door? What would I say? He'll freak if I tell him about the appointment with Skeelie.*

Zoe yowled and yapped in the bushes.

"What is it?" I shouted. "Where are you, silly dog?"

I called out, but she didn't appear. "Oh, don't make me come and find you, Zoe. I'm not in the mood today."

Zoe woofed, but still I couldn't see her. Her frantic barking then echoed from the direction of an old, abandoned croft house.

"Okay, Zoe, I'm coming."

The old ruin looked awesome in the golden winter sunlight, a very picturesque find. I snapped a photo. Its glowing sandstone walls partially fell to rubble; only three walls remained. A rusty, corrugated tin roof had long since tumbled inward and lay semi buried amid boulders inside, which I gingerly clambered over. Zoe wasn't there but I scouted around inside, regardless.

Peering out of the old windows, I raved at the awesome view and took some more shots. The rough lintels and sills framed a backdrop of bright blue sky, and distant, green, rolling countryside in front of majestic, snow-topped hills.

*Wow! What great photos!*

Abandoned farm machinery lay strewn around the front of the croft house; the tireless wheels, rusty vessels and old bottles spoke volumes about the croft's history. I took lots of photos.

*Who lived here?*

I closed my eyes and visualized an old woman, dressed in drab tweeds. Her back hunched forward and she limped, leaning on a stick. Hard facial lines, which engrained into her brow, told of worry, the loss of a husband, perhaps? Without his strength, she struggled to manage the croft house chores.

I sighed, opened my eyes and snapped a few last shots until I heard Zoe bark again.

To the rear of the croft house, I discovered an old derelict bus without tires. A crooked, bare branch hanging down from a neighboring tree scratched across the roof of its hollow, metal frame, sounding like chalk against a blackboard. The bus creaked in the breeze, calling out eerily for closer investigation.

Gingerly, I positioned my boot onto the first step of the bus and pulled myself up. Holding on to the doorframe, I peeked inside. Rows of seats sat moldy but still intact. Most of the floor had sunk to the earth and long strands of grass and thistles grew up into the spaces in the aisle. The driver's seat, though damaged, appeared in reasonable condition. I sat myself down and held onto the steering wheel. However, the minute my butt hit the chair the weirdest thing happened; the sound of an engine started to drone in my head.

*But this contraption has no floor, no tires, no wiper blades, no windows, and no door and so, for sure, it has no engine,* I thought. Yet, I could hear the low growl of an engine, ticking over smoothly at low revs.

Behind me, I sensed a congestion of . . . passengers. I felt their fullness, like we were all sardines packed into the same tin. I heard them chattering, like drones of worker bees. The bus was empty, yet I could *feel* that I had company, by the vibration of their emotions. Immediately over my left shoulder, in total silence, I felt the emotion of heartache sat next to heartache. Behind that seat I felt the pull of addictions. They sat perched in front of suspicion, whose seat backed onto innocence. To the right I felt a perilous pride sit next to confusion and farther back sat aggravation, hopefulness and determination. Spread across the very back seat... an array of playfulness that jiggled and teased. Together, the intensity of all these conflicting emotions overwhelmed me. I needed out of there, so I rose from the seat to jump clear of the bus.

Clutching the sides of my head, my brain screamed at the inside of my ears. "Ouch!" I cried. "My thoughts are going to burst. No more! Go away! Please, all of you, I feel out of control here."

*I need my stone back!*

As I dove clear, away from the bus, I expected to belly flop to the ground. To my horror, though, I found myself spread-eagled on top of Kyle MacKay. He lay there gawking up at me.

Kyle wore the same expression as a dim-witted peach seller that I used to see by Interstate 45 in Texas. I'd see him each summer, eating his own peaches to survive dehydration. The traffic on 45 moved far too fast for anyone to stop for peaches, yet the peach seller never gave up hope.

"Brucie! Why are you talking about peaches, like?" Kyle asked. He grinned beneath me now, apparently enjoying his role as my mattress.

I snapped from memories and scrambled to my feet, flustered. "Sorry. I didn't see you there," I said. "Was I talking out loud?"

We both talked at once, though, so I didn't hear his explanation as to why he'd stood there watching me. Zoe still barked up a storm, too, competing with Kyle, who twittered on.

"Didn't you hear me calling you, as you climbed the hill behind my house?" he asked. And, he added something about a family of wildcats inside the building behind the old croft house . . .

Too late!

A loud hiss preceded a yowl, followed by another hiss and a yelp, and Zoe shot out from behind a dyke, bounding toward me with her tail between her legs.

"Anyway," said Kyle reaching out to inspect Zoe's bloody nose, "Before the stuff about peaches, like, who were you telling to go away?"

*Oh, no . . . the people on the bus. He heard me talking to them, too?*

Zoe hugged in by my side. Her nose looked scratched, nothing serious. Mostly, her pride hurt.

I suddenly remembered to check the top of Kyle's head.

*Not a single orb in sight.*

"Brucie! I asked you a question."

"Ah, yes . . . about the bus. Who did I tell to go away?" I had to think how to tell him.

"Hmm. Well, you see . . . there were people on the bus, Kyle. I couldn't see them but I could feel all of their emotions very strongly. Too strongly, actually, and that's why I jumped off."

Kyle cautiously squinted toward the bus, shivered, and shook his head.

"Och, I don't understand," he said, and quickly changed the topic. "I talked to Donald today and he said that you went to see him, like . . ." Kyle paused before continuing, "he told me your visit had something to do with John Alexander, but he wouldn't say more, like."

"Oh, it was nothing." I kept schtum, as Gramps would say.

*Maybe looking for orbs is like trying to see an image within one of those three dimensional Magic Eye pictures.*

I practiced screwing up my eyes and then widened them again, and then relaxing my pupils as I looked above Kyle's head.

"Eek, Brucie, quit looking at me like that. It's weird, like." Kyle stepped back a pace. "And, please don't say there are dead people following me again." Kyle jittered and swiped at the air, as if stalked by an invisible wasp.

I pulled the camera from my pocket.

*I'd better show him the orbs.*

"No, I don't see dead people following you, but I have a photo here that I want you to see." I fumbled with the camera, flicking through the memory. "Look," I said, "I snapped this shot on Christmas Day, when you came to see me." I turned the camera round so he could see the screen.

"A photo of me, like?" he asked. Kyle wrinkled his nose, puzzled.

"Here, look closer." I zoomed in.

Kyle studied the image. "Very handsome; you definitely captured my good side, like."

"Yes, but do you see anything else in the picture?" I asked.

"Like what?" He asked, "A plate, a wall, a bit of my hand holding a fork? What?"

I pointed at the area above his head. "This is what I am talking about." I drew is attention to the transparent circles, laced with mauve patterns.

"What is that, like?" he asked.

"Orbs," I said, "Spirits."

He looked blank at first, then his face grew paler and he swallowed. "You mean ghosts ARE following me?"

Kyle suddenly spun around. He stepped back and looked up into the space above where his head had been. "Can you see anything there now?" Kyle hopped about like he'd scorched his feet. "Where are they?" He panicked. "Is something following me?"

"No. Honestly, I don't see anything," I said, and touched his arm for reassurance.

"Take a picture of me, then. So I can see for myself that they've gone, like. Go on, Brucie. Hurry."

I snapped a shot of him standing next to the window of the croft house.

"Look. Nothing there . . . okay?" I showed him the proof. "No orbs."

Kyle snatched the camera from my hand and switched back to the photo of the orbs. He studied the photo for ages, zooming in, zooming out, zooming in and zooming out.

I used the space within Kyle's silence to think.

*Should I tell him about his appointment with Fisher Skeelie?*

"Kyle, I have done a dumb thing and I am going to need your help." *Here goes!* I took a deep breath. "Only, once I tell you what I have done, I fear you're going to kick my butt and not speak to me again, far less help me to raise twenty pounds by Friday."

"What?" He handed back the camera. "Why do you need twenty quid by Friday?" He patted his pockets. "I'm skint, like."

"Because..."

Suddenly, all of the conflicting emotions from the bus, calmed to a baited hush. I still couldn't see the passengers, but I knew that they listened; hands clasped on knees, heads facing Kyle and me. All of the heartache, suspicion, innocence, pride, confusion, aggravation, hopefulness, determination, playfulness and teasing suddenly switched to a unanimous curiosity. I really felt their inquisitiveness.

*Calm, Brucie,* I spoke to my brain.

"Because why, Brucie? You're dreaming again," said Kyle.

I sat down on a large boulder, inviting Kyle to join me. My back leaned against the old bus. He hesitated with his hands pushed down firmly into his trouser pockets, but eventually he accepted my invitation and shuffled his butt onto the rock beside me.

As I thought about where to begin, I felt the vibration of an engine accompany me. When I struggled for words the engine dropped a gear, providing extra revs to push me onward and upward. When an idea flowed, the bus cruised alongside, steadily, effortlessly, like the bus was being steered by a skilled driver, someone who steered me forward.

"Can I speak frankly to you 'bout something personal, Kyle?" I asked.

"Okay," he said, "as long as it has nothing to do with girl's menstrual cycles, like. That stuff really freaks me out, you know what I mean?" He laughed.

"No. Nothing as gruesome as periods, I promise." I breathed out heavily.

"I know your situation is a bit different from mine but . . . how old were you when your dad died, Kyle?"

"I was twelve." His cheeks flushed pink. "Brucie, what has this got to do with the awful thing that you did?" he asked, changing the subject.

Kyle rose and walked a few paces ahead, changed direction and then shot a distrustful glance back toward me. He stared straight into my brain.

I had to think carefully. *How can I explain myself better?*

"I just wondered if your Mom changed when you lost your father. You see, my Mom has turned weird since she and Dad split." I felt sad. "She used to be so energetic, teaching me interesting stuff; we'd have such crazy laughs together. But, now she sits indoors drinking bitter, black coffee and smoking endless cigarettes." I felt a tear in my eye and wiped it away quickly. "Her doctor prescribed antidepressants. They helped a bit but she's lost in a cloud of negativity." I stopped sniffing and stared ahead. "She's not living her life any more, not really, not if you knew how she used to be." I searched into his face, hoping he would help me.

He broke his silence.

Finally, Kyle began to share. "I kind of know what you mean," he said. "I think my Mom took sick, too, like. She doesn't keep well, though."

"But Kyle, my Mom dated Jake MacKinnon! How sick is that?"

"Yep, right enough," His eyebrows rose. "That's bad, like," he muttered, shaking his head.

The bus engine stalled to a halt.

"But, I swear she isn't seeing Jake any more, Kyle." I wished I hadn't mentioned creepy Jake. This all proved harder to speak about than I had first realized.

Kyle shrugged, without agreeing or disagreeing.

I reminded Kyle, "Jake's in jail now."

"No, he's not, actually. Jake is out of The Nick. He got bail. Frank only charged Jake for being drunk and disorderly and for breach of the peace."

"But, he threatened me and I'm a minor!" I said, indignantly, standing up. "He scared the be-jeepers out of me! He should be in jail!"

"Yes, but your Grandpa cracked his scull with a rock, like," said Kyle. "Think about it, Brucie. What if Jake pressed charges for assault against your Grandpa and Bunty Blackhead? Your Grandpa caused the only injury that night. Jake has half a dozen stitches in his head, you know?"

"But, that's not fair!" I screamed and whacked the bus with my fist. The engine sparked to life then stalled again.

Kyle said, "Look. Jake won't touch you again, Brucie." He paused. "I won't let him." Kyle flexed his muscles and then, blushing with red cheeks, he asked again, "Now PLEASE…what is the awful thing that you wanted to tell me? What have you done?"

*Man, this explanation gets tougher by the minute.*

"I need to ask you a question first," I said. "Jake is a nephew of Fisher Skeelie, isn't he?"

As Kyle nodded, I said, "Remember my stone?"

Chug! Chug! The bus engine spluttered.

"Aye. I remember. After the dance you said that Bethany MacKinnon and her mates stole it. Didn't they give it to Fisher Skeelie, like?"

"Yes. She's using it, posing as some sort of phony seer, giving readings at twenty quid a shot," I said.

Suddenly, Kyle raised his voice.

"Brucie!" he shouted. "Will you get to the point and tell me what have you done?"

"Okay," I said, nervously. "My mother arranged an appointment for a reading with Fisher Skeelie, Kyle," I said.

"So?" he asked.

Chug! Chug!

"So, she obviously wanted Skeelie to tell her things about her future, things about my dad, and things about Jake, and…"

"Wait. Wait. Wait. How do you know that she wants to discuss this?"

"I don't know," I answered. "But, I can't take the chance. I don't want that old hag anywhere near my Mom, telling her lies." I began to cry. "What if Skeelie tells Mom to forget my Dad and move on? What if she tries to get Mom to see her nephew, Jake, again? What if …"

Chug! Chug!

"I'm beginning to get the picture now," he said. "You want me to talk to your mother, don't you?"

"Not exactly, but you are close," I said.

"Then what, Brucie? Come on. Out with it. What have you done, like?"

"Kyle, I called Skeelie, pretending to be my Mom. I cancelled the appointment but Skeelie said that she'd want a cancellation fee?" I sobbed again. "So, I told her, as Mom of course, that I'd send someone else to the appointment, to avoid having to pay the cancellation fee."

I hung my head, waiting.

"And?" he asked. "So, who is going in place of your Mom?"

The chugging ceased. Silence.

"Ah, well, you see…" I thought, stammered and stuttered.

*How can I tell him when he's glaring at me like that?*

"It… it was … it was the orbs … that gave me the, the idea, Kyle, and … and…"

The specter engine coughed into erratic phantom power. Chug! Chug!

Brmmm! It spluttered with me, each of us trying to crank up to life again and restart.

Kyle's eyes open wide, really wide.

"Oh no! Brucie!" he cried out. "No way, like! Not me!" He walked around in circles flapping his arms in the air, "Not me!"

I wiped my eyes.

"But, if you went to see her, Kyle, talked to her about the orbs, then maybe afterward you could steal my stone back. She's bound to use it for your reading and ... I need it back so that ... so that ... I can use it to try and prevent a disaster involving Donald ..."

"Donald?" he gulped.

"Yes, I had this dream ... this vision ... whatever, I don't know which, but I saw Donald drown."

"What?!" Kyle's face baked white as bleached flour.

I grew desperate and raised my voice. "Kyle, I think that the ferry to the islands, the Hebrides, is going to sink with Donald onboard and I need the stone to try and use it to see into Donald's future, so please help me get the stone back ... Will you, please?"

He shouted this time. "Brucie! What's going on? Are you off your head, like? I can't steal!"

A loud choking cough blasted from the bus engine, and a cloud of blue smoke blew from the rear.

"What the...?" Kyle gawked at the bus in disbelief. "Did you see that?" He pointed. "Smoke!" He smelled the air. "Phew! What's happening, Brucie, like?"

When the smoke cleared I saw the culprit.

*This is a fabulous contraption,* said Coinneach. *You call it a "bus," don't you?*

"I might have known that you had something to do with this." I shouted at him, "Quit the smoke effects. You're scaring my friend, Kyle."

Kyle ran behind me. "Who in the hell are you shouting at, Brucie, like?"

"Coinneach, of course,"

"Where?" he asked. Still clutching my arm, Kyle peered into the bus. "I can't see him. Where did he go?"

"Let me ask him, Kyle."

*Where are you?* I demanded. *What are you playing at?*

Coinneach answered. *Tell the boy to stop staring at me. I hate staring. It's very rude,* he said. And then, he twittered on about transportation. *I remember stowing away on a cart full of pigs that left for market one day. Pigs are such lovely animals, very clean and not at all dirty like some people would have it. They make wonderful traveling companions. Pigs don't stare.*

"Well?" asked Kyle, shaking my arm. "What is going on? Is Coinneach there, like? Is HE the orb thing that follows me?"

*Are you, Coinneach… the orb thing in the photograph?* I asked.

*Not guilty,* he said.

"No. Apparently, he doesn't do orbs," I told Kyle, who now looked seven ways to sundown. His feet suddenly magnetized to north, the direction of home, in case he needed a quick get-a-way.

"Come on, Kyle," I said. "Let's go."

As we left I could see Kyle was shaking.

"I'm just cold," he lied.

I said "It's okay to admit that you are scared, Kyle." Then I regretted it.

He threw his arms in the air and shouted angrily. "I'm not scared, right!" He paused, "Look, I'll even go and see Fisher Skeelie; I'll keep this appointment if you want." He kicked a tin can on the road. "But, I don't know about getting your stone back. I'd need to think about that, like." Kyle calmed momentarily and then fidgeted, tightening his belt buckle. "I'm meeting the twins at the Sheddie tomorrow." He hitched up his jeans but they fell back down on his hips. "Why don't you and Rhiannon come along and we can ALL talk about getting your stone back?"

I cheered up. "Can we?"

*Kyle has lost weight.*

"Yeah, I guess," he said. "But . . . I don't have twenty quid to pay Skeelie, so you'll need to work that one out for yourself."

"That's okay, Kyle. Thanks." I gave him an awkward hug.

*Yes, he's definitely thinner.*

"Kyle … I dread telling Rhiannon … she hates me talking about anything weird." I hesitated, picking at my fingernails. The skin chilled from pink to blue on my hands.

*How can I put this?*

"Kyle, there are SO many reasons why I need the stone back."

"More reasons?" he asked, apprehension mounting in his eyes.

Zoe whimpered.

"Yes. I'll tell you more tomorrow," I said. Now was not the time to risk upsetting Kyle again, so I said, "I'm sure you need to go home and eat now."

"Yeah, I'm starving, like," he said, and then paused. "Brucie, maybe we can find you another stone."

"You don't understand, Kyle. That one is special. Without it, I feel like I'm out of control. If I had the stone back I could learn to use it and ..."

"Listen, Brucie." He said. "What is for us won't go by us."

I screwed up my face, puzzled, "What'cha mean?"

"I mean, concentrate on today and leave tomorrow alone. Fate won't pass you by, no matter how many stones you have. Don't start playing with chance, guessing the future and trying to tell people's fortunes," he said. "That sort of stuff should be good for a laugh, like, but it's making you miserable. Why don't you start to be normal?"

"But, my dream... I need to know if it's a warning. I saw Donald... He drowned at sea when a ferry sank." Tears pooled in my eyes again and no matter how much I rolled my eyeballs, or widened my eyes, or blinked, a giant tear spilled over my bottom lashes and trickled down my cheek. "Kyle, I saw him drown."

Kyle stared at me, stony silent.

"Donald gurgled under the water, as his lungs filled up, 'Save me! Save me, Brucie!'" I sniffed and wiped my nose on my sleeve.

"It's probably just a dream, like," he said, and then gulped. Kyle's face grew pale again.

"Kyle ... Donald told me that he's going on the ferry to Lewis soon. I can't ignore this. Maybe my stone will help me see. It's special, with powers that I can tap into, if only I learn how to use it. I want to learn, Kyle."

Kyle shrugged without answering.

I needed to convince him. "Look, I understand what you mean about concentrating on today. I'm not playing games here. This is not about joking around with Ouija boards any more or charging twenty quid to trick folk. This is about my destiny, about seeking out my life direction. The stone is special. It holds a gift, and Fisher Skeelie is using the gift for selfish reasons. I think my destiny is to help others. I want to help Donald," I said. "But don't tell him about this, will you? Not yet."

Kyle didn't answer and didn't promise anything.

Zoe pawed at my leg.

"Wait, Zoe," I said. Zoe sat. "Look, Kyle, I want to help the woman in the wall, too."

"What woman in the wall?" he asked, fidgeting with his belt again.

*He's bored. He doesn't believe me. He thinks I'm nuts.*

"Oh," I hesitated. "Didn't I tell you about her, either?" I said, knowing full well I had not.

I checked my watch, avoiding his question. It said one minute past eleven and I now felt completely and utterly exhausted.

A horn tooted from behind us. Johnny MacKay, the building contractor, passed in his white van. He drove slowly and I could see that he wore the same thin checked shirt again.

*Weird! Why did I get a déjà vu feeling when I saw Johnny MacKay?*

"Brucie?" said Kyle. "I'm talking to you and you're miles away again."

"Sorry." I checked my watch again. It said nine minutes past eleven.

*Mental! Where did those eight minutes go?*

Zoe barked, looking up at me with a dog gone bored expression. "I need to take Zoe home." I said. "Gramps will wonder where I've got to. I'll think about Fisher Skeelie. I hope Donald will be okay. I should call Rhiannon. I'll see you tomorrow at the Sheddie."

"Brucie, your brain is multi-tasking again and I can't keep up," he said. "Guys can only think about one thing at a time."

I turned to leave, and then stopped. "Kyle . . . sorry. I need more balance don't I? Like learning to walk a tightrope, I guess. I need to learn when to concentrate on my feet and when to concentrate on looking ahead."

Kyle shrugged. "See you tomorrow," he said, and he walked away in the opposite direction shaking his head.

Walking with Zoe, I thought about tightropes, and Mom and Dad.

*Mom and Dad ... how can I get them to stop arguing? How can I?*

"OUCH!"

Passing the war memorial, something hard hit the back of my head. It hit me and then splattered to the ground behind me. I jumped aside, peered down toward the pavement. The carcass of a dead crow lay at my feet. Freaked, I bolted forward urging Zoe, "Quick, Zoe! Run!" and I charged up Ardcarron Brae, racing home as fast as I could.

"Caw! Caw! Caw!" They shouted behind me, Goth and Cough, followed by a loud "Caw!" from Bethany MacKinnon.

## Crow magic

"And we threw a dead crow at her, Gran." Bethany MacKinnon laughed. "Pwahahaha!"

"Crows is magic, so they is!" said Skeelie to Beth. "Crows is everywhere, squawking from all around. And you knows why crows is everywhere? Because magic is all around us."

"Yeah right." Bethany scoffed.

"Honest! Crows is smart. They is the blackest thing that shines in the sunlight. Sun makes their feathers shine with deep blues and purples, even though they're really black. That's to remind us that black magic is alive during the day."

"Who cares?" said Beth.

"They is watchful, crows. They build nests high and they post a sentinel to watch. If a sentinel crow doesn't watch good then the rest of the crows will kill him dead. Must've been a dead sentinel you found."

"Nah, just a crow. I killed it. He had his back to me and I smacked him with a stone," said Beth. "Pwahahaha."

# Chapter 18

## *Remember to Love Yourself*

The Misses MacGregor's shop opened late for business. The thin sister contracted flu, so their shutters did not lift until the late hour of 11:00 am. By happenstance, Rev. MacLeod bought the first morning paper. I watched from the opposite side of the street, as he entered their door. He didn't wait inside very long, so I knew thin Miss MacGregor would be okay. The minister then stood outside the shop with his head buried in the paper, probably reading the obituaries column.

*He looks like a black vulture scanning for pickings, in his black coat, grey bobbled hat and grey trousers,* I thought.

I stood at the same spot where the dead crow hit me the day before. No sign of it now.

*Where did you go, Mr. Crow? Were you swept into a shovel by a street cleaner? Dragged to a ditch by a feral cat? Or, did the vulture across the street find you and offer you a Christian burial?*

*Poor crow,* I thought. *Where did those creeps find a dead crow?*

Rather than answer my own thoughts, I checked my watch and made for the Sheddie to meet my Besties.

"'Morning, Reverend," I said, in passing. I don't think he heard me.

The cold air nipped at my ears. Gramps had said that there was snow in the air. 'I can smell it,' is what he actually said.

"How can you smell snow?" I'd asked Gramps. "It's frozen water."

I sniffed the air as I walked, but could only smell carbolic soap from Rev. MacLeod and chicken soup, coming from the Misses Macgregor's kitchen. I stood still, shut my eyelids, cleared my mind from all thoughts, and concentrated harder. Ready . . . steady . . . sniff again. Nothing!

When I opened my eyes, Sissy stood in front of me, clutching her usual basket. This time a red and white dish cloth draped over the top.

*Why does she suddenly appear like that?*

As I looked closer, the cloth in her basket moved, and then it moved again.  I fixed to ask about the moving cloth when she spoke.

"Snow is on the way, lass," she said.

I asked, warily.  "Can you smell it?"

"Aye," she said.  I felt her watch me as I stared down at the cloth in her basket.

"It's a crow," she said.  "Near dead it wuz.  A spell by the fireside soon had it rested up."

Nodding, I said, "Of course . . . the crow."  My brain lurched.

*What the freck!  How many people do you meet carrying injured crows around in baskets?  Is it THE same crow?  What does she mean by "a **spell** at the fireside"?  Does she mean "a period of time" or "a magic spell; a charm; an incantation?"*

As Sissy walked away, I trained my ears to hear a caw.

*Nah.  It can't be the same crow.  THAT crow lay stiff as a starched collar.  And,* then I dared myself to accept that Sissy might be a witch.  *Nah! She can't be.  I* pondered back and forth.  *Of course.  Yes, that's it!  I changed my mind.  Nah! She can't be.  But, then... Sissy is certainly very different.  It's weird that none of my friends know her.*


I made my way to the Sheddie, walking and talking to myself.  By the time I reached the far side of the railway bridge, snow began to fall.

Rhiannon scowled and quipped, "You're late."

*Ouch, why is she so nippy?*

Checking my watch, I replied, "It's only 11:05."

When she rolled her eyes and turned her back, I bit my nails.

*Why is she like this?*

The twins brought a large flask of coffee and five assorted plastic cups.  Donald handed a blue one to me.

"Here, Brucie," he said, easing the tension.  "Have a coffee."

Inside the shelter of the Sheddie, we huddled together on the wooden bench seats.  I shuffled to the middle, with the twins to my left, Kyle and then Rhiannon on the other side.  We watched the falling snow, hypnotized by its beauty.  All around, the day hushed.  Silence.  No cars drove by, no people walked, no seagulls swooped, no jets soared, no wind howled, no sheep bleated, no music blared, no dogs barked, and none of my friends spoke.  Nothing echoed in my ear, only calm white noise and falling snow.

But, Rhiannon's moody face began to tie knots in my stomach.

*Who spat on her grits?*

"I guess we are here to talk about Brucie's *psychic nonsense*," she said, and then sighed.

*Maybe I should cut to the chase.*

"Rhiannon, are you still mad at me for skipping off on Hogmanay?" I asked.

"Brucie..." She stopped to think. "I'm just going to say it. Brucie, I think you are crazy and I'm not sure I want to hang out with you anymore. You're too freaky."

*Boy howdy, she's proper pissed at me. This is gonna take me from hell to breakfast to fix. How am I going to get my stone back with only Kyle to help?*

When I thought about the stone, my chest ached. I saw pink and green waves in my head. I watched the colors float around me, like bright buoyant clouds.

Rhiannon looked at me and made a "Tch" sound, clucking her tongue off the roof of her mouth. "Look at her. She's off in a dream again."

I jumped, startled . . .

*What the . . . ?*

A shaft of pale blue light bounced from Rhiannon's throat and reverberated off the walls of the Sheddie. It swallowed the pink and green clouds. Gone! No one else appeared to notice this phenomenon.

Rhiannon's face scowled. "Kyle told us what you said to Fisher Skeelie, Brucie. You're playing with fire, and I don't want any part of the plan. You promised me... you promised you would stop all of this psychic crap."

My heart sank.

Rhiannon sighed and then softened her stare.

"Oh, Take this." She held out her hand, "I've got seven pounds and fifteen pence. Put that toward the cost of the appointment. If you get that stone back, do us all a favor and return to being a normal friend again, will you?" She tossed the money onto the floor in front of me, folded her arms and shook her head.

I wanted to thank her but I didn't know how.

Duncan drew breath, pulled his hand from his coat pocket and slowly held out his palm. "Five pounds and twenty six pence in change," he said, and threw his contribution on top of Rhiannon's.

Donald followed, "Add four pounds and ninety to that." He smiled.

Kyle blushed and emptied out all of his pockets onto the seat beside him. "A bus pass, a library card, two pieces of gum, a broken watch, a pair of nail clippers, a guitar plectrum, a green button, and twenty nine pence," he said.

I felt a bit like a reprieved convict. "Gee, thanks. Thanks for letting me off the hook."

"That's seventeen pounds and sixty pence," said Duncan.

"I have two pounds that Gramps gave me, so that leaves forty pence to find," I said. Gathering up the money, I handed it to Kyle, "Here. You keep it."

Kyle shook his head, "Nah! Not me, like," but then his eyes widened and he backed down. "Okay." He gathered up the cash. "I'll hang on to it."

No one spoke for a while and in the pause that followed I shuffled my feet, awkwardly.

Donald spoke first. "Brucie, Kyle said you had some sort of bad dream." He paused. "What's it about?"

*Shoot! How can I answer this, with everyone staring at me?*

I squirmed. "Well… em…"

"Speak up, Brucie," said Kyle. "Tell Donald about the dream."

"Look, quit pushing me, Kyle! I asked you not to tell Donald. I feel VERY uncomfortable now."

"Me too, Brucie," said Kyle. "I'm totally freaking about what you said to Fisher Skeelie. You dropped me right in the sharn." He looked toward the others for support.

I twiddled a lock of hair between my finger and thumb, and hid my face in my hands. Rhiannon and the twins sat quiet as bed bugs.

*Sharn? That's cow shit, isn't it? Hmm, he's right. I did drop him in it.*

I checked Kyle's face again. "You'll still go to see Skeelie, won't you?"

"I guess so," he said, "but I'm not doing this alone. You need to fess up, and get me some support here." He stood up and leaned against the Sheddie wall. "Come on, Brucie. Tell Donald about the dream where he drowns."

"Kyle, stop it," I said, but he kept saying 'Fess up.'

When he said it a fourth time, I snapped, hurling my coffee cup over their heads. Steamy liquid splattered over the Sheddie window and dripped down the far-off wall. Bolting for the footbridge, I stomped up the steps over to the other side of the railway track. There, alone on the northbound platform, I slouched down onto a blue seat and cried. I quivered, panting fear and rage, and kicked my shoe at the wall of the old station house.

"Why me?" I cried. "Why me?"

A hot flush rose up my neck into my cheeks, and I squinted out from under the mop of red hair that had flopped over my face. Back at the Sheddie, no one had moved. In a tight clique, they huddled together, muttering stuff I couldn't hear.

"You've no right to push me like that, Kyle!" I screamed.

Suddenly my view was obstructed.

*Between them they've raised most all of the money you need,* said Coinneach, posing like a jerk in his silly wide-awake hat again. He strutted regimentally up and down the platform, holding the brace of cast-away pistols and his Mexican powder horn.

I sighed. "Git! Git out of here, Coinneach."

*You never mention my medals,* he said. *I always wear medals with the wide-awake hat, the brace of pistols and the Mexican powder horn.*

"Go away!" I protested. "I can't do this today, Coinneach."

*Can't do what?* he asked. *I came here because I thought you might need some assistance.*

"I can't tell Donald about the dream . . . not with everyone staring at me. He'll think I'm a loony."

*A little embarrassment never hurt anyone,* said Coinneach, jingling his medals in my ear.

"Stop it! I can't tell him because then . . . then. . ." I lowered my voice. "Donald will know that I'm . . . I'm . . . in love with him." My face flushed hot again.

*Oh? I didn't realize the situation was that serious,* said Coinneach.

"Neither did I?"

*Then maybe it isn't that serious. Maybe you simply fear that you love him, Brucie.*

"Why would I fear love?" I twiddled a lock of my hair again.

*Why not? He said. Lots of people fear love. Let's test you.* He paused to think. *Who else do you love, Brucie?* he asked. *Think hard before you answer. Then ask yourself if you fear loving these people?*

I didn't want to answer his stupid questions. Across the railway line, my friends hated me.

*I'm waiting.* Coinneach prompted me.

"Okay, okay, keep your wide awake hat on. I love Gramps. I stopped to think. But, I don't fear loving him."

*Who else?* he asked.

"Mom . . . I love my Mom . . . and I love my Dad."

*Ah, now I'm smelling fear,* he said.

"Oh, quit, will you? I only fear that life is not the same, now that they live apart. Everything changed so quickly between them. They treat me differently. **Their** love changed."

*So, do you fear their love or do you fear the change?* he asked.

"That's a dumb ass thing to say. I don't fear their love. It's losing their love that I worry about."

*But your parents DO still love you, don't they?* he asked. *And, yet . . . you always look scared to me.*

"Get lost. I'm NOT scared. It's not what you think. Mom and Dad don't love me like they used to, that's all. It's not the same as when I was younger. Other people came along and changed them, and changed their love; Michaela changed it, and Little Pike changed it, Jake MacKinnon changed it, Scotland changed it."

*So do you fear that Donald's feelings toward you will change, too?* he asked.

"Stop prying, Coinneach!"

*Well, do you fear that?*

"Yes, I fear that," I said, and I cried. "He's gonna change when he finds out that I love him. I'll probably lose his friendship, because Donald's not into love, and all that sort of stuff. He's more into books and religion and math and chemistry and mechanics and football ... He likes me because I act different . . . probably because he thinks I'm not into slushy stuff, like love and romance."

*And what about YOU?*

"What about me?" I asked him back.

*Will you change . . . if you tell him about the dream?* he asked.

"Of course I'll change. How can I act the same after I cry or if blush or if he finds out what my true feelings are?"

*How much do you think he will change if he finds out your true feelings?*

"That is such a silly question," I said. "All I know is what I feel. That's the problem. I don't know how he feels. I don't know what he'll do."

He asked me, *Did you change when you feared a difference in your parent's love?*

"Of course I changed. Wouldn't you, if your parents split up and you had to move so far away from your father?"

Coinneach paused. *Maybe you have forgotten but Lady Seaforth burned my father in a barrel of tar before I ever got to know him.* Then, he asked. *Why did you change, Brucie, after your parents' divorced?*

I shouted the answer out loud, "I changed because I'm angry with them!"

*You are shouting. That's wonderful. Who else are you angry with right now?* he asked.

"Apart from you?" I asked.

*Yes, apart from me.*

"I'm angry with them over there, my so-called friends." I pointed. "I'm angry with them, because they're sitting huddled in the Sheddie and I'm standing here alone in the snow, shouting because I am angry, freezing my ass off, and I'm struggling to know what to say to them. I'm shouting because I fear how they will react when I bear my soul to them all, yet again." I shouted even louder, "the smell of putty ... colorful butterfly wings... the taste of birthday cake flavor ice cream... HAGGIS! 123 – 45 and all that stuff."

I paused for breath, relieved by the release of anger.

"Yes, okay, Coinneach, I get it now. It's me that has changed more than them, and, yes, I'm angry." I looked back over toward the Sheddie. "I guess they look the same, all sitting there waiting for me to come back. They are wondering what to do about me, too."

*I'd say that was a fair assessment of the situation,* he said.

I hugged my sides with my arms. "It feels like my own shadow is trying to pick a fight with me these days. I get so angry with myself."

Coinneach stayed silent.

"I love my friends, all of them, but I fear them and how they'll react to me. My parents, too, I've grown apart from everyone, haven't I?"

Coinneach didn't answer.

"My friends think I'm aloof...Distant as Texas, that's me, isn't it? No one knows how to react to me because I don't know who I am, yet. Only Gramps – he knows what to do. He knows that soon I'll decide who I am. He's giving me time to decide. It's like that destination thing that you said, Coinneach. You can't guide me because I don't know where I'm bound yet."

*Correct!* He said. *"What is your destination? What do you believe in? What is your passion? What makes you want to fight? What makes you sparkle?"*

I hunted around my emotions, searching for one that didn't hurt.

"Where did all these conflicting emotions come from, Coinneach? It's like Grandpa said, when he tried to explain loneliness, we have all of these different people inside of us: as a daughter I feel one kind of hurt, as a friend I hurt a different way, in school I hurt from the pressures of being a student, my American identity hurts in a different way to how Scottish people hurt. All these parts of my personality feel so complex when mixed together, like a tangled spider's web."

I told Coinneach, "I guess the only way to find peace is when all these parts of me stop fighting with each other. I long for the day when I can be a daughter, student, friend, American and everything else, without one part of me upsetting another."

*How will you do that?* asked Coinneach.

"I guess I'll have to learn to accept all parts of my personality equally."

*You mean love yourself as a whole person?* he asked.

"Yes, love myself. That's it. I need to love myself. That will bring me confidence. I love you, Brucie Bice," I told myself. "I love ALL of you."

And with that thought in my head, I decided it was now or never and I crossed back over the bridge, toward my friends.

I stood before them and cleared my throat to speak.

"Okay, the dream terrified me, Donald," I told him, in front of everyone. "You were crossing a wide body of water and a storm blew up. The ferry that you travelled on capsized and you hit the water. You flapped and flailed, desperately searching for something to grab. Finding nothing, you drowned right in front of my eyes and I couldn't save you. I've been unhappy ever since. I don't know what the dream means. All I know is that I am scared of losing you." I blushed, and then continued. "Should I take the dream literally? And if this is fate, can I change it?"

Donald sat wide-eyed but gave no other clue as to how he reacted inside. I started to tremble so I said into my brain, *I love you, Brucie Bice.*

He gulped before speaking. "What a bummer, Brucie. You mean I'm going to die and Duncan will inherit my new football boots? No way."

*Why is he being so flippant?* I thought.

I maybe didn't love myself enough, because faster than a scalded cat,

I snapped at him.

"Look forget it, okay? I felt frightened, that's all." I turned away, so no one could see my eyes well up.

"I'll tell you what..." he said. "We'll send Duncan on the ferry instead."

"No thanks, brother," said Duncan, "If the ferry is going to sink then you can go down with it." He turned to me. "What about me, Brucie? Did I appear in your dream?"

"No, only Donald," I replied, wearily.

Rhiannon sighed and I worried about aggravating her with my psychic-babble, but she put her hand on my shoulder and spoke softly. "Brucie, I heard you shouting over the other side of the track, something about being frightened of changes?"

"Yes. So?" I asked.

"Well, something radically changed in your behavior then," she said.

"I know. I'm sorry." I said.

"No," she said. "I don't think you do know. You yelled, spitting mad, and for the first time you didn't get mad in a Texan accent. Nothing "burned your britches". You had no "conniption fits". You didn't "cloud up and rain knuckles." No "horn tossing moods." Your feet stayed firmly on Scottish terra firma, not "sod-pawing;" no "dancing through the hog trough;" and no "stomping baby ducks" and getting "all cross-legged over it." Well done, Brucie Bice! You spouted steam from every joint but you didn't get 'so mad that you could eat a horny toad backwards'."

I laughed.

Donald laughed, too. "Don't worry, Brucie. The next time I go on a ferry I'll wear a life vest all the time under my coat. I'll tie the buttons so that no one can see, and I'll pretend to be very fat. Would that help?"

Duncan pinched his stomach. "You don't have to pretend, Donald."

"I'm freezing here in the Sheddie," I said. "I feel like I'm sickening for a cold," I said. "Is there somewhere warmer where we can go to talk?" I asked, nervously, showing my pink and blue hands to Rhiannon.

"Listen guys..." said Kyle. "When do I have to go and see Fisher Skeelie?" He stammered, "and wh... wh... what am I supposed to say to her? Do I ask her about the orbs? Do I show her the picture? She scares me!"

*Yes! He's going to do it. What a nice guy.*

"Let me think about it, Kyle," I said, and I dug my cold hands into my pockets. I felt something chink together in the bottom of the lining and pulled out two twenty pence pieces, "Forty pence! I don't believe it." I handed them to Kyle to add to the pile of money. "We have exactly twenty pounds here between us. What are the odds of that happening?"

Rhiannon shook her head and hunched her shoulders, but I swear she also smiled.

"I'd say that my reading with Skeelie is meant to happen, then, like" said Kyle.

"Yeah," I said, pulling Mom's appointment card from my coat. "It's on January 6th, at 2:30 p.m."

"That only gives you two days to come up with a plan for getting your stone back," said Duncan.

"Wait a minute," said Kyle, "Slow down and back up a bit. I don't want to get caught stealing, especially not from her. She'll curse me. So, can I make one suggestion first?" He looked at me with a serious expression. "Why don't you simply go and ask Skeelie to give the stone back to you?"

Rhiannon mocked, "Yeah right, as if that is going to happen, Kyle. She'd guard it even more closely."

"Are you sure that she doesn't suspect anything?" asked Kyle. "I mean, did Skeelie really believe that she spoke to your mother on the phone? What if she's twigged that she actually spoke with you, Brucie? I mean, why would your mother send me, a 14-year-old guy, in her place? Think about it."

"I have thought about it, and I think she honestly believes that my Mom spoke to her. Me and Mom do sound very alike on the phone." I turned to Rhiannon for support, but she was busy pulling a loose thread form the hem of her coat.

"I can tell the difference," said Kyle. "It's easy, because your mother is too lazy to answer the phone." He laughed.

*Ouch! That's my mother he's talking about.* I glowered at Kyle.

He changed the subject. "You still haven't told us about the woman in the wall yet."

Donald whipped the kick out of Kyle's horse when he spoke for me, "Oh, that's simple; a woman lives in the wall of our house, a ghost." Rhiannon stopped fumbling and paid attention, too.

"John Alexander saw her. He stayed awake, frightened to go to sleep at nights, so I asked Brucie to come and speak to him and to the ghost. She got rid of the woman, told her to leave John Alexander alone. He's been fine ever since." Donald turned toward me and said, "John Alexander thinks you're bionic now, Brucie. He thinks you can do anything. He won't shut up about you. He even tries to speak with a Texan accent. I'm tired of hearing about you. It's beginning to drive me insane."

*What does he mean, tired of hearing about me?* I felt deflated.

"I'm only Brucie MacKenzie-Bice, no one special really."

Coinneach cleared his throat. *What happened to loving yourself?*

"Actually, cancel that last bit of self-criticism. Maybe I AM special. We're all special in our own ways, aren't we?"

"Come on then, 'special people'," said Donald, mocking me sarcastically. "Let's go to my house, where it's warmer. We can be 'special' there by the fire. Hopefully, John Alexander will speak normally today, and not in his phony Texan accent."

I squirmed, uneasy with his tone. Rhiannon caught the look in my eye, too.

"You mean at Gargoyle House?" She laughed. "That's what Brucie calls it, don't you, Brucie?"

My face reddened, in answer to the question.

"I like that," said Duncan. He smiled, "Yes I like it very much, 'sounds great. I live in Gargoyle House."

We crossed the road, each of us making fresh footprints in new snow.

Hanging back a bit, I caught Donald's arm. "Did I spook you? Are you worried about the dream?"

He said, "No, I'm fine," but in his eyes I detected an edginess. He pulled his arm away from me and paced quickly forward to join the others.

I tagged along behind. *Love yourself, Brucie,* I thought. *Remember to love yourself.*


## The Lookout

**The sentinel crow watched Brucie from its post, high up in the trees behind the church manse.**

**Her red hair caught its eye -- red for danger, red for fire, red for**

the pumping of hearts.

"Baboom!  Baboom! Baboom!" it cawed to its fellow crows.
A whole murder of crows now watched Brucie, too.

# Chapter 19

# The Reverend and the Big Bang Theory

Inside the study at Gargoyle House, Duncan held a match to newspaper beneath wood kindling in the hearth. Soon, the logs crackled. Coal hissed and ten shoes sat side by side as everyone warmed their feet by the flickering light. Except, my feet refused to warm; I still felt chilled to my bones.

Johnny MacKay, the local builder, banged and hammered up in the attic, and Duncan made us laugh, ribbing Kyle about the holes in his steaming socks.

"AAAAAAAAAH!"

A scream ripped through the wall. The noise pierced my soul.

*Ouch!* I cupped my hands over my ears.

No one else reacted. My friends seemed oblivious.

Thud! Thud! Thud! Thud! Thud! Thud!

Everyone's eyes turned toward the door.

Small feet bounded down the stairs. The door swung open and John Alexander screeched and wailed, hysterically. He opened his lungs and yelled with all his might. "Boocie! Boocie, help me!"

He flung his little arms around me, trembling, and wouldn't let go.

"What's wrong?" I asked.

"Tell her to leave again," he sobbed. "Tell her to go away."

My friends hung back in varying degrees of paralyses, unsure of what to do.

Bang! Bang! Bang! Johnny's hammer hit off the floor above.

Suddenly, the wall beside the fireplace burst open and the woman in the red shawl screeched into the study, wailing hysterically, too.

*Baby!* She opened her lungs and yelled with all her might. *Baby! Tell the man to go away! He'll hit the baby.*

She, too, flung her arms open and, although I felt nothing, she appeared to wrap herself around the other side of me. Both she and John Alexander clung to me like white on rice.

"Whoa!" I said, overwhelmed.

"Stop it!" John Alexander pleaded with the woman in the red shawl. "Go away. Leave me and Boocie alone."

*Baby! He's going to hit the baby!* The woman from the wall wailed. *Make him stop banging!*

"Tell the lady to go!" screamed John Alexander from my left.

*Tell the man with the hammer to go,* screamed the woman from my right.

They both tugged at my sleeves but only the child succeeded. Wafts of cold air brushed off my right arm, as the woman's bony fingers clawed in the direction of my hand.

"It's okay John Alexander." I tried to calm him, but he sobbed hysterically. "Donald, take him, please?" I asked. "I can only concentrate on one thing at a time!"

My friends all stared at me in blank horror. Rhiannon demanded to know what happened, but I had no time to speak to her. Kyle, scared witless, held onto Duncan's shirtsleeve, using Duncan as a human shield. Donald grabbed little John Alexander.

Bang! Bang! Bang!

As the banging continued upstairs, the woman wailed, *No! My baby!*

Rhiannon shouted, "What's going on Brucie?" but in the mayhem I couldn't answer her because John Alexander screamed.

"Who?" I asked the woman. "Tell who to go? Where is your baby? I don't understand." As I shouted in the direction of the standard lamp, my friends' eyes widened and their jaws hung open.

In desperation, the woman lunged at me blowing icy gusts across the room.

The standard lamp flew onto the hearthrug, landing next to Rhiannon. She screamed, "Stop this Brucie, NOW!"

Duncan squealed, jolting Kyle, who bolted for the door, vaulting onto Donald, who shouldered John Alexander, and they all folded like a broken clutch of deck chairs onto the ground.

The Reverent MacLeod tore into the room.

"STOP THIS UNGODLY RACKET!"

*Oh No! He's going to blame me.*

His temples boiled red and bulged with blue popping veins. "What's going on, Brucie?"

*I knew it.*

He paused to loosen his collar with his index finger. "Stop these antics or I will have to ask you to leave. You are frightening John Alexander again."

"Again?" I protested. "But, I'm not doing anything." I shivered even more.

*Gee Reverend! Quit looking at me like I'm a dead frog in your guacamole.*

And then I caught my reflection in the large gilt framed mirror. My hair blew backward. It was *her* fault. She was the one blowing wind. I ducked to avoid objects that she launched toward me; magazines, flowers from a vase on the mantelpiece, and the minister's paperwork from the desk flew at me, too... page by page by page.

*Stop it! Stop it NOW!* I told her.

Thinking on my feet, I pointed to the window, "Better shut it. There's a gale blowing outside."

The Reverent chased across the room to slam the window shut. Simultaneously, the woman stopped the wind, but when the minister returned to stand by the mantelpiece, he stared me down with cold, calculated suspicion.

John Alexander intervened. "She's not frightening me, Daddy. It's the lady that's doing it. Over there! The lady is over there!"

*Bang! Bang! Bang!*

*Oh No! The builder, again.*

*Stop him. Stop him banging,* the woman screeched. I winced and plugged my ears.

"Tell Johnny MacKay to stop hammering," I said.

"WHAT?" Reverent MacLeod retorted, indignantly.

"Tell Johnny MacKay to stop hammering," I said again. "Something is wrong up there."

"My only concern is down here, with all you hooligans! You're trying to trick me into believing you've conjured up some sort of poltergeist, and in this... I mean in my... I mean, the Good Lord's own house!"

The minister breathed in deeply, widening his nostril. He held the breath until he found composure. His voice lowered, but he still glowered at me, furious. "Johnny MacKay has much work to do, so I'll thank you to leave him be."

I tried to interrupt but he wouldn't have it. He launched into a lecture.

"You need to leave, Brucie. Something very wrong is happening here and… Time is of the essence with builders these days. Tradesmen are hard to come by, Brucie."

*Blah, blah, blah . . .*

Stepping toward him, I raised my voice. "NO!" I cut him dead in his flow. "You MUST tell him to stop hammering. He's disturbing something in the structure of the wall. Trust me," I pleaded.

"Tell Johnny to stop, Daddy," said John Alexander.

The minister's eyes bulged from their sockets, again. He mumbled, shook his head and threw his hands in the air. Caving to pressure, he left the room, calling out to the builder from the bottom of the stairway.

"Johnny! Can you take a break for a minute, please?"

Silence.

In my peripheral vision, I saw the woman wrap her shawl around her shoulders and rock herself back and forth. I longed for warmth and security, too.

*He nearly hit the baby*, she protested.

Reverent MacLeod burst back into the room like a bulging boil in bright tones of angry purple. His dog collar bit at his neck, so he wrestled it with his finger again. I watched as his temper infused with his church-grey soul. They growled and snarled at each other, till he quashed the fight between his palms. His praying hands became the mediators. Composed, he knelt down beside John Alexander, and softened his voice.

"Is that better, son… the quiet?"

The little boy nodded.

He then asked his son, "Why must Johnny stop banging?"

John Alexander repeated what the woman had said, "Johnny was going to hit the baby in the wall."

The minister called for his wife to remove the child from the room. His head spun toward me. He growled like a grizzly bear. "Get thee behind me Satan!" he shouted. The temper in his soul burst free, with ravaging claws. "Out! Out of my study! All of you." He ground his teeth together and spat fury.

Scuttling out of harm's way, we stood in the hallway at the bottom of the winding staircase. The twins, especially Donald, trembled with alarm.

"Could you all leave now, please?" Donald asked.

Duncan attempted to re-enter the study. "We're sorry, Father…" but the door slammed in his face.

Johnny Mackay stood on the top landing peering down. "Is there anything wrong? Did something break with the hammering? "

I tried to say, "You have to stop the hamme…" but Donald insisted, "Please, Brucie. You really need to leave now."

Rhiannon pulled my sleeve, "Come on."

"No. There is something in the wall upstairs. I need to see what it is."

"BRUCIE!" She shouted. "They'll sort it out. Let's go now. Please?"

"You don't understand. If we check out the wall, then the woman will stop frightening John Alexander. She said that her baby is inside the wall."

Rhiannon yanked my sleeve harder, "BRUCIE! You don't listen, do you? LEAVE, NOW!"

Reluctantly, I followed Rhiannon and Kyle to the door. Donald closed it firmly behind us.

In the driveway, Kyle piped up, "We can forget seeing the twins now, Brucie. They'll be grounded for weeks."

"Why?" I asked, but no one answered. "No one did anything wrong."

Rhiannon shrugged, "No. We didn't, but *you* did."

She walked off, without turning around.

Kyle ignored Rhiannon's departure. He hopped from leg to leg, like he needed to pee. "What's this baby in the wall stuff?" His eyes opened wide and scanned my expression like giant, satellite receivers.

"I'm not sure, Kyle," I admitted, stifling a sneeze. "I need to get back inside the house and have a look around upstairs."

Kyle skipped to the next question. "Could you really see a woman in the wall, like, because I didn't see anything, like… but I saw all that stuff flying about? I thought I'd crap myself," he said. He clasped his hands behind his head and breathed deeply as if he were about to faint. "Manic! Pure, absolute manic, like!"

I asked, "Kyle, will you help me get back inside?"

"Brucie! How? They told us to leave."

I pointed to a ladder lying in the snow, and then looked up to an open window above the porch.

Kyle followed the direction of my eyes, "NO! Don't even think about it." He tried to pull me away. "Look, it's cold and you're sneezing. Why don't we call it a day, like?"

"Let go, Kyle," I ordered. "You don't have to come, too, but I'd sure appreciate if you'd stand here and keep an eye out."

He let my arm go. "Brucie! You are crazy," he said, but I was already half way up the ladder. Luckily, I slipped in the window with ease.

On the upstairs landing, I sneaked up behind Johnny MacKay and poked him on the shoulder, just as his arm fixed to swing his hammer. Johnny's feet sprung from the ground and he squealed with fright, like a pig newly chosen as this year's Christmas ham.

"What the ...?" he called out.

"Shh!" I begged. "Listen, I need to tell you something." I cupped my hand to his ear and whispered.

Johnny Mackay stood short for a man. With my nose no more than a few inches away from his ear, he smelled 'well scrubbed' as Gramps would say, like a mixture of Fairy Snow washing powder, homemade soup and sawdust. When I finished speaking, he dropped his hammer to the ground, narrowly missing my toe.

"I can't . . . Oh, no . . . What the . . . You're k . . . kidding me?"

I raised my right hand to God. "Honestly!" I swore as I lied to him, but I held my fingers crossed behind my back.

"Th... Thanks f... for w... w... warning me," he stammered.

Johnny MacKay seized his toolbox, spawning a flurry of flying screws and nails. His bolts bolted, plum-lines plummeted, and springs sprung to the ground, as he stumbled and wrestled the lid closed. In haste, Johnny wrapped his whole arm around the large metal box and staggered to the front door. He spilled an array of various metal objects from under his armpit, as his legs clambered down the staircase.

"S... sorry R... Reverend, I'll have to leave for the day," he called, adding some excuse about a stomach upset. "Too much turkey," he lied.

I snuck into the attic space, where Johnny had been working. Limited daylight, from a grubby skylight window complicated my search. I fumbled around, unsure what to look for. Suddenly, she appeared beside me.

"My baby. . ." She pointed to the wall.

"IN the wall?" I asked, but she didn't seem to know.

"How can it be IN the wall? I can't . . . AH!" I jumped. "Ouch! Who's there?" Someone caught hold of my arm and squeezed into the attic space beside us.

"Oh good, are we playing hide and seek today?" said the happy, pink-gummed lady, with the buttoned-up coat. I'd seen her before at their Halloween party.

*Oh no! It's Donald's grandmother, the old lady from the island of Lewis that pees in their potting shed.*

The old dear closed her eyes. "Go and hide," she said, and she began counting very loudly, "One, two, three, and four."

*Darn! I need to leave before someone hears her and finds me in here.*

I clambered back down the ladder and joined Kyle behind the woodshed, out of sight.

In the yard, Johnny MacKay's taillights disappeared out of the driveway.

"Wait!" the minister called. "Come back Mr. MacKay. He shouted after Johnny, "When can I expect you to come back?" but his words fell on deaf ears. Johnny sped away.

The Rev. MacLeod threw his hands into the air and muttered aloud, "Lord PLEASE give me strength." He shut the door again, returning inside. We heard him call the twins to meet him in his study. Metal curtain hoops scraped across the curtain pole, as the heavy drapes shut, blanking out my view. I feared for the twins.

"Let's go, Kyle," I said.

Kyle looked at me and asked, "Did you find anything up there?"

I shook my head in reply.

Kyle walked backward in front of me. "Is Johnny MacKay really sick?"

"No, he's not sick," I answered. "I'm going to step on you, if you don't stop walking in front of me."

"Then what?" Kyle looked totally confused. "What did you do to make him rush off like that?" He stopped walking, blocking my path so that I had to stop and answer him.

I refused to say, which drove Kyle totally nuts.

He folded his arms. "I'm not going to help you get your stone back unless you tell me what you said to him."

I thought for a minute. "I'll tell you AFTER we get the stone. Deal?"

"Okay, deal," he said, unfolding his arms again and shaking his head. Kyle laughed, "You really are crazy, aren't you?"

"Probably," I said. "But I've bought us a few hammer-free days so that we can try to work out what "baby in the wall" means."

"You mean you're going to sneak back in to look around?"

"I don't know yet," I answered. "I have to do something to stop that woman wailing at me and John Alexander."

"Can't you leave this to the Rev. MacLeod? After all, he is a minister and he should know how to deal with spirits. Maybe he can perform some sort of exorcism on the house."

"Yes, but only if he *believes* there is a ghost. He thinks we are mucking about to aggravate him." I added, "He's so angry. Listen to him shout at the twins. Would you like to step back in there and tell him his house is haunted?"

Kyle shook his head, "No way, Jose!"

"Kyle, I…" I stopped and sighed.

"What is it now?" he asked.

"I still need to talk about how to get my stone back. We've got such little time left till the appointment on the 6th!" I said.

"Tell me about it!" he stressed.

"What if you go to the appointment and I phone her midway through? When she gets up to answer her phone, you can nab the stone and run out of the door."

Kyle said, "Nah, like." He shook his head. "What if she puts the stone into her pocket while she answers the phone? Maybe she won't answer the phone, you know… if I'm with her. Or, what if she has the phone right beside her, like?" he said, woefully. "Or, what if she doesn't even use the stone?"

"She will," I said. "I know it."

"This is not going to work, Brucie," he said. "It's wrong to steal. Folk that steal always get their comeuppance. I don't want anything bad to happen to me."

"But, she stole from me first, Kyle." I felt my eyes well with tears. "I just want my stone back. There won't be any comeuppance. Nothing bad will happen."

But, I spoke too soon.

## From The Crow's Nest

Bethany and her uncle Jake crouched behind the shed in Fisher Skeelie's garden. Sickly sweet, musky smoke swirled up into the cold air around them and the pair giggled childishly.

The sentinel crow watched from its nest, high up in the trees beyond Fisher Skeelie's house. It swooped down closer.

Beth squealed. "Aw rank! Did you see that?"

Jake laughed.

"The bird shat on our joint!" she said.

Jake knocked the joint out of her hand and laughed.

"Come on. Let's get to work while it's daylight," he said.

The two slunk off into the woods and returned with armfuls of firewood.

The red roof of Skeelie's house was fixed prominently in the sentinel's gaze -- red for danger, red for fire, red for the pumping of hearts.

"Baboom! Baboom! Baboom!" mocked the gathering crows. A whole murder of crows circled above, watching Bethany and Jake as they chopped up the firewood with Fisher Skeelie's axe.

## Chapter 20

## *The Flu and the Chimney*

Part of my comeuppance arrived early, when overnight I burned a fever of 102 degrees. My throat cut like fire. Each bone ached in turn and my skin burned so raw that I could hardly roll over. Even the soles of my feet hurt. I had more pains than an old window.

"A week in bed is the best cure for flu, Lassie," said Grandpa.

*A WEEK! But, the appointment with Skeelie is tomorrow,* I thought.

He urged me to stay warm and to sip one of his famous hot toddies.

"What's in a toddy?" I croaked.

"This toddy is made of hot blackcurrant juice with lemon, ginger and a drop of whisky," he said, handing me two painkillers to boot.

"Stone the buzzards, Grandpa!" I said, choking on a sip. "How much whisky did you put in this?"

Mom intervened, grabbing the cup from my hand. "Dad! She's only sixteen."

Maybe fever parched my brain, or maybe I needed to speak up. "You're no role model to lecture me about alcohol," I said.

She struck back quick as a cottonmouth. "What do you mean?"

I slid down the bed and pulled up the covers for protection. "I mean, lately, you drink too much."

Too late… For the first time ever, Mom cuffed me. Whack!

"Fiona!" Grandpa hollered. "Enough! I won't tolerate this in my home. Can't you see that your daughter is ill?"

With tear-filled eyes Mom retorted. "Can't you see that YOUR daughter is ill, too?"

"What do you mean?" he asked.

Stunned, I rubbed my ear. I'd never seen her as explosive as this before.

"What I mean is that you spend all your time fussing over Brucie. I need someone to fuss over me, too. Neither you nor Brucie respect me any more. I'm ill, too; I'm depressed."

Grandpa guided her out of the room where they argued further.

*It's true; I have lost respect for you, Mom. I wish I could tell you how I feel when you argue with Dad on the phone. Why can't you spend time with me instead of locking yourself away in your room? You've lost all your sparkle. And I know how many empty bottles you take to the recycling bank.*

I called through the house, "Nothing justifies you hitting me, Mom!"

The words had hardly left my lips when I vomited all over the bed.

The doorbell rang and Kyle entered. "Hello, can anyone hear me?" he called out. Kyle breezed straight into the middle of the Mom and Gramps' row. He opened my bedroom door in a panic, "Eh, your mother has thrown a cup of something at the wall and stomped out of the back door, grabbing her coat and her car keys."

What a beamer! As if the embarrassment of our family fight wasn't enough, but . . . No! A boy just walked into my bedroom, as I lay in a pool of vomit.

Kyle stood gawking at me.

Grandpa, with regained composure, now guided Kyle from my room.

"Sorry for walking in, Ali, like," I heard Kyle say. "Only... there's something important that we have to do tomorrow and..."

Grandpa said something back, which I didn't hear

"Tell you what, Ali. I'd offer to help you clean the puke but..."

The front door opened and shut again, as Kyle left the house.

I tried to get up to change the bedding but the room spun around and I vomited again. Gramps came to my rescue with a bowl of soapy water, some fresh towels and sheets. Soon, I sunk back into bed, clean but exhausted.

Fever dragged me into a fitful sleep, spat me out with cold sweats, and then boiled me up till I shivered again. Hot and cold, up and down, in and out of dreams. The day passed in an exhausting rollercoaster of heat, chills, aches and pains. When Coinneach appeared at the foot of the bed, I couldn't decide if I was hallucinating or not.

*I see you have some sort of foreign plague, so I need to depart. Got any spots on your belly? Boils on your back? Any rancid pus flowing from your ears?*

*No, I haven't.* I huffed, indignantly. *And it's flu, NOT plague.*

*Regardless,* he said. *How are you going to persuade your young friend to retrieve the stone, now that you are too sick to make plans with him?*

*I'm not too sick!* I said. *I can get up if I want to.*

But he knew I lied, so he disappeared to leave me rest.

Gramps watched over me. He brought bowls of chicken soup. But I couldn't eat, so he returned with glasses of cooled boiled water. "You must try to drink, or I'll have to call the doctor," he said.

I remember sipping the water, but I don't recall Gramps leaving the room. Each time I fell asleep, I spiraled into a nightmare. Down and down I tumbled, into a dark and murky blindness. Choking, I struggled to escape from a muddy swamp that filled and bloated my lungs. Behind me, I heard the cry, "Save me! Brucie, save me! Please!"

"It's Donald!" I panicked, and tried to get out of bed again, but this time I fell on the floor. "My God, it's Donald! He's going to drown. I have to call Kyle." I struggled, so dazed that I couldn't think where I left my phone. And then, I remembered Jake's heel crunching my phone into the ground. I climbed back into bed and slept.

My watch on the bedside table read fifteen minutes past twelve o'clock. "But, is that a.m. or p.m.?" I asked myself. "How long have I lain here?"

Gathering my thoughts, I called out.

"Grandpa!"

The door opened and he smiled. "Yes?" he asked. I figured it must be 12:15 p.m.

"What's the date today?" I asked.

"It's the 6th January," he said.

"Holy Cannelloni! Then there's only one hour and forty-five minutes left," I cried. ... *fluffy grey kittens with bright blue eyes... chocolate fountains ...jumping over waves with Dad on the beach at Galveston ... 1234 – 567 ...och, darn it... I can't count when I'm this stressed.*

"Forty-five minutes until what?" asked Grandpa, but I didn't answer him.

"Nothing, but I feel better now," I lied.

Wobbling my way toward the shower in the bathroom, I clung to the wall for support.

*I'm not fooling Gramps. Am I?*

Regardless, he handed me a couple of soft fluffy, white towels that had been warming on top of the radiator. "Brucie, whatever you are planning, are you sure you are up to it?"

"Yes, I feel great now." Stopping short of the bathroom door, I asked Grandpa, "Did Kyle leave any messages for me?"

"He only said to get better soon." Grandpa smiled.

Mom never spoke but I could smell her cigarette smoke wafting in at the back door. I popped my head round the corner. "Glad you're back," I said.

Mum smiled.

*How am I going to contact Kyle? She'll hear me if I use the house phone.*

After my shower, Gramps handed me a cup of hot coffee.
After the coffee, he jingled his car keys in his pocket.
After I refused a lift, he tied a thick scarf around my neck.
After Gramps kissed my cheek, I stepped outside into the cold.
After he told me to, "Take care," I said, "I will, Gramps."
After that . . . he looked SO worried about me.

Down at the telephone box, on the corner by the railway station, I dialed Kyle's mobile. The call diverted straight to his answering message, "If you get this message it means I'm skint. Lend me a fiver and you can leave me a message. Otherwise, I won't be able to get it."

"Darn!" I replaced the receiver. The large, metal framed clock at the station said seventeen minutes remained until the two o'clock appointment with Fisher Skeelie. I wondered what to do, when suddenly a familiar figure appeared to my left.

*Get off the railway line, will you?* I said to Coinneach. He had one foot on each of the track lines.

*How do those big iron horses balance on these bars?* he asked. I didn't have time to explain.

*It's not a horse; it's called a train. Now please help me, Coinneach. Do you think that Kyle has gone to see Fisher Skeelie?* I asked him.

Lying on his belly inspecting the railway sleepers, he shrugged. *Don't know.*

*Then, I'll have to go to her house and find out.*

He looked up at me with a concerned expression. *I don't think you have the strength to walk all the way up that hill.*

*I have flu, Coinneach. That's all. I can make it.*

*You've been warned,* he said, tapping the railway track with his cutlass.

*Can't you forget about the railway line for a minute and help me?* I coughed up goop into a large white handkerchief. My head spun.

He said nothing, saluted quietly, tipped his wide-awake hat and vanished. I waited for his return, shivering, but as the minute hand on the big clock shifted another minute closer to two o'clock, I couldn't risk hanging around.

The steep climb made me wheeze until my breastbone ached. *Maybe Coinneach was right.* I doubled up on the road, panting in shallow breaths, hands on my chest, in pain. Rhiannon's horse nuzzled up to the fence beside me and whinnied.

"I'm ill, Bracken," I said. "How I wish you'd carry me on your back." He nodded his head.

"Yes, I know. You can't get out of the paddock. I guess I'm nearly there now, though. Thanks anyway." I trudged on.

Rounding the bend at the top of the hill I felt strangely surreal and I panicked as my heartbeat thumped in my ears. I stopped to lean against a large oak at the entrance to the woods. Behind me, something moved.

*It's the stag!*

A large black crow cawed overhead. I fixed my stare on the stag and kept perfectly still.

*Wait, I must be feverish. No. It's not a stag; it's a person. How weird! They're wearing a deerskin-colored coat.*

Cold shivers engulfed my body.

*I can't stop. I need to push on. It's almost time.*

But, as I neared Fisher Skeelie's house, I hung back for a minute, determined to get a better look at the figure in the wood. I shaded my eyes from the light with my hand, peering out ahead. My breath steamed in the frosty air around me. The person in the coat, an old lady, bent down to pick something up off the ground and I screwed up my eyes to see what it could be.

*I'm too far away. Darn it.*

Straining hard, I recognized the object that she lifted; a basket, she lifted a cane basket.

"Sissy!" I croaked, but she couldn't hear. Sissy scuttled into the woods.

*She's maybe collecting kindling, or pinecones for her fire.* I thought for a second or two. *But, where does she live?*

My curiosity about Sissy ceased when I spied Kyle's moped, parked by Fisher Skeelie's gate. I beamed, elated. "Yes. He's here!"

*But, what now?* I thought. *I can't follow the plan because I've no mobile phone to call Skeelie.*

Carefully, I eased open the gate and tiptoed down the narrow path, beside the gable end of Skeelie's house. I didn't know the layout of her house, so I simply held my head low, aimed for a holly bush beneath the nearest window, and dove in behind it to hide out.

"AHHH!"

I screamed when I bumped into Rhiannon. She sat crouched under the window ledge, too.

"What are you doing here?" I asked.

"SHH!" she urged, clamping her hand over my mouth. "You'll get us caught."

But, the minute she removed her hand, I bombarded her with questions.

"What's going on? Can you see Fisher Skeelie? What's the plan? Can you see my stone? What is Kyle doing? Why…?"

"SHH!" she said, again, this time with knitted brows and a clenched fist. I thought she was going to thump me, but she stopped and stared at my face. "My God, you look awful."

"Thanks a lot," I sniffed.

"Shh! What is that noise?" she asked.

We listened beneath the window. I couldn't hear anything except my own heart beating, my lungs heaving, and the occasional crow cawing.

Footsteps.

We both pressed our backs further into the wall and I grabbed Rhiannon's hand.

Voices.

We held our breath.

Bethany and Jake MacKinnon emerged from a clearing in the woods, grinning. Skeelie's front door opened, the two entered and clicked the door latch behind them. When the key turned, Rhiannon and I looked at each other in horror.

I squealed, "Oh my God! Kyle's locked inside the house with Skeelie, Beth and Jake."

"What can you see?" Rhiannon urged, as I stood up to peer in the window.

"Nothing, yet," I said. My throat burned like fire again. Every word I spoke cut my gullet like a razor blade. Then…

"Woah!" I gulped. "Oh no!"

As I'd peered inside, the net curtain flipped aside and Bethany MacKinnon stared back out at me.

"Let's get out of here," said Rhiannon. "Run for it."

"But, what about Kyle?" I asked.

Suddenly Jake blocked our path. Quick as a whip, he pounced, locking his hand onto Rhiannon's forearm.

"Let her go, Dog Breath!" I coughed at him.

The usual spent match protruded from the gap between Jake's front teeth. He laughed a mean, wicked laugh. I smelled him, even with a blocked nose – smoky, musky, and meaty. Jake looked smug and sinister in his long, black, leather coat. On his head a dirty felt hat sat cocked to one side. Beneath its brim, his raven-dark eyes flashed with teasing glee. His face amassed with shadows of unshaven stubble. A gold loop, pierced through his bottom lip; it sparkled and flashed as he taunted me by licking his tongue around it. His presence threatened every inch of my being and yet he lured me, too; horrifically so, with his sharp cheekbones and long hair, which he tied back with a band. Jake knew every inch of his scary potency, the sleaze and fear that he burrowed into my brain. My eyes dared not look at his for more than a second, in case . . . well, just in case. I swear my fear fed his lust. He enjoyed harassing us this way.

"Where's that pretty mother of yours?" he asked. "How come she's not here for her appointment with our new Ardcarron Seer? Eh?"

Ignoring any reference to my Mom, I fired back, "That old lady ain't the New Ardcarron Seer… she's the New Phony Crony, maybe." I raged mad, but scared to death. My cough gurgled up phlegm from my chest.

Jake threw his head back and laughed even louder. "Why don't you come inside, Little Red Nose, and tell her that yourself. I'm sure she'll be delighted," and, knowing I'd follow; he marched Rhiannon to the back of the house and shoved her inside. "Look what I found," he called out. "These visitors were queuing up in the garden, behind the holly bush, waiting for their turn to see you."

Skeelie opened her mouth wide, exposing a pair of blackened teeth as she laughed.

I stepped into the dimly lit kitchen, and felt a shove from behind. Beth, standing behind the door, quickly fastened a bolt on the back door. CLUNK! Now all three of us were trapped, me, Rhiannon and Kyle, abducted by these slimy people. My heart pumped against the fluid in my chest and I wheezed.

Rhiannon spoke. "You can't simply kidnap us like this. I'm calling my dad to come fetch us."

But Beth snatched Rhiannon's phone from her hand and threw it to Jake.

Kyle remained speechless and goggle-eyed, perched nervously on the very edge of a wooden stool. He faced an old armchair where Skeelie sat by the fireside. Incense sticks burned in holders on the hearth; jasmine. *I hate the smell of jasmine. It reminds me of cat's pee … speaking of cat's pee… Coinneach! Thank God you are here. Help us, please.*

He hovered in the shadows behind Fisher Skeelie, watching over her left shoulder. My guide put his finger to his lips, *Shhh!* and then mischievously blew on The Skeelie's ear.

"Why are you grinning at me, girl?" asked the old crone, batting her left ear with a boney hand. She stood up and shivered.

I wiped my nose with a tissue and tried to cover the smirk on my face. But, my grin soon faded when Skeelie withdrew my stone from the pocket of her apron.

I felt a shimmering vibration, calling me, like a precious jewel. When my watery eyes widened, she laughed at me.

"D'ya like me loverly stone?" She chuckled.

"Give that to me!" I said. "It's mine."

"Oh no, no," she said. "Finders keepers."

*Grab it, Coinneach! Please grab the stone for me. You can reach. Then we can find a way to get out of here.* I begged him but he shook his head.

*I can't. Blowing air is as far as I advanced in my poltergeist class. You'll have to work this one out for yourself. I'm only here for moral support.*

*If air is all you have then keep blowing on her neck, till I think of something. If nothing else it'll make her uncomfortable.*

Coinneach tipped his wide-awake hat and dutifully blew.

Fisher Skeelie reached for a cardigan. She draped it over her shoulders and shivered again. "Throw a few more logs on the fire, Bethany dear," she said. While her smirking niece obliged, Skeelie turned her attention to Kyle. She spoke directly to him, ignoring the rest of us.

"Now, before we wus so rudely interrupted, I wus telling you about the orbs, wusn't I?"

Kyle protested, "Please don't do this. Don't make a fool of me in front of everyone."

"I don't make fools. Fools make themselves." The Skeelie laughed a mocking tease. "You all came here together now, didn't you? Ha! Ha! Ha!" she laughed again. "What fools! What fools!"

Kyle squirmed and shifted in his chair, as Skeelie spoke again.

"Ah yes, I see it's your father. He says "Hello" and to tell your mother "Hello" as well. Tell her to stop spending all her money at the bingo."

Tears welled up in Kyle's eyes. "Can't we do this alone … I mean without everyone watching …" he gulped.

Skeelie drew the stone out again and gazed inside it. "Ah! Ha! Ha! Ha! Yes, your dad had a great sense of humor. He says he seen yer reading those rude men magazines and ye'll get it from yer ma if she finds then in yer room. Ha! Ha! Ha! And, here's the best one… he's says he's not really yer da anyway. He says yer da could be any man in the village, b'cause…"

"Leave him alone," I said to Skeelie.

Distraught and humiliated, Kyle struggled to sit still.

I gazed at my stone in Skeelie's hand.

*Help me, Eye Stone. If only I could touch you.*

The small sitting room enclosed around me, drab, dark and dreary, like the walls moved in on us. I gazed toward the window for inspiration from the light outside, but I felt as weak and ineffective as the pale, winter sun as it hung low in the sky to the west.

*Help me sun. I'm so cold and tired.*

To the right of the front gate, silhouetted by the sun, a crow landed on the fence, and it hopped on one leg.

*Help me crow.*

I watched Sissy cross the road, toward the fence from the direction of the wood.

*Help me Sissy.*

Suddenly, she picked up the crow, held it in her hand, and stroked the bird, talking to it. When she released the crow, it flapped a bit and circled above Sissy's head, and then flew north over the wood to join a large group of its friends.

I thought about screaming out, "Help, Sissy, we're being held prisoner in here!" but I feared that Jake would clamp one of his dirty hands over my mouth. Anyway, after the crow flew off, Sissy seemed to vanish, too.

Back inside the room, Kyle looked at the floor, humiliated.

"Your father says he's standing to your right hand side, Kyle," she told him.

*Lies! She's telling Kyle lies, Coinneach.*

Jake and Bethany, such a weird and inappropriate pair, moved to a sofa by the kitchen door. They flopped to the seat, next to each other. She raised her feet up on a table, nudging Jake. He copied her and they sniggered like infants. Rhiannon and I stood awkwardly. I wondered when their games would end, when they'd unlock the doors and let us go. Inside, I hissed like a cornered Cajun rattler, but my soul weighed heavy with guilt. It was my fault that Kyle endured this torment, but I didn't know what to do, or how to stop it.

*Coinneach, do something to stop her... Blow on the old hag again, HARDER! BLOW!*

Outside, the crow had returned. It circled and then landed on Skeelie's fence again. It looked at me, cocking its head, staring in the window.

*PLEASE. Help me crow,* I begged. But, again he flew away.

As Coinneach blew, Fisher Skeelie shivered.

"Another log, Bethany! And some coal too," said Skeelie.

Beth stacked yet another log onto the fire, and added a good half bucketful of coal, which she banked up into a full, black, smoking heap.

Skeelie continued to poke fun at Kyle, while he sat there like a plastic duck at the fairground. She took aim and popped one cheap, cheating lie after another.

"Ah yes, laddie. Your dad is speaking again." Skeelie put her hands to her neck and pretended to choke. "Oh, I feel your dad's pain as he lay dying. He's strangling. Did he hang himself? No, wait, he choked on a bone, or is it drowning that I am feeling? That's it! No wait…"

Kyle drew his knees up to his chest and hugged them like an infant. "Stop it! Stop it!" With elbows on his knees, he cupped his hands over his ears and cried.

Rhiannon exploded at Skeelie. "STOP IT NOW!" She turned to Kyle. "Kyle, this is nonsense. Don't listen to her." Looking back to Skeelie, she shouted again, "Leave him alone. You're a cruel old witch!"

Kyle bolted for the door, but Jake yelled at him, "Sit! And, don't move until I tell you to go."

The rattler in me rose ready to strike. "Why don't y'all..." but I stopped mid-sentence. Outside the window, something caught my eye. A black shadow formed above the trees.

The sky above the house filled dark with crows. A full parliament of large black birds cackled and cawed. At first I didn't understand. Their beaks held twigs, like they were building nests for the coming spring. But, the crows landed on the roof. I heard a chink and then a dunk on the top of the chimney pot. Chink. Dunk. Chink, again and again. Dunk. Chink. Dunk.

*I gotcha! I know what's happening now.*

*QUICK! BLOW ON THE FIRE, COINNEACH.*

*BLOW HARD!*

Smoke bellowed inward from the hearth and we all coughed.

*Yes!*

I jumped for joy.

*BLOW AGAIN, COINNEACH! The crows have blocked off the chimney with twigs.*

I covered my mouth and concentrated my thoughts. *That's it. Keep blowing!*

More and more smoke filled the room. Fisher Skeelie stopped talking and wheezed, fanning her face with a handkerchief. I moved in beside her, ready to take action.

*God, this smoke is going to kill me! My lungs are ready to burst.*

"Here, let me help by opening a window," I offered to Skeelie.

Jake lunged forward to block my path, but seeing his aunt struggle for breath, he nodded at me, "Go ahead, then." He spun around, turning his back on me to help his choking aunt.

*This is going to be my only chance, Coinneach. Blow once more, and with all your might this time.*

Thick smoke + Confusion = Time to act.

I thrust Jake aside, ramming him with my shoulder, and shoved both hands hard against Fisher Skeelie. As she toppled backward, I shot my hand into her apron pocket and yanked out the stone. "YES!" I rejoiced. But, I'd pushed Fisher Skeelie too hard. She tumbled onto the fire hearth and . . . WOOSH . . . her clothes ignited.

*SHOOT! SHE'S BURNING! SHE'S ON FIRE!*

Fisher Skeelie screeched in agony as flames lapped up from her skirt and on to her face.

"What do I do, Coinneach? RHIANNON? KYLE? WHAT DO I DO?"

But, I couldn't hear their replies on account of Skeelie's screams.

Seconds felt like minutes, where nothing moved fast enough. I panicked, hopping from one foot to the other, stupidly flapping my hands in the air, as if such a silly thing would extinguish her flames. Suddenly, I bolted up onto the window ledge and leapt out the window, head first into the holly bush. "Hurry, guys. Follow me," I called. My skin tore up, but I wrenched free and leapt for cover toward a clump of trees to my right, and then bounded across the road like a petrified fox fleeing hounds.

Gasping for breath, I clung with white knuckles behind a large oak, digging my fingernails into the gnarly bark.

*Oh my God! Where are Kyle and Rhiannon? Did they follow?*

Breathing slower and deeper to steady my nerves, I stretched my neck out and quickly sneaked a look. I darted back.

*Oh no! I can't go back for them. Jake will kill me.*

With a deep breath, I clutched the stone in my pocket to steady my nerve.

*I've got you back now, Eye Stone, but at what cost?*

I glanced again at the house. But, the bellowing clouds of choking smoke grew thicker, engulfing the whole area and obscuring my view.

My eyes bulged in their sockets, stinging like giant, red jelly fish. I punched myself on the side of my head. And then, again. "You stupid idiot, Brucie!"

Suddenly, one unholy, nerve-slicing scream ripped out from the old crone's house. "AHHHH!"

I envisaged Skeelie's skin, scorching and searing.

*Oh, no! This is my entire fault.*

Gagging, I threw up on the grass.

Gazillions of horrors stabbed my brain until I brandished my fists, hollering to the Heavens, "HELP ME GOD! Please?"

But God said nothing.

The sky was still astir with crows.

*I can't see Kyle and Rhiannon anywhere.* I looked again. *That's it; I have to go back for them. I can't leave my friends. I'm going back in.*


### The Morrigan Crow


The Sentinel called upon the Morrigan crow. "It is time," cawed The Sentinel.

Her majesty, The Morrigan Crow, had not yet joined the battle. She flew overhead, inspiring fear or courage in the hearts of warriors below, choosing favorites according to their valor.

In past battles, warriors, whose shields she stole, she cast to the depths of the earth. Others, the chosen ones, she set free to run away from harm.

The Morrigan swooped. She appraised the girl with the dark raven-colored hair. The boy beside her looked up. His blonde eyelashes moved like butterflies. A third hid somewhere. The Sentinel had told her about the hair of red with booming heart. The Morrigan spotted her. Hair of Red stood separated from Raven Dark and Butterfly Blonde, anxious and alone. Ba Boom! Ba Boom! Ba Boom!

"It is time," said The Morigan Crow. And so, her poem began. She cawed.

> "Raven Dark, Butterfly Blonde,
> Run free! Run free! Run free!
> Graven harks multiply. Abscond!
> Abscond! Abscond! Run free.
> Hair of Red with Booming Heart,
> Run free! Run free! Run free.
> Despair and dread now looms. Depart!
> Depart! Depart! Run Free!"

# Chapter 21

## *The Life of a Tree*

A large black crow swooped down in front of me, as if trying to get my attention, but I needed to find my friends.

"Rhiannon?" I called, "Where are you?" I coughed, fanning the smoke away from my face. "Is that you?

I found her, shaking like a small dog with tremor disorder.

"Brucie, look..." She pointed toward the path outside Fisher Skeelie's back door. "It's Bethany's grandmother. She's badly burned."

I saw Beth hunched over, crying into a writhing pile of rugs and blankets, which lay on the ground outside the house. "It's okay Granny," she sobbed into the blanket. "Don't move now. The ambulance is coming. It's on the way."

My gut wrenched with guilt and I covered my nose from the smell of barbequed skin.

*Should I go and help Skeelie?* I moved forward. *Wait . . . where's Kyle?*

He stood at the far end of the back yard, wrists rope-tied like a steer. Jake held a stick in one hand and jolted the rope end with the other, shouting, "You're gonna pay for her pain, Boy."

"We have to get out of here, Brucie," said Rhiannon. "Jake'll kill us all."

The pesky crow swooped at me again and I ducked.

Smoke belched from the house and flames lapped upward through the slates, like red tongues licking up to the point of the roof. Skeelie continued to sizzle and groan on the ground.

"I'm NOT leaving without Kyle," I said.

"Are you mad? If Jake catches us he'll rope us up, too." Rhiannon shook with terror.

"No he won't," I said. "Bethany is busy tending to her grandmother. Jake might be strong enough to hold down Kyle . . . but he can't wrestle three of us on his own, not if you and I fight like cats." I hissed and curled my fingernails inward like claws.

"My God, Brucie!" she cried, with her palms against her forehead. "You're totally serious, aren't you?"

"Yup," I said, and swiped my nails in the air. "Come on . . . after the count of three."

I grabbed Rhiannon's arm, denying her time to stall and think. "One… Two…Three…" I counted. "Let's GO!"

We leapt forward snarling and spitting, "TSSSSSSS!" I slashed at Jake with my finger nails splayed.

"Woah! Woah! Get off!" Jake gasped. He threw his hands in the air, dropping the stick and the rope. He stumbled backward.

"Run free, Kyle!" I shouted. Slicing my nails across Jake's cheek, I fought like an alley cat.

As Kyle ran free, the crow swooped again and knocked Jake's hat to the ground.

I quickly spun around. "Run, Rhiannon, run!" We ran out of the gate.

Kyle stopped on the verge outside Skeelie's house, unsure where to go. I screamed directions, "This way!" and led them across the road. "Hurry!" We tore into the thicket and uphill. "Run! Fast as you can."

*Is Jake following? Is he?* I asked myself.

But, then I heard Jake behind me, swearing at the crows. "Get off! These effing crows are attacking me!"

*Don't look, Brucie. Keep running.*

Kyle and Rhiannon panted and squealed at my heels, as I jumped over rock, bog and tree roots. Blood coursed through my heart, which pounded and throbbed from my chest to up inside my head; Ba Boom, Ba Boom, Ba Booming. Each new beat grappled to pump faster than the last. I recalled the stag's warning about fire.

*No! What if my heart stops? What if it stops?*

I scrambled up to higher ground where snow lay underfoot. My lungs droned like a squeezebox. *Wheeze!* My skin drenched wet, yet my tongue rasped dry as chalk. Pushing on, I sprinted on the flat and strode to climb. I staggered, going and going, then lagged and lunged till my right leg muscle locked and I fell to the ground, squealing with cramp.

"AH!" I grappled for my leg.

"Brucie!" Rhiannon stopped dead and reached out to catch me. "Are you okay?"

I nodded up to her from the ground, clutching my calf in anguish.

Behind us, back down the hill, an eerie siren wailed. Another siren sounded from the same direction. The two wails grew louder as they drew closer.

"Ambulance and Fire Engine?" said Kyle, hands still tied. His wrists flared swollen and pink. Kyle indicated with his head, "In my back pocket, Rhiannon...get my pen knife, will you?"

"Oh my God, Kyle, your wrists are bleeding!" I cried. "How did you keep up, running in that state with your hands tied?"

"No choice, like." He panted.

Rhiannon dug into Kyle's jean pocket, opened the small knife and hacked at the rope until Kyle snapped free.

"Is that a bruise on your face, Kyle?" asked Rhiannon. "Did Jake hit you?"

Kyle turned his blue cheek away from her. "Nah, like. It was the other way around . . . well nearly, like . . . I was getting ready to deck Jake when you two pussy cats arrived on the scene."

"Liar!" Rhiannon threw the closed penknife back to Kyle. "If Brucie hadn't saved you..." She stopped.

Kyle buried his face in his hands and looked away.

"Feck, Brucie, we can't keep running," she said. "We'll end up lost in the hills." My friend broke down and wept. "I'm SO scared. What are we going to do?"

Kyle wiped his eyes on his sleeve, too, and turned back toward us. "I don't even know where we are anymore," he said.

He climbed up onto a large bolder, straining to see over trees. "Jeez, what smoke! I can see a fire engine down there, a small white Fiat-type car and a cop car."

Rhiannon flapped her arms. "Oh no! Do something, Brucie."

My leg cramp eased but my head and chest ached. I could hardly speak, and my throat hurt, but I had an idea.

"I know where to go," I said, rising to my feet again. "Follow me."

As I limped ahead, Kyle asked, "Where are you taking us?"

"You'll see," I replied.

Closing my eyes, I held my stone to my heart. I clutched it tightly and spoke inside my head.

*I need to find the Barracks. Show me the path I need to follow. If there is a guardian in these woods, I'm asking for help. Please show me the tree orbs to light the way?*

When I first opened my eyes I saw nothing different, but I'd been looking for globes, like in the pictures; transparent shimmering balls with glowing purple veins that laced inside. My disappointment soon gave way to elation, when sparkles shimmered and spangled to my left. They looked like fairy lights.

"Cool!" In awe, I asked my friends, "Do you see the orbs?"

They shook their heads.

"I really wish you could see this. It's beautiful. There's a pathway ahead, lined with twinkling fir trees," I said. "The trees are all lit up. Quickly. Let's follow the path. This way guys."

A crow appeared over our heads again. It flew in the direction of the lights, as if guiding us forward.

The lights led us straight to the Barracks.

Hiding inside the Barracks bought us time to discuss our options. It felt safe in there, tucked in between my two friends.

"Brucie, this place is so awesome, like. Where did you collect all this stuff from?" said Kyle, inspecting the Kilmarnock bonnet to his left.

I shivered and coughed, snatched the hat, and placed it on my head. "It's not mine. Everything here belongs to Coinneach. He calls this The Barracks."

Rhiannon edged away from a nest of black feathers and crow poop. "It's getting dark out there, and will you listen to your cough, Brucie." She wrapped her arm around me.

*God, I'm freezing here. If only I'd taken one of Grandpa's old oilskins. Don't you have any coats here, Coinneach?*

No one answered.

A pair of boots hung above me, so I pulled them on over my shoes.

The powder horn and the cutlass sat to my left and beside these I found a tin box, containing an old knife and a flat stone. *What's this?* Then, it struck me ... Sulfur; the powder horn contained a mixture of sulfur.

"Hey!" I held up the knife, the stone and powder horn. "If you chop some dried wood with the cutlass, Kyle, I could light us a fire."

"Brucie, if you light a fire, they'll see it down at the village." Rhiannon sighed. "We might as well go home and give ourselves up to the police."

"Give ourselves up? But, we haven't done anything," insisted Kyle. "I thought we were here hiding from Jake."

Rhiannon glared at him again. "Kyle, Fisher Skeelie could be dead and we're to blame."

"But, I didn't do anything, like. It was Brucie who did it."

Rhiannon snapped. "Yeah but Brucie came back and saved your butt. In fact, she saved us both. God knows what could have happened."

"I had to go back for you," I said. "How could I leave two of my best friends?"

"I know," said Rhiannon. "Thanks."

I buried my face in my knees, exhausted. Haunted by shame, guilt and anger, I suddenly called out, "Oh, I didn't mean to hurt her!" With tears rolling down my cheeks, I asked my friends, "You know that, don't you? You were witness that I didn't mean to hurt her? We were trapped. I was just trying to get my stone back and…"

"It's okay, Brucie." They both agreed, "We know."

"But, it's only a matter of time," I said, "before the police hunt us down. I'm probably a murderer by now. There's no way Skeelie survived those burns, Rhiannon."

She looked at me. "We're going to stick together in this. Either we all take equal blame or none of us do." She looked at Kyle. "Right?"

Rhiannon hugged me again, "Thanks for coming back for us. That took guts."

My breath steamed out in front of me and I shivered. We sat in a semi-circle inside the tree. Not a sound filled the air. Then, suddenly a pair of owls hooted in the dark and we huddled even closer together.

My cough hacked again, draining the oxygen from my brain and causing my head to spin. Instinctively, I reached into my pocket for the stone, seeking whatever comfort I could find. I drew it out, cupped my hands around it and closed my eyes. *At least I got you back.*

"Can I see your stone, Brucie," asked Kyle, so I showed him.

He handed it back. "Here, like . . . why don't you try and use it to see how much trouble we're in?"

"But, I've never practiced with the Eye Stone before… I mean, not intentionally."

Inquisitively, I removed one of Coinneach's shoelaces and tied it on to the Eyestone. "I have an idea," I said. Dangling the Eyestone in front of me, like a weighted plumb line, I spoke to it.

"Help me Eyestone. Move if you can hear me." I waited and held my hand very still. "Swing back and forth like a pendulum if you can hear me."

The stone began to rotate clockwise, in small circles.

"Are you trying to tell me something?" I asked.

The stone spun faster and in wider circles.

"Is Skeelie dead?" I asked.

The stone stopped flat still and began to swing back and forth, left to right.

"Does that mean no?" I asked.

Suddenly the stone began to rotate in wide clockwise circles again.

"Oh I'm confused," I said, clutching the stone in my hand. "I'm sorry, guys, I'm still learning. I don't know what to do yet."

Almost immediately after clutching the stone, I charged full of electrical tingles and buzzes. Wedged inside the hollow of its trunk, suddenly, I felt a deep connection with the tree. Spiritually, the tree encased and protected me. I remembered the lesson that Coinneach taught me about grounding myself. Grounded inside this tree, feeling its roots buried firmly beneath my feet, I felt solid, safe and strong. Above my head, the bare winter branches began to waken. I felt the birth of spring buds within me. Soon, after the spring equinox, the buds would burst forth. In awe, and from within, I envisioned their vibrant greens, and tasted the sweet sap on my tongue. The tree's energy flowed through me, head to toe. I felt so protected. I felt so loved.

*I think I have courage now.* "I'm ready, Eye Stone." I said aloud. "Please begin to teach me."

My first hazy vision seeped through. When the cloudiness cleared in my mind, I saw myself sitting by the Clootie Well, with an open book.

*The handwriting is familiar. It's my diary.*

I told Rhiannon and Kyle what I could see and I read a few lines from the diary aloud to them. "What is my destination? What do I believe in? What is my passion? What makes me want to fight? What makes me sparkle?" I exclaimed with excitement. "Hey! That's stuff that Coinneach asked me to think about. I noted that down a couple of days ago, just before I took sick."

Kyle interrupted, "Tell us more. Read on, Brucie."

"The next page says... Darn I can't read it."

"You have to, Brucie," said Rhiannon. "We need to know what happens next."

Pages blurred, words blurred, all illegible.

"Grr! Why can't I see what I've written in the future?"

"Maybe we are not meant to know that part yet, like?"

It seemed impossible to read beyond what I remembered writing a few days previous. The tease frustrated me.

"Try again," said Rhiannon.

I still saw myself holding the diary and I still saw page after page of writing, none of which I could read . . .

"It's no use," I told them. "But . . . at least I'm not wearing a jailbird suit, so maybe that's promising."

Rhiannon kept encouraging me, "Keep going. It might take time, Brucie."

Concentrating again, suddenly, I recoiled back against the tree. I saw Fisher Skeelie's face, horribly burned, skin welded and twisted over her left eye. Rhiannon squeezed my hand, whispering, "It's okay, I'm right here with you." I searched desperately into the future to see if I could find out anything more about Fisher Skeelie, but saw nothing.

"I can't see any more. I think she's alive, but each time I try to think about Skeelie, the vision ends and the stone loses its power. Maybe the stone only works when I relax, without trying to control what I see. Maybe, as Kyle says, I'm not ready to see some things."

Returning the stone to my pocket, I blinked and suddenly caught a vision of Mom in a satin, ivory-colored dress. I gripped the stone again. Mom held flowers . . . and smiled, with a shiny new ring on her finger. Someone stood by her side . . . a man, wearing a checked shirt.

"It's . . . it's . . . Johnny MacKay, the joiner!" I gulped. "What on earth!" I clutched harder at the stone.

"Brucie . . ?" My friends begged me to tell them what I saw.

I blurted, "I think my Mom is going to marry Johnny MacKay!"

"No way!" said Kyle. "But, hey . . . speaking of Johnny MacKay,

Brucie…you promised, like, if I helped you get the stone…" He nudged me. "…You know, that you'd tell me how you got Johnny leave the twins' house."

I laughed. "Of course, yes. Well, it took me a while to twig, but you see, that day I recognized Johnny as someone I had previously known. The familiarity of his checked shirts gave him away; I'd met him in the waiting room, back when Mom had an appointment with the psychotherapist. When I engaged him in conversation about his obsessions and phobias, the poor man shook and trembled."

Rhiannon laughed. "I can't believe you questioned a patient about his mental health in the waiting room of a psychiatric clinic."

I thought about that for a second or two. "I guess. Anyway, later, when I needed the hammering to cease in the twins' house, Johnny's phobias served as a pure gift. 'Don't move, Johnny,' I said. 'I think there is a spider on you.' He leapt up and then froze to the spot, before reaching for his toolbox. As I dusted his shoulder with my hand, I couldn't help embellishing. 'I'm surprised you're able to work in this attic, since the twins lost their pet tarantulas.'"

"Brucie!" squealed Rhiannon. "You are so…so…mean."

The more I thought about Johnny Mackay, the closer I returned to the vision of him standing with my mom. *Yup, it definitely appears like they are an item.* But, I thought about Dad, my heart ached, and I couldn't look any more.

"Well, you see, I needed to help John Alexander get rid of the lady in the wall." I clutched the stone as I spoke and . . .

Smokey blue wafts of light swirled inside my mind. The colors, dull at first, then sharpened to red -- shawl red. And, once again movies rolled in my mind. With eyelids loosely shut, I continued to peer inward.

Looking across to my immediate left, and then to my right . . . I saw the red shawl begin to wrap around my shoulders. I touched where I imagined it lay, and felt its coarseness. A mirror presented in front of me, into which I gazed. In the reflection I saw her face, the face of the lady in the shawl, not mine. For that moment, I became the lady in the wall. Hot, yet shivery and weak, my belly ached with a strange, intense pain. My eyes closed even tighter and I looked down toward my swollen naval. In my arms I now held a small bundle, which I unwrapped to reveal the lifeless little body of a beautiful baby boy.

*Where am I?* I checked around. *I'm in an attic room in Gargoyle House.* I looked back at the baby again. My heart ached, as I covered his small face and laid the cold, little bundle behind a box in the corner of the attic by the wall.

Suddenly a voice bellowed up from a room below. As I choked back tears, the master of the house raged downstairs. "Where's that damn lazy servant girl?"

*That must be me he's talking about. I must be the servant girl.*

The more I relaxed and adopted the servant's identity, I found myself able to read her thoughts, by the vibrations and fear that she emitted. *Once I've raked out the hearths, scrubbed the steps, and served the master's breakfast, I'll return to bury my secret; my poor, little, stillborn son.*

But, the master roared furiously about his hunger. "Servants sleeping late? Throw the lazy wretch from my house!" he ordered.

I felt a tight grip on my arm. Someone tossed me outside into the yard of Gargoyle House. They slammed me up against an outer wall, where I felt my head crack against the brick. *Ouch!* A door banged behind me. I sobbed, hopelessly, and ached for the little bundle that I'd left in the attic.

"Brucie! Come back to us. What's happening? Why are you wincing and holding your head?"

Wiping my eyes, I coughed into the present. In the bone-piercing cold, I sat motionless inside the tree.

Kyle and Rhiannon sat goggle-eyed, staring at me, waiting for a report. I told them what I'd seen.

"Poor woman!" said Rhiannon, her voice tinged with guilt. "No wonder she haunts the building." Rhiannon paused. "I'm sorry that I... well, you know... I didn't understand. I thought you were causing trouble down at the manse."

I nodded. "It's okay. I didn't fully understand until now, either."

Dog tired, I pulled my thoughts away from the servant in the attic room and offered back the stone to the depths of my pocket. But my mind wouldn't leave the parameters of Gargoyle House. I felt tied there, to the house.

I saw Gargoyle House now in its present form. The Eye Stone was not ready to switch off. I saw the staircase, the minister's office, and . . . Donald's face appeared in front of me, expressionless.

Kyle's voice faded into the distance, "Oh-oh, Rhiannon." I heard him say. "Brucie looks dazed again. She's going into another trance."

243

My hand caressed the stone.

*Maybe if I could become Donald, I could read his thoughts, too.*

The vision engulfed me but Donald wouldn't let me near him. With eyes closed again, I imagined myself step forward toward him, but even though I couldn't see him move, no matter how many paces I took, he remained one lengthy stride away from me. And, when I looked into his face…. each time I moved my head to catch his gaze… I couldn't see his eyes, not square on. Yet, I did not see his head move. So, I studied the area around me, looking for clues.

*Why does Donald treat me with such complacency and disdain?* The whole MacLeod family stood in total silence, all looking away from me. *But, wait . . . John Alexander is watching. Wow! He's much older, standing apart from his family, unshaven, smoking a cigarette, glass in his hand, tattoo of a single eye on his arm.*

He belched beer as he spoke to me. I could smell it. "They'll blame you for my demise."

*Your demise?* I asked him. *I don't understand. Why?* I thought.

John Alexander shrugged. "One day my family will look back and say that I turned bad ever since the day I found the little corpse in the attic." He paused. "You see, I'll bring the bundle of bones to Dad. The lady in the wall will stop bothering me then. But, I'll become more curious, and I'll start sitting in the graveyard, talking to the tenants there, dabbling in the occult. Dad will blame you, unless, of course, you . . ."

He vanished. The whole family vanished. Donald, too.

"Wait!" I said aloud. "…unless I do what? How do I stop this happening? And, what about Donald . . . will he drown?"

The vision ended abruptly.

"Brucie!" I could hear my friends, saying, "What's happening?"

Shivering, I panicked and searched back to study my thoughts, so I could share my concerns. They waited, more patiently now, to hear.

"John Alexander appeared as a young man, around twenty. I saw Donald in the same vision, so can I safely assume that he's going to be around for many years, too? Oh, why did I dream about him drowning, then? I don't understand."

"Maybe you should take a rest now, Brucie, like," said Kyle. "Leave it all to fate."

"Yeah, Brucie," said Rhiannon. I wonder what's going on down in the village."

"What are we going to do, guys?" I asked. "I wish Coinneach would show up. It's his fault, too, you know." I sighed. "All I've ever wanted, you know, is to stand up tall and be proud of who I am. We're in trouble way over our heads. If we get arrested, how will I ever take pride in myself again?"

"I'm proud of you, Brucie," said Kyle.

Rhiannon agreed, "Me, too."

"I feel haven't deserved friends like you. Thanks, guys," I said. But, I struggled to stay in the moment.

*What is it? Why am I being pulled back to the vision again?*

Tossed within a wild and turbulent sea, again, I relived the shock of the sudden frigid cold, the desperation of grabbing for something to hold, the helpless sinking feeling, the gagging and...

"Of course!"

I left the tree and stood outside of the Barracks. Lowering the stone to the end of the bootlace, I made it into a pendulum again and held it up.

I asked, "If dreams differ from visions, will I experience the swirling smoke before I **DREAM**?"

The stone swung from left to right.

"Okay. "If dreams differ from visions, will I experience the swirling smoke before I have **VISIONS**?"

The stone changed its movement and swung in a wide clockwise circle.

I spoke aloud to my friends. "I think I'm almost on the right track here. I think the smoke comes before visions but not before dreams."

*Hmmm...then why did I see those symbols in the teacup?*

I continued to think aloud. "What if my brain concocted the drowning dream from the jumble of all my fears?"

My mind jumped from one fear after another that I had struggled with over the last few months; lack of confidence, ghosts that jumped out of walls, my arrival in Scotland, leaving Dad behind, bullies in a Scottish school, Mom and Jake... As I reflected, the panicky feeling of drowning returned.

*I think that's it!*

Kyles' shoulders sagged, "You mean it's you that fears you are drowning and not Donald, you know like that symbolic stuff we're taught in English class... what's it called again when one thing is used to describe another ... a metaphor. Maybe you had a metaphoric dream."

Then, he sliced straight to my core. "You love Donald MacLeod, don't you?" He sighed.

"Wow! Well done for the big words, Brainbox," said Rhiannon, stunned.

My cheeks started to glow. "I don't know if I love him, Kyle." I gazed away, to think. "I'm confused now."

"Kyle?" I asked, "Do you remember the day we'd been up to the old croft house, where the bus sat. You said, 'Don't start playing with chance, guessing the future and trying to tell people's fortunes'?"

Kyle nodded. "Yes."

"I think you were right, Kyle," I said. "Before I can successfully predict the future, I think I need to handle the here and now first – I need to handle the present."

*Clap! Clap! Clap!*

I jumped.

Coinneach stood to attention in front of me, clapping his hands. *Well done*, he said. He emerged in his full grandeur, wide awake hat tilted slightly left, and the full set of medals puffed out on the chest of his coat. On his shoulder sat a crow, while various frogs and toads hopped on his shoes.

"What is it? Why are you looking over there, Brucie?" said Kyle. "Is it the police? Is someone coming?"

"No, it's Coinneach and…" I looked again. "He's with Sissy."

Sissy clapped, too . . . Sissy with the cane basket.

"Sissy?" I said, aloud. "What are you doing here with Coinneach?"

*He and I are… Well, I'm a travelling woman, ain't I? I only comes back from time to time to visit Ardcarron, and the house where I moved to when I left my life of travelling.*

*So you're a ghost?* I asked, quietly in my thoughts.

*Apparently so,* she answered, and laughed.

"What are they saying?" asked Kyle. "I can't hear them speak?"

"Shh," said Rhiannon to Kyle. "Give Brucie some space."

Eying Sissy suspiciously, I asked aloud, "So, how did you and Coinneach meet?"

Coinneach spoke, *I told you about her already; she washed my shirts and I brought her a dead cow to butcher? Remember now? You asked me where I found the dead cow, and I answered, I shot it with my brace of pistols but missed, so I used the gun powder.*

*Remember?*

"That was Sissy that you spoke about?" I asked.

Coinneach nodded.

I looked at Sissy for confirmation, but she busied herself dusting Coinneach's wide awake hat. "So where is your house in Ardcarron, Sissy, the one where you used to live?" I asked.

She looked downhill. *My hoose? ... Hmmm, that's the house doon there. The one that's on fire! And, er ... ehm ...* Sissy hesitated. She turned away and I couldn't see her eyes. *I'm sorry that me granddaughter took your stone. She aye had a wicked streak in her, that one.*

"What?" I exclaimed. "Fisher Skeelie is your granddaughter? You lived in that house once, too?"

She nodded. Turning to Coinneach, Sissy said, *But we fixed her wi the crows, didn't we, my lovely man?*

He smiled.

"But she's your family Sissy, and you..."

She finished my sentence. *Yes, I 'elped you wi the crows. The crows helped you to get away from her.*

"Why?" I asked. "Why help me and not her?"

*Ah, you see, when she wuz a young un, she done a rotten thing to me.*

Rhiannon paced back and forth. "Brucie, Tell us what's going on? We can only hear one half of the conversation."

"Sissy says she's Fisher Skeelie's granny. She helped block the chimney."

Rhiannon shook her head, totally bemused. "Eh? Why would a granny do that?"

This Sissy spoke aloud, so that my friends could hear. "Okay, 'old yer hair on, young 'uns ." Sissy pointed at me. "I've been looking out for ye, lass. You see... I caught a pike before you did. Since I wis young I used to 'ave the giftie. I did good with it. I 'elped folk. Travellers are like that. We work hard for people and we help people. My wicked granddaughter, the one you call Fisher Skeelie, she isn't really born of Travellers. She ain't got our bond wif family nor our respect for animals and nature. All she wanted wis me stone. One day she asked me to take her to the place where I found it. She tried to snatch me stone, she wrestled me and pushed me in the loch, but I held on to me stone tight as I hit the water. We sunk together, me an' the stone."

"What? You mean . . ."

"Yes, that's right. The same stone that you found, I found it before you. No one ever knew what happened to me, cuz they never found me body. Of course, me granddaughter told nuffin' to no one. When me lungs filled wi water and I's dead, I got stuck in an old sunken upturned boat beneath the water, so my body never surfaced. Didn't 'ave no fancy divers in those days, luv."

*Wait a minute...drowning... stuck in a sunken, upturned boat...I think I've found the last missing piece of the puzzle. Could my dream have been partly about Sissy, too?*

"I still wanders the shores of Loch Ussie, sometimes I does," she said. "Just for laughs, to frighten folks. Not too much, and just folks who are hunting deer. Ha ha ha. You see, I love deer and I loves animals, so I do."

"So that's why Skeelie wanted my Eye Stone so badly," I said.

"Part of me wants to stay beside the loch, because I always wondered how different my life would have been if that little guttersnipe 'adn't drowned me."

I wanted to hug her. Poor Sissy. "So, were you there the day that me and Gramps went fishing? Did you see me catch the pike and find the stone again?" I asked Sissy, gently.

"No. Not exactly," she said. "I speak wi the fish and the birds. As I said, I've always had a kindly way with me animal friends. A family of swans that live on the loch . . . they told me about you."

"I remember the family of swans," I told Sissy. "The day I went fishing with Gramps the swans made me sad because they reminded me of Dad, Mom and me, when we were still a family." I hung my head and shuffled my feet, awkward because my friends were listening.

As Rhiannon squeezed my shoulder, Sissy turned to walk away.

"Hey! Don't go yet," I said. "I've got more questions."

*Isn't it weird about all these family connections; me and Gramps, Coinneach and The Brahan Seer, and Fisher Skeelie and Sissy?*

She waved at me. "Time to leave, darlin'. You'll be okay love."

Sissy lowered her basket to the ground, left it next to the opening of the Barracks, and walked away. As she moved, she hunched her deerskin coat up over her shoulders and raised her arms into the air with fingers spread. Slowly, her fingers shifted shape into antlers, until before me stood the same beautiful stag that I'd met before. As I continued to watch, the deer's antlers grew even more until they turned into branches and the stag became a tree. I continued to watch.

"Wow!"

And they all became one; Sissy, the Stag and the tree.

I gulped and looked around to see where Coinneach had gone. He shuffled about in the midst of a pile of dead tree limbs that he'd stacked.

"What are you doing?" I asked.

*I see you've found the flint and the gunpowder,* he said. *Do you need guidance on how to light a fire? Gunpowder is my specialty, you know.*

I stopped to ask the guys. "He wants to know if we want him to light a fire for us."

Rhiannon shivered, "I dunno. I really want to go home but let Kyle decide."

"I'm totally freezing, like, but they'll see it down at the village," said Kyle. "They'll come for us."

"I know," I said, "but they are going to find us eventually anyway." I shook with the cold, and wrapped my arms around my body to try and retain some warmth. "I can't stand this cold all night. I'm still sick."

Coinneach shrugged. *It's up to you.* He also turned to walk away.

"Wait! Please don't go, not yet." I tried to catch his arm but my hand slipped straight through. "Earlier . . . I need to know why you were clapping, earlier."

*I clapped because of what you said. You guided yourself toward the answer. You did it yourself, without me doing any guiding for you.*

"What are you talking about?"

*You said, 'it's all very well being able to predict the future, but in order to do that you realized that you'd have to learn more about how to handle the here and now first?' and so I clapped.*

"Then help me, because I don't *know* what to do about the here and now," I said.

*None of us do. The present is all about choices. Right now, I have to make a choice, too: do I follow my darlin', Sissy, or do I try to find that wretched sailor who stole my prize Glengarry bonnet?*

I turned my back on Coinneach, gripped my stone and looked at my friends.

*Poor Kyle! He endured a lot of humiliation to help me get this stone back. I need to take the blame for what happened to Skeelie. It's not these guys' fault. Look at them. They are here because they are willing to share the blame with me. They're cold and they're scared.*

I straightened my hunched shoulders and spoke to my friends. "If I'm ever going to learn to read the future, I need to be honest. So, let me start being honest right now. This is my entire fault, not yours."

Satisfied with my decision, I turned to give instruction to Coinneach. Ready to accept my fate, I opened my mouth to say, "Light it! Light the fire," but he had already read my thoughts.

KABOOM! KABOOM! KABOOM!

The gunpowder exploded, shaking the forest floor and blasting me back against the tree. Blackened, coughing, I lay on my back in the Barracks. Kyle and Rhiannon lay to my left, stunned.

"Awesome, like!" said Kyle.

Looking out toward a large blazing campfire, the dark silhouette of a weird, old tramp with a crow on his shoulder leapt and jigged around the flames, clicking his heels together as he jumped next to frogs.

"Look Rhiannon, can you see him?" said Kyle.

"Wow! Mental!" said, Rhiannon.

*Oh I do love gunpowder*, Coinneach sung, *I really do love gunpowder*. He danced off into the distance, and then vanished, leaving the three of us alone.

I sat up straight in the opening of the tree next to my friends. I pulled off Coinneach's large shoes, and then my own shoes from my feet. From my pocket, I pulled out my Eye Stone, placed it in on my knee in front of me and watched it sparkle in the firelight. My toes, in bright green socks, wiggled to life when they felt the heat off the fire. Rhiannon picked up Sissy's basket filled with pinecones and tossed the cones one by one onto the fire. We sat back ready to accept our fate.

Overhead branches creaked, as they touched onto neighboring branches. They, in turn, scratched the backs of other trees, till soon it seemed all the limbs in the forest joined hands. I reached for the hands of my friends.

Together we did what forests of trees and what best friends do best; we grew together, reflecting, connecting, with power, focus, grace, and awareness, balanced, in truth, and with endurance, we sacrificed with calmness and gratitude.

The first voice I heard was Frank's. "This way, everyone," he ordered sternly. "They must be close by. I see the fire ahead."

Close on Frank's heel a woman in a red duffle coat followed. She had red-framed glasses and wellington boots. Her oversized shoulder bag made it difficult for her to walk, and she clutched a large folder to her chest.

The second voice, the one that called out, "Brucie," belonged to my Grandpa, the fisherman. He'd come to help reel me in.

Yup, having a grandpa can be handier than hip pockets on a haggis. I hope that's a compliment because that night, when Gramps searched the wood for me, I felt so glad to have him near. Once upon a time, Gramps was my only friend. Now I had Rhiannon and Kyle, too.

I reached out to reclaim my stone, held it tight and prayed. Rhiannon, Kyle and I linked arms before the approaching search party spotted us. Suddenly, ancient voices from the past echoed down from the Scottish hills and up from the glens, joining me in prayer:

Our Faither in heiven,
hallowt be thy name;
thy Kingdom come
thy will be dune
on the yird, as in heaven.
Gie us our breid for this incoming day;
forgie us the wrangs we hae wroght,
as we hae forgien the wrangs we hae dree'd;
an sey-us-na sairlie, but sauf us
frae the Ill Ane.

And, I knew from that day on, no matter the hardship, no matter the location, no matter about Mom's depression, no matter if teenage love proved unrequited, no matter how much I missed my dad; I'd always walk in the company of friends.

P.C. Frank Anderson leaned over, squinted inside the Barracks, bit down on his large bottom lip and said, "I think you all better come with me."

THE END


(Coming soon – 'Distaff – Book Two of Eye Stone')